DAVID DICKINSON was born in Dublin. He graduated from Cambridge with a first-class honours degree in classics and joined the BBC. After a spell in radio he transferred to television and went on to become editor of *Newsnight* and *Panorama*. In 1995 he was series editor of *Monarchy*, a three-part examination of its current state and future prospects. David lives in Somerset.

For Colin and Rosie.

DAVID DICKINSON

Constable • London

Constable & Robinson Ltd
3 The Lanchesters
162 Fulham Palace Road
London W6 9ER
www.constablerobinson.com

First published in the UK by Constable,
an imprint of Constable & Robinson, 2008

First US edition published by SohoConstable,
an imprint of Soho Press, 2008

Soho Press, Inc.
853 Broadway
New York, NY 10003
www.sohopress.com

A copy of the British Library Cataloguing in Publication
Data is available from the British Library

UK ISBN 978-1-84529-603-2

US ISBN 978-1-56947-503-4
US Library of Congress number: 2007038616

Printed and bound in the EU

1 3 5 7 9 10 8 6 4 2

PART ONE

THE WILD GEESE

Consider Ireland. Thus you have a starving population, an absentee aristocracy, and an alien Church – and, in addition, the weakest executive in the world. That is the Irish Question.

Benjamin Disraeli, 1844

1

The box was brown and tightly bound with string. It sat happily on a small table in the front hall of the Powerscourt residence in London's Chelsea. Indeed it looked as if the person in charge of wrapping the parcel believed it would only survive the journey if virtually encased in strong twine. The top had so many lines criss-crossing it that it resembled a master cobweb. Occasional loops under the knots bore witness to the fact that the wrapper might have preferred a different profession, pastry cook perhaps, or ornamental plasterer. Lord Francis Powerscourt approached the object gingerly. The box bore his name on the front. He knew what was inside. He felt reluctant to open it. Maybe, he said to himself, the expectation is always better than the reality. And he knew that one of the many divisions into which the world's population is split – those who can whistle and those who can't, those who adore Venice and those who complain about the smell, those who can order drinks in theatre bars at the interval and those who can't – was the distinction between those who can unwrap parcels neatly and those who can't. Powerscourt knew that his wife Lucy would have the thing open, the string tied neatly into a ball, the box itself virtually intact and available for reuse, in a minute or two. And he knew, as night followed day, that his own efforts would be similar to those of his three-year-old twins, torn strips of cardboard lying all over the floor, pieces of string also strewn on the ground to trip the unwary, a general sense of mess and disorder. Sighing slightly, he opened the drawer of the table and brought out a pair of scissors. Why did they have to put on so much bloody string? he said to himself after a few minutes, with only three of the fetters broken. And why was the top of the box so hard to open? With growing irritation he forced the lid open at last.

The Cathedrals of England, Volume One, by Francis Powerscourt, it said on the cover of the book. He stared at it in wonder and disbelief. His name. His book. His cathedrals. Had he not visited them all, walked their cloisters and their clerestories, climbed up their towers where the great bells rang out over fen and plain? Had he not worshipped at Matins in the morning and with the sombre beauty of Evensong as the light faded from the day? He began to smile as he unpacked his treasures. There are a few great moments in a man's life, he said to himself, catching your first fish, scoring your first century, getting married, looking at your own newly arrived children so small and cross in their tiny white clothes. This was another, opening the first book you had written. He remembered his oldest friend and companion in arms, Johnny Fitzgerald, telling him about the intense joy these occasions called forth, how for days afterwards you would be drawn to the place where these very special first editions were being displayed, to touch them, to open them at random, caring little for the content, to smile once more, maybe even to laugh. Johnny had compared it to the first time he tasted Chassagne-Montrachet, a sensation he, Johnny, had described as being akin to being received into heaven with a band of angels serenading you with anthems of celestial glory.

There was a sudden burst of noise coming down the stairs. The twins, Christopher and Juliet Powerscourt, seemed to have escaped the attentions of whoever was meant to be guarding them. They were singing some strange song that might once have been a nursery rhyme. They stopped when they saw the remains of the parcel and the string. Christopher

4

pointed at the box and nudged his sister in the ribs. He looked, his father thought, like a person who has forgotten the word for something in a foreign language.

Juliet eyed the object carefully.

'Box,' she said with a great effort, as if some mammoth feat of mental arithmetic had just been performed. 'Box.'

'Box good,' said Christopher and led the charge down the rest of the stairs. Powerscourt noticed that their clothes were still clean even though they had been up for an hour or more, a minor miracle where the twins were concerned. He thought of trying to explain to them that he had written the book but decided that it was no use. He might as well tell them that a man from Mars had just landed in their back garden. They pulled the box on to the floor and Christopher climbed in. Juliet began gathering bits of string and said 'Pull' firmly to her father. Quite what they had in mind was not apparent for at that moment two things happened simultaneously. Powerscourt's wife, Lady Lucy, appeared at the top of the stairs and began summoning the children back to their normal place of confinement at the top of the house, and there was a firm, confident knock at the front door.

Powerscourt ushered into his hall an immaculate footman, clad in black breeches and a black jacket with a rather daring yellow waistcoat and brilliantly polished black boots.

'Lord Powerscourt?' said the apparition with the yellow waistcoat.

'I am he,' said Powerscourt, smiling at the young man.

'I have a message for you, my lord.' The clothes, Powerscourt thought, might be the clothes of Mayfair and the West End, but the vowels were pure Whitechapel. 'From my lord, my lord,' and he pulled an envelope from his inside pocket with the panache of a conjuror.

'Forgive me,' said Powerscourt, 'and who might your master be?'

'Sorry, my lord,' said the footman, 'forgive me, my lord. I work for Lord Brandon, the Earl of Lincoln, my lord. And forgive me,' the young man began to stammer slightly as if the whole ordeal of two lords in one sentence might be proving too great a burden, 'my lord wonders if you could give an answer straight away, my lord.'

Powerscourt opened the envelope. 'Dear Lord Powerscourt,' he read, 'I wish to take advantage of your wisdom in a troubling and troublesome matter. I do not feel able to vouchsafe any details in this letter. Ill health leaves me unable to come up to town at present. I would be most grateful if you could feel able to come down and see me here at Kingsclere as soon as possible. The matter appears trifling at present, but I fear greatly for the future. Your experience and your expertise are badly needed. Yours, Lincoln.'

'Is there any reason, Lucy, why I shouldn't go to Kingsclere in the morning?' asked Powerscourt.

'None at all,' said Lady Lucy, seizing a twin firmly in each hand.

'Please send the Earl my best wishes,' said Powerscourt, 'and tell him that I will call on him round about eleven o'clock tomorrow morning.'

The young man bowed and took his leave. The twins were transported to the top floor. Powerscourt grabbed half a dozen of his books and brought them up to the drawing room to show his wife. *The Cathedrals of England*, he read on the title page, by Francis Powerscourt, published by Constable, Orange Street, London, MCMV.

Lord Francis Powerscourt had been an investigator for many years now. He had served in Army Intelligence in India and South Africa and had recently returned from investigating the murder of a British diplomat on the Nevskii Prospekt in St Petersburg. Apart from the twins, he and Lady Lucy had two older children, Thomas, aged twelve, and Olivia, aged ten. He had written the book during a two-year gap when he gave up detection at the request of his wife, after he was nearly killed investigating a couple of deaths in one of London's Inns of Court.

'Oh, Francis,' was all Lady Lucy could say when she saw the books. 'Oh, Francis,' she said again, and began to flick through the book and the illustrations. 'I'm so proud of you, Francis, we'll have to have a party. But tell me, what did that yellow waistcoat man want with you? Why are you going to Kingsclere in the morning?'

'I don't know, my love,' said Powerscourt, handing over the letter. 'When you have read that, you will know as much as I do.'

'A troubling and troublesome matter.' Lady Lucy looked up at her husband. 'Do you suppose it has to do with divorce, people running off with other people's wives and husbands, that sort of thing?'

'I do hope not,' said her husband. 'We shall find out tomorrow.' Powerscourt stretched out in his favourite armchair by the fire and began to read his book. He began, as is only proper, with the introduction. He did not feel it necessary to tell his wife that, as well as vast properties in the south of England, the Earl of Lincoln also had great estates in Ireland.

Gervase St Clair de Bonneval Brandon, eighth Earl of Lincoln, was waiting for Powerscourt in what the butler told him was the Great Ante Chamber of Kingsclere, a vast Palladian mansion just outside the little town of the same name. Powerscourt had often wondered why most of these people ended up living somewhere other than their names. The Dukes of Norfolk were not to be found near Diss or Fakenham or Cromer, but in the heart of rural Sussex. The Earls of Pembroke were nowhere close to Haverfordwest or Fishguard but outside Salisbury. And these Lincolns you might expect to see near Boston or Grantham or Louth were nestling happily in the peaceful county of Hampshire.

Brandon was in his early sixties with a formidable shock of black hair on top of a broad forehead. His jowls were very heavy, his eyes dark brown. Powerscourt thought they showed a lot of pain. He was wearing dark trousers and a rather raffish black smoking jacket over a cream shirt. Behind him Powerscourt glimpsed a vision of gold leaf and elaborate plasterwork, of proportions made in heaven, of red Chippendale chairs and a painted ceiling, of marble-topped tables and embossed doors, of Axminster carpets and the seventeenth-century heiresses and long-faced aristocrats created by the Court painter to Charles the First, Sir Anthony Van Dyck. Ladders and great planks were being moved around the room and there was a subdued muttering in French which Powerscourt couldn't quite catch. He felt privileged to have caught even a fleeting sight of one of the great rooms of England, the Double Cube Room, made, he believed, to designs by Inigo Jones. The owner of this slice of earthly paradise stared at Powerscourt from his deep red leather armchair. There was a small table beside him with papers scattered across it as if the Earl had been reading them before Powerscourt's arrival.

'Damned doctors!' said Brandon, trying unsuccessfully to rise from his chair to shake his visitor's hand. 'Damned medicines!' He placed his hands on the side of his chair and made another attempt to lever himself upright. His face grew red from the exertions. Powerscourt felt that offers of help would be inappropriate for this grounded aristocrat.

'Damned gout!' he spluttered. 'Why does the bloody thing have to come back the day you come to call? Damn my calf! Damn my other calf! Damn the bloody medicine! Damn the bloody doctors!'

'Please don't trouble yourself,' said Powerscourt emolliently. 'Please stay right where you are,' and he leaned forward and shook Brandon by the hand in his sitting position.

'Damned doctors!' said the irascible Earl. 'Do you know I once got this bloody gout in my big toe? Not once, twice, now I think about it. Do you think those damned medicine wallahs could do anything about it? Of course not!'

Powerscourt wondered if the whole morning would be spent on an extended philippic against his physicians. There was a loud bang from next door and the sound of a body falling to the floor. A string of French expletives followed, most of them completely new to Powerscourt who would, until now, have described himself as reasonably fluent in Gallic oaths. The accident seemed to cheer the invalid up, somebody perhaps more seriously handicapped than himself and about to be equally dependent on the passing whims of the medical profession.

'Damned picture restorers!' he said. 'Cost me a bloody fortune and all they can do is fall off their ladders all day.' With enormous effort and a continuous salvo of oaths the Earl managed to put one leg over the other. It appeared to bring some relief.

'Damn my leg, Powerscourt,' he said, 'damn the bloody gout, we'd better get down to business, what!'

'By all means,' Powerscourt replied, accompanied by a groan from the picture-restoring department next door.

'Don't know if you know this, Powerscourt, but we own large estates in Ireland as well as round here.' Brandon waved an arm in a circular fashion as if to indicate the range of his English holdings. 'Good land, Westmeath and places like that, none of your damned peat bogs and perpetual rainfall out there in the mists of County Mayo. Damn this disease!' The unfortunate Earl had apparently just endured a twitch of great ferocity in his lower leg which he was rubbing incredulously, as if in amazement that a part of his own anatomy could cause him so much distress.

'Thing is,' Brandon winced as he carried on, 'there has recently been a series of robberies. Not just at our place but the one next door as well.'

Powerscourt felt slightly let down. If asked, he would have said he didn't do burglaries. Murders, yes. Blackmail, yes. Disappearing diplomats, yes. But men with blackened faces climbing through a downstairs window and making off with the family silver, no. Some of his distaste must have made itself apparent. Brandon almost managed a laugh.

'Don't go looking down your nose at our little bit of crime yet,' he said, holding firmly on to his calf. 'Wait till you hear what they took, these Celtic burglars.'

'What did they take?' said Powerscourt, feeling like the feed man in the music hall.

'They didn't take the obvious things,' Brandon carried on, interrupted by a torrent of French from the Double Cube Room. 'They didn't take the silver, they didn't touch any of the antiques, they didn't look for any cash, they just took paintings.'

'Paintings?' asked Powerscourt. 'What sort of paintings?'

'In my place, called Butler's Court, the family is called Butler. We own a great heap of land there, the Butlers own another great heap, they're our relations, they live there, they farm the land for us. They've been there for hundreds of years and they're related to those other Butlers who own half of Munster. Come to that, they're related to about half the quality in the south of Ireland. So damned few of them left they'll all be bloody well interbreeding soon.' He paused briefly as if contemplating incest rife from Offaly to the Kerry peninsula. 'I digress,' he went on. 'Eight generations of Butlers have disappeared from the walls, going right back to a Sir Thomas Butler in the seventeenth century. Four more Sir Thomases have gone – Butlers win no prizes for originality in naming their sons. And a Caravaggio. And a couple of Rubens.'

'Do you know, Lord Brandon, if any of these portraits were by famous artists, any Romneys, Gainsboroughs, Reynolds, that sort of thing?'

'Damned if I know, Powerscourt,' said Brandon, eyeing his leg suspiciously. 'I can just about keep it in my head that the stuff on the walls next door is by some character called Van Dyck. Not a clue who did these Irish daubs at all. Funny thing, here I sit, surrounded, they tell me, by all this priceless stuff, and it doesn't mean a thing to me. My father said they should have bought horses with the money the ancestors spent. His father believed it would have been better invested buying vineyards in France. Never mind.'

Powerscourt wondered if the Caravaggio and a couple of Rubens were the real target and the portraits a diversion. Or was it the other way round?

'And what about the neighbours, Lord Brandon? Did the same thing happen there?'

'Ten out of ten, Lord Powerscourt. I can see now where your reputation comes from.' Powerscourt wasn't sure if he was being ironic.

'Damn and blast these doctors!' Another spasm had taken over the left leg. Brandon turned very red as he fought the pain and reached into his pocket for a bottle of pills. 'Not meant to take one of these for another two hours,' he said bitterly, gulping down his medicine, and washing it down with a glass of red liquid from the lower shelf of his table that might have been claret, or port. 'Afraid we'll have to be quick now, Powerscourt. I call these pills Davy Jones's Lockers. Send you straight down in ten minutes or so.'

'The other pictures?' asked Powercourt.

'Six generations of Connollys gone. One Titian. One Rembrandt. That's it.'

'Were the Connollys also in a straight line? Father to son to son without a break?'

'They were,' said Brandon.

'Were there any requests left for the families? Any letters, any demands that they leave the country or anything like that?'

'Not that I know of. Why should the thieves leave letters? Thieves don't leave letters. Not as a rule. Not round here.'

'They might in Ireland,' said Powerscourt. 'It could be the first stage in a rebel campaign to get them to hand over their money or their land, or sell it. You can get excellent terms now if you want to dispose of your Irish estates.'

'Damned if I see why we should have to sell our land if we don't want to, to some Irish peasant or the Christian Brothers or the bloody Roman Catholic Church. Do you?'

'I don't think that's the point at the moment,' said Powerscourt, reluctant to plunge into the thickets of the Irish land question where so many had perished before him. 'How are the families taking it?'

'That's just the point, Powerscourt,' said Brandon. 'The women are terrified. If the women go, they'll take the children with them. The families will be destroyed. The bloody rebels will have won without firing a shot. Will you take the case, Lord Powerscourt? I think they would all feel easier if they knew you were coming.'

'Of course I'll take the case, Lord Brandon. Be delighted to.' Powerscourt did not say how ambivalent he felt about the whole thing. In one sense, these were his people. He had been born into that class and that caste and their values must run in his veins. He had, earlier in his life, sold the great house in Ireland that carried his name because he and his sisters could not bear to live there any more after their parents died. With that break had come a different break, a break with the anomalies and injustice that could, from time to time, tear his country apart. Why should one man own fifteen thousand acres and another one only be allowed ten?

'I've had my people make copies for you of all the correspondence so far. All the addresses and so on are in there.' He handed over a large envelope which, for some reason, reminded Powerscourt of the box with his books. 'Next time you come,' he waved a hand dismissively towards the Double Cube Room as if it were the servants' quarters, 'I'll show you all the stuff.'

Brandon rubbed his leg once more. 'I'm obliged to you, Powerscourt. Any time you need anything, money, influence, the House of Lords, just let me know.' Powerscourt dimly remembered his friend Lord Rosebery telling him that the gout-ridden aristocrat was a formidable fixer in the Upper House.

As he made his way down the staircase towards the front door he wondered just how strong Lord Brandon's pills actually were. He was pursued by the familiar cry, 'Damned doctors! Damned gout! Damned pills!'

'So there we have it,' said Lord Francis Powerscourt, as he finished recounting the story of his trip to Kingsclere to Lady Lucy and Johnny Fitzgerald early that evening in the drawing room at Markham Square. He left the documents lying on the table. Johnny had spent the day working on his next book, called *Northern Birds*. He had just finished the first draft, he told the company, and proposed taking a break from birds before revising it. Powerscourt was astonished to see that his friend, a great consumer and connoisseur of wine, a man with an account at no fewer than three of London's leading wine merchants, was drinking tea.

'Francis, Johnny,' said Lady Lucy, 'what do you make of it?' She sensed, even at the very beginning of this case, that there was something about it, perhaps the return to Ireland, that was making her husband uneasy.

Powerscourt looked at Johnny, who seemed to send him a nod that said the floor is yours.

'It could be any one of a number of things,' he began. 'It could be a practical joke. The Irish landlord class are rather better at practical jokes than they are at many other things.'

'But not twice, surely, Francis?' said Lady Lucy.

'If you were a serious practical joker in Ireland, Lady Lucy,' said Johnny, who was also of Irish extraction, peering sadly at his empty teacup and making a preliminary reconnaissance of a bottle of Fleurie on the sideboard, 'you could keep going till you'd done four or five or maybe even six houses. It would show people you were serious, if you see what I mean.'

Lady Lucy wasn't sure that she did see.

'The real question, in a way,' said Powerscourt, 'is who is behind it. If it is a practical joker, then that seems to me, from the point of view of the Butlers and the Connollys, to be tremendous news. An apple pie bed is infinitely preferable to a bullet in the back. One possibility is that the thieves are in it for the money. Either the pictures will turn up in some gallery, probably in America, in the next year or so. Or there will be a blackmail note asking for so many thousands of pounds for the return of the paintings. The Irish landlord class have always been devoted to their ancestors, they believe that the longer the line the more secure their claim to their lands.'

'Do you think, Francis,' said Fitzgerald, 'that the same people would be as interested in buying the portraits as the Old Masters? The Old Masters could be the real target after all, and the portraits just a series of red herrings on canvas. These Americans are paying fabulous prices just now.'

'Or it could be the other way round,' said Powerscourt. 'Tomorrow morning I have an appointment to see a Mr Michael Hudson at the art dealers Hudson's in Old Bond Street. He is said to be London's leading expert on the transatlantic market.' Powerscourt paused to open the bottle of Fleurie and fill three glasses.

'We're tiptoeing round the problem, you know,' he said. 'We haven't faced up to the truth that dare not speak its name in this affair. The women in the Connolly and the Butler families are not frightened because one of their ancestors may end up on a wall in Boston or New York. The real issue is quite different.'

'And it is?' asked Lady Lucy quietly, wondering if this would provide a clue as to what was upsetting her husband.

'Violence,' said Powerscourt and he felt the word change the atmosphere. 'Men of violence. Men who used to hough or maim cattle or horses in the night when they wanted the landlords to leave. They have had many names, Whiteboys, Steel Men or Hearts of Steel, raparee men, Fenians, Irish Republican Brotherhood, Clann na Gael if you're American. They all believe in solving the land question or the political question by violence. They have rebellions or uprisings in Ireland almost as often as the French – 1798, thirty thousand dead, 1848, 1867. Who is to say it is not time for another bout in the long battle against the landlords and the English

14

garrison? This could be a refinement in tactics. You wouldn't have put money on the Irish inventing something so sophisticated and brutal as the boycott, would you? After all, there was no physical violence associated with boycotts. Maybe this is some further refinement. Paintings go today, maybe people go tomorrow. God knows. And there's one thing I find very confusing. Lord Brandon with his gout assured me there had been no letters. Letters, whether threatening or warning, have always been associated with agrarian violence in Ireland.'

'Do you think he was lying, Francis?' asked Johnny.

'I don't think he was lying, I think the people in Ireland may have been lying to him.'

'So what are your plans, Francis?' asked Lady Lucy.

'Well,' said her husband, 'I think you should stay here for the time being. When the situation is clearer I hope you will be able to join me. I am going to see the good Mr Hudson in the morning and a day or so after that I shall set off for Holyhead and the Irish Midlands. Johnny,' he paused to refill his friend's glass, 'could you do something for me? Go to Dublin and make a mark with the picture dealers so they will let us know at once if anything appears on the market. Better send it to me care of the Butler house for now.'

'It'll be a pleasure.' said Johnny Fitzgerald cheerfully. 'I haven't been to Dublin for years. They say it's one huge slum nowadays but there are great birds down in the Wicklow Mountains.'

Later that evening Lady Lucy found her husband staring moodily at a map of Ireland spread out on the dining-room table.

'What's the matter, Francis?' she said in what she hoped was her gentlest voice.

'It's all this,' said Powerscourt, waving his hand in the general direction of Powerscourt House, Enniskerry, County Wicklow. 'This is my past. This is where I was born. This is where my parents lived and died. They're buried there, for

15

God's sake. If you could belong to one of the great pillars of the Protestant Ascendancy, the landlord class, the Anglo-Irish, call it what you will, then I belong to it. Don't get me wrong, Lucy. I love Ireland very deeply. Those Wicklow Mountains where I was brought up, the west with its rivers and lakes and the dark ocean, they are among the most beautiful places in the world to me.' He paused and looked down at his map again.

'Forgive me, my love, I don't see why that should be upsetting you.'

'Sorry, Lucy. I'm not explaining myself very well.

'Much have I seen and known: cities of men
And manners, climates, councils, governments . . .

'I've been lucky enough to see all kinds of societies all over the world. But where Ireland is concerned I don't know whose side I am on. Who am I? Irish or English? Can you be both? History tells me I am one of the Protestant Ascendancy. I should be on their side. But I'm not. Or I think I'm not. I'd like to be neutral. But if that's not possible I think I'm probably with the other side. In a democratic age, after all, only the Catholic side can win. The Protestants are so heavily outnumbered. But I'm not Catholic. I'm Protestant. Even so, if you think the Catholic side should win, if anybody wins at all in these circumstances, don't you see that in this case maybe I should be advising the people who stole the paintings rather than the other way round?'

Lady Lucy didn't know what to say. She took her husband by the hand and led him upstairs. 'It's a long time since you've been to Ireland, Francis,' she said brightly, trying to sound more cheerful than she felt. 'Perhaps it'll all seem very different when you get there.'

At nine o'clock the following morning a group of three bedraggled men and an even more bedraggled donkey were

16

making their way up Ireland's Holy Mountain. The mountain was Croagh Patrick, some seven miles outside Westport on the Louisburg road in County Mayo, about as far west as you could go in Ireland without setting sail for the New World. The Reek, as the locals called it, was wreathed in cloud this morning, a light rain falling. Below it the waters of Clew Bay with their three hundred and sixty-five islands, one for every day of the year, were almost invisible. Even before Christian times Croagh Patrick had been a place of pilgrimage and mystery to the inhabitants of ancient Ireland. St Patrick himself, Ireland's patron saint, had fasted on its barren slopes for forty days and nights, giving the mountain its name. Every year on the last Sunday in July a great throng of pilgrims, many of them brought by boat or by special train, climbed to the summit and celebrated Mass nearly three thousand feet above ground. All of the three men could remember the words of the Archbishop of Tuam, the Most Reverend John Healey, the previous year. He had been standing on the roof of the old, rotten church to address the faithful. The Archbishop was a great bull of a man and within minutes a Westport bookmaker was offering odds on whether he would fall through before he finished. Healey was a passionate believer in pilgrimage, which he linked to the sufferings of his people.

'Think of this mountain,' he roared forth to the assembled multitude, over ten thousand strong, 'as the symbol of Ireland's enduring faith and of the constancy and success with which the Irish people faced the storms of persecution during many woeful centuries. It is therefore the fitting type of Irish faith and Ireland's nationhood which nothing has ever shaken and with God's blessing nothing can ever destroy.'

Charlie O'Malley, Tim Philbin and Austin Ruddy were all builders from Westport. They were part of a team of a dozen men charged with the construction of a new oratory for the celebration of Mass on the summit of Croagh Patrick. Three men, including the contractor, Mr Walter Heneghan, lived in a tent on the summit complete with cooking and cleaning facilities stolen from the British Army. Wages were paid on a Friday afternoon in Campbell's public house at the foot of the mountain, the tented party descending to make sure that the porter had not changed its taste or been diluted while they had been on vigil at the summit. Everything that could be pre-fabricated or part fabricated was assembled at the bottom of the mountain and carried up by man or beast later.

This morning, as so often, it was Charlie O'Malley's donkey who raised the standard of revolt. The beast was heavily laden with sand and cement. It sat down and refused to move.

'For God's sake, Charlie,' said Tim Philbin, 'what's the matter with your bloody donkey this morning? This isn't the same beast we had up the mountain yesterday. How many bloody donkeys do you have anyway?'

'I had three at the beginning,' said Charlie defensively. Charlie was a well-built man in his early forties, his brown hair growing thin on top. 'As you well know, I said we shouldn't have laden one of the animals so heavily last week. It took one look at Saturday morning and passed on straight up to donkey heaven.'

'What do you want with so many bloody donkeys in the first place?' said Austin Ruddy.

'I am operating on a very important principle,' Charlie replied haughtily, 'taught at school with great pain from that evil black strap of his by Brother Gilligan.'

'And what was the principle?' asked Tim Philbin, poking the donkey's back to see if he would get up. He didn't.

'It was first set out,' said Charlie rather pompously, as if he had been turned into Brother Gilligan for the morning, 'by a man with a strange Christian name, like Swede or Carrot, something like that.'

'Potato?' said Tim sarcastically.

'No, it wasn't Potato,' said Charlie. 'Cabbage maybe? Parsnip? Bean? Pea?'

A smile of triumph spread across Austin Ruddy's face. 'You

boys can't have been paying attention to Brother Gilligan. I shall have to drop him a line when I'm next in Westport. Turnip, that's the name of the fellow. Turnip Townsend. Lived in the early 1800s, I believe. No record of him coming on pilgrimage to the mountain.'

'The christening must have been very strange,' Charlie mused. 'John Joseph Turnip Townsend, I baptize thee in the name of the Father and the Son and the Holy Ghost.'

'It was a nickname, you fool,' said Tim, giving the donkey another prod.

'And what, Austin,' said Charlie O'Malley, 'was the theory that the great vegetable man gave to the world?'

'Well, you have me there,' replied Austin Ruddy defensively. 'I can remember that classroom clearly, I can see that great brute Gilligan in his black soutane or whatever they call it, but the theory of your man with the turnips has gone from my mind. I can't have been paying attention at the time.'

'I'll tell you what it was,' said Charlie triumphantly. 'The Rotation of Crops, that was his thing. Turnips one year, carrots the next, then cabbages. All change every year. I had an Uncle Fergus who used to go on about it. His wife used to say that he should rotate his drinks as well as the bloody vegetables for he was a walking whiskey distillery by the end.'

'It's just grand to hear about your Uncle Fergus, Charlie,' said Tim, 'but what in God's name has the theory to do with donkeys?'

'Simple,' said Charlie. 'Rotation of donkeys. With three of them you could work them one day in three. Better service from the donkeys. Longer life for the donkeys. Lower replacement costs for me. Just like the man Swede said. Sorry, sorry, not Swede, Turnip. Now with two, if you bastards don't load them up with too many bits and pieces, they work every other day. Rotation principle, only less of it.'

The animal at the centre of this learned discussion gazed sadly up the mountain as if it were a climb too far. The three men scowled at it.

'Should we pray?' asked Austin Ruddy.

'Don't be stupid,' said Tim.

'Should I give the beast a good kicking?' asked Charlie O'Malley.

'No,' said Austin quickly, 'if you kick this brute as hard as you kicked that last beast, it may die on us here and we'll have to carry all that stuff up ourselves.' He delved deep into an inside pocket and produced a half-bottle of whiskey, created in a Dublin distillery and rejoicing in the name of John Jameson.

'Have a sip of the hard stuff here. Maybe we'll get some ideas.'

As an experiment, Charlie waved the open bottle of John Jameson's finest under the donkey's nose. The animal looked about him as if searching for the source of the smell. Charlie set off up the mountain, holding the whiskey in front of the animal. The donkey followed happily. By eleven the three men and the alcoholic donkey had reached the summit. The low cloud began to clear and the sun came out as they worked. Way beneath them Clew Bay was laid out like a magic carpet, the blue waters like glass in the sunlight, the islands winking to each other in the bright morning air.

An outsider, looking at the window and reception area of Hudson's, the art dealers of Old Bond Street, would not have thought they had anything to do with paintings at all. There was just one picture in the street window, a rather smudgy Impressionist. There was one other in the foyer, a rather dreamy Madonna that Powerscourt thought might have been a Murillo.

Michael Hudson had just celebrated his thirty-fifth birthday but he looked ten years younger. He had light brown hair, regular features and bright blue eyes. He looked as though he could model for a page or a young courtier in a Renaissance painting.

'What a pleasure to meet you, Lord Powerscourt. Are you returning to detection in the world of art? Many may close down if they hear news of your arrival.'

Powerscourt smiled. Some years before he had been involved in a case involving fakes and forgeries along this very street, culminating in the unmasking of a forger in the Central Criminal Court. He explained his problem to the young man and handed him lists of the paintings which had been taken. 'These are very rough lists so far,' he said, 'but I thought it only sensible to bring you on board at the very beginning. Once I obtain more information about the pictures – size, name of artist, if known, and the subject matter of the Old Masters – I shall, of course, let you know. I have a colleague gone to make discreet inquiries in Dublin.'

'I only know a little about the Irish art market, Lord Powerscourt. In my youth I was employed for a couple of weeks to make a catalogue of paintings at some castle in Waterford. The owner forgot that he had promised to pay me. Let me tell you first of all of the obvious ways in which we should be able to assist. We shall put the word out in London and the principal centres in Europe about these missing paintings. We shall tell our offices in New York and Boston. I shall write this afternoon to Farrell's in Dublin. Michael Farrell has a small gallery in Kildare Street. He does a lot of business with the Protestant gentry over there. But tell me, Lord Powerscourt, a man of your reputation is not normally employed to look for a few missing family portraits. Is there something you haven't told me about yet?'

'If this was Sussex, or Norfolk,' said Powerscourt, 'nobody would be very concerned. But it's not, it's Ireland. I think there were letters that accompanied the thefts. Not simultaneous necessarily, maybe a couple of days later. What those letters said I have no idea. I suspect they were blackmail of one sort of another. Violence lies so often just beneath the surface of events in Ireland. It's like those noises bats make that humans cannot hear. These thefts are a minor form of

21

violence. Worse may follow. The wives in these houses are terrified. That suggests to me that there was a threatening letter and that it was the letter, not the vanishing paintings, that made them lose their courage.'

Michael Hudson had pulled a catalogue from his desk. 'Let me show you this, Lord Powerscourt. This comes from an exhibition held recently in New York which transferred to Boston and, I believe, Chicago. These people, McGaherns, are very respectable. They operate a long way down the scale from ourselves. The works they sell are cheap and tawdry, they might cost five or ten or twenty pounds rather than the same number with thousands added. They operate,' and here Hudson looked up from the paintings, 'in areas with very heavy concentrations of Irish settled in them. I worked in our office in New York for two years and I must have walked all over the city by the end. The pictures they sell in such quantities are never originals, but the subject matter doesn't change very much, attractive colleens, horses of every shape and size with or without their riders, those wonderful lakes and mountains Ireland is festooned with, small cottages with smoke coming out of them in the wild wastes of Mayo and Connemara. The ancestral home or the fantasy of the ancestral home, no doubt. The real home might have been a Dublin slum. Many, if not most, of these people have never been to Ireland in their lives, but they live very Irish lives in America, Mass, Christian Brothers, walls draped with pictures of the Blessed Virgin Mary, family piety, all that sort of thing. Oddly enough, their Ireland is often a generation or a generation and a half even behind the real one. The parents pass on what they remember of the world they left twenty or thirty years ago. Forgive me, I'm wandering off the point.'

Michael Hudson closed his catalogue and put it on his desk. 'I have no idea if the McGahern works are turned out in Dublin or New York, but one thing is clear, Lord Powerscourt. There is an artistic connection between the two countries. It is possible there is an innocent – well, not innocent, but certainly non-violent explanation for what has been happening to these portraits.'

'You mean, they may end up in the McGahern catalogue? And get sold off like that for twenty pounds each?'

'Not quite, Lord Powerscourt. The Irish who buy the McGaherns are not poor, but they're not well off either. Sixty years on, some of these Irish families have become quite rich, a number of them very rich. Suppose you're an ambitious Irish family living in New York. Suppose somebody comes along and offers you a bundle of your ancestors. They're probably not your ancestors at all, but the neighbours aren't going to know. Think of eight of these hanging in your parlour or dining room. The prestige would be terrific. In a society composed entirely of immigrants of one sort or another, how great would it be to show off a family history that went back a couple of centuries?'

'You wouldn't even have to be related to the people in the pictures,' said Powerscourt. 'You could say they were O'Shaughnessys or Carrolls from years gone by and nobody would be the wiser.'

'Exactly so,' said Hudson, 'and I suspect you could charge a great deal of money for a complete eight-place-setting set of ancestors, as it were.'

'I think there's a snag in this theory,' said Powerscourt. 'I'm not sure that the Irish immigrants, who are Catholic, would want to have portraits of Protestant landlords on their walls, however rich they had become. Those people in the Big Houses would be, if not actual enemies, then the oppressors of the poor tenant farmers who had fled to America to find a better life. Somebody in America might like ancestor portraits, mind you. The old might have an appeal for some in the land of the new. How on earth would we find out what the situation is?'

'At this moment,' said Michael Hudson, smiling at his visitor, 'I have no idea. We could,' a smile spread slowly across his handsome face, 'try placing a few advertisements in the kind of papers the wealthier Americans might read. Set of eight Irish family portraits, eighteenth to nineteenth century, available, that sort of thing. I think we'd need to put a fairly hefty price on them to deter the McGahern clientele, say fifteen hundred pounds. What do you think of that, Lord Powerscourt?'

'I think it's rather clever,' said Powerscourt, smiling back to the young man, 'but tell me – what happens if you are inundated with potential customers? Suppose thirty or forty come knocking at your doors? What do we do then?'

'Find a forger perhaps? That would be a good trade, you know. Forge them all over here, send them to America, I don't think you could be prosecuted there for something done over here. Your forging friend could do very well. Seriously though, I think we wait and see.'

'I am most grateful for your time and your help, Mr Hudson,' said Powerscourt, rising to take his leave. 'Perhaps you could be so kind as to send any news to my London house with a copy to me at the Butler house whose address is here.' He handed over a small sheet of paper then paused as he was about to open the door and turned back to the art dealer. 'One last thing, Mr Hudson. Every time I have anything to do with paintings in a professional capacity, the same questions arise. Is this a real Romney? Did Gainsborough actually paint this portrait? That red mess over there, is that really a Tintoretto? You know the question of attribution far better than I. If it comes up, would you be willing to come to Ireland and help me out?'

'I would be delighted, Lord Powerscourt. After all, they say Ireland is very beautiful at this time of year.'

2

The gate lodge of Kincarrig House, ancestral home of the Connolly family, recently deprived of the painted records of six of their own ancestors, was set back slightly from the road. On either side the stone walls that marked the outer edge of the demesne seemed to stretch away into infinity. Powerscourt was beginning his investigation here as Kincarrig House was closest to Dublin and the Holyhead boat. He had made his appointment before leaving Markham Square. Then he planned to move further west to Butler's Court. Powerscourt's cabby was a cheerful soul, pointing out the places of interest as they went along.

'This gate lodge now,' he said, 'and the arch and the drive here, sure they're among the finest in Ireland.'

Powerscourt made appreciative noises. He gazed upwards at the Triple Gothic Arch that towered above the road. It was completely useless. All over Ireland, he thought, at the entrance to the Big Houses with their long drives of beech and yew curling away to hide the property from the prying eyes of the public and people of the wrong religion, the owners had built monumental gates of one sort or another. Anglo-Irish mansions were guarded by a strange stone menagerie of lions and unicorns, of falcons and eagles, of hawks and harriers, tigers and kestrels and merlins. Powerscourt had heard stories of a house with a stone dinosaur on guard. The animals were often surrounded by great stone balls, as if, in times of emergency, they might return to life and begin hurling this weighty ammunition at their enemies. Powerscourt remembered his father telling him of one estate belonging to a Lord Mulkerry in County Cork where the demesne walls and the monumental gates became one side of the town square. And on the side of the town square was a large plaque on which was written: 'Town of Ardhoe, property of Lord Mulkerry'. Badges of ownership, marks of superiority, symbols of arrogance, Powerscourt disliked them intensely. And as his cab rattled along this very long drive he remembered too the prestige that attached to the length of the approaches to the Big House. Less than half a mile and you were virtually going to a peasant's cabin. Half a mile to a mile, pretty poor, little better than a cottage you'll find at the end, a mile to a mile and a half, there might be a pillar or two to greet you at the end but nothing much, anything over two miles and respectability is attained at last. Over to his left he could see the sun glittering on a fast-flowing river which must, he suspected, pass the Connolly house to enhance the Connolly view.

The house was Regency with a front of seven bays and a Doric entrance porch with eight pillars. Well-tended grass ran down the slope towards the river. Inside was a magnificent entrance hall with a marble floor that ran the whole length of the front of the house with a dramatic enfilade of six yellow scagliola pillars and dozens and dozens of drawings and etchings and paintings of horses. A huge elk head guarded the doorway. A very small butler greeted Powerscourt, asking him to wait while he found his master.

The architecture of this house and the houses like it whispered a strange language of their own, a language that came back to Powerscourt from years before.

It spoke of parapets, and turreted gateways, of rectangular windows with mullions and astragals under hood-mouldings, of quatrefoil decoration on the parapets, of vaulted undercrofts and great halls, of carved oak chimney pieces and

26

overmantels, of segmental pointed doorways, battlemented and machiolated square towers, of portes cochères and oriels, of ceilings in ornate Louis Quatorze style with much gilding and well-fed putti in high relief supporting cartouches and trailing swags of flowers and fruit, of entablature enriched with medallions and swags and urns, of halls with screens of Corinthian columns and friezes, of tripods and winged sphinxes, of quoins and keystones, of Imperial staircases and rectangular coffering, of rusticated niches and doorways, of scaglioli columns, of friezes and volutes and many more, stretching out across centuries through hall and drawing room and dining room the length and breadth of the country.

Out in the parks and walkways, many of them by lakes or rivers, were great fountains, houses with obelisks in their grounds, gardens guarded by forts with cannon to fire salutes on family birthdays, conventional orangeries and unconventional casinos, ornate gardens, Japanese gardens, Chinese gardens, Palladian follies, in one case a herd of white deer to mark the exclusivity of the Big House and the Big Garden.

This, Powerscourt thought, was architecture as political statement, an arrogant damn your eyes architectural declaration of superiority. We are the masters here. Don't even think, any Irish Catholic peering through the trees at the house over the top of the wall, that one day this might be yours. It won't. And yet, Powerscourt thought, and yet . . . The temples and the churches and all the great palaces of Rome were still standing the day before the barbarians came to town. He wondered if those stone sphinxes that adorned the Ascendancy Big Houses might not have one or two riddles left for their masters, riddles that might rather speak of Descendancy.

'Mr Connolly is in the library, sir,' the butler said, rousing Powerscourt from his reverie, as he ushered him into a handsome room with great gaps on its walls. The word library can have many different meanings in Ireland, Powerscourt remembered. Put a great many books in them and nobody will ever use the room in case they're meant to read a book. But hostesses like to have libraries in their houses. It adds an air of learning to the predominant themes of hunting and shooting. Hence there are many libraries in these houses with very few books in them. And as Peter Connolly rose to give him a very short and rather perfunctory handshake, Powerscourt realized he was in the latter category of library. He had seen bedrooms in England with more books in them. A solitary bookshelf, no more than waist high, gave its name to the room.

'Thank you for coming to see us, Lord Powerscourt. How can I be of assistance?'

Even before the man finished the first sentence, Powerscourt knew something was wrong. There was a coldness that was on the edge of rudeness. Never mind the traditional Irish hundred thousand welcomes, he was hardly getting a single one in the Connolly household.

'I would like to see where the pictures were, and any details you have of them, who the artists were, that sort of thing.' He noticed suddenly that there were four picture cords hanging from the rail above, but no paintings in them. Connolly noticed his glance.

'The police asked us to leave everything as it was,' he explained. 'Not that they will be any use. The oldest Connolly was placed just above the fireplace, the others followed him in line of inheritance. The last two of the sequence were in the dining room with the Titian and the Rembrandt in the gold drawing room.'

'Do you have any details of the artists who did the portraits? Do you have any records of what the gentlemen were wearing?'

'I fail to see how that is relevant,' said Connolly coldly, looking pointedly at his watch.

Powerscourt felt he was on the verge of losing his temper.

'Look here, Mr Connolly, I presume you want to get your pictures back. Suppose the thief sells them in Dublin or they are carried over to one of the big London firms. The proprietors know that six male Connolly ancestors have gone

28

missing and a couple of Old Masters. I have made it my business to see that they are so informed. If one of your ancestors were to appear, how in God's name are they going to know that he is a Connolly? He could be an Audley or a Fitzgibbon or a Talbot or anybody at all in Christendom. Without descriptions the whole attempt to recover them is a waste of time.'

Connolly looked at him very coldly. 'I do not believe the pictures will ever be recovered. The villains will destroy them. Soon they will come back here for more, whether for more pictures or for the people who live here, I do not know. Our time has come, Lord Powerscourt, and all that is left to us is to face it with the courage of our race. I have asked for police protection and the sergeant laughed in my face. All this talk of descriptions of pictures is futile, fiddling while Rome burns.' Connolly was working up a fine head of steam. His wild talk sounded even stranger in such elegant surroundings, the marble fireplace, the intricate plasterwork on the ceiling, the distant whisper of the river through the open windows.

'Are you not jumping to conclusions, Mr Connolly? You had two other paintings stolen, I believe, one Titian and one Rembrandt. Taken all together, those pictures could fetch tens of thousands of pounds. It's perfectly possible that this is the work of a gang of art thieves who are even now arranging the dispatch of the paintings to New York. It would help enormously if you and your family could manage to write out descriptions of all the paintings. It would help to recover them.'

Connolly was shouting now. 'You just don't understand! You haven't lived here for years! You're not even Irish any more! We made it our business to find out about you, Powerscourt, betraying your past and your people to swan about in London playing at being a detective! You've no idea what it's been like to live here these last thirty years, the Land War, the boycotting, the plan of campaign, the betrayal of a

Protestant people by a Protestant government in London trying to force us to sell our land to appease the Catholics. Well, we have lived through all that here in this house. I do not believe that a gang of art thieves broke into my home to steal our pictures. I just don't believe it. This is the final act, Lord Powerscourt. Who is there to defend us any more? Politicians? The Irish Members of Parliament want Home Rule for Ireland, that means Catholic rule with no room for Protestants. To a man, they're all Papists, Rome rulers all, waiting and waiting for their day to dawn. There's a hunger for land out there, Powerscourt, our land. Sometimes on market days in the town square, you can almost smell it.'

Powerscourt was suddenly struck by a thought that had absolutely no relevance to the conversation. He was not going to be asked to stay. He was certain of it. There had been no mention of green bedrooms or the most comfortable room in the attic. In landlord Ireland, famed for its hospitality and its generosity, this was unthinkable. He knew the stories, of houses where over a hundred guests would stay for weeks at a time, head after head of prime cattle slaughtered to fill the table. One apocryphal story concerned an assistant surveyor who had come to do some work on the house and stayed for a year and a half. After a week the family forgot his name and felt it rude to inquire again. Short of a slap in the face, a refusal to invite a visitor to stay for the night was one of the biggest insults you could offer.

'I'm sure you're being too pessimistic, Mr Connolly,' said Powerscourt. 'I thought things had been relatively peaceful here over the last few years. But tell me this, did you get a letter from the thieves? Demands of some sort? Blackmail perhaps?'

'I have not,' said Connolly and something in his downward look told Powerscourt the man was lying. 'You talk of peaceful times over here. Things are never what they seem in Ireland, never,' said Connolly darkly. 'And now, if you will forgive me, I have work to do. We can't all spend our time swanning round other people's houses asking damn fool questions. My coachman will take you into the town. I booked a room for you in the Kincarrig Arms. It is a perfectly respectable hotel. I do not wish to have you staying in my house. Good afternoon.'

With that Peter Connolly ushered Powerscourt to the door and vanished into another part of the house.

The Connolly house had a little river running past its front door. Butler's Court, the Butler residence a few miles south of Athlone, stood a couple of hundred feet above Ireland's greatest river, the Shannon. Visitors to the house could arrive by road or water. In summer the river meandered gently south towards the sea; in spring and autumn when the rains were heavy it flooded slightly. In winter it looked sullen, dark and forbidding, its waters swirling their way into black eddies as it rumbled down to Limerick and the Atlantic Ocean.

Powerscourt's first thought as he looked at the house was that he had seen it before. He was in some great square in Italy, in Siena or Perugia perhaps, looking at the great town house of some local aristocrat. Dimly, he remembered that the principal architect of Butler's Court was Italian. He felt relieved that the front of the house appeared to be unchanged. So many Irish houses had been altered, defaced in his view, in the previous century by a fad for neo-Gothic that included turrets and battlements and fake towers. Maybe it was because the leading architects of the day preferred this style of building. Maybe it was keeping up with your neighbours. Powerscourt had the rather fanciful notion that somewhere in the back of their minds these Irish patricians felt threatened by the world around them. The peaceful Regency fronts, all proportion and good taste, would not be enough to defend them from the hostile forces that surrounded them. So they felt safer with their walkways and their turrets. Nobody had taken the style so far back in history as to have a moat and a drawbridge, but Powerscourt thought these would have sold well.

Butler's Court's central block was built of grey stone with thirteen bays along the front. Two curved colonnades of golden Ardbroccan stone linked the main building to two flanking pavilions which contained the kitchen and the stables. There was no pillared porch to mark the front door of the house. The front door sat unobtrusively in its place as if it were just another window. A set of steps led down to the gravel drive. It should look heavy, massive, Powerscourt thought as he approached the front door, but it didn't. Butler's Court looked light and graceful.

In the Connolly house he had only met the diminutive butler and the disagreeable Mr Connolly. Here it was rather different. A Butler's Court footman, a tall and imposing fellow called Hardy with military bearing, had scarcely opened the door to him when a balding middle-aged gentleman shot forwards from one of the many doors to shake him firmly by the hand.

'Lord Powerscourt, welcome to Butler's Court! Delighted to meet you! I am Richard Butler and this is my house.' Powerscourt was just about to reply when he heard the singing. The front hall had a chequered black and white marble floor and a mighty staircase of cantilevered Portland stone. The sound was coming from a gallery on the first floor.

'We soldiers of Erin, so proud of the name,
We'll raise upon rebels and Frenchman our fame.
We'll fight to the last in the honest old cause
And guard our religion, our freedom and laws.
We'll fight for our country, our King and his crown
And make all the traitors and croppies lie down.
Down, down, croppies lie down.'

The children were coming into the gallery, holding hands,

boys and girls together. There were so many that Powerscourt wondered if he had wandered into a school.

> 'The rebels so bold, when they've none to oppose,
> To houses and haystacks are terrible foes.
> They murder poor parsons and also their wives
> But soldiers at once make them run for their lives,
> And whenever we march, through country to town,
> In ditches or cellars the croppies lie down.
> Down, down, croppies lie down.'

'They're not all mine,' whispered Richard Butler as the leading couple in this strange procession reached the top of the stairs and began the descent into the hall below past one of the few remaining portraits of an early Butler and elaborate rococo stuccowork on the wall.

Powerscourt wasn't sure he would teach his children this song. It referred to the defeat of the rebels in the rising of 1798. Croppies were called croppies because they wore their hair cut short in the style made popular by the French Revolution. Croppies, with a few exceptions, would have been Catholic. It was, in effect, a cry of triumph, particularly popular with the Orange Lodges and the Protestant hardliners in the north of Ireland.

The front rank were now passing the chimney piece of black Kilkenny marble and heading straight for the front door, looking neither to the right nor to the left of them. Richard Butler was smiling affectionately at them all as they passed. At last the supply of singers seemed to have dried up. Then Powerscourt saw who was in charge. Bringing up the rear was a tall, almost emaciated young man in a black suit that had seen better days.

> 'Oh, croppies, ye'd better be quiet and still,
> Ye shan't have your liberty, do what ye will.
> As long as salt water is formed in the deep,

A foot on the necks of the croppy we'll keep,
And drink, as in bumpers past troubles we drown,
A health to the lads that made croppies lie down.
Down, down, croppies lie down.'

The tall thin young man with the fair hair and the soft blue eyes saluted Powerscourt and Richard Butler gravely as he passed into the garden to join his charges.

'James, James Cuffe is the young man's name,' said Richard Butler. 'He's the eighth son of a family nearby. Poor woman always wanted a daughter. She ended up with a cricket team of boys and a twelfth man. A dozen boys! Can you imagine it! James comes here to teach some of the younger children like the ones in the garden. We've got cousins' and neighbours' children as well. He's wonderful with them. Never seems to raise his voice at all. Don't know how he does it. Wife believes the small children think he's a giant and will cast wicked spells on them if they misbehave.'

Butler began to steer Powerscourt towards a pair of double doors. The noise inside seemed to have stopped. 'Forgive me, Powerscourt, let's get things sorted. We've put you in the green bedroom on the first floor. There's a good view of the river and the housemaids are all convinced it's haunted by a man with his head in his hand. Don't believe a word of it myself. No work for you today. There are three people who knew the lost pictures well, myself, Hardy the senior footman and the parlour maid Mary who dusted the frames. We're all going to assemble for you at ten o'clock in the morning. Now then,' he showed Powerscourt into the Green Drawing Room, so called because the walls were lined with green silk, 'the young people have all gone off for a walk, so there's just the three of us for tea.'

Sylvia Butler looked about forty and still retained most of the beauty that must have dazzled her husband into marriage all those years ago. She captured Powerscourt's heart with a charming smile as she indicated he was to sit beside her.

34

'How was our cousin Brandon when you saw him?' she inquired sweetly. 'Was he afflicted with that gout at the time?'

'Alas, Mrs Butler, it was bad with him, very bad. I think he suffers a great deal.'

'The doctors tell him he must stop drinking. That would be the best cure,' Mrs Butler said, 'but I think he would find it difficult. Tell me, did he have to take any of those special pills of his, the ones he calls Davy Jones's Lockers?'

A footman entered with a tray of tea, laden with cakes and scones and barm brack, a fruity sort of cake to be consumed with butter as if it were toast, very popular in Ireland.

'The last time we saw cousin Brandon,' Mrs Butler went on as the footman disappeared out of the door, 'he had to take one of these pills. After a quarter of an hour he collapsed on a sofa and slept for five hours.'

'He took one just before I departed,' said Powerscourt as Mrs Butler began to pour the tea, 'but he was still compos mentis as I left the house. I think he must have had a minute or two to go. He was still swearing at the doctors as I went down the stairs.'

'Scone, Lord Powerscourt? Barm brack?'

Powerscourt suddenly wondered how many teas were served in an afternoon in a grand house like Butler's Court. He put the question to Mrs Butler.

'Three,' she said. 'Otherwise the whole thing gets out of hand. We have one for the children, one for the servants and one for us.'

'You must be remembering the stories,' said her husband with a smile. 'There's a family near here where the servants valued the distinctions in status between themselves so much that they ended up serving lots of different teas every day. On most afternoons tea would be served in ten different places. The Lord and Lady and their guests had it in the drawing room. The elder children and their governess had it in the schoolroom: the younger children and their nannies and the nursery maids had it in the nursery. The upper servants, together with the visiting ladies' maids, had it in the house-keeper's room. The footmen had it in the servants' hall. The housemaids had it in the housemaids' sitting room, the kitchen maids had it in the kitchen and the charwomen had it in the stillroom. The laundry maids had it in the laundry and the grooms took it in the harness room. Once a week a riding master came from Dublin to give the children a lesson and the number of places where tea was served went up to eleven; for while he was too grand to have tea with the servants or the grooms, he was not grand enough to have it with the gentry in the drawing room, so he was given a tray on his own.'

Powerscourt laughed. His eye was drawn to three gaps on the walls. Over the mantelpiece was an enormous hole, with two smaller ones on either side of it. He supposed all would be revealed in the morning. At dinner that evening – he had forgotten how much food was consumed in these houses – he noticed another eight empty spaces on the green walls, dark lines marking where the edges of the paintings had met the wall, the paint a paler green than the surrounding area, the squares or the rectangles looking like undressed wounds.

All through the afternoon and evening a great number of people asked Powerscourt the same question. 'Have you met Great Uncle Peter yet?' The children asked him with great interest, running away in fits of giggles when he answered. The grown-ups would smile to themselves when they too learned that Powerscourt had not yet made the gentleman's acquaintance. With great difficulty he managed to discover that the great uncle was extremely old, so old that even he had forgotten how old he was, and that he was writing a history of Ireland.

James Cuffe, Young James as everybody called him, the tall thin young man who looked after the children, played the piano after dinner. He was unobtrusive, rattling through some pieces by Chopin with restraint. Then he was persuaded to

36

accompany a young army wife, Alice Bracken, as she sang some songs by Thomas Moore.

> 'Believe me, if all those endearing young charms,
> Which I gaze on so fondly today,
> Were to change by tomorrow, and fleet in my arms,
> Like fairy-gifts fading away,
> Thou wouldst still be adored, as this moment thou art,
> Let thy loveliness fade as it will,
> And around the dear ruin each wish of my heart
> Would entwine itself verdantly still.'

Powerscourt felt himself sinking into a languid draught of nostalgia. His mother used to sing this song, leaning on the edge of the piano with the drawing-room doors wide open to the garden in spring and summer, the waters of the great fountain just audible from the bottom of the steps, faint evening noises blending in with the music. His father would be playing the piano, rather badly, for he had taught himself to play and his finger movements would have appalled the fastidious music teachers of Dublin. And Powerscourt himself, a small boy of eight or nine, rather an earnest child, he thought, would be staring at his mother and praying that she would not stop and send him to bed. Sometimes when more expert hands were available at the keys, his mother would sing duets with some of the guests, two voices twinning and twisting round each other and floating out into the Wicklow air. He thought that was his favourite memory of his mother. His mind turned suddenly to Lady Lucy. Maybe he would bring her over and she too could sing for Ireland in this great house by the river.

> 'It is not while beauty and youth are thine own,
> And thy cheeks unprofaned by a tear
> That the fervour and faith of a soul can be known,
> To which time will but make thee more dear;

37

No, the heart that has truly loved never forgets,
But as truly loves on to the close,
As the sunflower turns on her god, when he sets,
The same look which she turned when he rose.'

Richard Butler along with his footman and Mary the parlour maid were on parade in the dining room promptly at ten o'clock the next morning. Hardy the footman looked even more military today, standing to attention as if he were a sergeant major on parade. Mary was shuffling anxiously from foot to foot as if she were about to undergo some disagreeable medical procedure.

'Now then,' Richard Butler was brisk and cheerful this morning, 'let's begin with this full-length over the door. Can you remember who it was?'

There was a silence from his two experts, the footman who saw the painting at least a dozen times a day and the girl who dusted the frame every morning except Sundays when she was given time off to go to Mass. Finally Hardy coughed slightly.

'There was a name on the bottom right of the frame, sir, but I can't remember what it said.'

'Very well,' said Butler, pausing to write something in a small black notebook, 'what was the gentleman wearing?'

'Blue?' said Hardy hesitantly.

'Black?' said Mary.

'I thought it was green, a green cloak over his shoulders,' said Richard Butler, a slight irritation beginning to show. He made some more notes. 'How about this other full-length Butler, the one over the fireplace?'

'He was sitting at a table, that one,' said the footman, 'with papers all over it.'

'No, he wasn't, he was sitting on a horse,' said Mary defiantly. 'An enormous horse.'

'That was your man on the other wall, opposite the door,' said Hardy, 'not this fellow here.'

'The man on the horse, surely,' said Butler, frowning slightly now, 'was in the drawing room by the door. Big black horse.'

'Brown,' said Hardy, 'the horse, I mean.'

'Well,' said Richard Butler, 'I'm not sure we're making much progress. If the one on the other wall was on a horse, then this one can't have been on a horse too, can he? What was he doing?'

'No reason why he shouldn't have been on a horse,' said the footman, 'logically, I mean.'

'Are you saying,' asked Butler, 'that this one was on a horse too?'

'No, I'm not,' replied Hardy, 'I was only pointing out that there was no reason why he shouldn't have been on a horse.'

'Well,' said Butler, a note of exasperation coming into his voice now, 'if he wasn't on a horse, what was he doing?'

'Sure, he wasn't doing anything,' said Mary, rejoining the argument, 'he was just standing there, looking at something, like those country fellows leaning on a gate.'

'You're not saying my distinguished ancestor was just leaning on a gate, are you, Mary?'

'No, no, sir, it was just the look of him.'

'I think you'll find, sir,' said Hardy with a note of finality, 'that this gentleman here, over the fireplace, was the legal gentleman, with a judge's red cloak and a lot of papers on a table in front of him.'

'No, he wasn't,' said Mary with spirit, 'your man with the wig and stuff was above the other door, so he was. There was a crack in his frame, you see, and I always remember thinking that the legal man was going to sentence me to be transported to Tasmania or some dreadful place.'

'You sound very definite about that, Mary,' said Butler. 'Are you sure?'

'I am sure, so I am,' said the girl firmly.

'Not so, you are mistaken,' said the footman firmly. 'The legal party was not above that door. He was by the mantelpiece here, watching his descendants eat their meals, so he was.'

'The devil he was, Augustus Hardy. Isn't it your eyes that need testing now, and you hardly able to read the headlines in the *Freeman's Journal*?'

'Please, please,' said Richard Butler, 'let us not fall out. Why don't we have a look in the drawing room next door?'

Another gaping wound stared at them from above the fireplace. 'I'm sure we can agree about this one,' said Butler hopefully. 'This was the painting of the hunt, done fairly recently. I forgot to mention it to Lord Brandon, Powerscourt. Most of the county hunt, all in their scarlet coats, were assembled by the front door of the house, mostly men, including myself, of course, but a few women as well. The house was in the background.'

Both footman and parlour maid agreed about that. They ventured back into the dining room. But that was all they could agree about. On the dispositions and dress of the other two portraits they disagreed violently. One, according to Hardy, showed a Butler leaning on his fireplace, a book in his left hand, a dog asleep at his feet. Nonsense, said Mary, none of those Butlers were shown with a book, heaven only knew if they could read or not, some of them, it was all so long ago, and if anybody thought she, Mary, would not remember whether one of the gentlemen was reading or not, they were a fool. The other painting, the footman maintained, showed a Butler resplendent in cricket clothes, a cap over his head, a bat in his hand, pads on his legs, obviously waiting to stride out to the wicket. Mary agreed that there had been such a Butler, but it was a smaller Butler and he had been positioned between the fireplace and door. There was, Powerscourt thought, very considerable disagreement among the witnesses. If it had been a court case the judge might well have thrown it out because of the gross confusion about the evidence. The only thing the participants agreed on was that the people in the paintings were Butlers. Their hair might be black or brown or grey or silver or white or non-existent. Their jackets, likewise, might be blue or black or brown or red; they might be wearing cloaks of dark blue or red; they could be lawyers or hunters or cricketers. They could be smiling or scowling, their noses great or small, their eyes any colour of the rainbow, their chins clean shaven or covered with a beard that might also be black or brown or even white. There was no certainty about any of these Butlers. They were changelings to the footman who tended them and the girl who dusted their frames. Richard Butler was looking very cross indeed.

'There is confusion everywhere,' he said. 'How can I give an accurate description of the vanished pictures to the authorities?' Powerscourt thought Hardy and the girl had looked at the paintings so often that they didn't really see them any more; they had all merged into a kind of composite Butler for all rooms and for all seasons in their minds. Once the paintings had gone from the walls, they rearranged themselves in the footman's and the girl's brains until they were seriously confused. They might have been clearer had they only seen the paintings once.

'I wonder,' said Powerscourt, 'if you have many visitors to this house, people who like looking at old houses, that sort of thing?'

'We do,' said Butler, 'we have them all the time. Most of them are very well behaved.'

'Do you have any architectural people, Butler? People who might take photographs of the house and its rooms?'

'I see what you're driving at, Powerscourt,' said Richard Butler, beginning to look much more cheerful. 'We have had such people though I don't think they ever sent us any photographs. But we did have a chap ourselves, now I come to think about it, a chap to take photographs of the place about five years ago. I'd completely forgotten about the fellow. We wanted a record of how the place looked at the turn of the century. I've still got them in my study. Hold on, I'll be back in a second.'

Richard Butler departed at full speed. The footman was looking rather disappointed, as if he thought the parlour maid

41

had got the better of him in the discussion about the missing paintings. The girl was looking defiant.

'Tell me, Hardy,' said Powerscourt, 'could one man lift one of those full-length portraits off the wall and carry it outside?'

'He would have to be very strong, my lord,' Hardy replied. 'The things are a very awkward shape, if you see what I mean. Much easier with two.'

The owner of Butler's Court returned with his wife and the biggest photograph album Powerscourt had ever seen. 'It's a pretty big house,' he said to Powerscourt apologetically, laying the album out on the dining-room table.' Powerscourt wondered if he had brought Sylvia, as charming in the mornings as she was in the afternoons, to keep the peace between the squabbling servants. Gradually, over an hour or so, the various Butler ancestors were restored to life as they had lived it on the walls of their dining room and their drawing room. Hair of the right colour was finally restored to the right head. The hunter, the lawyer and the cricketer all returned to their proper places. Clothes that had been blue were finally adjudged to have been black, clean-shaven men were transformed into men with beards and vice versa. It was, Powerscourt thought, a most pleasing transformation, and he joined Richard Butler in entering all the details in his notebook. Mary the parlour maid departed to dust the rest of the paintings. The footman shimmered off to his own quarters. Mrs Butler went upstairs to change for a picnic lunch on an island in the river. Mr Butler carried off his giant album back to his study. Powerscourt announced his intention to walk all round the ground floor and inspect the windows. He would, he said, follow them to the island. He might be late as he had some more notes to take.

A determined burglar could have found his way into the house easily enough. There were one or two places where the windows were not quite secure. After half an hour or so Powerscourt returned to the dining room. He perched on the edge of a chair and stared at the empty patches on the walls.

He checked the notes he had made of the Butler inventory of the paintings. A number of blank rectangles marked the spaces where the second, third, fourth, sixth and seventh Thomas Butler had claimed their places to a surrogate eternal life on the walls of their dining room. The first Thomas, Powerscourt had been told by the seventh, had been too busy building his house and establishing himself in the extra acres given to his grandfather by Cromwell so that he never had the time to sit for his portrait. Another Thomas had flatly refused to sit for his portrait at all. He was constitutionally incapable of sitting still, Richard Butler said, his restless irritability only soothed by sitting on a horse, or rather, charging around on his horse more or less permanently, which is why he hunted six days a week when he could and even threatened to hunt on Sundays as well until the local bishop intervened with telling quotations from the Book of Genesis about six days shalt thou labour. All those family portraits gone from here altogether, all male, the women still demure in their places. And a few Old Masters.

The great house was very quiet now, the inhabitants all departed in high excitement on their trip on the river, rowing boats prepared for the journey to the island in the middle where, by long tradition, the family had their picnic lunch during the summer in some style with three sorts of wine and a bottle of port that could solve the problem for the more elderly among the Butlers of what to do in the afternoon. Powerscourt walked down to the library and stared out of the great windows, the air very clear this morning, the Shannon bright and close, the line of the trees where the forest began sharp in the light.

Powerscourt was looking at the books now, column after column of them marching silently towards the ceiling. Many of his favourites were here, Thucydides and Tacitus, gloomy chroniclers of the failings of their great powers, George Eliot, Tolstoy. But it wasn't the contents of the leather volumes that interested him. It was words, the words that made up the books, the words the authors used to tell their stories. Words, he thought, words were very dangerous in Ireland. Theobald Wolfe Tone, a not very successful barrister in the Dublin of the 1790s, became intoxicated with words that had crossed the seas from France. Liberty. Freedom. Equality. They featured large in the thinking of the United Irishmen, formed to unite Catholic and Protestant and set Ireland free from English rule. Some men made their living by cutting cloth or growing corn or selling provisions or dealing in livestock. Lawyers looked at words on a page and invested them with meaning. Illiterate peasants in the west of Ireland swore the Oath of Tone's United Irishmen, not understanding what most of the words meant. 'I will persevere in endeavouring to form a brother-hood of affection among Irishmen of all persuasions.' Freedom or Equality meant little when you lived in a mud cabin and had scarcely enough food to feed your family. Freedom meant little when a man with a different religion whose ancestors came from England to take your land, a man who lived in a great stone house with lakes and tall windows and libraries with portraits of his family, could throw you out of your tiny patch of earth and pull down your stinking hovel. Liberty. Equality. Fraternity. Words. Words written on a page by lawyers. Words that took those Mayo peasants far from their homes in the rebellion of 1798 to fight their last battle at Ballinamuck in County Longford, slaughtered by the English dragoons on the hillside or butchered in the bog. Words had killed them. And those who were taken prisoner by the English that day? Words killed them too. A word called treason saw them hanged. Powerscourt wondered what might have happened if Theobald Wolfe Tone had been more successful as a lawyer. Or, indeed, that other lawyer associated with freedom, liberty, equality, Maximilien Robespierre, a man so drunk with words that he tried to abolish religion and replace it with rituals and celebrations in honour of reason. Reason, another word. God wasn't dead yet. Not that time anyway. He was soon back, if he had ever really gone away. It was

Robespierre who perished instead, consumed on the guillotine by his own words.

Words were dangerous in Ireland. Catholic. Protestant. Mass. The Virgin Mary. Fenian. Informer. All had been dangerous in their time. Some still were. Now new words were coming, boycott already officially entered in the dictionaries. Captain Charles Boycott was a land agent in the west of Ireland who refused to grant a reduction in rents to his tenants in 1880 after two years of bad harvests. Powerscourt strolled over to one of the bookshelves and pulled out a biography of the Irish political leader Charles Stewart Parnell which included his description of what boycott meant at a huge meeting in Ennis in County Clare. This was what was to happen to a landlord who refused to reduce rents or a man who took over the farm of an evicted tenant: 'You must show what you think of him on the roadside when you meet him, you must show him on the streets of the town, you must show him at the shop counter . . . even in the house of worship, by leaving him severely alone, by putting him into a sort of moral Coventry, by isolating him from the rest of his kind as if he were a leper of old, you must show him your detestation of the crime he has committed.' Many people in Ireland other than Boycott were boycotted. Powerscourt's father had told him of Ascendancy families who had refused to reduce their rents. Unable to bear the psychological strain of the ordeal, they had fled their houses and their lands, conceding victory to the foe. They settled instead in quiet English towns like Cheltenham or Tunbridge Wells where the respectability of the suburbs could atone for the eternal silences of the Irish shopkeepers and the defection of their own servants. But, Powerscourt thought as he returned the book to its place, it was the abstract words that were the most dangerous. The words that represented ideas that could send men to deaths as it had those Mayo peasants in the 1798 rebellion. He thought of another category of words, designed to describe the proper functions of society as if it were a well-made watch or clock. Political economy. Laissez-faire. People being forced to stand on their own two feet. Words written by people in great libraries like this one perhaps, remote from reality, that encouraged the British Government in the 1840s to believe that it was wrong to interfere with the workings of the market, that the starvation in Ireland was an act of God and the Irish needed a lesson to tell them how to farm their land properly. One million Irish dead in the famine testified to the wisdom of those words and the political economists who wrote them and gave that advice. Another million or more fled to America in the next generation. More words on a page, the flies' feet of an alphabet that could send men and women to mass graves, unmarked and unmourned, thrown into fields by the hundred and left to rot in the Irish earth that had failed them.

There was the sound of loud complaint coming from the garden. Another Thomas Butler, this one only seven years old, had apparently fallen into the water and was being brought back to the house for a change of clothing. This he regarded as a monstrous injustice, depriving him not just of the company of his brothers and sisters, but of the innumerable fish of unimaginable size he would have caught during his time of banishment. Powerscourt smiled as the argument moved past his windows and into the great hall. He looked round the library once more, filled with words, millions of them. The most dangerous word in Ireland, he decided, inspecting critically a section devoted to theological works, was God. God or perhaps Nation. On balance, he thought, God had it.

3

Mrs Alice Bracken was lying on her back on the grass circle in the middle of Butler Island in the centre of the River Shannon where the Butler family had repaired for lunch. It was a beautiful day. The sun was beating down on Alice's face though she thought she would only have to move a couple of feet to her left to be in the shade. A young cousin of the Butlers, currently staying at Butler's Court, John Peter Kilross was lying on the ground at right angles to Alice and dropping strawberries into her mouth very slowly. They were cool and fresh as she bit into them. The girl rather liked receiving her fruit in this fashion, though she thought it would be more difficult with the larger specimens like the melons or pineapples currently ripening in the great glasshouses at the back of the house.

Alice Bracken had been born Alice Harvey twenty-three years before, third of five daughters of Mr and Mrs Warwick Harvey who owned an estate at Ballindeary near Castlebar in County Mayo. Many people thought all Irish patricians lived in enormous mansions like Butler's Court, with vast estates, innumerable horses and virtually uncountable wealth. It was not always thus. Often in his cups Mr Harvey would mutter to his children about the Encumbered Estates Court and how close they were to being delivered into it. When she was very young Alice had thought an Encumbered Estates Court was just another big house with a demesne like Florence Court in

47

County Fermanagh where her cousins lived. Only later did the terrible truth dawn on her as her elder sisters told her what it really meant. It was, she reflected ruefully at the time, rather like learning the truth about Father Christmas, only worse. The Encumbered Estates Court was where the law sent people who were bankrupt, who owed so much money they could not pay their debts. They could languish for years in these insalubrious surroundings while the lawyers collected their fees and decided what do with the land and the house. Warwick Harvey's father and grandfather had both borrowed large amounts of money to extend their house. Their grandson and son had to pay the interest and the bills. When the harvest was bad, the diet in Ballindeary Park was little better than that of their poorest tenants. When they were invited to the local hunt balls only one girl was able to go at a time as there was only one ball gown fit to be seen in public and it had to be altered to fit one of five different shapes every time it left the house. Most of the girls' days after they reached maturity were spent wondering if they could ever escape, if their lives were to be spent in something worse than genteel poverty, eking out the tea leaves for another afternoon, water the only drink in the house apart from the cheap whiskey which her father consumed to ease his sorrows. Even then he diluted it so heavily that the taste of the whiskey was like a noise heard far away, remote and distant as though a visitor was tiptoeing away from your house in the dark.

In these circumstances it was not surprising that the thoughts of the girls should concentrate on young men. Maybe middle-aged men. Even older men if they had an income and a roof to put above their wife's head. Any visitor who came to see their father, surveyor, bailiff, parson, was inspected in minute detail by ten voracious eyes. Young curates, when they could be found, were often a source of fevered speculation, but their mother had to remind the girls that young curates in the parish of Ballindeary, soon to be united with the neighbouring parish to form the larger unit of Ballindeary and Carryduff, were not

48

likely to be rich men. One of the curates appeared to be so poor that he could not even afford a horse and walked everywhere. Officers provided the most regular source of fantasy and imaginary escape. The neighbouring town of Castlebar was a garrison town, regularly furnished with English soldiers. The officers, almost all English with a sprinkling from Scotland, were forever looking for excuses to dance with the local young ladies, to flirt with them, to pass the time in whatever romantic entanglements they could manage. Very occasionally one of the officers would overstep the mark, or one of the girls would forget herself, and the young man would be transferred so fast that the girl's family might never find where he had gone, the girl herself sent off to Dublin to stay with her aunt for a while. Into this slightly desperate world of longing, where both parties longed for completely different things, came a tall, very handsome young officer called Captain Rufus Bracken with soft brown eyes and perfectly twirled moustaches. It was the moustaches rather than the face that most people remembered, should they chance to think about the Captain in his absence. He was the fifth son of a small landholder in Derbyshire, and though he talked loud and often to the young ladies about his vast estates in England, he was entirely dependent on his family for of fortune he had none at all.

One fateful Saturday nearly three years before it had been Alice's turn to wear the ball dress and she had been swept off her feet by Captain Rufus Bracken, so tall and slim, so handsome in his uniform, so distinguished with his moustaches, so obviously rich with his estates in Derbyshire. Six weeks later they were married after a whirlwind romance. The cynics or the realists hinted that Alice must have been pregnant. It was widely known that his commanding officer at the time, unlike his predecessors or his successors, was a convinced puritan who did not approve of conniving at the sudden dispatch of young Englishmen about to become fathers off to far distant shores. In his book they had to stay and do their duty. And, in fact, the cynics were wrong. Alice was not pregnant. She was, however, not entirely pleased with her first glimpse of the vast estates in Derbyshire. The house, she declared, was little better than a fishing lodge in Ireland; the income, she realized all too soon, was non-existent. They returned to Ireland where they were eventually given a small house to live in and a modest allowance by her mother's second cousin, Richard Butler of Butler's Court.

The wooing, the pursuit, the chase had interested Captain Bracken greatly. The reality of marriage did not. He had no interests apart from masculine pursuits. It was perfectly fine to woo a girl with tales of the past heroism of his regiment. As the marriage lengthened from weeks into months, the stories began to pall. On his time away from military duties at Butler's Court he found it hard to relate to the Butlers with their endless talk of horses he hadn't seen or hunts he hadn't attended. After one terrible row about money Captain Bracken had applied, in his fury, to be posted abroad. He had been sent to India, to the North-West Frontier, where his relations with the Pathan tribesmen were no more satisfactory than they had been with the Anglo-Irish gentry. The Captain was an indifferent correspondent, his letters sometimes taking months to arrive and containing little but inane gossip about army wives and the tiresome intrigues at The Club. Alice did not mourn his passing, except in one respect. She missed him physically. Of the loss of his conversation she was not concerned. Sometimes she wished he would never come home and would leave her to a lifetime of flirting with Ireland's young men. Sometimes she even wished he was dead so she could marry again. Then she would reproach herself greatly and tell herself that she was a wicked person who deserved no portion of God's grace in this world or the next.

And so it was that she came to be lying on the ground with John Peter Kilross dropping strawberries into her mouth as she toasted herself in the sunshine. Had she thought about it – but Alice was not a great one for thought – she might have realized that this Johnpeter, the two Christian names usually run together for reasons nobody could now remember, was remarkably similar to the departed Captain Bracken of the moustaches. Only it was the voice with the young man Kilross, a voice so soft and charming that the young ladies would flock round him to hear the latest poetry or listen to him singing. Like the absent husband, Johnpeter was the fifth son of a moderate estate in County Kildare and, like Alice, a cousin of Richard Butler on his mother's side. And while the Irish peasants divided their holdings among their children so they became smaller and smaller over time, the Anglo-Irish landlords always passed the estate on intact to the eldest son in the hope that it would grow larger and larger. So Johnpeter had few possessions apart from a pair of fine hunters and a set of silver goblets left him by his grandmother.

'I wish I could lie here for ever,' said Alice languidly, as the strawberries continued to drop into her mouth.

'Don't worry,' replied the young man, and his voice was like honey in the girl's ears, 'there are still plenty left.'

Some fifty feet away, Lord Francis Powerscourt was sitting opposite Mrs Butler in the island's summerhouse. Normally, when the grown-ups remained in their proper places on the mainland, this summerhouse was an Indian camp out in the wilds of Wyoming, or a beleaguered British outpost in South Africa like Ladysmith or Mafeking, under siege to the terrible Boers. The children would crouch in it, firing imaginary guns from its windows, assaulting it from the roof, a position perilously reached by jumping some six feet from a nearby tree. Today the grown-ups had taken it over and the children played elsewhere, recreating great naval battles with a couple of canoes or disappearing completely up into the tops of the tall trees. It wasn't even, the children said to themselves, as if the grown-ups did anything sensible in the summerhouse when they took it over. They just talked to each other, apart from one memorable evening when Alice and Johnpeter had been spotted kissing vigorously as the light faded when the

Butler children were meant to be going to bed, but had decamped to the island instead for a midnight feast of buns and biscuits liberated from the kitchen.

'This must be a very worrying time for you, Mrs Butler,' Powerscourt began, 'with all these pictures disappearing.'

Sylvia Butler smiled. 'I've been trying to find out,' she said, 'if there is any history of this sort of thing. I've often wondered if the ancient Celts had a tradition of this kind of activity. You steal my pelt or my club or my best stone and there is some sort of curse placed on me. Like voodoo or whatever it's called in the West Indies. The stealing of the paintings is meant to be a mark of doom for the family. Sometimes,' she laughed what Powerscourt thought was rather a false laugh as if she was trying to conceal her real feelings, 'I do feel cursed. I feel not wanted. I feel some people want us to go. But it never lasts very long.'

Powerscourt wondered if this wasn't precisely the effect the thieves had wanted. It would be impossible, he thought, to have lived in Ireland for the last thirty years or so without realizing that some, if not a great many people wanted you to go. He thought it prudent not to mention the fact.

'Your steward was mentioning to me yesterday,' he said, 'that one of the Christian Brothers at the school in the town down below is a great expert on the ancient Celts. Apparently he spends his holidays digging around in old ruins or ferreting about in the bogs for relics of those times.'

'They always strike me as being rather sinister, those Christian Brothers,' said Mrs Butler, 'especially when they move about in packs. They look like ravens or crows about to do some damage or attack somebody. He is called Brother Brennan, the antiquary fellow. They say he hopes all the young farmers who pass through his hands will search their land for antiquities for him. He has great hopes of opening a museum some day with all his treasures in the main square down in Butler's Cross, the town at the bottom of our drive. Perhaps you should go and see him, Lord Powerscourt.'

'Tell me, Mrs Butler,' Powerscourt shifted slightly in his seat to catch a view of the river through the trees, 'who do you think is responsible for these thefts?'

Sylvia Butler paused. Should she tell him the truth? She had only known him for twenty-four hours or so. She had met too many Irishmen with charming and plausible manners in her life who had later turned out to be men of straw. Powerscourt, she decided suddenly, was not a man of straw. Lord Brandon had spoken of him in the most glowing terms. 'If it was a joke, a practical joke,' she began, 'we would know by now. Even in Ireland the practitioners would have put us out of our misery after all this time. That leaves an interesting choice, Lord Powerscourt. Thieves who intend to make a great deal of money from selling the paintings? Or men of violence, advanced nationalists as I believe they call themselves nowadays, though why it should be advanced to break into innocent people's houses and steal their possessions I do not know.'

She paused suddenly, as if conscious of the contrast between what she was about to say and what surrounded her, the birds singing happily in the trees on their island, the Shannon gurgling quietly on its long journey to the Atlantic, the distant laughter of the children, the heat growing stronger as they passed into early afternoon.

'I'm sure it's the men of violence,' she said very quietly, 'they want to get rid of us. They always have. Our land is very fertile. Richard has made it much more profitable with his improvements and his educated farm managers. We even had one from Germany once, you know, Lord Powerscourt, a very earnest young man who wore enormous black boots all the time. I remember wondering if he wore them in bed but I never found the answer. Richard said he had a great feel for horse breeding. We did have one horse after he left, I recall, who won everything at the Punchestown Races three years in a row. Richard called it Wolfgang. Everybody gets richer these days, the tenants, the shopkeepers in the town, ourselves.

We've cleared all the debts now. Richard looks so proud when he tells people that the Butlers don't owe anybody a penny. I'm sure those Fenians or whatever they call themselves these days – the vicar is convinced their new name is the Irish Republican Brotherhood, but I wouldn't trust the vicar to know about a thing like that – they all want to drive us out. It's been going on for centuries. We may lose in the end, Richard and I tell ourselves in our darker moments, but we won't go out without a fight. We'll dance until dawn at the last hunt ball, we'll drink the last of the stirrup cup and finish the port in the cellar, we'll kill the last fox in Ireland and exhaust ourselves at the last tennis party. We'll go out in glitter and glory, dressed up in our finest with Young James playing the Dead March from *Saul* on the piano.'

She laughed, a rather desperate laugh, Powerscourt thought. 'Tell me,' he said, looking at her small delicate hands, 'are you frightened?'

Mrs Butler paused and looked closely at Powerscourt. 'I thought you were going to ask me that sooner or later,' she said. 'It's not an easy question to answer. Of course I could tell you that I'm not frightened at all, but that wouldn't be true.' She paused again. 'Sometimes I am very frightened indeed. I think I can say in all honesty that I'm not afraid for myself. It's the children I worry about. If these dreadful thieves can steal into our house and take the dead from the walls why can't they take the living children from their beds? Sometimes in the night when Richard is snoring away beside me – I shouldn't have told you he snores, should I? – and I hear the creaks and strange noises all these old houses make in the night, I think the thieves have come back. Twice now I have crept into the children's rooms to make sure they are still there.'

She looked at him defiantly. 'I know what you're going to ask me now. You'd better ask me, Lord Powerscourt.'

'I'm not going to ask you that question just at the moment,' said Powerscourt, smiling across at her, 'I want to ask if you

54

are sure your husband has not had a note from somebody, asking him to do something to get the pictures back. You see, Mrs Butler, surely, I have said to myself many times now, they must want something, these thieves. Why go to all the trouble of organizing these thefts, unless, of course, you want to sell the paintings and I'm not convinced that is the case, though I wouldn't rule it out altogether. Why bother? So what do they want? They have to tell us at some point.'

Mrs Butler folded the hands Powerscourt admired so much together and looked down at the grass. 'I know Richard doesn't tell me everything. It wouldn't be natural if he did. But he hasn't mentioned a word to me about any messages. Is he telling the truth? To be perfectly honest with you, Lord Powerscourt, I just don't know. He might be or he might not. He can be quite devious sometimes, though not,' she giggled like a girl at this point, 'when he's snoring. I'm sorry,' she went on, 'I know that's no help to you at all.'

Now Powerscourt asked the question. 'Would you think of taking the children away, Mrs Butler?'

'Please call me Sylvia,' she said inappropriately, perhaps playing for time. 'I've thought about that a lot. I think if any more pictures are stolen from any more houses – why stop at two, after all – then I might take all the younger ones to England. Except I would miss Richard terribly, even when he snores away in the middle of the night. There I go again. I can't give you a straight answer to anything, Lord Powerscourt. How very Irish of me!' And she laughed a nervous little laugh but her eyes were locked on Powerscourt's face and they were very serious indeed.

'I wish I could offer you some reassurance,' Powerscourt said, 'but I wouldn't want to give you false comfort.'

Their conversation was suddenly interrupted by a couple of fiendish war whoops as two small children with blackened faces shot across the grass and disappeared up a tree.

'I've taken up enough of your time,' said Powerscourt, rising to his feet. 'I've got an idea. I think I'm going to have a look at the opposition, or what might be the opposition. Time to seize the initiative,' although even as he said it, he knew he didn't quite believe it.

'Are you going to see the antiquated Christian Brother, sorry, I mean the antiquary Christian Brother?' Sylvia Butler asked.

'Nearly,' Powerscourt replied, 'nearly, but not quite. I'm going to call on the parish priest, who rejoices, if your steward's information is accurate and I'm sure it is, in the name of O'Donovan Brady. With a name like that he could have fought in the Williamite wars or fled to France with Patrick Sarsfield.'

One bribe to an angelic child had Powerscourt rowed back to the mainland. Another, slightly larger one, sent a young footman on horseback to ask if it would be convenient for Lord Francis Powerscourt to call on Father Brady later that day. And so, shortly after five o'clock, Powerscourt had walked down the long drive and was standing in the main square of the little town of Butler's Cross. Mulcahy and Sons, Grocery and Bar, seemed to be the main shop, dominating one side of the arena. It was flanked by O'Riordan, Bookmaker and Bar. Opposite them was the emporium of Horkan and Sons, Agricultural Suppliers and Bar. A pretty eighteenth-century house next door carried the discreet message, Delaney, Delaney and Delaney, Solicitors and Commissioners for Oaths. Just in front of the Roman Catholic church was MacSwiggin's Hotel and Bar, fine rooms and wholesome Irish food. That meant ham and eggs, Powerscourt remembered, served twenty-four hours a day. Only in the legal establishment, he noted wryly, was it not possible to obtain alcoholic refreshment on the premises. Even then, the solicitors in their dark suits would probably whip out a bottle of John Powers finest whisky from their bottom drawer to close the transaction.

At precisely five thirty Powerscourt rang the bell of the priest's house. The door was answered by a remarkably pretty girl, presumably the housekeeper, in her early twenties who showed him into what she assured him was the Father's study. The walls were lined with books, some of them in Latin, some printed in Rome. The walls carried a heady cocktail of political and religious messages. Directly above the fireplace was a full-length portrait of Daniel O'Connell, the man they called the Liberator, widely credited with securing Catholic Emancipation some eighty years before and the final repeal of the Penal Laws that had discriminated against his co-religionists. To the left of it, in a much smaller frame – Powerscourt wondered if this indicated the true strengths of the priest's convictions, politics looming larger than God in his mind – a weary-looking Christ was dragging his cross up the hill they called Golgotha. To the right, the empty tomb, brilliant bursts of light pouring from its depths and the women kneeling in awe on the stony ground. Opposite them, posing in front of a barricade in the fashionable clothes of a French revolutionary of the mid-1790s, Theobald Wolfe Tone, leading member of the United Irishmen who fomented the rebellion in 1798. And a Protestant. A Protestant, moreover, from the unholy city of Dublin. Powerscourt thought that there must be rejoicing, even for the sinner that repenteth. Perhaps, after this passage of time, Tone had become an honorary Catholic, received into the faith with the compassion the Church was famed for from the hellfires where his heretic religion would have undoubtedly carried him. Powerscourt was not surprised that there was no place on these walls for Charles Stewart Parnell, Protestant leader in the Westminster Parliament of a group of largely Catholic MPs who almost brought Home Rule, a form of self government, to Ireland, only to be brought down by his adultery with the married Mrs Katherine O'Shea, an adultery condemned from the pulpits of most of the Catholic churches in Ireland.

'Good afternoon, Lord Powerscourt, how can I be of assistance?' Father O'Donovan Brady was a short tubby man of about forty years, red of face, bald on top and with small suspicious eyes. His tone was polite but cold. Powerscourt thought he looked like Mr Pickwick, a billiard ball of a man, might have done had he been employed in the rack and thumbscrew department of the Inquisition, a priest more interested in sniffing out sin than in offering the consolation of salvation.

'Thank you very much for seeing me at such short notice, Father,' Powerscourt began. 'I am staying with the Butlers up at Butler's Court.'

Father Brady interrupted him. 'I know who you are, Lord Powerscourt, and I know the nature of your business here with us.' Of course, Powerscourt remembered. Word of his arrival and his mission would have travelled down the long drive to the little town as fast as the kingfishers that flew across the river. Johnny Fitzgerald had once observed that the sending of telegrams or maybe even important and interesting letters was not a safe practice in Ireland – the contents might have been read long before they reached the intended recipient.

'A fine family, in spite of their religion, the Butlers,' the priest went on. 'The local people will always remember them for the work they did here in this barony at the time of the famine, slaughtering their cattle and handing over their crops to feed the starving. Not that you could say that about most of the landlord class, not by a long way.'

'I was wondering, Father,' Powerscourt was picking his words very carefully now. He had spoken more truthfully than he knew when he talked to Mrs Butler earlier that day about entering enemy territory, 'if you could offer me any advice about the missing paintings, whether or not this has happened before, that sort of thing.'

Father O'Donovan Brady walked over to his sideboard and took out a full decanter and two large glasses. 'Would you care for a small glass of sherry, Lord Powerscourt? I normally take one myself at this time of day.'

Powerscourt noted with interest that the Reverend's glass was filled to a much higher level than his own. He wondered if the need for alcohol could overcome suspicion or even dislike of Protestants.

Father Brady sat down with his glass and drank deeply. 'I fear,' he shook his bald head as he spoke, 'there will always be mischief in Ireland as long as the landlords are here.' Powerscourt wondered suddenly if the man was actually a Fenian, or a secret member of the vicar's Irish Republican Brotherhood, inciting revolt from the pulpit perhaps, withholding the sacrament from supporters of the status quo. 'You ask if I can be of assistance to you in your sordid inquiries. Would you have me incriminate members of my own congregation, if I knew anything germane to the matter, which I do not? Are you asking me, in effect, to become an informer, virtually a spy for the Intelligence Department up at Dublin Castle?'

Tout, informer, Judas, there were few more dangerous words in Ireland where hatred of informers was as prevalent as the willingness of the native Irish to betray their own for money. The United Irishmen, Powerscourt recalled, had been riddled with informers, like a rotting honeycomb.

'Of course I would not ask you to incriminate one of your own flock, Father. I was merely seeking information of a more general sort,' said Powerscourt, watching Brady take another deep draught of his pale sherry.

'Perhaps we can be clear about things, Lord Powerscourt. I cannot complain if you come to me looking for help in your squalid activities. But I am under no obligation to help you. I refuse to incriminate or betray any member of my congregation. I understand you reside most of the time in England now, Lord Powerscourt. Perhaps it would be better for this poor benighted country if all the Protestants, even the Butlers, went to live in England. Ireland is a land largely populated by Catholics, it always has been. One day, I am sure, God willing, it will be a proper Catholic nation. Whether or not there will be any significant place in that Catholic nation for other faiths is not for me to say, thank God.'

59

He went and poured himself a generous refill. He did not offer one to his guest but Powerscourt's glass was hardly touched. 'We have had landlords too long in Ireland, Lord Powerscourt, far too long.'

Powerscourt thought the time had come to beat a retreat. 'Thank you very much for your time, Father,' he said, heading for the door. 'I can see little point in continuing this conversation.'

The priest showed him out. 'We have conversion classes here in this house every other Thursday, Lord Powerscourt. Church of Ireland Protestants, Presbyterians, Methodists, all are welcome. It is never too late to welcome the sinner and the heretic into the true faith.' With that he slammed the door shut. As he left Powerscourt was just able to see through the window Father O'Donovan Brady pouring himself another refill. It was only a quarter to six.

As he approached the steps leading up to Butler's Court Powerscourt was passed by a carriage travelling at considerable speed. The passenger rushed inside. As Powerscourt entered the great white hall with its glorious staircase he heard Richard Butler cry, 'Oh no! Oh, my God! How dreadful! How truly dreadful! How many this time?'

'Ten altogether this time, Richard,' the man from the carriage said. 'Seven ancestors, all male, a Titian and couple of Gainsboroughs, well, maybe Gainsboroughs or attributed to Gainsborough as they say. I never did understand anything about this damned painting business.'

'Allow me to make the introductions,' said Richard Butler. 'Lord Francis Powerscourt, come to investigate the theft of the earlier pictures, Mr William Moore, of Moore Castle in the neighbouring county.'

Just as they were shaking hands, they heard the sound of another pair of boots racing up the steps. The boots appeared to be in as great a hurry as the carriage had been earlier.

'Francis,' said a panting Johnny Fitzgerald, nodding politely to the others. 'I have news. Important news, I think.' He fished a note from his pocket. 'This,' he said, 'from a leading New York newspaper several days ago. The text was sent over by cable. "Eight Anglo-Irish portraits by distinguished Irish and English artists, eighteenth to nineteenth centuries. Four full-length, four half. Available for sale as a group or individually. Price on application to Goldman and Rabinowitz, Picture Restorers and Dealers in Fine Art, 57 Fifth Avenue, New York City."'

4

Richard Butler led them rapidly out of the hall, talking loudly about a horse he had seen that morning. The beast, he declared, was a most promising animal, the finest he had seen since the German-bred Wolfgang years before.

'Didn't want the women to hear,' he said, panting slightly as he reached the security of his study. 'Sylvia would be on the first boat to Holyhead if I told her this evening, so she would. God, this is terrible news.'

Further introductions were effected, William Moore telling Johnny Fitzgerald that he had known a cousin of his at school. 'Tell us, William, in God's name,' said Butler, 'tell us when it happened, how it happened.'

'The theft took place sometime in the middle of the night. There's a broken window down in the kitchen. That's where they came in, I think. One of the footmen noticed the vanished pictures on his rounds first thing this morning.'

'Was anything else taken?' asked Powerscourt, sitting himself down on a small sofa by the fireplace.

'Nothing at all,' said Moore, a small wiry man with red hair and a bright red beard, 'and the silver in that room is worth a fortune, far more than the bloody pictures.'

'And how did the family take it?' asked Butler.

'Well,' Moore said, 'the wife initially didn't seem to mind very much. Said she'd never really cared for the portraits anyway. She's always maintained they make the place look like a bloody mausoleum, like the one Victoria built for the dreadful Albert over at Frogmore, all those damned dead men looking at her every time she entered a room. I thought it wasn't going to bother her very much. She ate a huge breakfast, eggs, bacon, tomatoes, sausages, fried potato bread, mushrooms, toast, and I began to feel a bit better myself. Then I found her an hour later crying on the terrace, saying the rebels were back and we'd all be murdered in our beds. Her people came from Wicklow, you know. They had a terrible time there with those rebels back in '98. I think three of them were killed.'

'What are we to do, Lord Powerscourt? What on earth are we going to do now?'

Richard Butler was twisting his hands round and round each other, as if he were in pain. He and Moore looked at Powerscourt with the air of children expecting a parent to rescue them from some especially unpleasant predicament. Powerscourt had no idea what to say. Temporarily, he was lost for words.

'Let us begin with the practicalities,' he said at last, trying to sound more authoritative than he felt. 'The first thing is to decide what to do about the women and the wives. I do think, Butler, that you will have to tell them, and tell them as soon as possible. For all we know Mrs Moore may arrive here at any moment to pour out her woes to your wife. You know what women are like about talking to each other, talk all bloody day if you give them half a chance.'

Richard Butler peered anxiously out of the window in case another carriage was bringing a distraught Mrs Butler to his quarters. All he could see was an old man raking the gravel on the drive.

'I suggest,' Powerscourt went on, 'that Mr Moore should stay the night here, and, with your approval, Johnny and I will accompany him back to Moore Castle in the morning. We can make a full inspection of the house and an inventory of the missing pictures and so on.'

The prospect of another guest and activity of some kind seemed to restore Butler's spirits slightly.

'Very well,' he said, 'I'll get that sorted in a moment. But tell me, Powerscourt, are you certain I have to tell Sylvia? Tell her that more paintings have disappeared?'

'In my opinion,' replied Powerscourt, sure of this if of nothing else, 'you have no choice. Or rather, you have two very disagreeable options. Either you tell her yourself, or you wait for rumour to reach her. News, as you know as well as I do, travels very fast over here. You wouldn't want her to hear about it from the cook as they're discussing the menus for the week first thing in the morning now, would you?'

Richard Butler looked racked by the choice. 'I'll tell her in the morning,' he said finally. 'She'll be able to bear it better in the morning.'

For a moment nobody spoke. The only sound was the methodical swish of rake on gravel.

Then Johnny Fitzgerald tried a diversion. 'These are wonderful horses you have here on your walls, Mr Butler,' he said. 'Are any of them yours?' Powerscourt wondered briefly if one of the horses lining three walls of the study was the fabled Wolfgang, triple winner at the Punchestown Races. He knew that horses were the only subject that might distract attention from the calamity of the vanished paintings over at Moore Castle. A vigorous debate followed, Butler telling the two strangers to Ireland that all the horses on the walls were, or had been, his and that he thought he had spent far more money on them than his ancestors had on the paintings.

'There's a thing,' said Moore, suddenly animated, 'why haven't they taken any of the horses? In Ireland you can turn horseflesh into cash faster than almost anything else. How would anybody know, Richard, if some of your animals turned up in Tipperary, or Waterford or Cork?'

'It's a poor eye for a horse they have down there in Cork,' said Richard Butler darkly. 'Those buggers wouldn't know a racehorse from a dray.'

'Forgive me for bringing the conversation back into the human world, gentlemen,' said Powerscourt, 'but did the thieves leave you any kind of message, Mr Moore? A ransom note? Demands for money, that sort of thing?'

William Moore blinked rapidly. 'No note, no ransom, nothing at all. Do you think it's going to be like the boycott all over again, Powerscourt? Not that nobody's going to talk to us, though with some of them that would be a blessing, but a new . . .' He paused briefly, searching for the right word. '. . . a new tactic, a new device to confound the landlords? Do you think it's that, Powerscourt?'

'I don't think we should alarm ourselves with talk of boycotts and fresh campaigns at this stage, Mr Moore,' said Powerscourt diplomatically, wishing he could believe it. 'I know this is all very difficult to bear, but only three houses have been affected so far. And nobody's lives or livelihoods are affected.'

On that note the little party broke up, Butler and Moore going to sort out his accommodation and the loan of a pair of pyjamas, Powerscourt and Fitzgerald to walk by the river in the late afternoon sun.

'That advertisement from the New York paper, Johnny. How did you get hold of it?'

'Do you think there's something wrong with it, Francis?' said Fitzgerald.

'I can only answer that when I know how you came by it,' Powerscourt replied, staring across the Shannon from the bottom of Butler's gardens.

'Well,' said Fitzgerald, 'I'd made the rounds of most of the Dublin art dealers, shysters most of them. Then there was this man called Farrell in a gallery of the same name in Kildare Street, just along from the Kildare Street Club, Dublin's answer to the Garrick and the Reform. He thought I was you, to start with, Francis. Seemed most disappointed that I wasn't you, if you see what I mean. Damned unfair of him, I thought, nothing wrong with me. Anyway, when I said I was a great friend of yours and that we'd worked on all sorts of cases together, he relented a bit. He said nobody had been trying to sell any ancestor paintings at all, so maybe the thieves are keeping their powder dry. Then he gave me the advertisement but he wouldn't say where it came from. He said, the Farrell man, that he could only tell you in person. It was all very secretive, like we were all trying to sell him a couple of fake Leonardos. He even bolted the door and closed the shop up for a few minutes while he talked to me. What do you make of that, Francis?'

'I'll tell you what I think it means, Johnny,' said Powerscourt, bending down to trail a hand in the water. He told Fitzgerald about his conversation with Michael Hudson in Old Bond Street some time before and Hudson's idea of placing an advertisement in one of the American newspapers. 'Appropriately enough, from where we're standing now, this is a fishing expedition. Hudson's trying to see if there is a market for these ancestral portraits in New York. If there are a number of replies, then we will know there is a market for these things, a market that the thieves might have known about.'

'And what happens if they are queuing up round the block to buy the bloody things?' asked Johnny. 'Goldman and Rabinowitz don't have a heap of Irish landowners lying about in their basement, do they?'

'I don't think that matters very much,' said Powerscourt. 'Paintings gone for cleaning, unavoidable delay in transshipment from Ireland, customs formalities to be finalized, you could keep the ball in play for months.'

'By God, Francis,' said Johnny Fitzgerald, 'your lines of communication here are longer than they ever were in South Africa or India. London, New York, London, Dublin. That's a bloody long way. Are you going to tell them in the Big House about it?'

'Certainly not,' said Powerscourt firmly. 'That would be like putting it on the front page of the *Irish Times*. Father O'Donovan Brady down in the town, my favourite Catholic priest in all the world, would hear of it inside twenty-four hours.'

Dinner that evening was a rather subdued affair in Butler's Court. The blank spaces reproached them from the walls. Butler carried on a desultory conversation with Alice Bracken about the prospects for the forthcoming hunting season. Powerscourt had a halting discussion with the tall thin young man called James about Irish songs and ballads, a subject on which the young man possessed an encyclopedic knowledge. Only Johnny Fitzgerald seemed to be on top form, entertaining Sylvia Butler with anecdotes about the Dublin art dealers he had recently met, all of them, without exception, he maintained, thieves and villains of the darkest hue, not a single one of them a man you would buy a tea caddy from. After the consumption of a spectacular trifle, almost all the ingredients originating on the premises, Richard Butler proudly told the company, the ladies withdrew. As their host placed a bottle of port in the centre of the table they were joined by a very old gentleman with white hair, a straggly white moustache and a thin white beard. He shuffled slowly to an empty chair, bringing with him a large black notebook. He was wearing a faded dinner jacket under a very old green dressing gown decorated with Chinese dragons of considerable ferocity. Powerscourt wondered if it had come from the East with Marco Polo.

'Uncle Peter,' said Richard Butler rather wearily. 'How good of you to join us.'

'Didn't feel like the whole thing, dinner, I mean,' said the aged uncle, eyeing the port greedily. 'Had something in my rooms.'

By the look of him, Powerscourt thought, he had been doing rather more drinking than eating in his rooms. His eyes were bloodshot and he carried with him a general air of faded dissipation, like an old sofa that had been left out in the rain.

'Heard you had visitors,' Uncle Peter went on. 'Educated men. Cambridge, one of them. Young James told me.'

The old man nodded firmly at this point, looking with even greater interest at the glasses and the bottle. 'Thought they'd like to hear some of my book.' He patted the volume in front of him.

'Uncle Peter's been writing a history of Ireland,' Richard Butler said loudly in the tone he might have used when talking to a small child. 'He's been working at it for the past fifteen years.'

'Really?' said Powerscourt, wondering what was to follow. Johnny was eyeing their visitor with a look of fellow feeling for a man who so obviously liked a glass of something every now and then to ease the pain of the day.

'Parnell's funeral,' said Uncle Peter, rummaging about in his book. 'That's the end of my story. That's the bit I thought the gentlemen would like to hear.'

Butler filled four glasses and handed them round. 'Moore,' he said, laying down the lines for his escape, 'I want to ask your advice about a piece of land that's up for sale over at Carryduff. I think it's quite promising. Did I tell you, by the way, that the bloody man Mulcahy down in the square tried to buy some of my land? Bloody cheek!' Land, Powerscourt remembered, a subject almost as dear to these people as horses. Powerscourt was to learn later that William Moore was said to have the sharpest eye for a piece of land in the four provinces of Ireland. With that, and a slight bow, Richard Butler led his neighbour from the room.

'Why did you finish your book with Parnell's funeral?' asked Johnny Fitzgerald. 'That's nearly fifteen years ago now.'

'Will you tell me,' the old man said, downing most of his glass in a single gulp, 'what's happened in Ireland since? I'll tell you now, so I will. Power, real power, flowing away from the landlord class like an ebb tide. More priests, more bloody nuns, more schools, more of the young playing those stupid games of Irish football and that ridiculous hurling they go in for. Who's ever going to give them a proper international match in hurling, will you tell me that now?'

'We'd be most interested to hear about Parnell's funeral,' said Powerscourt politely. 'You see, we were both there, Johnny and I.'

'Maybe you'll be able to give me some advice then,' said Uncle Peter. 'You'd be amazed at how hard it is to find accurate information in this country. It's the newspapers, you see. They can't even agree on the date the great Charles Stewart Parnell was buried. I'm sure the man from the London *Times* was there on the spot, and the man from the *Irish Times* and the fellow from the *Freeman's Journal*, but I don't think the chap from the *Cork Examiner* was there at all, or the man from the *Mayo News*. Some of them have got the funeral on a different day. One of them, can't remember which one now, memory's going like a clock winding down, said Parnell died on a Tuesday and was buried the next day, on the Wednesday. Would you believe it? As if they could put his body in a coffin, transport it from Brighton to Holyhead and then get it on a boat from there to Kingstown inside twenty-four hours. The thing's not possible. Do you think they make it up, the newspapermen, I mean?' During this speech Uncle Peter had extracted a pair of battered spectacles from a dragon's pocket in his dressing gown and was ferreting about in his book, looking for the right place to start.

'Sunday it was,' said Powerscourt, 'the day they buried him.'

'Friday, I'm sure it was Friday,' said Johnny.

'There you are,' said the old man triumphantly, 'and you're not even newspapermen. Young James would have told me if you were newspapermen.'

Richard Butler made a brief reappearance in his dining room. He was carrying a large tray with three further bottles of port and an enormous jug of iced lemonade.

'I thought it might be a long evening, boys,' he said, depositing his precious cargo directly in front of Uncle Peter. 'This should keep the vocal cords in working order.'

69

'The commissariat has arrived,' said Uncle Peter thankfully to the departing Butler. 'Supplies.' He had the air of a man who has just found the Ark of the Covenant. As he looked again in his book for the right place to start, his eyes peering down at the pages, his right hand, guided by apparently unseen forces, reached out for the port bottle and refilled his glass. Not a drop was spilt. Even Johnny Fitzgerald, a man with some experience in these areas, nodded his appreciation.

'Excuse me, Uncle Peter,' said Powerscourt apologetically, 'don't you think it would be helpful if you gave us a brief biography of Parnell before we start? You and Johnny and I have lived through it, after all, but Young James here was only a child when the man died.' Powerscourt watched as the old man's mouth opened and closed several times.

Then Powerscourt understood. This was a change of plan. Old men didn't like changes of plan. In his mind Uncle Peter was already lost in the details of Parnell's funeral. Now he was asked for the view from the mountain top.

'Let me try,' said Powerscourt, 'it won't be very good but it might help.' He paused briefly, marshalling his thoughts. 'Born in famine times. Protestant landowner from County Wicklow. Elected to Westminster Parliament mid-1870s. By the end of that decade two bad harvests in a row filled the island with the terror of another famine. With Michael Davitt Parnell founded the Land League. Farmers asked their landlords for reduction or cancellation of their rents. Widespread agrarian violence. Landlords who refused were sometimes boycotted. Two results. Gladstone passed a law that made it easier for the tenants to purchase their land. And he imprisoned Parnell in Kilmainham Jail for inciting violence, which guaranteed Parnell immortality in Ireland. Became Leader of Irish Parliamentary Party in 1880. Turned it from undisciplined rabble into formidable fighting force. Parnell and his MPs fought for Home Rule for Ireland. Gladstone was converted to Home Rule, a form of devolution. Through the '80s Parnell carried on a passionate affair with Katherine

O'Shea, wife of another Irish MP. Cited as co-respondent in 1889 divorce case. Savaged by hostile publicity when details of the adultery came out in court. A few MPs stayed loyal, remainder fought him tooth and nail. Pro- and anti-Parnellites contested three by-elections in Ireland through 1891. Parnell lost them all. Married Katherine O'Shea June 1891.'

'Admirable,' said Uncle Peter. 'Now then,' he went on, wiping his mouth quickly with the sleeve of his jacket, 'let us begin.' He read in a light tenor voice that gradually filled the dining room. '"Chapter Twenty-Seven,"' he said. '"Charles Stewart Parnell died at a quarter to midnight on 6th October 1891 in Mrs Parnell, formerly Mrs O'Shea's house at Number 10 Walsingham Terrace in Brighton. He had been ill for some days. The months of strain as he campaigned unsuccessfully to hold on to his political base at those three by-elections in Ireland, the Irish Parliamentary split into bitter faction fighting after the shock of his divorce case, must have taken their toll. He had endured levels of abuse and hostility unparalleled even in Ireland. Lime had been thrown in his face. On another occasion eggs had been hurled at him and his trousers were torn in a scuffle in a hotel, the waiter repairing his breeches under the table while Parnell ate the remains of his supper. Everywhere he went he was pursued by the national anthem of his opponents, 'Three Cheers for Kitty O'Shea'. Sometimes his enemies would shake battered clothes on poles at him, proclaiming to all and sundry that these were Kitty O'Shea's knickers.

'"On his last evening he asked his wife to lie down on the bed beside him. His old dog Grouse, at his request, was also present in the bedroom. He had not slept for two days and a local doctor had given him some medicine. Throughout his life Parnell was a superstitious man – the colour green had always been anathema to him – and he believed that his lack of rest was a bad omen. And it was October, a month he always said was his unlucky time of year. During the evening he dozed and Mrs Parnell thought she heard him mutter

'Conservative Party' as if he were planning some further political manoeuvre. If she touched him, he smiled. Later he said, 'Kiss me, sweet wifie, and I will try to sleep a little.' Those were the last words on earth of the man who changed the face of Irish politics. Just before midnight he was gone. He was only forty-five years old."'

Uncle Peter's voice began to crack towards the end, whether due to lack of refreshment or emotion unclear. As he topped up his glass he turned to his little audience of three.

'What do you think of it so far?' he asked. 'Do you like it well enough?'

'Excellent start,' said Powerscourt.

'Splendid,' said Johnny.

'Let's have some more, Uncle Peter,' said Young James in an uncharacteristically long speech.

'Short sentences wherever possible,' the historian declared, 'nothing too ornate in the prose style department. Gibbon. Always liked Gibbon. Never got to the end of that *Decline and Fall of the Roman Empire*, mind you. Don't suppose many people did.'

He peered down at his black book once more, checking on the way that there were still plentiful supplies of port to hand. '"The news of his death travelled round the world. In New York's fourth ward, heavily populated with Irish immigrants, portraits of the dead leader appeared in the windows, draped in black. About twelve o'clock on the morning of Saturday 10th October Parnell's body set out on the long journey back to Dublin for his funeral and burial. A number of Irish MPs accompanied him on his journey. Mrs Parnell was too upset to travel, but her wreath went with him every step of the way: 'My true love, my darling, my husband.' Rain was falling heavily as his coffin, almost covered with wreaths of large white flowers, was carried out to an open-sided funeral carriage drawn by four black horses. The umbrellas of the small crowd were useless in the violent squalls of rain. They took shelter in the doorways and in the rooms of houses being redecorated close by, saluting the coffin respectfully as it passed. The route went along the King's Road on the sea front, past Regency Square and the West Pier whose great girders were being pounded by the waves, its promenades totally deserted, and up West Street to Brighton station. The coffin was lifted into a van attached to a special saloon on the 1.45 to Victoria station in London. En route to the capital it was decoupled at Croydon and diverted to Willesden where many Irish men and women came to pay their last respects. Another wreath bore the message, 'Charles Stewart Parnell, Salutation. He died fighting for freedom.' Shortly before seven o' clock the train set off from Willesden on its melancholy eight-hour journey through the dark heart of England to Holyhead and the Irish boat. Sixteen men carried Parnell's coffin on to the steamer, the *Ireland*, where it was wheeled on a trolley into the smoking saloon on the lower deck, an appropriate, if temporary, resting place for a man so devoted to cigars. A black cloth was laid over it, covered in its turn by a green flag. Twenty-eight more wreaths, which had travelled north with the coffin, were placed alongside it. 'Died fighting for Ireland'. 'In fond memory of one of Ireland's greatest chieftains who was martyred in the struggle for her independence.' At two forty-five in the morning, nearly fifteen hours after the corpse left the house in Brighton, the *Ireland* set off to carry Charles Stewart Parnell on his very last crossing of the Irish Sea to Dublin."'

'Still awake, are ye?' croaked the old man, pouring himself a tumbler of iced lemonade. 'Plenty more to go.'

Johnny Fitzgerald rose and took one of the bottles of port from in front of the old man. 'Thought we'd better keep you company,' he said cheerfully.

Powerscourt was thinking that the political questions raised by Parnell in his lifetime, the land question, the precise relationships to exist between England and Ireland, the thorny conundrum of Home Rule, had not been answered yet. Gladstone had promised that it would be his life's mission to bring peace to Ireland or perish in the attempt. It had been one of the chief political objectives of his long career. Well, Gladstone had perished. Ireland still did not have peace. Maybe another act in the long drama was being played out in these Irish rooms with the great holes on the walls where ancestors from centuries before had rested in their great houses. Maybe the theft of these paintings was the start of another chapter. Maybe they were all part of a story that went back eight hundred years.

'"The *Ireland* was late arriving in Kingstown,"' Uncle Peter continued, staring down at his book, 'still battered by the storm, angry waves lashing at the harbour walls. Great crowds had often welcomed Parnell home from his Parliamentary triumphs here in the past, bands playing 'The Wearing of the Green' or 'A Nation Once Again'. They were silent this morning except for a low moan as the coffin came into view. Among the crowd in Kingstown early that morning was the young Irish poet W.B. Yeats, come to greet his friend Maud Gonne who had met Parnell in Ireland in the days before his death."'

'Bitch goddess!' said James, with sudden and unexpected force.

Uncle Peter looked up at him like an elderly bishop whose sermon has just been interrupted by a junior member of the choir. 'I beg your pardon, Young James? What did you say?'

'Bitch goddess!' James repeated with the same vigour as before. 'Maud Gonne is Yeats's bitch goddess. She wouldn't marry him and she wouldn't leave him alone. She's tormented him for years, the cow!'

'Maybe,' said Uncle Peter, 'but perhaps it's just as well the poet man met his bitch goddess. Answer me this, Young James, would we have had Homer's *Iliad* without Helen of Troy? She was somebody's bitch goddess, though I'm damned if I can remember whose just at this moment. Would your man Shakespeare have written *Antony and Cleopatra* without Cleopatra and her snake, best thing that ever happened to her in my view? Or John Donne written his verses without all those mistresses of his? What would have happened if they had married anyway, Yeats and Maud Gonne? Maybe they'd have lived happily ever after, taking out the tarot cards under the fruit trees in the garden in the afternoon and writing obscure papers for the Theosophical Society in London in the evening. No pain, no poem. I've never had much to do with the women myself,' he admitted, 'too temperamental for me, but I've always understood that the one thing they're good for is a bit for inspiration for the poetry writing classes when the normal things like drink have failed.'

'Anyway,' Uncle Peter went on, fuelling his cynicism with another large gulp of Cockburn's finest Old Tawny, 'your man Yeats, so a professor from Trinity told me once – don't ask me his name, that's gone too for the present – he told me Yeats thought he and his friends could create an alternative version of the Irish past to fill the political vacuum left by the death of Parnell and the squabbling of his associates. Horse manure!' He paused for just one more mouthful. 'Horse manure and gobshite! How many people from Carrick-on-Shannon or Ballywalter know where the bloody Abbey Theatre Yeats founded actually is? How many people have bought tickets for the performances? How many Catholic farmers and shopkeepers and solicitors are ever going to buy a book of poetry, any damned poetry, let alone stuff with titles like "The Song of the Wandering Aengus" or "The Valley of the Black Pig" or "The Host of the Air", for God's sake? And how many Christian Brothers are going to teach poetry written by a Protestant from Sligo, if they teach poetry at all?

'Damn. I'm lost now. Where was I?'

'Parnell's just off the boat, Uncle Peter,' said Johnny, 'and it was still raining. This was Ireland, after all.'

Uncle Peter looked as if he was going to continue his diatribe, but he went back to his book.

'"The body was carried quickly ashore and placed on the waiting train. There was a short delay while the mail was unloaded from the *Ireland*. Charles Stewart Parnell began his last journey into Ireland's capital on track laid in 1834 by the Dublin and Kingston Railway Company, at the time the first commuter line in the world. At seven thirty on Sunday morning it reached Westland Row station. As the coffin, six feet four inches long, was finally removed from the large deal case which had protected it on its rough journey across the sea, the crowd surged forward and hacked the case to pieces, breaking the wood up into fragments to be treasured as relics, as if they had come from a dead saint. A soaking escort of nearly a thousand members of the Gaelic Athletic Association, a nationalist body devoted to Irish games, widely believed to be infiltrated by Fenians or members of the Irish Republican Brotherhood, more devoted to insurrection than to ball games, formed an honour guard round the bier as it was laid on its hearse. They were all dressed in green and carrying hurling sticks tied with black crepe and green ribbon. Here was a blatant warning to any anti-Parnellites who might have thought of trying to disrupt the proceedings. Violence would be met with violence."'

Johnny Fitzgerald had been holding his hand up and waving it for a minute or so. 'Those bits of the deal case enclosing the coffin, Uncle Peter,' he said, 'I know something that might be useful for this section of your book when you next revise it. You could buy bits of them, the relics I mean, in many of the Dublin pubs that evening when the funeral was over. They were changing hands in some places for a pound or more. Mind you, one of the publicans told me afterwards that there was enough wood on sale that night to cover fifty coffins. Maybe they increased and multiplied, like those loaves and fishes on the mountain.'

'Thank you, Johnny,' said Uncle Peter. 'I am seriously thinking of banning all interruptions in the manner of a French teacher of mine who punished any disturbances when he was giving dictation with a severe thrashing.' Uncle Peter took advantage of the diversion to open another bottle.

'Anybody else wish to interrupt? Young James, have you further comments on the personalities involved you would like to impart to us? Powerscourt, you have been commendably quiet so far?'

All three shook their heads.

Uncle Peter's appearance was rather wild now, wisps of hair falling down on to his lined forehead. He looked, Powerscourt thought, like an aged prophet come out of the wilderness with his book to lead his people on a last crusade, or a man who had spent too long in solitary confinement. A large drop of port had fallen on to his green dressing gown. At any moment, Powerscourt felt, a dragon's mouth might dart forth and gulp it down. Uncle Peter's drinking continued regularly, like the beat of a metronome. From outside the dining room came faint noises of doors being bolted and creaky sash windows closed. The household was going to bed.

'"Parnell's last journey across the city resembled a secular version of the Stations of the Cross, the stops at the great memorials to Ireland's past replacing the final stages of Christ's journey. The procession moved slowly away from Westland Row station, outriders on either side, the honour guard of the hurling stick youths surrounding the coffin, crowds marching six abreast behind them, the pavements packed with mourners, women kneeling down and crossing themselves as it passed by. Down College Street they went, stopping at the Old Parliament building on College Green. Here, until its abolition in 1800, an Irish Parliament had sat, composed entirely of Protestant members and looking after entirely Protestant interests, able to pass limited amounts of legislation. Parnell's great grandfather had been a prominent member of this Assembly. Now the cortège rested for a minute to honour the great grandson who had nearly secured the return of an Irish Parliament to Dublin, one that would have been dominated by Catholics. Nobody in an Irish crowd would have failed to see the symbolic significance of this moment. At the rear one of the thirty-three bands on duty that day began playing the Dead March from *Saul*. The procession continued through the rain, crossing the river Liffey and advancing along the northern quays to St Michan's Church, one of the oldest in the city. As the coffin entered the church one of the officiating clergy said at the porch, 'I am the Resurrection and the Life, he that believeth in me shall not perish but have everlasting life.' As the coffin went through the church it passed under the archway of the organ which, according to legend, Handel himself had played at the first performance of the *Messiah*. Down in the crypt of St Michan's, some special atmospheric properties, unique to the church, had kept a number of corpses in a state of remarkable preservation, the wooden caskets cracked open to reveal skin and strands of hair. There is even a figure, deep from Ireland's past, known as The Crusader. Up above, as the prayers for the dead were intoned, Parnell's own body was beginning its long rot towards eternity. For most of the congregation this was the first, and probably the last, Protestant funeral service they would ever attend.

'"Elsewhere in the city groups of mourners began forming up for the final procession. Societies and clubs assembled on St Stephen's Green at twelve, members of Dublin and provincial Corporations gathered in Grafton Street. The Parnell Leadership Committee, the small remnant of his Parliamentary supporters, met in the National Club. Fresh mourners were still pouring into the city on special trains from all over Ireland, the carriages filled with people wearing the black armband with a ribbon of green."'

'Still here, are ye?' Uncle Peter asked, pausing to pour another glass. 'Not dropping off yet?'

No, no, his little audience assured him, they were all fine.

'"The most dramatic farewell of all the farewells that day came in the City Hall, the municipal headquarters of Dublin Catholicism where Daniel O'Connell himself had been Mayor back in the 1840s. Parnell's coffin was placed on a catafalque on the marble floor of the great circular chamber, ringed with statues of dead heroes from Ireland's past. He lay in front of a statue of O'Connell himself. There were railings round the body, guarded by members of the Dublin Fire Brigade with their polished helmets to allow the mourners to pass round it to pay their last respects. Some thirty thousand were believed to have done so. All around were flags from that earlier Protestant Parliament which had been brought up from Parnell's family estate at Avondale in County Wicklow. Behind O'Connell's statue was a huge Celtic cross of flowers, six feet high, of arum and eucharis lilies, white chrysanthemums and ferns. It came from Parnell's Parliamentary colleagues. The building was draped with black all the way up to the dome and a great white banner ran across the room bearing what was meant to be Parnell's last message to his country, 'Give my love to my colleagues and the Irish people.' There were other wreaths, of course, from Limerick, from Navan, from Waterford, from Arklow, from Tralee, from Kilkenny, from Donegal, but none more poignant than the simple three of lilies and roses, from the children of Mrs O'Shea, now Mrs Parnell, which said, 'To my dear mother's husband, from Nora,' 'From little Clare,' and 'From little Katie.' Few in the City Hall that sad Sunday would have known it, little Clare and little Katie themselves did not know it at the time, but it was Parnell who was their father. Other inscriptions spoke of murder and martyrdom in Erin's cause. Parnell, a man who spent more time in his lifetime cultivating the Roman Catholic hierarchy than he had his own Protestant bishops, was being turned into a human sacrifice in the sacred cause of Irish freedom. The torch of heroic martyrdom had passed in apostolic succession from Wolfe Tone to Daniel O'Connell and from O'Connell to Charles Stewart Parnell. Who would be next?"'

'That's good,' said Johnny Fitzgerald, 'that's very good, Uncle Peter.'

'Do you like it now?' Uncle Peter replied, gazing at them like a very old owl over the tops of his battered spectacles, as eager and hungry for praise as authors usually are.

'Oh yes,' Powerscourt said, 'it's very good indeed.'

'"Now came the last journey,"' Uncle Peter went on, '"the last apocalyptic journey to the graveside. As the procession moved out from the sombre gloom of the City Hall the weather changed and sunshine arrived to bless Parnell's last moments on the streets of Dublin. The young men of the Gaelic Athletic Association formed up in their honour guard around the hearse once more, many of them now holding their hurling sticks like rifles on a drill parade. Behind them came the City Marshal on horseback and in full uniform. Behind the Marshal, Parnell's horse, riderless, saddled, with the boots in place in reverse position, tribute and symbol to the dead leader since the days of Genghis Khan. Then the carriages, over a hundred of them, with the Mayor and the members of the Corporation and Parnell's family. There was one carriage, observed but not apprehended by the plain clothes men from Dublin Castle who mingled with the crowds that day, believed to be carrying three veteran Fenians, with whom Parnell had enjoyed ambiguous relationships through-out his life. They, along with the members of the Corporation, had organized the funeral. Behind them a vast procession, most of them wearing black armbands with a green ribbon, said to be two hundred thousand strong.

'"The great cortège left the City Hall and moved slowly through Christ Church Place into Thomas Street. Here were two more symbolic stops, the first at the house of Robert Emmett, another martyred Protestant rebel who had launched a pathetic postscript to the '98 Rising in 1803 and been executed for his pains. Emmett's true claim for inclusion in the pantheon of Irish saints and heroes was his speech from the dock at the close of his trial where he declared that no man should write his epitaph until Ireland was free. Emmett's epitaph,"' Uncle Peter looked up at them sternly at this point, '"remains unwritten to this day. A little further up the same street came the last stop, the last of Parnell's Stations of the Cross, at the house where another Protestant rebel, Lord

Edward Fitzgerald, was betrayed and fatally wounded at the end of the 1798 rising. Lord Edward had been born into the bluest of blue-blooded Irish families. His father was the Duke of Leinster and he was a child of the vast wealth and splendour of Carton House in County Kildare. Even after he was betrayed for his role with the United Irishmen, his relatives were arranging with the authorities for blind eyes to be turned at selected ports while Lord Edward fled the country. He died in prison several days after the shooting.

'"It was now taking an hour and three-quarters for the procession to pass a given point. The bands were playing with muffled drums, many of them now working their way through Chopin's Funeral March. From Thomas Street they took the body of the man they had called The Chief or The Uncrowned King of Ireland in a great loop around the city, showing Parnell Dublin as if he were a living visitor, east into James Street, across the river at King's Bridge, back along the northern side of the Liffey, running brown and dirty after the rains, over the river once more at Essex Bridge, down Parliament Street, close to the City Hall where they had started, back into College Green for a last look at the old Parliament building, north up Westmoreland Street and over the river again, past O'Connell's statue at the bottom of Sackville Street and along Cavendish Row to the last resting place at Glasnevin Cemetery.'"

The last bottle of port was open now. Young James was looking tired. Johnny Fitzgerald had a slight smile on his face as if some other memories of the day had come back to him. Uncle Peter's voice was slowing now, on the last lap of his marathon read.

'"It was evening by the time the hearse finally stopped at the gates. A group of pallbearers, some of them Parnell's colleagues in the Parliamentary party, carried his coffin to the grave. Mrs Parnell's wreath was first into the ground, 'My true love, my darling, my husband,' followed by many more. The rest of the funeral service was read by a Reverend Fry from Manchester and the Reverend Vincent, the Chaplain of the Rotunda Hospital in Dublin. Parnell's last resting place was not far from O'Connell, the two ready to lead Ireland once more when the dead shall rise from their graves at the last day. The crowd, after a last look at the grave, peeled off to make their way back to their pubs or their tenements or their homes, 'their homesteads' as Parnell had called the peasant cabins at the time of the Land War in the early 1880s. Maud Gonne,''' Uncle Peter stared balefully at Young James at this point, daring him to speak, '"told her friend Yeats later that evening that a shooting star had appeared in the sky during the actual burial itself. Both she and the poet were greatly impressed, discussing the astral significance for some hours. Another poet, Katherine Tynan, also a friend of Yeats, began a poem about the apparition.

> '"That night our chief we laid
> Clay in the ice cold sod,
> O'er the pale sky sped
> A strange star home to God.
> Ran the East sky cold,
> The bright star glistened and went,
> 'Twas green and glittering gold
> That lit the firmament."'

Uncle Peter closed the book. He folded his dressing gown around him and shuffled towards the door, pausing only to grab the remains of the last bottle of port. He didn't bother with the glass.

'Goodnight to you all,' he said. 'I couldn't say another word. Thank you for listening,' and then he was gone, the sound of his feet shuffling slowly across the marble floor of the hall gradually fading.

'I met a man,' said Johnny, 'on the way out of the cemetery that day, selling hurling sticks with that ribbon round them like the boyos had. He must have had teams of women making them up for him all day. He reckoned he'd sold hundreds and hundreds of the things. He thought he might have made enough money for the deposit on a pub, the man. Said he'd always wanted to own a pub. He was going to call it the Parnell Arms.'

Johnny and Young James departed, Johnny telling stories of pubs with strange names. Powerscourt went to the window and pulled back the curtains. There were no shooting stars by the Shannon this evening. A fox was patrolling by the edge of the river. He opened the window and peered sideways at the façade of this great house, built in the early eighteenth century when any talk about Home Rule for a Catholic Ireland would have sounded like the ravings of the insane.

That night he had a strange dream. He was looking at a great long beach that he thought was Silver Strand in a wild and remote corner of Connemara. At the end was a pier with a small sailing ship. There was a crowd of gentlemen on the beach in those long frock coats worn centuries before, coats of scarlet and black and dark blue, with great white and cream stocks at the top. Their brightly polished shoes with heavy buckles were being slowly stained by the sand. They had just finished building a large number of sandcastles, formidable structures that looked as though they could withstand the Atlantic waves. The more imaginative of them had placed shells along the front to denote where the doors and windows would have been. Some had elaborate turrets and tower-like structures on the top. Gentlemen's houses in a gentlemen's Ireland. They clapped as he watched and went off together, arm in arm, towards the pier to board their boat. They sailed slowly away towards the south. Perhaps these were the Wild Geese, Powerscourt reflected, a great body of Irish lords and their followers who fled the country after the Elizabethan Wars. Suddenly Powerscourt began to run after the vessel, shouting helplessly as he went. The wind took his words and blew them back past his face towards the mountains. He wanted to tell them. He so much wanted to tell them but it was too late. They had misjudged the tide. Their castles were not safe. The waves were beginning to lap around the foundations now, to swirl along the sides, to curl relentlessly around the back and turn the structures into small islands, cut off from the main. The sandcastles lasted longer than he would have imagined possible. In the end it was hopeless. Undermined at the front, falling away at the back, they were overwhelmed by the sheer volume of the waves. They began to collapse, slowly at first, and then erosion lapped away at them until there was almost nothing left. By the time this tide went out, Powerscourt was certain, the sands would be like the ones in Shelley's poem 'Ozymandias', lone and level and stretching far away.

PART TWO

THE BLACK ROOM

No man has a right to fix the boundary of the march
of a nation. No man has a right to say to his country,
'Thus far shall you go and no further.'

Charles Stewart Parnell, 1885

5

There was more trouble at the summit of Croagh Patrick, Ireland's Holy Mountain. The men building the chapel at the top, a place where pilgrims could rest and celebrate Mass after climbing the twisting two thousand seven hundred feet to the summit, had lost some vital supplies which they needed that day for a key stage in the construction. Rather, they hadn't lost the supplies, they had lost the donkey that had carried them up. In their haste to get started before the weather broke and the rains came that day, the workmen had only unloaded one side of the animal. The other side, along with the donkey, had disappeared.

'Jameson! Jameson!' Charlie O'Malley shouted in despair. 'Where the divil are you, in God's name?' After the earlier occasion when one of his two donkeys, working in rotation according to the principles of the great agriculturalist Turnip Townsend, had been persuaded to abandon its sit-down strike and proceed to the summit by the aroma from a whiskey bottle, Charlie had christened the animal Jameson after the makers of the golden liquid in Dublin. The other beast, currently munching contentedly at what was left of the thin grass in the O'Malley back yard, was called Powers in honour of the John Powers whiskey establishment in Cork. If he was ever able to afford a third, Charlie was going to christen it Bushmills. Bushmills, Charlie thought, would be a fine name for a donkey, giving his stable a neat geographical balance with donkeys and distilleries placed at Cork and Dublin and one in Bushmills in the north.

'You can't lose a bloody donkey on the top of a mountain,' said Tim Philbin. 'It's not possible. It's ridiculous. There's nothing higher than the top of my boot between here and the water down below.'

'You shouldn't have hit it yesterday, Charlie,' said Austin Ruddy, staring helplessly towards the mountains behind Croagh Patrick. 'I'm tired of telling you. You're not kind to the beast, never have been.'

'Eats enough, so it does,' said Charlie O'Malley. 'They'll eat me out of house and home, those damned donkeys, the wife says.'

'What's all this?' A great roar came from inside the tent where the contractor, Mr Walter Heneghan of Heneghan and Sons, Builders and Surveyors of Louisburg, had his head-quarters. A small wiry man with grey hair emerged, clutching in his hand a little book which contained, as all his workmen knew, what Mr Heneghan referred to as The Skedule. He had never been a master in the reading and writing department, Walter Heneghan, in spite of all the best efforts of the straps and the canes of the Christian Brothers, and the maintenance of this document, its daily updating with the latest develop-ments, kept him occupied at a rickety card table in the tent and seemed to fill most of his days. He did not actually do much of the work himself, leaving his mind free for his more important duties and calculations. The rest of the men were convinced Walter spent most of the afternoon sleeping under his canvas roof while they laboured on in rain or sunshine but they never dared open the canvas flap to look inside.

Heneghan's immediate employer was a very difficult man, even for a priest. The Reverend Michael Macdonald, Administrator of Westport, was a nervous churchman. He worried. Every day he worried. Eight years after the event he still remembered as if it were yesterday the disaster that had struck him in his previous incarnation as parish priest in Ballinrobe. He had been responsible there for the erection and consecration of a new convent for the Order of the Immaculate Conception a mile or so outside the town. One of the nuns, a Sister Mary Magdalene, had been his particular friend in those times. Six months before the completion date he had organized the grand opening. The bishop was to come. A couple of local MPs had promised to attend. Nuns of every sort to be found in the west of Ireland were coming in their finest wimples to bless their sisters in their good fortune. In the months that followed he believed the assurances of his building foreman that all would be finished on time. All, as the Reverend Michael Macdonald remembered far too clearly, even now, was not going to be finished on time. Only three days before the ceremony did he discover that the dignitaries would be opening a building where the cells had no walls, the kitchen had no cooking facilities and the chapel had no windows. Everything had to be cancelled, the invitations withdrawn, Galway's and Mayo's nuns instructed to stay in their places. The bishop had shouted at him. The *Mayo News* ran the story for three editions in a row, coming as close as Irish journalists dared in those days to criticizing the clergy. Every night for the next two years he had included in his prayers a plea to his God that never, never again should he be called upon to supervise the construction of a building, secular or religious. He would not even contemplate the erection of a badly needed shed in the garden of the priest's house. And now he was lumbered with it all again. God had singled him out for punishment once more. His sins were not numerous, he knew, but the penance for them was huge. A late convent was one thing. A late chapel on the summit of Ireland's Holy Mountain would be far far worse. He might be expelled from the priesthood in disgrace, or sent on the worst punishment any Irish bishop could deliver, a life sentence to a parish in the slums of Dublin which had ruined many a better man than he.

This was the origin of The Skedule. Once a week Father Macdonald would pore over it with Heneghan, checking every entry and every planned completion date of every section of the work. Heneghan, whatever his other qualities, was a deeply religious man – his faith, he was sure, had won him the contract, after all – and he too feared for the late completion. The wrath of the priests would be as nothing compared with the wrath of God. And at that moment Walter knew that they were two weeks behind Skedule. With luck, they could make it up, but a spell of bad weather could prove fatal. He too joined the search for Jameson.

'Bloody donkey gone? With all that glass still strapped to its side? You stupid buggers, why didn't you unload it all? God in heaven, what fools am I given to carry out His wishes! Fools!'

He strode to the other side of the half-finished building and peered down at the waters of Clew Bay beneath. 'Jameson!' he roared. 'In the name of St Patrick, come back here at once, you daft animal!'

Jameson did not choose to reply.

'Jameson! In the name of St Patrick and all the saints of Ireland, come back here at once!' Charlie O'Malley sent his message to the other side of the Holy Mountain. Still there was neither answer nor sighting of the donkey.

'Jameson! In the name of the Blessed Virgin Mary and St Patrick and all the saints of Ireland, shift your bloody arse up here!' Not surprisingly, Tim Philbin's message found no answer either. Walter Heneghan thought of gathering his little band together and leading them in prayer to St Anthony of Padua, Hammer of Heretics and patron saint of all things lost, but he thought it might work better if he said it to himself when he was safely back in the tent.

The men were sullen for the rest of the day. Charlie O'Malley would go on sad little missions a couple of hundred yards at a time looking for Jameson and calling out promises of extra carrots, or a fine cauliflower for the donkey was strangely fond of cauliflower. Only at the end of the day, when they were taking a well-earned rest in Campbell's public house at the foot of Croagh Patrick, did Walter Heneghan realize that his prayer under canvas to St Anthony, Hammer of Heretics, had been answered. The landlord took him to one side.

'Have any of youse lost a donkey?' asked the landlord.

'A donkey?' said Heneghan, as if he had just heard the word for the first time. 'We bloody well have lost a donkey.'

'Well, it's here,' said the landlord. 'It's out the back, so it is.'

'Thank God for that,' said Walter, shaking the man firmly by the hand. 'What'll you have? A donkey found is worth a drink any day in my book. But tell me this. Did the beast have any glass with it?'

'Glass?' said the landlord. 'What sort of glass, for God's sake? Beer glass, whiskey glass, that kind of thing? Does the animal drink like a human?'

'No, no,' said Heneghan. 'Glass for building, windows, that sort of stuff.'

'That sort of glass?' replied the landlord innocently. 'What would a bloody donkey want with window glass, for Christ's sake?'

'It's for the chapel,' said Heneghan sadly, 'the chapel at the top of the mountain.'

'Glass with the donkey, is it now?' said the landlord. He turned to the crowd in his bar, most of whom looked as though they had spent the entire afternoon, if not the entire week, on the premises, 'We haven't seen any glass with that donkey, boys, have we?'

'No no, no glass. Donkey yes, glass no,' they chorused.

As he trudged back up to his tent, clutching half a dozen beer bottles, Walter Heneghan added a spiritual question to the long list of temporal ones he had to ask Father Macdonald. Why was it that St Anthony of Padua was so good with donkeys and so bloody useless with glass?

Powerscourt and Johnny Fitzgerald and William Moore were on their way from Butler's Court to Moore Castle to inspect the site of the vanished paintings. Moore Castle, its owner proudly informed Powerscourt and Fitzgerald as they approached its entrance, had been in his family since the days of Cromwell. The place, Powerscourt realized as the carriage drew to a halt at the Castle's lower section, had had many builders over the years. Somewhere there must be a bit of Georgian, but it was in Victorian times that every single generation seemed to have extended, rebuilt, knocked down or restructured. Architects must have regarded the place as a treasure trove, Kubla Khan miraculously translated to County Roscommon.

'I'll show you round the place later,' Moore said, leading them up an enormous marble staircase, adorned on both sides with the inevitable antlers of elk and stag. 'Pictures first.' Moore brought them through an astonishing entrance hall, a vast, long, high room with a gallery running round the top and a stained-glass window off to the left halfway up the stairs, and into the dining room, a beautiful room, the walls painted in pale yellow, adorned with well-fed putti and elaborate highly decorated plasterwork.

'This used to be the drawing room,' Moore began, 'but my grandfather thought it would work better as a dining room. Used to be seven portraits, four full-lengths in here,' Moore said sadly, nodding at the series of blank spaces on his walls, 'oldest the one above the fireplace there, Josiah Moore from the 1720s. Then on the opposite wall, his grandson, Joshua, 1770s, on the other two walls his son and grandson. I don't know if the money ran out, but the other three, my grandfather and his brother and great grandfather on either side of the fire, were much smaller, portrait size is what I believe you call them, head and shoulders only, no greatcoats or uniforms.'

Outside they could hear the noises of grass being cut. There was a distant view of dark mountains.

'I'm quite lucky in one respect,' Moore went on, sitting himself down at the head of his table and waving a hand inviting his guests to be seated too. 'I heard about the difficulties they had over at Butler's Court in identifying their pictures. I actually had a great uncle who was interested in Irish portraits – can you believe it? – and he made a catalogue of them all.' Powerscourt thought he made his ancestor sound like a man who claimed he could fly to the moon or empty the Irish Sea. 'He tried to cover all the paintings in all the great houses in Connaught, you know,' Moore went on. 'Mind you, he went mad before he could finish it.' Fitting fate for the fellow, in Moore's book at any rate, Powerscourt thought. 'Anyway,' Moore nodded at a neat pile of papers in front of him, 'here are the details of all the ones that went missing. This is for you, Powerscourt, obviously.' Powerscourt saw that the entries were full and comprehensive, easily sufficient for any art dealer to identify a picture if it passed through his hands.

'This is most impressive, Moore,' he said. 'I am very much obliged to you. Tell me, is there any evidence that they broke into this room here, to effect the theft?'

'Not in here,' said Moore, 'but let me show you something next door.' He led them out through the baronial hall into a long room looking out towards the fountain, adorned with three pairs of grey marble columns. 'This used to be the front door,' he said, nodding at the great window in front of him, 'and this used to be the entrance hall. My grandfather changed all this lot round. Now, if you look carefully at the sash on the window next to the one that was the front door, you can see dirty smudge marks on it. The parlour maids noticed them the morning after the robbery and I told them to leave them where they are. It's my belief that they took the pictures out this way to some kind of conveyance round the corner. It would have been easy to do – the grass would have muffled the noise.'

'Do you know how they got in?' asked Johnny Fitzgerald.

'There's a broken window in the kitchen down below,' Moore said. 'I think they came and went that way. There is another room where they could have passed the pictures out of the house, mind you, but there are no telltale smudges in there. Come, I'll show you where the other paintings were.'

He took them into a billiard room opposite the dining room, a full-size table with a couple of balls lying on the green baize, waiting for the next match. 'This used to be the library,' he said sadly, 'but my grandfather threw all the books out one day. He said they were annoying him so they all had to go. He organized a great bonfire outside on the same day and they all went up in smoke.' Life, Powerscourt thought, was never dull in Moore Castle.

'Our three Old Masters,' Moore pointed again to further gaps on the walls, 'the Titian and the two Gainsboroughs, were here. They used to be in what was the entrance hall, but my father moved them in here.'

'I believe you said when you arrived at Butler's Court that the Gainsboroughs might not be authentic,' said Powerscourt. 'Did your great uncle establish that, before he went mad, I mean?'

'He did and he wasn't at the time, mad, if you follow me. He was said to have been in good health when he said the Gainsboroughs weren't painted by the hand of Gainsborough, if you see what I mean. One artist's hand looks very much like another, if you ask me.'

'And the Titian?' Powerscourt carried on. 'Was that real?'

'Nobody ever said it wasn't,' said Moore defiantly. 'Not to me at any rate.'

He led them back out into the galleried hall with its great timbered roof. 'This,' he waved expansively at the enormous space, 'used to be the main staircase. Then my grandfather threw that out.'

'Before or after he burnt the books?' asked Johnny Fitzgerald.

'After,' Moore laughed, 'he must have got into the swing of it by then. This other double staircase' – an enormous Victorian affair, made of oak, beckoned – 'used to be where the wall on the side of the old stairs was. They extended the house backwards, if you follow me, to put the new staircase in.'

William Moore took his visitors round the rest of the house, the dark wood panelling, the strange over-decorated Victorian chapel where Powerscourt felt God would not stay for long if ever he called at all, and out into the gardens by the fountain. Moore talked continuously, giving the names of his ancestors and the dates of construction. High up on the outside of the third floor Powerscourt saw a strange contraption like a bosun's chair, hanging from the roof by a series of ropes and pulleys. Standing rather precariously inside was a small young man with torn trousers who waved happily at them and shouted Good Morning.

'What on earth is that?' asked Johnny Fitzgerald, pointing upwards.

'That's John,' said Moore. 'Normally he works in the stables but today he cleans the windows. His elder brother Seamus used to do it but he kept falling off the ladders. They're not very good with ladders for some reason, Roscommon people. No head for heights at all. I rigged the thing up myself – naval fellow told me how to do it. But come, I think it's time for some coffee, or something stronger if you would prefer.'

Powerscourt and Fitzgerald assured their host that coffee would be fine. It came in the long room with the pillars that used to be the entrance hall.

'Now then, Moore,' Powerscourt began, 'all these pictures gone, smudges on your window, your wife upset, I don't suppose you have any idea at all who is responsible?'

'No idea at all.'

'Tell me, pray,' said Powerscourt, resolved to try a different tactic with Moore than he had employed on the other two victims, 'what do you say in reply to the letter they sent you?'

Moore turned red and began rubbing one side of his face as if that would make his discomfort go away. 'Letter?' he said in a querulous tone. 'I had no letter.'

'I think you did, Moore, I'm virtually certain of it.'

'No, I did not.'

'Consider this,' said Powerscourt. 'Somebody spent a lot of

time planning these robberies. Maybe they are common or garden thieves but I doubt it. There is a great deal of stuff lying about these houses, silver and so on, which would be worth a lot more than your ancestors. It's possible they were just burglars but I don't believe it. I think they want something. I have no idea what the something is, but I think you do. Because they told you. In a letter.'

'How many times,' said Moore, still red in the face and sweating slightly now, 'do I have to tell you, Powerscourt, there was no letter.'

'Let me make a stab,' said Powerscourt, not giving up, 'at telling you what the last sentence said. This or something like it. If you do not comply – maybe they would have said agree rather than comply – with our requests, your wife is next. That also applies if you tell a single human soul about this letter.'

'How on earth –' Moore began and then stopped suddenly. 'There was no letter,' he hurried on as if trying to retract what he had just said, 'no letter.' He sat back in his chair. Johnny Fitzgerald took up the attack. He and Powerscourt had carried out interviews like this many times in their lives. They knew the moves so well they hardly needed to communicate with each other, like tennis partners who have been playing doubles together for years.

'How about this then?' said Johnny, in the manner of a man trying on another coat in a gentleman's outfitters. 'You took the paintings yourself. You crept down in the middle of the night and removed them to some hiding place or other. God knows, you could hide the Crown Jewels in a place this size and nobody would find them for years, however hard they tried. You're broke, or you're nearly bankrupt like so many of your fellow landlords, in hock to the banks and the insurance companies and those seedy moneylenders in Dublin. The art market's booming, even for Irish ancestors I shouldn't wonder. You were going to sell the pictures when all the fuss has died down and pay off some of your debts. There must have been enough debt after all this building work to float a steamer on the Shannon. Admit it, man, you did the whole thing yourself!'

'I did not,' said Moore. 'There are all sorts of things I would sell before I sold those paintings. They're part of our history, part of our family heritage going back to Cromwell's time, let me tell you. It'd be like selling members of my own family.'

Powerscourt was suddenly visited by the bizarre image of Michael Henshaw Moore or Casterbridge Moore from Thomas Hardy's novel, selling off his wife in the marketplace in Sligo town.

'Anyway,' Moore went on, 'I'm not broke. Richard Butler certainly isn't broke. Your man Connolly isn't broke either. Between us we hold some of the finest land in Ireland. You may not know it, living across the water as you do, but the Government has been passing laws for years encouraging tenants to buy the land they rent off their landlords. They've just passed another one called the Wyndham Act which actually bribes the landlords to sell out. People can make a packet. There's a whole lot of new houses going up down in Carlow and Kilkenny with Wyndham money, the bonus they call it. Well, let me tell you something, Powerscourt. They can do what they like down there in Carlow and Kilkenny, but we're not selling. No, sir. We may not be the masters now but we're damned if the bloody Government is going to decide the future of our property. Like the pictures, it's our history and our heritage too.'

Powerscourt thought it was time to call a halt. 'All right, Moore,' he said, 'we'll leave it there for now. We didn't mean any of it personally. I hope you understand that.'

'I know you have to ask your questions,' said Moore, pouring himself a generous glass of John Powers. 'I'm just upset you thought I might have done it myself, that's all.'

'We've come across stranger things than that in our line of work,' said Johnny Fitzgerald delphically.

'I suppose you'll want to get back to Butler's Court,' Moore said. 'Let me arrange for a couple of fresh horses for you.'

Another Anglo-Irish house, Powerscourt thought ruefully, where the welcome was not as warm as it might have been. Two out of three of them were keen to get him off the premises as fast as they could.

6

Alice Bracken and Johnpeter Kilross were sitting on a bench by the river Shannon at the bottom of Richard Butler's garden. They were both hot after an energetic game of tennis which Johnpeter had won 6–3, 7–5, coming from 5–2 down to take the second set. Maybe it was this unexpected defeat that had put Alice in a bad mood.

'I'm sure that backhand of mine was in,' she said grumpily, 'the one down the line when I was leading 5–4 and 40–15 in that last set.'

'No, no,' said Johnpeter, patting her hand as sweetly as he knew how, 'it was out.'

'Didn't look out to me,' said the girl.

Johnpeter wished he had let Alice win the second set. He had had every intention of doing so. That, after all, was why he had let her build up such a big lead in the first place. But then she had laughed at him when he fell over at the net, trying for an acrobatic smash, and his heart had hardened. Alice began kicking the side of the bench.

'Don't be in a bad mood, Alice,' he said, trying and failing to hold her hand. 'It's only a game.'

'That's what everybody says when they've won,' she said. 'I've never heard anyone say it when they've lost. Nothing's going right for me at the moment. Everything's so boring.

There's no sign of the Captain returning, no sign at all. And it's months and months before the hunting season starts. And I haven't got any money for a new hunter.' She went on kicking the side of the bench.

'Well, there's all this business about the paintings,' said Johnpeter. 'That's not boring.'

'If I hear another word about those wretched paintings,' said Alice, 'I'm going to scream. Anybody would think the paintings were more important than everybody having a good time. Mind you,' she turned to look around to make sure they were not overheard, 'Richard Butler is worried sick. He's been riding over to see that man Connolly every other day without telling anybody about it. One of the stable lads told me. Very early in the morning he goes. Maybe they've lost some paintings over there too, though nobody talks about it. You'd think we were in a war.'

'Maybe we are,' said Johnpeter. 'And what do you make of our investigating friend, Lord Francis Powerscourt? His wife is coming tomorrow to join him for a few days, you know. I heard him discussing it with Mrs Butler. And she's worried sick too, Sylvia Butler, though she tries to put a brave face on it. When she thinks nobody's looking her face goes from cheerful to miserable in one second flat.'

'They'll turn up when nobody's expecting them, those paintings, so they will,' said the girl.

Johnpeter thought she might be in a slightly better mood now. 'I know, Alice,' he said brightly, 'why don't we take a boat over to the island? You know you always like it over there.'

'I'm not in the mood for the island today,' said Alice haughtily, as if island escapades were beneath her.

'Do come on, Alice,' said Johnpeter, 'there won't be anybody there. The children have all gone off to their cousins.'

'I told you, I'm not in the mood.'

Johnpeter wished he could find somewhere less exposed than the island, some little place where he and Alice could be alone. More than anything, for the moment anyway, he regretted not having let her win that second set.

Pronsias Mulcahy, sole proprietor of Mulcahy and Sons, Grocery and Bar, of the main square in Butler's Cross, was peering over his ledgers in the back room of his shop. Pronsias was a well-built man of about fifty years, his hair turning grey, his figure growing stout as if he partook too liberally of the provisions, both solid and liquid, that he dispensed in his shop. He was surrounded this afternoon by some of the raw materials of his trade, great hams hanging from the ceiling, boxes of cheeses about to make their way on to the tables of Butler's Cross and its neighbouring villages, tinned stuff from England and America, fresh barrels of stout. Today was half-day in the shopping community, thirsty citizens having no choice but MacSwiggin's Hotel and Bar if dehydration overcame them on a warm afternoon. Pronsias was an eldest son and had inherited the business from his father. Over time he had built it up into a thriving concern. The locals said that Pronsias was the wealthiest man in the county, even including Richard Butler. There was a black book open in front of him now where all the grocery accounts were kept, Pronsias able to work out the precise level of profit on every entry merely by looking at them. This facility was known to a select few in Butler's Cross who had happened to see it in action, and it had gained him a remarkable reputation for financial wizardry. Any normal person, the locals said, would have to write everything down, suck heavily on the pencil, maybe have a drink or two to improve the mental powers, and then take about five minutes to complete the complex calculations. And Pronsias could do it in his head! Truly it was a gift from God.

One of Pronsias's brothers, Declan, was a solicitor out west in County Mayo. Another was a police sergeant down in County Kerry where the police station, for some unknown reason, had one of the finest vegetable gardens in the south. A third was a priest up in Donegal. His two sisters had made good marriages, one to a schoolteacher and another to a man who worked in a bank. Next to the black book was a red one where the entries and the accounts for the bar were kept. And next to that, the most secret volume of them all, the blue book where Pronsias kept the details of his loans. By now he had a more substantial portfolio than the bank in North Street on the far side of the square. His customer base was far wider than you might have expected, reaching out into levels of society that did not normally buy their groceries in the main square in Butler's Cross. The loan business had begun in a very small way, regular customers unable to pay at the store. From then it gradually expanded into small tenant farmers behind with their rent, worried parents anxious to pay for their sons or daughters to take passage to England or America or Australia. Weddings, he had discovered by accident, were a fruitful source of business. About half of the local receptions were now paid for by the generosity of Pronsias Mulcahy, Grocery and Bar of Butler's Cross. Pronsias charged slightly more than the banks in interest, that was admitted, but he never fore- closed on a loan, a little help for a friend in need as he would put it to his customers. He would let the loans go on for years if necessary, fully aware that if he ever foreclosed his business might dry up. He looked on himself as a great benefactor, oiling the wheels of local commerce and giving young people a chance to make something of their lives. When necessary, the youngest Delaney of Delaney, Delaney and Delaney, solicitors in law across the way, would draw up the necessary paperwork and keep the documents in their storeroom.

Once a week on half-days like this one Pronsias would take himself off to the priest's house at five o'clock for a refreshing glass of John Powers. Pronsias always took a fresh bottle with him, reasoning that Father O'Donovan Brady might need whatever was left to succour unhappy parishioners who had fallen foul of their God. Pronsias thought that the Powers would be more comforting than the priest in those circumstances, but he shared that thought with nobody. Father Brady was a useful fount of local information, pointing out to Pronsias who might be having trouble with the rent. It was an arrangement of mutual benefit to both sides. Both felt that whiskey in exchange for customers was a fair bargain, especially for Father O'Donovan Brady who appeared to have an inexhaustible supply of John Powers stored in his cellar, some bottles nearly full, some a third full, others half full, however hard he tried to exhaust his supply.

Lord Francis Powerscourt had collected his wife Lucy from the railway station. She brought news of the children and of her relations, one of whom had fallen into financial difficulties and might be in need of rescue. Lady Lucy had a great many relations. After the formalities were completed at Butler's Court, Lady Lucy admiring the furniture and the decoration in their enormous bedroom, Powerscourt took her down to the river and filled her in with the details of his investigation. The Shannon was very smooth that afternoon, flotillas of baby ducks on manoeuvres by the riverside under the watchful eye of a parent, the ducklings occasionally diving in unison underneath the water and reappearing together at exactly the same time, as if an invisible conductor was teaching them synchronized swimming.

'I didn't like to say anything in the carriage, Francis,' she said, taking his hands in hers, 'but you're looking worried. Is the case not going well? Are you not making any progress?'

Powerscourt laughed bitterly. 'I was saying to Johnny only yesterday that I think we should give up, go home, pack our tents. We haven't made any progress at all.'

She squeezed his hand and led him to a bench in the shade. 'You mustn't give up, Francis, you've always said that, you and Johnny.'

'I just don't know what to do,' said her husband helplessly. 'What have we got here, after all? Well, we've got a whole heap of empty squares on the walls of these houses. Fine, you might think, but the abandoned plaster and the black smudges where the edges of the pictures were can't actually tell you anything. The problem with the humans is worse. Normally there are lots of people you can talk to. Here the ones you can talk to who might tell you something, the owners, don't tell you the truth. I'm sure all three of them have had, in effect, a blackmail letter from the thieves, but they all deny it. The other ones you can talk to, the servants and the local people, may not talk to you or they may, as it were, be in the pay of the enemy.' He told her of his sulphurous encounter with Father O'Donovan Brady.

'But surely, Francis,' Lady Lucy was holding firmly on to her husband's right hand, 'the servants and people all trust the families in the Big Houses – they work for them, after all. I'm sure that wouldn't be a problem in England.'

'Ah,' said Powerscourt, 'but this is Ireland. It's different here. Let me tell you a story Richard Butler told me the other evening. It concerns a man called Blennerhasset, old Ascendancy family, living on a great estate down in Tipperary, family here since Elizabeth's time, that sort of thing. Every general election this Blennerhasset was returned to Westminster with a big majority, his tenants and the people connected with the land all turning out to vote for him. Then the franchise changed. More and more people got the vote. Parnell and his crowd came along and changed the rules, Home Rule – what a comforting couple of words they are, images of a contented family sorting out their affairs in the parlour at home – now the order of the day. At the first of these elections under the new rules, Blennerhasset went off to the local town to make sure the voting was in order and check that the proceedings were properly conducted. All his tenants were very polite to him as usual. He was back home when the results were known, and he saw all the tenants having a party, a huge bonfire and fireworks in the main square. He thought it was to celebrate his victory in the normal fashion. But he hadn't won. He'd lost. His opponent had won by a huge margin. All his tenants had doffed their caps to him, metaphorically speaking, but they'd voted for the other man. Blennerhasset was heartbroken. He couldn't believe his tenants, his tenants, for God's sake, had voted for the other fellow. They had betrayed him. His whole view of everything was shattered. He died not long after. Now do you see what I mean, Lucy? If you take the wrong people into your confidence you could be giving comfort and succour to the enemy and telling them what is in your mind. It's like operating in a foreign country where you don't know the language or where the same words have different meanings for the speaker and the listener. I'm in despair, Lucy, I really am.'

'What does Johnny think about it all?' asked Lady Lucy. But she never had time to find out what Johnny thought. For at that moment a huge shout of 'Powerscourt!' rang round the garden.

'Powerscourt, where the hell are you?' Richard Butler came into view, red-faced, running at top speed, panting from his exertions, waving a piece of paper in his right hand. 'Powerscourt, Lady Lucy, thank God I've found you. Powerscourt, there seems to have been another one, another theft, I mean.' He stopped and sat down on the edge of the bench. 'Read this!' He shoved the telegram into Powerscourt's hand.

'Crisis meeting tomorrow lunchtime. Ormonde House. One o'clock. Bring Powerscourt. Train from Athlone 10.15 or 11.05. My people will meet you. Ormonde.'

'This doesn't say anything about paintings being stolen, Mr Butler,' said Lady Lucy brightly. 'It could be about anything at all.'

'Ah, Lady Lucy, but this is Ireland. If it was something unimportant you would feel free to mention it in a telegram. If it was something important, you wouldn't dream of mentioning it. You could never tell who might be reading it, so you couldn't.'

'I see,' said Lady Lucy, who didn't.

'Crisis, that's the key to the thing now,' said Butler, mopping his brow with an enormous handkerchief. 'Crisis, Dennis Ormonde is telling us. That can only mean one thing. More paintings have gone.'

'I fear you may be right,' said Powerscourt. 'We'll find out tomorrow.'

All through that evening the word seeped through the floorboards of Butler's Court. It travelled invisibly along the long passages. It flew up the great staircases and whispered along the attic corridors. The kitchen maids heard it in the kitchen as they prepared a great rhubarb pie for pudding that evening. The junior footmen heard it as they polished the silver in the pantry. Out in the stable block the grooms heard it as they prepared the horses for the night. More paintings have gone. Ormonde House is the latest house to be visited with the affliction. The Master and Lord Powerscourt are going there tomorrow. God save Ireland.

Rain was falling steadily as their train travelled slowly across the province of Connaught. There were glimpses of great lakes as they passed by, of dark mountains glowering across a barren landscape. Richard Butler had given Powerscourt a brief history of the Ormondes, Earls of Mayo, the previous evening, the Ormondes the greatest power in the west for centuries past, their great mansion, Ormonde House, nestling on the shores of Clew Bay some five miles from the town of Westport, the finest house in Connaught. Powerscourt was to say afterwards that his first impressions of the place were a blur, so fast had events unfolded.

The Ormonde carriage drove them at breakneck speed along the Louisburg road. Butler pointed out Croagh Patrick, Ireland's Holy Mountain, towering over the landscape, brooding over the dark waters of the bay, imposing itself on the grey frontage of cut stone that was Ormonde House. A tall figure with black hair and prominent black eyebrows was pacing restlessly in front of the steps of his home.

'Butler,' he said, pumping his visitor's hand, 'glad you could come. Powerscourt, I presume you are Powerscourt, welcome to Ormonde House. And a sorry welcome it is too!' There was, Powerscourt thought, a terrible anger flowing through this man, a rage that he was going to share with his visitors. 'Come with me,' he said. 'Come and see what the bastards have done!'

He brought them into an elegant entrance hall and through a door on the right into the Picture Gallery. Or, Powerscourt thought sadly, what had been the Picture Gallery. It was a beautiful room, long and broad with a polished parquet floor and great windows looking out over the gardens at the far end.

'Look at it!' roared Ormonde, pointing to the five gaps on the blue wall, one after the other as if they had taken a sudden burst from a machine gun. 'Look at what they have done, God damn their eyes! Two full-lengths, three portrait-sized paintings of my ancestors! All gone! Stolen by some thieves whose own ancestors probably rotted to death in the workhouse with the typhus in the famine years! And a bloody good thing too!'

Dennis Ormonde was literally shaking with fury. His face was almost purple. 'When I think of what they did, my family, for this county and for this country, I despair. I tell you what I would like to do, what one of my forebears actually did,' he pointed, his hand shaking as he did so, at the first of the full-length gaps in the wall, 'in the last rebellion in these parts. The authorities – my people have always been the authorities round here – brought the punishment triangles out in the main square over there in Westport. If the bastards talked before the action started they were released. If not they were lashed to the triangles, stripped and flogged by the yeomanry till their blood was running in the gutters and they were screaming for their mothers. But they talked after a while. My

107

great grandfather got the names of the rebels from the victims on the triangles. And when they were caught, the bloody rebels, they were hanged, hundreds of them. Bloody good thing too. Too soft a fate for some of them, hanging!'

Dennis Ormonde walked back down his gallery and closed the door. He went back to stand by the empty spaces once again. They seemed to reignite his anger.

'I'm bloody well not going to take this lying down, I can tell you. They may be taking over the land, they may have all the bloody MPs in that useless bloody Parliament in Westminster, but they can't steal my property, they damned well can't. I've talked to the local police, might as well have talked to the man who referees the hurling matches for all the good that'll do. I've wired to Dublin Castle and an inspector and his colleague from the Intelligence Department are on their way. I've sent word to the Grand Master of the Orange Lodge and the man who runs the Royal Black Preceptory in Enniskillen asking for one hundred men, aged between twenty-five and forty and in good health, to come and report for orders. They're to bring their own weapons. One hundred stout Protestants to carry the battle to the foe. Croppies lie down. And I've asked the Apprentice Boys in Derry to stand by with another hundred if we need them. I'm going to station guards on duty all night at every Big House with reasonable paintings in Mayo and the neighbouring counties. And, one last thing, I'm going to post a notice in Westport and Castlebar tomorrow afternoon when the thing's back from the printers, offering thirty pounds reward for information leading to the return of the paintings, all of them, mine and yours, Butler, and Connolly's and Moore's, and the capture of the bastards who took them. They've always betrayed their own for money in the past, the spineless scum, maybe they'll do it again.'

The look of fury never left Ormonde's face. If the thieves had known the response they were going to receive, Powerscourt thought, they might have stayed in bed. Posting a reward for such an enormous sum was one thing, importing one hundred armed Protestants into a predominantly Catholic county was another, fraught with dire political consequences. Orthodox Catholic opinion would be appalled and might contemplate reprisals. The Church itself might feel bound to take a stand. They could not watch from their pulpits and their altars while armed Protestant gangs patrolled the countryside and threatened their parishioners. As for less orthodox Catholic opinion, Powerscourt was filled with foreboding. The men who came out in the night in these parts knew all about houghing or mutilating their landlords' cattle and lighting up the night sky as they torched the Big Houses. Not far from here, not all that long ago, they had invented the boycott at Lough Mask House. Would it travel twenty or thirty miles and devastate the Ormondes of Ormonde House? If the angry man with the black hair and the black eyebrows went ahead with all his plans, it could plunge the west of Ireland into a political crisis. Powerscourt felt he had to try to prevent his investigation ending up in a whirlpool of sectarian violence.

'Lunch,' announced Dennis Ormonde. 'Can't let the bastards put us off our food.'

The Ormonde House dining room was one of the most beautiful in Ireland but Powerscourt had little time to admire the plaster glories on the ceiling. Still muttering to himself, Ormonde began to carve a great side of beef, the blood dripping down on to the serving dish. 'Got to have it rare, this Mayo beef,' he said. 'Well cooked it tastes like roasted string.' He paused and looked around the table, heavy with ornate silver.

'Horseradish!' he shouted at the butler. 'Where's the bloody horseradish, for Christ's sake? Twenty years I've been eating beef in this house with you serving at the table and you still manage to forget the horseradish!' He shook his head. 'Wife's fond of it too, oddly enough,' he added, nodding at his guests and heaping enormous portions of Mayo beef on to the three plates. 'She's even planted some of the stuff in the kitchen garden so we can make our own.'

Two footmen sidled in and began serving roast potatoes and peas. The butler who had fled the room at great speed reappeared with the offending horseradish. Ormonde took a giant's helping. 'Now bugger off,' he shouted at the servants. 'Come back in twenty minutes with the pudding. And if I catch any of you listening at the doors, you're fired!'

'Now then, Butler,' he said between mouthfuls of meat, 'what do you think of my plan? Shake the bastards up a bit, don't you think, when they find a brace of Orangemen waiting for them as they creep out of the shrubberies?'

'Well,' said Butler in a hesitant tone of voice and Powerscourt knew it was going to be a difficult afternoon, 'it's certainly bold. It has merit. But I just wonder if it might not be a little inflammatory.'

'Inflammatory? Inflammatory?' Ormonde yelled, pausing to lower his fork. 'Just tell me this, who's doing the inflammatory round here? Is it me? Have I been inflaming things? I have not. These bastards are the ones with the inflammatory, breaking into people's houses and stealing their pictures. If that's not inflammatory then I don't know what is!'

'I have every sympathy with your plight, after all I am in the same position as yourself,' said Butler, 'but I do think we have certain responsibilities as landlords not to start something which could lead to a great deal of violence.' Powerscourt saw Butler was pressing himself back into his chair as hard as he could as if it were a defensive wall or rampart.

'Responsibilities as landlords?' Ormonde was in full cry again, his face as red now as his beef, 'What horseshit! And what about the responsibilities of those bastards out there to keep the law? You keep talking as though I was about to commit some sort of crime. I am not. My Orangemen will be sworn in as militiamen or special constables or some other damned thing the lawyers can invent. Those bastards out there broke the law when they broke into my house. They started it, not me. You're being most unhelpful, Butler, you really are.'

'I've got another idea,' said Butler, 'I thought of it in the train on the way over. Why don't we just collect all the paintings from the Big Houses and lock them away in a vault in Galway or even in Dublin? That way there won't be any paintings for the thieves to steal.'

'That,' Ormonde snarled, 'is just about the feeblest and most defeatist talk I've heard in months. Lock the paintings away? For one thing we'd never catch the thieves that way. For another they'd just take to stealing something else. Why don't we take ourselves away too while we're at it and lock ourselves up in some vault in Tunbridge Wells or Wells-next-the-sea? The Orangemen, one hundred Orangemen, that's what we need.'

'You seem to forget, Ormonde,' said Richard Butler in the tone he might have adopted if he was talking to a small and rather stupid child, 'the laws of action and counter action that have always applied in this island. You mutilate my cattle or damage my land and I'll have a Coercion Bill through Parliament inside three months and a whole lot of those bastards, as you call them, are going to be locked up, many of them perfectly innocent people. At the end of it everything will blow over but the amount of hatred each side has for the other in the deposit boxes of their collective memory will have increased yet again. So the next round will be even worse.'

'So what do you suggest I do?' Ormonde was shouting now. The butler and the footmen, Powerscourt thought, wouldn't need to be listening at the door, they could probably hear him if they were halfway up Croagh Patrick. 'Ride into Westport with a fistful of Treasury notes in my pocket and hand them out to the local gombeens, asking them to be nice to us in future? Have an Open Day in Ormonde House? Come on in, boys, take all you want, everything must go?'

'That's absurd, and you know it.'

'And you,' Ormonde turned to glower at Powerscourt, munching loudly on a roast potato, 'the great investigator, what do you have to say for yourself? What do you think we should do?'

111

Powerscourt paused for three or four seconds to add weight to his question.

'Did you get a letter?' he asked, in what he hoped was his mildest voice.

'A letter? Of course I got a bloody letter!' Ormonde pointed a finger at Butler. 'He got a letter, Moore got a letter, Connolly got a letter, all God's children with the stolen paintings got letters. It's in the rebel rule book, sending letters on occasions like this.'

Out of the corner of his eye Powerscourt noticed Richard Butler turning a bright shade of pink. Ormonde noticed it too. He stared at Butler, and suddenly he knew.

'You bloody fool,' he said, speaking very quietly now. 'You had a letter too but you didn't tell our investigating friend here anything about it, did you? And the same goes, I'd bet a hundred pound, for Connolly and Moore. You were all in it together, fools all of you. How do you expect the man to find out anything when you don't give him the facts? God in heaven!' In a gesture of the more worldly sort he leant forward and helped himself to two more slices of his beef. He took more of his horseradish too.

'It seemed for the best,' said Butler. 'It was done for the best of motives, I promise you.'

'And what, Ormonde,' said Powerscourt, 'did the letter say?'

'Damned if I'm going to tell you that,' said Ormonde indistinctly, his mouth full. 'Blackmail, that's all you need to know, bloody blackmail.'

'Let me ask you just one more question about the letter, if I may. Did it contain any bloodcurdling threats about what would happen if you did tell anybody about it?'

'Didn't curdle me,' said Ormonde, still chomping at his beef, 'didn't curdle my blood at all. Obviously curdled Butler and all the rest of them. Well curdled, they are, all three of them. Ask yourself, Powerscourt, you're obviously an intelligent man, the kind of thing a blackmailer would say if he wanted his bloody letter to stay a secret.'

And with that Ormonde gave his attention to his previously neglected peas. Richard Butler was looking at Powerscourt, his eyes pleading for support.

'I really do feel, Ormonde,' said Richard Butler, preparing, Powerscourt thought, to place his head in the lion's jaws once more, 'that this plan with the Orangemen is unwise. Understandable, of course, but unwise. I would like to consult with my relation Brandon over in England, to see what his view is. He owns some of the land I farm, after all. They say he has great influence in the House of Lords, you know.'

'Your man Brandon,' Ormonde had completed the rout of his peas now and was staring at Butler with thinly disguised contempt, as if he too was about to join the ranks of the bastards, 'your man Brandon is scarcely able to get out of his seat. The gout's got him. The chances of Brandon's managing to get out of his house and park his arse alongside all the other well-upholstered arses on the red benches in the House of Lords over there in Westminster are pretty remote, if you ask me. Nobody's walked into his house in the middle of the night and made off with his bloody Van Dycks, have they? Brandon wouldn't be able to stop the thieves even if they walked up and shook his hand as they left with the canvases under their arm. Wouldn't be able to get out of his bloody chair. Ask him his opinion if you want, I can't stop you. Any more than you can stop me bringing in my Orangemen.'

The butler and the footmen glided in and removed the plates. A great dish of meringue and cream and fruit replaced the beef at the place of demolition. Ormonde began hacking large portions out of the pudding and handed them round.

'And you, Powerscourt,' he said, 'what is your view of my Orangemen? Are you in favour?'

'I must ask you a question first,' Powerscourt replied, trying to look as grave as he knew how. 'Will they be wearing those dark suits with the Orange sashes? Will they have those hard black hats on their heads? Will they bring a marching band

113

with those terrible Lambeg drums? Will they sing "The Sash My Father Wore" as they march along the Mall in Westport?'

For the first time that day Dennis Ormonde laughed. He laughed with the same energy with which he carved his beef or cursed his enemies.

'Lambeg drums! "Sash My Father Wore"! That's good, Powerscourt. Very good. I say,' he went on, crunching his way through a mouthful of meringue and cream, 'this pudding's good, damned good.'

There was a brief moment of silence as he enjoyed his sweet course. Powerscourt was trying to find a way to buy time. The hands of the clock were ticking fast towards those two hundred Ulster boots stamping their way down the Louisburg road towards Ormonde House. Even a couple of days would help. He had a sudden vision of Father O'Donovan Brady mounting the steps of his pulpit to harangue the faithful after Mass. He shuddered when he thought of what the priest might say about an invasion of Protestant heretics from the north. Ormonde returned to the assault, siege engines refuelled by the cream and fruit.

'Seriously though, Powerscourt, what do you think? Out with it, man!'

'In one sense it is an admirable plan, Ormonde,' said Powerscourt. 'You should congratulate yourself for having thought of it. I say admirable because for one purpose, that of catching these thieves, it is the best plan possible. Mind you, I do have certain reservations about the possible side effects. However, I have a suggestion to make.' Ormonde was helping himself to a third helping of the pudding. Powerscourt hoped it would ease his anger. 'Please continue with the arrangements with the Grand Master of the Orange Lodge and the people from the Royal Black Preceptory, but with one slight change of plan. They are not to set forth immediately. Rather they are to be on standby, ready to go at a moment's notice, boots polished, sashes cleaned, all that sort of thing. Because, gentlemen, we have forgotten a couple of very

114

important people who should be with us in a day or so. I refer to the inspector and his colleague from the Intelligence Department in Dublin. They will have access to sources of intelligence and information in the local community which we do not possess. They will need time to conduct their investigations in as low a key as possible. I am certain that they will find it easier to carry out their work in what you might call a low temperature. Once the Lambeg drums begin to beat, as it were, the temperature will rise dramatically, it may go right off the scale, and it will be much harder for them, people will be less likely to talk. If they fail, so be it. The Ulstermen set off the very next day.'

Powerscourt found himself praying that Richard Butler would keep his mouth shut. His prayers were answered. 'I need time to think about that suggestion, Powerscourt. It has merit, I can certainly see that. I thank you for it. What do you think are the chances of the intelligence people finding the thieves? Evens? Three to one against? Worse?'

'Difficult to say, Ormonde,' Powerscourt replied, remembering a commanding officer's advice that when the time came to blow your own trumpet you didn't pussyfoot around but gave it as big a blast as you could manage. 'I have been involved in intelligence work in India and I was sent out by the Prime Minister in person to reorganize the supply of military intelligence for the British forces in the early stages of the Boer War. And I had dealings with the gentlemen from Dublin Castle in an affair at the time of the Queen's Jubilee which must remain secret to this day. I have a great deal of respect for the Dublin Castle men. If anybody can locate these thieves, they can.'

'Didn't realize you had all that military experience, Powerscourt,' Ormonde said, rising from his seat and beginning to pace up and down his dining room as the remains of the pudding were cleared away. Up and down he went, Powerscourt and Richard Butler sitting as stiff as they could, like children playing a game of statues. At last he spoke.

115

'I'll do it, Powerscourt,' he said, 'I'll do it with one condition. Can we set a time limit for the intelligence people? Can't stand hanging about waiting for other people to do things myself, makes me nervous. If they haven't solved it in a given time limit, I bring in my Orangemen. What do you say?'

'What do you say,' Powerscourt replied quickly, 'to the time limit?'

'A week,' said Ormonde, 'would a week be satisfactory, from your experience of military intelligence?'

'A week would be splendid,' said Powerscourt, relieved that the man hadn't asked for forty-eight hours.

'Done,' said Ormonde, his mood lightening. 'Now then, what do you say to a walk in the grounds? Or we could take one of my boats out for a sail round the bay? Would you like to stay the night?'

'I would be delighted to stay the night,' said Powerscourt, 'but I have left my wife behind at Butler's Court and she has only just arrived in the country.'

'You should have brought her with you,' Ormonde was the genial host now, 'she could have kept my wife company. Always keeps well out of my way, the wife, when I'm in a mood. She calls them my Attila the Hun days. But you will bring her with you when you come back to confer with the intelligence people, won't you?'

Nothing, Powerscourt assured him, would give him greater pleasure. At Westport railway station he eluded Richard Butler for a moment and had a brief conversation with the stationmaster. Westport and the neighbouring parishes, the railway man assured him, were part of the Archbishopric of Tuam whose current incumbent was His Grace the Most Reverend Dr John Healy, resident in the Archbishop's Palace, Cathedral Street, Tuam, County Galway.

7

Lord Francis Powerscourt was sitting in the Butler library, staring intently at a sheet of writing paper. In ten minutes' time Lady Lucy and Johnny Fitzgerald were coming for tea and barm brack and a conversation about the way forward. It was difficult, he thought, to write a letter when you couldn't say what you meant. It was a contradiction in terms. Maybe he should have learnt Morse Code.

'Your Grace,' he began, for his correspondent was none other than the mighty prelate Dr John Healy, Archbishop of Tuam, 'I am writing to you on a matter of the gravest importance which could have dire consequences for your flock and for the politics of this country. I am reluctant to divulge any of the details in this letter.' Powerscourt was sure the man would know what he meant. 'I am an investigator, currently working on a case here in Ireland. In the past I have given service to the household of the Prince of Wales and to the previous Prime Minister, Lord Salisbury. I fear I must emphasize not only the gravity but the urgency of this matter. I believe the situation could turn very serious very soon. I would be most grateful if you could grant me an audience' – did one ask for an audience or an interview with an archbishop? Just have to take a chance – 'at your earliest convenience where I could lay the matter before you with all the details. I do hope you will be able to help, for your help, I firmly believe, could be pivotal. My apologies for such an importunate request, Yours, Powerscourt.' He wondered if there was some special formula you had to insert at the end of ecclesiastical correspondence as if you were writing letters in the French language, but there was no time to find out.

'I've been taking the lie of the land, as you might say.' Johnny Fitzgerald was munching his way happily through his third slice of barm brack and butter. Powerscourt and Lady Lucy smiled at each other. Taking the lie of the land for Johnny usually meant spending a lot of time in the local pubs. 'It's not bad, MacSwiggin's down in the square, though they start singing very early in the evening if you ask me. Anyway, the power in the land is that grocer man Mulcahy with his shop very near the hotel. It's not the bread and ham that make his fortune, it's the loans. Fall behind with your rent, Mulcahy's your man. Need some ready cash to marry off a daughter and give her a dowry, the Grocer's Bank has the answer. I don't think he'd lend you money to bet on the horses but I wouldn't be surprised. One fellow said Mulcahy had more money circulating, as he put it, than the Bank of Ireland.'

'Are you allowed to set yourself up as a moneylender like that, Johnny?' Lady Lucy asked.

'This is Ireland,' said Johnny Fitzgerald. 'Ask no questions, hear no lies.'

'Any word about the paintings at all?' asked Powerscourt.

'I'm coming to that,' said Johnny. 'I've absolutely no doubt that they all know something is going on, but the rumour factory has been working well. It's the stout, I've always believed that stout makes people exaggerate things. One old boy, sitting under the Blessed Virgin Mary all evening and not moving an inch, claimed it was the furniture that had gone. All of it. There's not a chair to sit on or a table to eat your bread off in the whole of Butler's Court. He was certain of it. Another fellow maintained it was just the table in the dining room and the big mirrors that had been taken. Said it had been lifted to order for some coal merchant in Dublin who wanted antique stuff to furnish his new house. This theory didn't take any account of the other robberies – maybe they went for the drawing-room furniture at Connolly's and the beds from Moore Castle. Word of Ormonde House hasn't reached them yet, which is surprising seeing that news usually travels faster than the railways round here.'

'And the Orangemen? Any word of the Orangemen?' Powerscourt wondered what they would make of that in the snug in MacSwiggin's Hotel and Bar.

'Not yet,' said Fitzgerald cheerfully. 'When that hits town it'll probably be an army three thousand strong, enough to take Galway in a siege. I tell you one sad thing, Lady Lucy and Francis. I was talking to the middle Delaney – who's one of the three Delaneys, solicitors with offices in the square, Lady Lucy,' – Johnny remembered she had only arrived recently – 'in the saloon bar of MacSwiggin's, a nice place to take a drink if you like to be surrounded by religious pictures, and he was telling me sad stories about the cricket team. He's a great fan of the cricket, Bartholomew Delaney, been playing for the local team for ages. He says it's dying out, the Butler's Cross Eleven, no new recruits coming in at all. Soon, according to Bartholomew, there won't be any young fellows left out in the field to chase the ball and cut it off before it reaches the boundary. The opposing batsmen, he said, will just have to hit the bloody ball and it'll go for four. Butler's Cross fielders will all be too decrepit to run after the thing. The opposing side will make hundreds and hundreds of runs. Butler's Cross cricket team, old age pensioners a speciality, will never win a match again.'

'What's happened, Johnny?' asked Lady Lucy. 'Where have all the young men gone?'

'They've gone Gaelic, that's what they've done. The Gaelic Athletic Association, or GAA as it's called, is very strong in these parts. They're allowed to play Gaelic football and hurling, but only Irish games. Once you sign up, you can't play cricket or soccer, it's against the rules. Ping pong, Bartholomew Delaney maintained sourly, was still allowed but the rest are proscribed as the games of the occupying power.'

'And who runs this GAA, Johnny?' Powerscourt had an improbable vision of the Pickwickian Father O'Donovan Brady, whistle in hand, refereeing a match, whiskey flask concealed in his baggy shorts.

'Ah,' said Johnny, 'there's a thing now. It's the Christian Brothers, so it is. Militant for independence and Home Rule, most of them. There's another thing, Francis, I nearly forgot. They've heard all about you down there in MacSwiggin's – well, in the public they have. I'm not sure about the saloon. They say you're a great detective man from London who's never failed to solve a crime, so they do. You've got almost magical powers, according to them, a Merlin come to Meath.'

'God in heaven,' said Powerscourt, 'I'm not sure I want my name bandied about in Diarmuid MacSwiggin's Bar and Hotel. I might pick up all sorts of unappetizing clients.'

'At least they'd be able to pay you,' said Fitzgerald. 'Quick loan from Mulcahy the grocer and they can pay you straight away.'

Powerscourt turned to Lady Lucy. 'Time to get serious. Lucy, we need some advice. This case seems to revolve around the men, Connolly, Butler, Moore, Ormonde, but I'm sure the wives are at least as important. Have you had time to have a proper talk with Mrs Butler? What would you do if you were the mistress of one of these embattled houses?'

'I know what I would do,' Lady Lucy said firmly, 'and I think I know what they are going to do. This being Ireland, you won't be surprised to hear that they are not the same thing. It's the children, you see, for me. And there seem to be so many of them running around. They would be even easier to steal than the pictures. Maybe the thieves would face such unpopularity if they kidnapped little ones that they couldn't do it. I wouldn't take the chance, myself. I'd take the whole lot of them over to England and wait till everything's blown over.'

'And Mrs Moore and Mrs Butler and the rest?'

'I think they will stay. You and Johnny would understand this much better than I do, coming from here in the first place. It's all this history, Francis. I've never known a place with so much history. They've been through so much of it, these families, wars in Cromwell's time, the Battle of the Boyne and all that, the rising in 1798 I think it was,' she looked at Powerscourt who nodded encouragement, 'the famine, the land wars, it never seems to stop. At any point these Moores and Butlers and Connollys could have sold up, packed their bags and left.'

'Wouldn't have got very much for the land, selling up during those upheavals,' said Johnny. 'Sorry for interrupting.'

Lady Lucy smiled. 'The point is, Johnny, that they didn't sell up. They stuck it out. Sticking it out seems to be a key component of the Anglo-Irish character. They've all inherited these places from their fathers. When they look at all these adorable children they can see the Big Houses passing on to them. The children are tomorrow. If you take them away you take away the future. What's the point of being here if you run away when a painting is taken from the walls?'

'Too much history, that's the trouble with Ireland,' said Powerscourt. 'Pity you can't sell bits of it off to some of these new places where they haven't got any at all.'

He rose from the tea table and went to the window. A loud game of tennis was taking place on the grass. Three small boys were having climbing races up the trees.

'Johnny,' he said, 'I'd like you to keep your eyes and ears open down in Butler's Cross. Somebody may say something they shouldn't one day soon. Lucy, can you keep us informed about the state of feminine opinion about the place? I'd be most interested to know exactly what was in that letter the thieves sent Richard Butler. If you can winkle that out of Sylvia Butler it'll be champagne all round. Now I must go down to the town to post this letter.'

Powerscourt went round to the far end of the stable block to collect his bicycle. It was a fairly old model with no known owner. He had been riding it for some days now and the stable lads kept it in a special place for him. He was thinking about what he might say to the Archbishop as he set off. The ground between Butler's Court and the town rose slightly as you left the house and then dropped down steeply towards the square. Heavily laden carriages had been known to slow to walking pace or less as they toiled up the slope. Cyclists preferred the outward to the inward journey. Powerscourt pedalled hard as he began the descent for the last post was but minutes away. About halfway down his hair was streaming out behind his head and he thought he should slow down. He pulled on the brakes. Nothing happened. He tried the other right-hand brake. Nothing happened. He was travelling very fast now as he tried both brakes again. Nothing. At the bottom of the drive there was a great stone wall. Powerscourt knew he couldn't control the bicycle much longer. It was never designed to move at this speed and it had begun to shake violently. Anything could happen now. He turned the handlebars slightly to the left and tried to steer a path into the woods where the undergrowth would slow him down. That wall at the bottom would surely kill him. Still travelling at slightly over twenty miles an hour he crashed into the brambles. The front wheel ran over a branch on the ground and Powerscourt was catapulted out of the saddle and dragged along the ground by the momentum until he hit a tree. For a moment or two he was unconscious. He had a gash on his right leg. His wrist ached. Blood was pouring from a long wound on his head. Briefly he thought of Lady Lucy. They were sitting in the drawing room in Markham Square. Then some sense of duty called him. He remembered his letter. Limping, lurching, occasionally dragging himself along the ground, he made his way to the end of the drive. He reeled across the street and posted his letter in the box. He turned and crawled back towards Butler's Court and Lady

Lucy. He collapsed by the ornamental arch at the gates, his blood dripping on to the hard hot ground. His last thought before he passed out was that if he was going to die, it was good that his last letter should have been to an archbishop. A stone lion with a stone ball stood sentry above him. Outside MacSwiggin's an elderly customer nursing his pint watched in astonishment as the apparition vanished from sight. He didn't think he'd been drinking that much. Later on, as he retold his story in the public bar, he remembered that the wraithlike figure reminded him of an engraving in his auntie's parlour. It was, he averred, and many believed him, the ghost of Theobald Wolfe Tone, the man had a definite look of Tone about him, come to post a last letter to the French, asking for reinforcements.

Johnny Fitzgerald found him at about a quarter to eight. He took one look at his friend and sprinted over to MacSwiggin's to find a doctor. The local doctor, Padraig MacBride, was, as it happened, having a quiet drink with his friend the vet in the saloon bar. As MacBride knelt down to look at Powerscourt Johnny wandered off to find the bicycle, or the remains of the bicycle. He looked very solemn when he returned.

'Well,' said the doctor, 'I think it's not quite as bad as it looks, so it's not. It's lucky he didn't hit that tree the moment he came off the bicycle. That might have killed him. As it is, being pulled along the undergrowth by the momentum isn't pleasant but at least you won't hit your head so hard.' The doctor was checking Powerscourt's pulse and peering at his head.

'Is it staying at Butler's Court you are, the pair of you?' he said. 'You look like the sort of people who stay at Butler's Court.'

'We are,' Johnny Fitzgerald, not sure if he was saying yes to the first or the second proposition on offer.

'Right then. If you could stop here with your friend a moment, I'll go and borrow some kind of horse-drawn transport to get him up the road to the house. I want to get that forehead cleaned up and I doubt we could carry him, with that hill and all.'

As Dr MacBride sped off towards MacSwiggin's there was a low moan from the prostrate figure on the ground. Powerscourt managed to sit up, swearing violently.

'Christ, my head hurts! Christ! Johnny, thank God it's you. What happened? Did somebody hit me over the head?'

'Francis, this is very important,' said Johnny, leaning down and whispering. 'Do you understand what I'm saying? Your wits haven't gone wandering, have they?'

Powerscourt wriggled slightly to make himself more comfortable. 'Wits present on parade,' he said, wincing from the pain in his head.

'Right, Francis, you must remember this, whatever else you remember. You fell off your bike and hit your head on a tree. It was an accident. Have you got that? You fell off the bike and hit your head on a tree.'

'I fell off the bike,' said Powerscourt. 'I hit my head on a tree.'

From the direction of the hotel they could hear voices raised in argument, then the sound of a horse's hooves.

'Quick, Johnny, tell me before they come. What really happened?'

'You mustn't tell a soul, least of all Lucy,' said Fitzgerald urgently. 'Somebody round here doesn't like you very much, Francis. You're running out of friends. Some bastard cut the brake cable on that bicycle. It could no more stop than it could take off.'

'Here we are,' said the doctor, sitting on top of a pony and trap driven by a youth who looked about twelve years old. 'This is Seamus, driving here,' said the doctor as they helped Powerscourt into the trap. 'Cheeky young bugger wanted sixpence to take us up the hill. I said it was an act of Christian charity, helping a fellow Christian in his hour of need. He said you were Protestants so that didn't count. I shall tell the Christian Brothers about him.'

Seamus spat expertly into the side of the road and they set off up the hill.

One hour later Powerscourt was sitting up in bed, sipping soup, his wife by his side. His head had been expertly bandaged by one of the parlour maids called Sinead who had won her nursing spurs bandaging the cut legs and bruised arms of the small boys of Butler's Court. Powerscourt was the first grown-up she had ever dealt with and she was proud of her work. The doctor had departed, prodding his patient in various places and peering into his eyes before he left. He was to return the following morning.

When she saw her husband being helped into the hall, the congealed blood on his forehead, the extreme pallor of his complexion, for one heart-stopping moment Lady Lucy thought he was going to die. Not again, she said to herself, please God, not again. She remembered the long vigils through the night, the weeping children sitting on her bed, when Powerscourt had been shot in one of his cases several years before, the certainty that he was going to pass away in front of her. He would drift from coma into death and she wouldn't even know the moment to hold him in her arms.

Johnny Fitzgerald had been quick to reassure her as they arrived. 'Don't worry, Lady Lucy,' he had said, putting an arm round her, 'it's not like last time. He fell off his bike, the silly old sod, and hit his head on a tree.'

'Dr MacBride,' the medical man had introduced himself and offered further reassurance: 'There is no cause for serious alarm, I believe. He'll be right as rain in a couple of days.'

'Francis,' Lady Lucy said, holding his hand, 'I'm so glad you're going to be all right. I was so worried when they brought you in, I can't tell you.'

'Don't worry,' said her husband, 'Maybe I just need some lessons in bicycle riding.'

'I always said,' Lady Lucy was firm on the point, 'that

125

Thomas was safer on a bicycle than you are. He concentrates, you see. Your mind is always wandering off, looking for murderers or playing imaginary cricket matches or whatever your mind does while the rest of you is in the saddle.'

Powerscourt laughed and grimaced at the same time as a salvo of pain flowed through his head. 'True, Lucy, very true. Maybe I shall get one of those motor cars, a great big one with a mighty horn.'

'You could kill yourself more easily in one of those than you could on a bicycle,' said Lady Lucy.

The mood was subdued in Butler's Court for the next couple of days. The news of the thefts from Ormonde House and Powerscourt's injuries seemed to take their toll. Sylvia Butler looked particularly subdued. Her husband tried to raise spirits with games of whist in the drawing room after dinner. Where the air had been filled before with the melodies of Thomas Moore, it was now filled with the shouts of the card players which grew louder with the passing of the port. 'You had the ace of spades, you bastard!' 'I didn't think you had any more trumps, damn your eyes!' 'Who would have thought you had all three of the buggers, ace, king and queen! You've won again!' Great Uncle Peter came down to play in his green dressing gown, raking in his tricks like a croupier in a casino. Powerscourt noticed that Young James refused all offers to play, saying quietly, 'I never play cards, never.' Powerscourt and Lady Lucy, playing together, took three shillings and sixpence off Richard Butler and his wife.

'We're going to have an entertainment soon,' Butler announced as the cards were folded away one evening, 'a sort of concert party. Young James is organizing the children to recite poems, sing songs, all that sort of thing. He was going to do it with those aged eight and upwards, but the six- and seven-year-olds ganged up on him and beat him up in a pillow fight. Now Young James says the little ones can't

126

remember their lines. He's going to fire the starting pistol when they can.'

Three days after his accident Powerscourt got what he wanted. There was a letter for him in a rather distinguished-looking envelope. He took Lady Lucy and Johnny Fitzgerald up to his room to read it.

'Dear Lord Powerscourt,' it began, 'His Grace the Most Reverend Dr Healey acknowledges receipt of your letter. As you stress the urgency, His Grace has spared time for you at five o'clock on Tuesday afternoon. If that is not possible another appointment can be arranged the following day. We shall expect you on Tuesday unless we hear to the contrary. Yours, Fintan O'Shaughnessy, SJ, Secretary and Chaplain to the Archbishop.' Johnny Fitzgerald disappeared for a moment or two and then returned.

'By God, Lucy, I'd better get my skates on,' said Powerscourt. 'It's Tuesday today. Where is Tuam, for Christ's sake? I've no idea. I've got a feeling it's up towards Sligo some place.'

'It's not up, Francis, it's down,' said Johnny Fitzgerald, grinning at Lady Lucy. 'Down towards Galway, the other direction entirely. I'm coming with you, Francis, to make sure you get on the right train. We don't want you ending up in Bundoran or Ballina, for God's sake. I've just been to look up the details of the trains. There's plenty of time but we need to get moving. I'll check out the hostelries while you're down on your knees with the Archbish, confessing your sins or being accepted into the true faith. Maybe they've got a Cathedral Arms or the Bishop's Mitre down there where a chap could quench his thirst. I've always wanted to have a drink in a pub called The Cathedral Arms. It'll make a change from the saloon in MacSwiggin's.'

Lady Lucy sat on the steps in front of Butler's Court and watched her men being driven off to the station. Why, she wondered, was Johnny Fitzgerald going with Francis today? He wouldn't normally accompany him on a mission to an archbishop. Francis might be pretty hopeless about directions

127

and that sort of thing, but even he could make his way on to a train. He'd been managing that for years now. Was Francis in some sort of danger? Even going to an archbishop, for goodness sake? Was Johnny going as some sort of bodyguard? Going to keep Francis safe? Then another terrible thought struck her and refused to go away. That accident on the bicycle, was it really an accident? Lady Lucy wasn't an expert on bicycles but she was sure there must be ways you could tamper with the things, loosening the saddle so the rider would fall off or unscrewing the bolts that held the wheels to the frame. Maybe you could do something with the brakes, she just wasn't sure. Throughout the morning she tried to put these fears out of her mind but they refused to go away. By lunchtime she knew that the knot was back, the knot in her stomach, the knot she had lived with for years, the knot she thought had gone away, the knot of anxiety and terror that her beloved might be in danger and might never come back from his journeys.

Father Fintan O'Shaughnessy, SJ, the Archbishop's Chaplain, was one of those irritating priests who don't walk. They glide. They shimmer, Powerscourt thought, as if the Holy Ghost has placed a slim buffer between them and the ground that ordinary mortals walk on. Father Fintan was definitely shimmering this afternoon as he led Powerscourt down a long corridor lined with Irish landscapes and religious paintings which led to the Archbishop's study.

The Most Reverend Dr John Healey was a great bullock of a man with grey hair, about six feet four with broad shoulders. One of his more irreverent curates once said that he looked like a cattle dealer from Mullingar. Certainly, Powerscourt felt, Dr Healey would be in the vanguard of his flock, an onward Christian soldier marching as to war. Powerscourt bowed slightly and shook Dr Healey's hand. There was a reproduction of a Renaissance crucifixion on the wall behind his desk.

More Irish landscapes lined the walls. Perhaps, Powerscourt thought, he liked collecting paintings.

'Lord Powerscourt, welcome to Tuam,' he boomed as if speaking to some mighty congregation. 'Have you been here before?' He waved his visitor to the chair opposite his own.

'I don't believe I've had the pleasure,' Powerscourt replied.

'Well, you must look round before you go, if you have time. A fine little town.' The Archbishop looked closely at Powerscourt's face as if sin or salvation could be discerned there by people like archbishops who knew what they were looking for.

'There's a definite likeness, you know,' he said with a smile. 'I met your father years ago now when I was at Maynooth, at the college there. He was a fine man, your father. You remind me of him.'

Powerscourt smiled. Maynooth, he remembered, was the principal seminary and Catholic college in Ireland. His father, a man with a deep interest in human nature, had collected parsons and priests and padres of every description. He always said he enjoyed their company, whatever their particular faith might be. Maybe a younger Dr Healey had been one of those.

'But come, Lord Powerscourt,' the Archbishop opened his hands out in front of him, 'to business. You must tell me of your concerns.'

Powerscourt told him everything. He told him about the stolen paintings and the letters that had accompanied them. He explained that he did not know the precise content of the letters, but said they were blackmail letters and that they contained a terrible threat if the contents were revealed to a third party. He mentioned the fury of Dennis Ormonde of Ormonde House and his threat to import one hundred Orangemen, possibly more, to guard the houses of the gentry of the west.

The Archbishop had been taking notes until the mention of the Orangemen. Then his jaw dropped slightly and he stared at Powerscourt.

'One hundred Orangemen,' he boomed once more, 'one hundred of them! God bless my soul!' His hands began stroking the great silver crucifix that hung from his neck. 'I'll come back to them in a moment if I may, Lord Powerscourt. Let me try to make clear in my mind the story so far, as it were. Some twenty portraits, all of them male, all of them the predecessors of these great landlords, have been stolen, and some Old Masters. Blackmail notes have been dispatched demanding we know not what. Do you know, Lord Powerscourt, if any of these blackmail threats have been met? Have the Butlers or the Moores paid up?'

'I wish I knew the answer, Your Grace. I think not. There is an air of desperation abroad in all these houses now, I think. There may be a deadline for payment. Again, I do not know. I suspect they are waiting for the threats at the end of the letters to be carried out. And they are hoping against hope that the thieves will be caught before they can carry out their threats.'

'These Orangemen now,' the Archbishop was taking notes again, 'you said they are, for the moment, a threat rather than a reality. Is that so? And, if so, under what circumstances will they come?'

'My apologies, Your Grace, I should have made myself clearer. Ormonde has sent to Dublin Castle for an inspector and a colleague from the Special Branch, or the Intelligence Department to come and investigate the thefts. Ormonde is giving them a week to find the perpetrators. If they fail, the Orangemen and their bands will set forth from Enniskillen. They could be here in a day. I believe Ormonde intends to charter a special train to bring them down.'

'Just one point, Lord Powerscourt, if I may, you're not serious when you talk of bands? There are all kinds of things I can put up with as a proper Christian pilgrim but Orange bands are not one of them. Please tell me you jest here.'

'I was speaking metaphorically, Your Grace, I have no idea if they propose to bring a band or not. But if you think about

130

their activities, those Orangemen are scarcely able to move about in any numbers in Belfast and their other strongholds without a band. It would seem to be part of the Orange mind.'

'You're right, Lord Powerscourt,' said the Archbishop sadly, 'they are hardly capable of leaving their front doors without those terrible Lambeg drums. Maybe they will bring a band. God save Ireland.'

The Archbishop frowned. His hands moved faster round his crucifix now.

'By my calculations, Your Grace, these Dublin Castle men should have arrived three days ago. There are four days left.'

'I can see your concerns, Lord Powerscourt. You were certainly right to come to me. Tell me, do you have particular fears or is it just the general situation that concerns you? And do you envisage any particular role for the Church in these events?'

Powerscourt paused for a moment. 'I think,' he began, 'that the situation becomes so combustible with the arrival of the Orangemen that anything might happen. But let me try out, if I may, some possibilities. Your Grace will, no doubt, be able to think of more. Look at it from the beginning. Suppose those Orangemen arrive in Westport station in their special train. At least they won't have had to share their carriages with anybody else. The most logical way for them to reach Ormonde House is to walk or march – even Dennis Ormonde hasn't enough carriages to carry a hundred of them there. Suppose they do bring a band and march out down the Mall in Westport towards the Louisburg road. Do you think they would reach the end of the town without bricks or bottles being thrown at them? I doubt it. Then suppose they arrive in Ormonde House and are put up in one of those great barns and outhouses out the back. How long before the buildings go up in flames? Or suppose these Orangemen go out drinking at one of those pubs like Campbell's underneath Croagh Patrick. They're nearly as fond of drinking as they are of marching. How long before a fight or a brawl breaks out and spreads?

131

How long before the Protestant houses with the paintings guarded by the Orangemen are torched? Or boycotted? Trouble could come in any one of a number of ways, Your Grace.'

'Trouble might indeed be coming, in battalions. What a terrible situation, Lord Powerscourt. The original wrong is done to the Protestants in the Big Houses. I don't approve of their presence here any more, I think their day is done, but having your ancestors stolen off your walls must be terrible. It's as if their past has been violated in front of them. I know how I would feel if somebody stole some of my Irish land-scapes and I'm not even descended from them. I think I can sense where you see the Church might fit in, but tell me your thoughts first, if you will.'

'I do not see,' said Powerscourt, 'how I can ask anything from you at all, Your Grace. You have been more than kind in hearing me out today and at such short notice too. I am not a member of your faith. I no longer live in this country. But I do care about it, about Ireland, I care passionately about it, and I pray that the peace should not be broken and more misery heaped on a population who have endured far too much of it already in the last hundred and twenty years. The people, Your Grace, will look to the Church for guidance. Moral leadership in Ireland today rests with you and your bishops and priests. The Church is more powerful today than it has ever been. When these outrages start, or rather if these outrages start between Orangemen and Catholics, the local priests will need guidance. You know far better than I do about the various ranges of opinion in the priesthood in your diocese, but I suspect that some of them would condemn any violence and others would condone it, either by word or by inaction.'

Powerscourt found the Archbishop's next question truly astonishing. 'Have you come across our local priest in the Butler's Cross area, Lord Powerscourt? Father O'Donovan Brady?'

'I have,' said Powerscourt.

'There are many like him,' said the Archbishop. 'Sorry, I interrupted you. Please continue.'

'Please don't think I would like the Church to turn into some kind of auxiliary police force, Your Grace, encouraging people to turn their neighbours in to the authorities or anything like that. But if there is no message, no instruction to the faithful through the priesthood, the men of the night may think they have the Church's blessing. If, on the other hand, the Church urges calm, encourages people not to resort to violence, then there might be hope.'

'I see,' said the Archbishop, closing his eyes briefly. 'I do not think I could give you any guidance on what my position might be until we have something more concrete to deal with. I do not believe that the men of the night, as you call them, would pay any attention to what the Church might say. Only at the end, when they need to confess their sins and receive the last rites, do they take any heed of priests at all. And then, of course, we cannot fail them in their hour of need. But the Church must give a lead, we must offer guidance. I am as concerned in a way – I speak freely in front of you as you have with me – with some of the priests and the younger Christian Brothers as I am with the men of the night. In many of them, second or third generation descendants of the dark years of the 1840s, the fires of hatred left by the famine burn very bright. They blame the landlords and what they describe as the English garrison. But we cannot build a new Ireland on theft and robbery by night and letters of blackmail by day. Certain principles will guide me. If these Orangemen come, with or without the bands, we must be patient. Our congregations must remember that however objectionable their presence may be, it was the actions of our own people that brought them here in the first place. Restraint and calm must be our watchwords. Of course, I shall have to be very circumspect in what I say. I shall pray for God's guidance to find the right language, and I shall pray that He guide me in the right path.'

133

'Thank you,' said Powerscourt.

Then the Archbishop produced another of his astonishing changes of tack. 'Tell me, Lord Powerscourt, how soon do you think your leg will be better?'

'My leg?' said Powerscourt in astonishment. Did the man possess healing powers?

'Your leg. I noticed you were in some difficulty when you came in.'

'Oh, that,' said Powerscourt, 'it's nothing. The doctors say it should be fine in a week or so.'

'In that case,' the Archbishop was smiling now, 'let me issue you an invitation. I shall explain. As Archbishop of Tuam I am charged, along with my other duties, with the supervision of the pilgrimage to Croagh Patrick, Ireland's Holy Mountain. It takes place on the last Sunday in July. I am sure you know of it. All these papers here' – he waved an enormous fist at the documents on his desk – 'are concerned with it. We are consecrating a new chapel on the summit this year. I think this pilgrimage is a very special event, Lord Powerscourt. Few who take part are unmoved by it. Surrounded by all these pilgrims, most of them saying their prayers as they go, some climbing barefoot, I have often felt very close to God. Certainly His Grace is present on the hillside that day, I am sure of it. I am inviting you and your wife and your friends to take part this year, as my guests. Of course I am not asking you to be in my party. We shall be many and shall stop many times for moments of devotion. Nor would I dream of asking you to take part in any of our services. But St Patrick is the patron saint of all Irishmen, whatever their particular denomination. As Protestants you would be most welcome. I think it would be good for your immortal soul, Lord Powerscourt, and I am certain you will find it a moving experience.'

'I am most touched and honoured, Your Grace,' said Powerscourt. 'I accept. Of course I accept. It will be a privilege to be your guest on that day.'

134

'And now, if you will forgive me, I must attend to three local MPs who have come to talk to me about secondary education. They have been waiting fifteen minutes already.' The Archbishop was ushering Powerscourt to the door in person. 'We must keep in touch. Write to me for another appointment if you need. Don't hesitate. I can find you through Butler's Court?' Powerscourt nodded. 'Good.' The Archbishop opened his massive front door. 'If we don't meet before I shall hope to see you on that Sunday. On the Holy Mountain.'

8

Johnny Fitzgerald was in the Mitre, a mere hundred yards from the Archbishop's Palace. Tuam, he said sadly, did not have a Cathedral Arms. He would have to wait another day.

'Satisfactory meeting?' he asked his friend. 'Archbishop well? Holy pictures in good order?'

'All well,' said Powerscourt. 'I'll tell you about it when we get back to Butler's Cross.'

After less than three minutes in the train Johnny Fitzgerald was asleep, possible tribute to the powers of the Mitre's ministrations. Powerscourt stared idly out of the window, thinking about the threat of violence that might erupt when the Orangemen came to town. He noticed a brown ruined tower with no windows, sitting in a field enclosed by the remains of the walls that once surrounded it, another memorial to the violence of Ireland's past. Ireland is a land of stone walls and ruins, he thought, Franciscan friaries, abandoned in Elizabeth's time, with jagged walls etched against the sky. A whole religious settlement at Clonmacnoise, founded in the sixth century, finally destroyed by the English garrison in Athlone a thousand years later, the remains of the buildings now lying open to the sun and the rain and the clouds by the side of the Shannon. Great Norman castles like Ballymote, square in construction with round towers for extra protection, where Red Hugh O'Donnell marshalled his forces in 1598 before marching south to defeat at Kinsale, ransacked and ruined. Only the crows are left, Powerscourt remembered, perched happily on the rough edges of the battlements. Manor houses and castles burnt in those wars like that of the poet Edmund Spenser who had composed his *Faerie Queen* in County Cork. After the rebels destroyed his house, his son burnt to death inside it, Spenser had written that Ireland would never find peace until all the native Irish were killed. Catholic abbeys and churches ravaged by Cromwell's men, raven and crow now living where the host had once been present and the peasant Irish had knelt to receive the sacrament. Anglo-Irish houses which had once been loud with music and laughter at the balls of the gentry, now stark ruins, torched in the 1798 rebellion. Tiny cottages in Connemara, roofless now and windowless, abandoned to death or emigration in the famine years. Cairns and dolmens that bore witness to earlier times, relics of earlier Irish in an earlier Ireland. Sprinkled all over the thirty-two counties of Ireland, like jewels fallen from a casket, bare ruined choirs where late the sweet birds sang.

Two days later Powerscourt and Johnny Fitzgerald were sitting in the library of Ormonde House, talking to Dennis Ormonde. His anger had faded slightly though Powerscourt thought it could erupt at any moment.

'No wife?' had been his first words to Powerscourt. 'Couldn't come? What a pity.'

'It's Sylvia Butler,' said Powerscourt. 'Lucy sends her deepest apologies but feels her place is with her at this time.'

'Women,' said Dennis Ormonde. 'Do you know what my one has done? She's gone and locked the Picture Gallery, both doors, and she won't let me have the keys, that's what she's done. If I want to work myself into a rage about the missing pictures I have to go and peer in through the window like a bloody burglar.'

Powerscourt and Fitzgerald made sympathetic noises.

'Now then,' he went on. 'Our friend from Dublin Castle is working on a bench in the garden. Doesn't come in here very much. Doesn't trust the servants, he says. Can't say I blame him really. Ulsterman, funny little man with one of those ghastly accents they all have up there. Name of Harkness, William Harkness, probably named after King Billy at the Battle of the Boyne. Seems strange to have one Ulsterman here one day when we may have a hundred of them the day after. Anyway, preparations are well under way for the reception and feeding and sleeping of the Orangemen in the barns and outhouses out the back. Cook is baking mountainous quantities of potato bread. She says they like potato bread, the Ulster people. Harkness does most of his business in the evening. He's got a lad with him, can't be more than twenty-five, comes from Dingle, name of O'Gara. One from one end of the island, one from another. God help us all.

'Now then ...' He rummaged around in a pile of papers on a table beside him. 'I've got a list of all the houses they'll guard when they come. This copy's for you, Powerscourt.'

Powerscourt looked at a neat list of grand houses. There was a line drawn halfway down.

'Don't think we can manage those places at the bottom of the list,' Ormonde said. 'Only got one or two pictures anyway. I'm banking on the thieves only going for houses with pictures. Can't think of any other means of elimination.'

Ormonde looked at his watch. 'You'd better go and make your mark with our friend from the Castle. He's got to go into Westport soon. Must be the only bloody policeman in the whole of Ireland with his office on a park bench.'

'Just one thing before we do that,' said Johnny Fitzgerald. 'Do you know if they're bringing a band?'

'Do I know if who is bringing a bloody band?' Ormonde sounded cross.

'The Orangemen,' Johnny persisted, 'are they bringing a band?'

'Do I know if the Orangemen are bringing a band? How the hell should I know?'

'I just thought you might know,' said Fitzgerald. 'Could be a bit tricky, having an Orange band marching about the place banging those big drums.'

'Bugger the band,' Ormonde was working himself up well now, 'why don't you go and talk to Harkness and I'll see what I can find out about Orange bands. Damn Orange bands!'

William Harkness's bench was strategically placed two-thirds of the way between the back of Ormonde House and the sea. If he looked to his right he had a clear view of any miscreants who might be foolish enough to approach the house in broad daylight. To his left he could spot any piratical invasion sailing across Clew Bay.

'How are ye, Lord Powerscourt, are ye well?' he began. 'It's great to meet ye. They've got a file on you back there in Dublin, you know, all of it very complimentary.'

'Have they indeed, Inspector?' said Powerscourt. 'Tell us this, sorry to be brief but I understand your time is short, what do you think your chances are of finding the thieves?'

Harkness looked at the two of them carefully. 'To be honest with you, to be truthful with you now, and I wouldn't say this in front of your man Ormonde, I don't think we're going to do it. Not in a week. Might do it if it was longer. The trouble is that the word has got out about these Orangemen. The constabulary here and in Castlebar are worried sick about them. The commanding officer of the Castlebar garrison has cancelled all leave for the foreseeable future. Everybody's clammed up.'

'I don't want to pry,' said Powerscourt, 'but do you have any informants inside the gang of thieves who stole Ormonde's paintings?'

'I couldn't swear that we do,' admitted Harkness. 'If we did they'd all be locked up and under interrogation.'

Powerscourt shuddered slightly. He knew what interrogation could mean in these parts.

'Are you able to tell us,' asked Johnny, 'how many informants you do have? Just so we have an idea.'

'I don't think that would be helpful at all,' Harkness replied.

'You mean you haven't got any,' said Johnny.

'I wouldn't say that.' Harkness's attention was suddenly drawn to a figure who must have been O'Gara from Dingle, ambling slowly towards the house. 'How's about ye, O'Gara, you hoor!' he shouted. 'What are you doing going over to the house, for Christ's sake? We're here, you fool, not there.' O'Gara broke into a slow run. 'What do you have to tell us, man? What news?'

'The policeman has done as you asked, sir,' he said. 'All the senior officers from Westport and round about will be meeting you when you go into Westport later this morning. It's all arranged.'

'I've been to Castlebar and Newport and lots of places talking to the police,' Harkness told Powerscourt and Fitzgerald. 'Some good may come of it. I'd better be off.'

The first stirrings of a plan were beginning to form in Powerscourt's brain. He didn't want to mention it to anybody yet, not even to Johnny Fitzgerald. But it might, it just might help to catch the thieves.

'When are you going back to Dublin?' he asked.

'The day after tomorrow,' said Harkness, tidying up the papers lying around on the bottom of his bench.

'I have an idea I may want to discuss with you,' said Powerscourt. 'I need to turn it over in my mind first, Inspector. Would you be able to break your journey home in Athlone? I am staying near there.'

'I would,' said Harkness, 'I'd be happy to. No bother.'

'In which case I shall send a message to Ormonde tomorrow, if I wish to proceed. No message, no meeting.'

'Understood,' said the man from Dublin Castle and fastened his briefcase with the most formidable lock Powerscourt had ever seen. 'Good day to you, gentlemen.'

Powerscourt and Fitzgerald watched them go.

140

'Do you think they know anything at all, Francis?' said Johnny.

'You can look at it in two ways, I think, Johnny. Either they know nothing at all, or they know a lot more than Harkness is letting on. If you forced me to place a bet either way I think I'd say they know more than they are letting on. But I could be wrong.'

They took an early lunch with the Ormondes, a clear chicken soup, roast lamb with redcurrant jelly that Powerscourt presumed was home-made, a fruit pie with cream. Johnny Fitzgerald had a long discussion with Ormonde about the local birds. Mrs Ormonde, a petite pretty woman in her early thirties with bright red hair, kept a firm but unobtrusive eye on her husband. The raging fury of days before, the Attila the Hun mood, had gone. You could see that he might easily be moved to anger but at this lunch table he was tamed. Just as she had done with the Picture Gallery, Powerscourt thought, Mrs Ormonde had locked her husband up and kept possession of the keys.

'In Dublin's fair city
Where the girls are so pretty
I first set my eyes on sweet Molly Malone,
As she wheeled her wheelbarrow
Through streets broad and narrow,
Crying cockles and mussels, alive alive oh.

Alive alive oh, alive alive oh,
Crying cockles and mussels, alive alive oh.'

The children's concert party in Butler's Court had begun. All the adults and a number of friends whose children were being cared for by Young James had assembled in the audience in the Long Gallery on the first floor. This was the most spectacular room in the place, nearly ninety feet long and twenty-five feet wide with huge windows looking out over the

141

gardens and the river. Richard Butler was in the middle of the front row, wearing a deep red smoking jacket and a bow tie, looking, Powerscourt thought, rather like a man about to introduce acts in the music hall. Sylvia Butler was beside him, the two smallest Butler children sitting on either side, resentful that they were not allotted a part in the performance. The vicar was there, Reverend Cooper Walker, with that cheerful air vicars wear to fêtes and parties. Johnpeter Kilross and Alice Bracken were sitting suspiciously close to one another in the back row. The first performers were three small girls in white dresses, aged, Powerscourt thought, about seven or eight. Maybe these were some of those who could not remember their lines. They sang a verse each on their own, all joining in for the chorus.

> 'She was a fishmonger
> And sure 'twas no wonder
> For so were her mother and father before,
> And they each wheeled their barrow
> Through streets broad and narrow,
> Crying cockles and mussels, alive alive oh.'

The child gave a great sigh as she finished as if it had all been a terrible ordeal. James, accompanying them on the piano, gave her a stern look. A makeshift stage, used in grown-up amateur dramatics, had been erected at one end of the room. To one side was a table with poles around it holding black cloth that ran round three of the four sides. It was open facing the audience. A set of steps led up to it and in front was what looked like a bath tub, also draped in black. Powerscourt wondered if there was going to be a mock execution.

> 'She died of a fever,'

the final singer, a dark-haired little girl with a very serious expression, put tremendous emphasis on the word fever,

'And no one could save her,
And that was the end of sweet Molly Malone,
But her ghost wheels her barrow
Through streets broad and narrow,
Crying cockles and mussels, alive alive oh.
Alive alive oh, alive alive oh,
Crying cockles and mussels, alive alive oh.'

Many of the audience were humming along to the final chorus. The three girls bowed solemnly and departed through the door at the back of the room. Great giggling and laughter could be heard coming from the children awaiting their turn.

'Didn't they look sweet, Francis,' Lady Lucy whispered to Powerscourt. 'I hope their parents are here to see them.'

Next up was a boy of about ten years, in a dark blue sailor suit. He delivered a short extract from a speech by Daniel O'Connell at Tara, home of the legendary High Kings of Ireland, which declared that the country was making its way towards reform with the strides of a giant. Seven hundred and fifty tousand people, the boy assured them, had listened to O'Connell that day.

There was a round of applause. 'Well said, wee Jimmy!' 'You tell them, son!' 'Three-quarters of a million, by God!' James was back at the piano now, two girls of about thirteen standing demurely on either side of him, but turned to face the spectators. James, Powerscourt noticed, was dressed entirely in black, black trousers, a black jacket that was slightly too small for him. Only the shirt was white.

'Down by the salley gardens my love and I did meet,'

they sang in unison,

'She passed the salley gardens with little snow-white feet.
She bid me take love easy, as the leaves grow on the tree;
But I, being young and foolish, with her would not agree.'

143

The girls were old enough, Powerscourt thought, to dream of love, but too young as yet to have known it.

'In a field by the river my love and I did stand,
And on my leaning shoulder she laid her snow-white hand.
She bid me take life easy, as the grass grows on the weirs;
But I was young and foolish, and now am full of tears.'

Another prolonged round of applause followed, loud cries of Bravo and Encore coming from the back of the room. How innocent it all was, Powerscourt thought, and how charming. How far removed from the world outside where thieves broke in and stole, and blackmail letters came in through the front door. Now he saw the significance of the table and the black drapes. Two tall boys in dark shirts were dragging a third, dressed in rags, his hands tied in front of him, to the front of the table nearest the audience. Everything about him, his posture, his gestures, spoke of defiance. He waited until there was complete silence in the Long Gallery.

'My lords' – the words were spoken with extreme contempt as the prisoner stared with hatred towards the front row – 'you are impatient for the sacrifice and my execution. Be yet patient. I have but a few more words to say.' The guards pulled viciously at his arms at this point. 'I am going to my cold and silent grave. My lamp of life is nearly extinguished; my race is run, the grave opens to receive me and I sink into its bosom. I have but one request to ask at my departure from this world – it is the charity of its silence. Let no man write my epitaph, for as no man who knows my motives can now vindicate them, let not prejudice or ignorance defame them. Let them and me repose in obscurity and peace and my tomb remain uninscribed until other times and other men can do justice to my character. When my country takes her place among the nations of the earth, then, and not till then, let my epitaph be written. I have done.'

With that the two guards pulled him away, crying, 'To the scaffold!', 'Death to the traitor!', 'Hurry up with the drawing and quartering, for God's sake!' but the boy managed to turn and face his executioners one last time. 'Robert Emmett, speech from the dock after his conviction, Dublin, 1803.'

A vast cheer went up. 'Hurrah for Emmett!' 'Hurrah for Johnny Mason!' 'Didn't he do well!'

Powerscourt suddenly remembered Uncle Peter's description of Parnell's funeral and his final journey through the streets of Dublin. The coffin and the vast crowds accompanying it had stopped for a minute or two outside the house in Thomas Street to pay their respects to the martyred Robert Emmett. Lady Lucy was whispering very close to his ear as the applause and the shouts went on.

'Was he a bad man, Francis, this Robert Emmett?'

'No,' said Powerscourt, 'yes. Depends whose side you're on.'

Now it was the turn of the girls again. Three willowy sisters, aged from ten to fourteen, with identical blonde hair came to the front of the stage and held hands. James was playing something very romantic on the piano with the soft key pressed down as far as it would go so the music sounded as if it came from far away.

'I will arise and go now and go to Innisfree,' said the smallest sister,

'And a small cabin build there, of clay and wattles made,
Nine bean rows will I have there, a hive for the honey-bee,
And live alone in the bee-loud glade.'

The audience had gone very quiet now. 'And I shall have some peace there,' the middle sister carried on,

'for peace comes dropping slow,
Dropping from the veils of the morning to where the
    cricket sings;
There midnight's all a glimmer and noon a purple glow,
And evening full of the linnet's wings.'

The eldest sister picked up the baton. She had a beautiful speaking voice, distinct and clear.

'I will arise and go now, for always night and day
I hear lake water lapping with low sounds by the shore;
While I stand on the roadway or on the pavements grey,
I hear it in the deep heart's core.'

James finished his piano solo with an elaborate twirl. The sisters bowed low and said as they rose, in unison, 'William Butler Yeats.'

Voices could be heard, breaking through the clapping. 'Peace comes dropping slow, that's really good,' said a woman from the second row. 'Linnet's wings?' said a cynic at the back. 'Did you ever hear linnet's wings? I ask you. Bloody poets.'

Then the room was suddenly filled with activity. Most of the children seemed to have a task to perform. Some went and closed the great shutters and pulled the curtains tight to block the late afternoon sunlight that had been pouring into the room, leaving long golden patches on the floorboards. Before the lights went out Powerscourt saw two children, dressed in very tattered clothes, lie down on the floor formed by the black draped table. Other children were putting some bulky objects into the bath tub. Others still brought wooden planks and laid them carefully from the edge of the table nearest the audience down into the bath tub. Four solemn children, two boys and two girls, took up their position at each of the corners of the table, each carrying a single lighted candle.

There were two great doors in the middle of the Long Gallery. One of these now opened to reveal a tall young man of about fifteen. He too carried a lighted candle and he had a small book with his words written in front of him. All he lacked, Powerscourt thought, was a bell.

'These are the words of a Protestant gentleman farmer on the potato crop of 1846,' he began. The young man checked his words.

'On 1st August I was startled by hearing a sudden rumour that all the potato fields in the district were blighted; and that a stench had arisen emanating from their decaying stalks. I immediately rose up to visit my crop and test the truth of this report, but I found it as luxuriant as ever, in full blossom, the stalks matted across each other with richness and promising a splendid produce. On coming down from the mountain I rode into the lowland country and there I found the leaves of the potatoes on many fields I passed were quite withered and a strange stench filled the atmosphere adjoining each field of potatoes.

'Five days later I went back up the mountain again. My feelings may be imagined when, before I saw the crop, I smelt the fearful stench. No perceptible change except the smell had as yet come upon the apparent prosperity of the deceitfully luxuriant stalks, but the experience of the past few days taught me that all was gone and that the crop was utterly worthless, the luxuriant stalks soon withered, the leaves decayed, the disease everywhere.'

The audience was whispering anxiously. 'My God, it's the famine.' 'What's James doing with these children and the famine, in God's name?' 'What are they going to do now, for heaven's sake?'

The answer came from right behind them. A tall girl with bright red hair had crept round to the back of the audience and was reading her account, the candle steady in her left hand and casting a dramatic light on her hair.

'An eyewitness sent to Skibereen in December 1846,' she began, 'found that there had been as many as one hundred and sixty-nine deaths from starvation in that little town alone in the previous three weeks. His report contained the following detail. On Sunday last, 20th December, a young woman begging in the streets of Cork collapsed and was at first unable to move or speak. After being given restorations and taken home to her cabin she told those helping her that both her mother and father had died in the last fortnight. At the same time she directed their attention to a heap of dirty straw that lay in the corner and apparently concealed some object under it. On removing this covering of straw the spectators were horrified on beholding the mangled corpses of two grown boys, a large proportion of which had been removed by the rats while the remainder lay festering in its rottenness. There they had lain for a week or perhaps a fortnight.'

'Oh, my God!' 'How frightful!' Lady Lucy was holding Powerscourt's hand very tight.

The next voice came from the centre of the stage. Another young man, another book, another candle, another report from the front line of the famine.

'The parish priest of Hollymount, County Mayo,' the young man said clearly. 'Deaths, I regret to say, innumerable from starvation are occurring every day. The bonds of society are almost dissolved. The pampered officials, removed as they are from scenes of heart-rending distress, can have no idea of them and don't appear to give themselves much trouble about them – I ask them in the name of humanity, is this state of society to continue and who are responsible for these monstrous evils?'

By the light of the candles on the stage the audience now saw two girls moving across the arena. The smaller one leant heavily on the shoulder of the taller one, her clothes in tatters, her hair streaked with dirt, her feet bare and bleeding, her face, what they could see of her face, ashen. They moved slowly and began to climb the steps at the back of the table.

'This is the Black Room,' said an invisible voice. Was it meant to be God? Powerscourt wondered. Surely not in a story like this. 'This is a County Roscommon workhouse in the year of our Lord 1848.' The rest of Europe was having revolutions, Powerscourt remembered. In Ireland people were dying in their thousands, or tens of thousands. 'The Black Room,' the voice went on, 'was where people were brought to die. Up to seven people were permitted in here at any one time.' As he spoke the girl in rags lay down on the floor to join the other two bodies already there. 'Nobody would disturb you in here. No efforts would be made to stop you dying.'

Now another voice came from underneath the shutters in the centre of the gallery.

'This is a Justice of the Peace, writing to the Duke of Wellington,' the young man said. 'Six famished and ghastly skeletons, to all appearance dead, were huddled in a corner on some filthy straw, their sole covering what seemed a ragged horsecloth and their wretched legs hanging about, naked above the knees. 1 approached in horror and found by a low moaning they were alive, they were in a fever – four children, a woman and what had once been a man.'

The audience were silent now, as if transfixed. A girl took up the story from one of the great doors opposite.

'An eyewitness from County Cork in April 1847 described how: Crowds of starving creatures flock in from the rural districts and take possession of some hall door or the outside of some public building where they place a little straw and remain until they die. Disease has in consequence spread itself through the town. There are now over four hundred afflicted with fever and dysentery. The graveyard has its entrance in the centre of the main street, and in several instances when the gates were closed and parties seeking to bury the remains of their friends, the coffins were placed on the wall and abandoned.'

Now a boy from the back of the room.

'Every avenue leading to and in this plague-stricken town has a fever hospital having for its protecting roof the blue vault of heaven. Persons of all ages are dropping dead in each corner of the town, who are interred with much difficulty after rats have festered on their frames.'

A girl from the back of the Black Room.

' A parish priest with five hundred out of three thousand dead in his congregation, most with no coffins. They were carried to the churchyard, some on lids and ladders, more in baskets, aye and scores of them thrown beside the nearest

149

ditch, and there left to the mercy of the dogs which have nothing else to feed on.'

Another young man, wearing a white coat and flanked by two burly attendants, now made his way across the stage and up the stairs into the death chamber. 'Medical staff,' the invisible voice resumed its melancholy commentary, 'made regular inspections of the Black Room.' The white-coated figure knelt down and inspected two of the wretches. He shook his head slowly. The two attendants picked up the first body and brought her over to the edge where the planks were waiting. 'It was necessary, to avoid infection, to remove the bodies of the dead as soon as possible.' The corpse was rolled down the planks into the bath. The second one followed immediately afterwards. The white-coated young man and his colleagues left. A girl wearing an apron and carrying a sack approached the bath and began emptying large quantities of what looked like flour over the bodies. 'The workhouse had no coffins,' the invisible voice went on, 'lime was thrown over the bodies as they were dumped in a pit outside the window of the Black Room and they were eventually buried in an unknown grave.' The voice stopped for a moment and then resumed. 'Over one million men, women and children died in Ireland in the famine.'

There was a pause for about five seconds. The tableau on stage remained absolutely still. The dead did not attempt to rise from the bathtub. Then there must have been some signal from James for the vicar rose to his feet.

'Let us pray,' he began. 'Let us pray for the souls of all those who departed this life in that terrible famine. Let us pray for their descendants, those who came after, whose lives were so deeply affected by the tragedy that had devastated their families. Let us pray for all those in poverty or sickness or hunger in this unhappy world today.' The vicar paused to let his congregation address their Maker.

'Lighten our darkness, Oh Lord,' he said, moving into the closing words of Evensong, 'and defend us from all perils and dangers of this night. May the Lord bless you and keep you, may the Lord make the light of his countenance shine upon you and be gracious unto you and give you His peace, in the name of the Father and the Son and the Holy Ghost, Amen.'

The Reverend Cooper Walker turned to the young people on stage. 'And now,' he said, 'let there be light!' As the curtains were pulled and the great shutters opened, he turned to Sylvia Butler. 'I've always wanted to make that announcement,' he said, 'let there be light, never have, until today.'

Richard Butler raised his voice above the hubbub. 'Interval time!' he cried. 'Punch! Cake! Jellies if you're small! In the garden!'

On his way out Powerscourt bent down to pick up one of the famine scripts that had fallen on the floor. It was written in a very distinctive, rather ornate hand, and had the reader's name at the top and 'Good Luck, James' at the bottom. He put it in his pocket. Outside he joined Lady Lucy and found Johnny Fitzgerald standing by himself with two glasses of punch, one in each hand.

'I was holding this one for a chap,' he explained, looking suspiciously at the drink, 'but he seems to have disappeared. Ah well, duty calls.' He began work on the glass in his left hand. 'Hasn't Young James a fine eye for the dramatic,' he went on. 'Quite moving it was, all those voices coming at you from all quarters. Maybe he'll be a great impresario fellow like that chap Beerbohm Wood over in London.'

'Tree,' said Powerscourt.

'Tree?' said Johnny, peering at the glass in his left hand, now bereft of liquid. 'Are you obsessed with trees now, Francis? Not content with bumping into them, you're now referring to them at every opportunity.'

'Tree,' said Powerscourt, 'the theatrical fellow, he's called Tree, not Wood. Beerbohm Tree.'

'Well, I knew it was something like wood anyway.' Johnny had started on his other glass. 'Will you look at this lot, Lady Lucy, it must be the memory of the famine. They're eating

151

everything in sight. You'd think they hadn't been fed in weeks.'

Sure enough the Butler spread was disappearing fast. Four whole cakes had been polished off in minutes. Three great salvers of sandwiches had nothing left. Two of the smaller children had collected three bowls of jelly each and were scoffing them happily underneath the tables where the food was set out.

'Johnny, Lady Lucy,' said Powerscourt, 'one of the things the Archbishop told me concerned the fires of hatred that still burn strong in the minds of some of the younger priests and Christian Brothers because of the famine. Do you think Young James feels the same thing? That famine stuff was pretty powerful. Do you suppose something dreadful happened to his family back then?'

'I think it's more likely he just has an eye for the dramatic, Francis,' said Lady Lucy. 'I have a cousin like that, always putting on amateur theatricals and rushing off to see the latest plays.'

Powerscourt resisted the temptation to say that any member of Lucy's family involved in amateur dramatics would always be able to command a large cast.

'I think I'll just get hold of a glass of this punch before the second half,' said Johnny, ambling off towards the drinks department. 'Maybe I should get two in case that fellow comes back. You never know.'

'Do you know what was in that bath tub, Francis?' asked Lady Lucy. 'Those little girls could have been hurt rolling down into it.'

'No, they couldn't, Lucy. Whole thing was filled with pillows. I looked at the time. Pillows everywhere.'

Lady Lucy tucked her arm into her husband's as they climbed the stairs. 'Let's hope there'll be some more songs and romantic poetry, Francis. Much nicer than the political speeches and all that.'

Some of Lady Lucy's wishes were granted, and some were not, in Part Two of Young James's entertainment. A lad of about ten with the voice of a choirboy gave a spirited rendering of 'The Minstrel Boy'. A lively reading from a novel by George Moore followed. James himself was involved in the finale. Powerscourt noticed with interest that the candles were back again, for the young man came to the front of the stage, surrounded by three girls, all with lighted candles. James waited for complete silence and then he began.

'When you are old and grey and full of sleep,
And nodding by the fire, take down this book,
And slowly read, and dream of the soft look
Your eyes had once and of their shadows deep.'

The first girl looked at James, blew out her candle and left the stage. James was now looking at Lady Lucy.

'How many loved your moments of glad grace,
And loved your beauty with love false or true,
But one man loved the pilgrim soul in you,
And loved the sorrows of your changing face.'

Powerscourt squeezed Lady Lucy's hand. The second girl had now blown out her candle and she too departed. James's eyes moved off to another female.

'And bending down beside the glowing bars,
Murmur, a little sadly, how love fled
And paced above the mountains overhead
And hid his face amid a cloud of stars.'

Powerscourt wondered if the words bitch goddess were about to appear but they did not. The third girl blew out the third candle of lost love and left. James said, 'William Butler Yeats' in a voice of great reverence and bowed. There was tumultuous applause and cheering. All the children came back on stage and formed a great semicircle. James returned to the piano. They gave a united rendering of 'Molly Malone' with the audience belting out the chorus. As the last Alive Oh was fading away, people beginning to rise from their seats and stretch themselves, there was a loud knock on the door in the centre of the Long Gallery. As it opened two footmen stood there, carrying a large parcel almost six feet across and about four feet high.

'This was dumped at the bottom of the drive, sir,' said the senior footman. 'We thought you'd like to see it straight away.' Everybody in the room, looking at the shape of the package, wrapped in brown paper secured with heavy string, knew what it was,

'My God, it's one of Butler's stolen paintings.'

'It's been recovered, thank the Lord.'

'One of the pictures, it's come back.'

One or two people cast admiring glances at Powerscourt as if he were responsible for the miracle but he was apprehensive, very apprehensive.

'Let's have a knife and a pair of scissors, by God,' said Butler, advancing towards his property.

Powerscourt had shoved his way through the crowd to stand at his side.

'Don't open it now, Butler, for heaven's sake. Not in front of all these people.'

'Damn it,' said Butler, 'it's my house, it's my picture. I'll open it whenever I bloody well like.'

'Don't you see,' Powerscourt pleaded, 'there's going to be some trick or other, maybe some horrible message contained in the thing. Please don't open it now. Do it later. Somewhere quieter.'

Everybody in the room was staring at the parcel left at the bottom of the drive. The scissors and knife had appeared. Powerscourt made one last plea.

'Please do it later, I beg you, when all the visitors have gone. You can open it then.'

'I'm going to open it now, damn your eyes,' said Richard

Butler, beginning to hack at the brown paper and string. When it was finally clear, he placed it on a chair for everybody to see before he turned and had a look at the contents.

In one sense this certainly was one of the stolen paintings. It was the one called *The Master of the Hunt*. There was Butler's Court, looking elegant as ever. There were the riders in their scarlet coats and the horses ready to ride off. There in the background were the hounds. But the faces were different. Richard Butler's had been replaced with a passable likeness of Pronsias Mulcahy, proprietor of Mulcahy and Sons, Grocery and Bar. The rider to his left now had the disagreeable features of Father O'Donovan Brady. Two of the Delaneys of the solicitors' firm of Delaney, Delaney and Delaney, down in the town square, were sitting happily on horseback to one side of Pronsias Mulcahy, formerly Richard Butler. Diarmuid McSwiggin of MacSwiggin's Hotel and Bar was there, and Horkan the man who sold agricultural machinery and offered drink in his bar. The cast of the original painting had been replaced with the leading citizens of Butler's Cross. The Town had replaced the Big House. 'I'm sure Papa was in the middle of that picture,' said a small Butler, his voice breaking the shocked silence that filled the room, 'but he's changed into that nice Mr Mulcahy who sells you sweets down in the square.'

'My God,' said Richard Butler and fled the room. Powerscourt and Johnny Fitzgerald managed to remove the painting before anybody could stop them. Sylvia Butler, assisted by Lady Lucy, ushered her guests down the stairs and out the front door. By the time they had all gone Richard Butler had reappeared in his Long Gallery. He looked as if he had been weeping.

'My God, Powerscourt,' he said, 'you were right and I was wrong about the painting. Forgive me. But what, in heaven's name, does it mean?'

'Mean?' said Powerscourt. 'It's a message. Your time is up. You're not wanted. Others are going to replace you.'

'I think it means something else too, Mr Butler,' said Johnny Fitzgerald.

'And what might that be?'

'It's this,' said Johnny Fitzgerald. 'It's the changing of the guard. Welcome to the new Ireland.'

PART THREE

PILGRIM'S PROGRESS

I do most earnestly beseech you, as Irishmen, as citizens, as husbands, as fathers, by everything most dear to you, to consider the sacred obligation that you are called upon to discharge, to emancipate your country from a foreign yoke, and to restore to liberty yourselves and your children; look to your own resources, look to those of your friends, look to those of your enemies; remember that you must instantly decide; remember that you have no alternative between liberty and independence, or slavery and submission.

Theobald Wolfe Tone

9

Lord Francis Powerscourt took himself for a walk by the Shannon the next morning. A mist was rising slowly from the waters. He was thinking about the returned painting and the havoc it had caused in Butler's Court. For Richard Butler, he felt, it must have been like a lash from a whip across his face, an assault this time not upon the faces of his ancestors but on himself and his family, and all the current residents of the Big House. There was, he thought, one small consolation. The painting left at the bottom of the drive was a copy, he was sure of it. He had checked it again early that morning. Where had it been painted? The unknown artist must have taken a good look at Messrs Mulcahy, Horkan, MacSwiggin and the rest of them. Had he been hidden away in the store rooms of the grocery or some unused part of Father O'Donovan Brady's disagreeable residence? Nobody, he was sure, nobody who was in on the secret would tell him a thing. Down there in the square where they sold sweets to the Butler children, that was now enemy territory. Then another terrible thought struck him. If there was one copy there could be another. Who would be the new faces next time? Would *The Master of the Hunt* effect a second coming into Butler's Court, adorned with the faces of Theobald Wolfe Tone and Robert Emmett and Charles Stewart Parnell and the martyred heroes of the nation's past? Even worse perhaps, would they replace the Master and his companions with the servants, the steward and the footmen now riding off to hounds, the cook and the parlour maids bringing up the rear? God in heaven.

He met Lady Lucy on his way back.

'Francis,' she said, smiling rather feebly at him, 'is there nothing we can do for these poor people? It's like a funeral in there only the corpse is still in the building. I've seldom seen people look so miserable. The only consolation is the children, they think the whole thing is the most enormous joke. They've a theory the other pictures will come back soon with famous cricketers in them or stars from the stage and the music hall.'

'I'll have to go and talk to Richard Butler about it all,' said Powerscourt. 'Maybe he'll show me the original blackmail letter now, though I rather doubt it. Have you seen him this morning, Lucy? How is he bearing up?'

'I saw him a few minutes ago. He was picking at his breakfast as if the sausages were poisoned and the tomatoes about to explode. Oh, I nearly forgot, Francis, there's a letter for you, forwarded from London. I don't know if it's important or not.'

'"Dear Lord Powerscourt,"' her husband read aloud, '"Thank you for sending me the details of the stolen paintings. I am writing to inform you of the results of our fishing expedition in the American art market with the New York firm of Goldman and Rabinowitz. You will recall that they offered eight Irish ancestor portraits for sale, four full-length and four half. So far, they have received sixteen queries about the works, all of them serious, none of them over-concerned about price. For the time being the dealers are fobbing off their potential clients with excuses about complications with customs, that sort of thing. But Goldman's have asked me to secure a dozen or more of these pictures with all possible speed in case their clients lose interest. I have therefore placed advertisements in a number of Irish newspapers offering good prices for such material. Mr Farrell, of Farrell's Gallery, is also looking for such portraits for me. Maybe, Lord Powerscourt, we have discovered a new niche in the art market! I trust the Irish air is refreshing, Yours etc, Michael Hudson."'

'What does that mean, Francis?' asked Lady Lucy.

'I don't think it takes us much further forward apart from finding this market for Irish ancestors in the United States. But if our thieves reply to the next round of advertisements with some of these stolen paintings, we'll be home and dry. We'd just have to wait until somebody turned up with them under their arm, as it were, and then we could all go home.'

Powerscourt found Richard Butler half an hour later sitting in his study, the door closed, staring at the horses on his walls, a bottle of Bushmills and a crystal glass sitting on the little table to the side of his desk.

'Powerscourt,' he said, and his voice was the voice of a beaten man, 'do you have any comfort for us all this morning?'

'Well,' Powerscourt replied, trying to sound more hopeful than he felt, 'perhaps you'd be able to show me that letter you had from the thieves now, the blackmail letter.'

Butler shook his head. 'Can't do that,' he said, the words slurring slightly, 'especially now, can't do it. Swore an oath, you see. To my father. Promised to keep all we had.'

'Let me try again in a different way then. Was there a deadline in the letter, a date by which you had to do whatever it is you're meant to do? I think there must have been a deadline.'

Butler nodded and poured himself a Johnny Fitzgerald sized slug of his whiskey. 'Yes, there was, bloody deadline.'

'Two more things then, if I may,' said Powerscourt. 'Whatever it was that they asked you to do, have you done it?'

Butler shook his head once more. 'Haven't done it. Couldn't do it. Told you. Impossible.'

'My other question then, has the deadline passed?'

'No, it hasn't,' said Butler, 'not yet.'

'But it's close now?'

'Very close.'

'How close is very close, Butler?'

160

'Can't tell you that either. Not safe.'

'What do you mean, not safe? Have they threatened violence? Have they said they'll take away some people rather than some pictures?'

'Can't say.'

'Can't say, won't say. Damn it, man, how am I supposed to find out what's going on if I don't know most of it?'

'Sorry,' said Butler, 'can't say.'

'Let me tell you a couple of things which I can say at any rate. That picture that came yesterday is not the one that was taken all those weeks ago. It's a copy. And, if you think about it, the thieves have got very cocky. I think they must have brought the artist into the town to look at the people and paint their faces unless Pronsias Mulcahy or one of the Delaneys is a dab hand with the paintbrush. He may have spent a couple of days here, staying perhaps in the best room in MacSwiggin's Hotel and drinking in his bar with the locals. Word may leak out in the next few days. You know, Butler, how everybody in these Big Houses thinks the servants listen in to everything they say? Well, I think the boot's on the other foot now. We must all listen in to whatever they're saying whenever we can, without being too obvious about it. You never know what we might find out.'

'I didn't sleep last night, Powerscourt,' said Butler, 'didn't sleep at all. Tell me, do you think that because Mulcahy and all those people appear in the painting, that means they are the ones behind it all?'

'The same thought occurred to me,' Powerscourt replied, 'but I don't think it does mean that. They may know every-thing that has gone on, some of those people down in the town, but that doesn't necessarily mean that they planned the whole thing.'

'I suppose I'd better try to cheer everybody up,' said Butler, locking his bottle of Bushmills away in a cupboard. 'Can't go hiding behind the whiskey bottle when times are hard. What would the ancestors have said about such behaviour?'

'That's the spirit,' said Powerscourt. 'Tell me, how many of those great battles in Ireland's past did you ancestors actually fight in?'

'All of them,' said Richard Butler, 'every single one that mattered. God save Ireland.'

Only one person in Butler's Court was grateful for the furore over the return of *The Master of the Hunt*. Johnpeter Kilross had discovered an empty cottage in a clearing in the woods about a mile from the main buildings. There was, he saw as he peered through the windows, a little sitting room, a kitchen, a tiny bathroom and a bedroom. The bedroom, oddly enough, was the only place that appeared to have clean windows. It was known as the Head Gardener's Cottage and the Head Gardener had indeed lived there until he secured a position close to Dublin to be near his sick mother. The place had been empty ever since, as the new Head Gardener already had a tiny house of his own near the town. Nothing seemed to have been moved. Johnpeter had infiltrated his way with a stable lad into the room at the back of the scullery where all the keys were kept and had spotted two stout specimens hanging on a hook labelled Head Gardener's Cottage. Under normal circumstances it was virtually impossible to get into this room alone and unspotted. Kitchen maids were forever bringing things in or taking things out to the scullery. But the curiosity aroused by *The Master of the Hunt* was so great that every single servant shot out into the hall or pretended to be busy in the gallery above on the first floor. Johnpeter had nipped down the back stairs and removed one of the keys. Now he and Alice would have a place where they could go in the afternoons. Or the mornings come to that. Johnpeter was certain he would be able to persuade her to join him there.

Powerscourt drove himself into Athlone early that afternoon. He had sent a cable to Inspector Harkness in Ormonde House requesting a meeting at three fifteen, the hour when the Westport–Dublin express was due to stop at Athlone. Harkness came striding down the platform, the briefcase with the enormous lock clutched firmly in his left hand.

'Are you well, Lord Powerscourt? Good to see you again.'

They drove out into the countryside for a couple of minutes and set out to walk by the river. Powerscourt told him about the return of the painting and its dramatic impact on the inhabitants of Butler's Court.

'Now then,' said the Ulsterman, 'you said you might have a wee bit of a plan to catch the thieves, Lord Powerscourt?'

'I do, and I would be grateful for your opinion of it. It depends on the list of houses Dennis Ormonde drew up for the Orangemen to guard. You remember the list, Inspector?'

'I do indeed,' said Harkness, patting his briefcase. 'Sure I have two copies of the thing in here.'

'And you will no doubt recall,' said Powerscourt, 'that there is a line drawn across the list. Underneath that line Dennis Ormonde does not have enough Orangemen to guard the houses and the houses do not have many old portraits anyway. Now then, I fully understand your reluctance to tell me the names of your informants, but do you have anybody close to the thieves, somebody who could be used to send them information?'

'I'm not altogether sure what you're driving at, Lord Powerscourt, but yes, it's only a guess, but I do believe there are a couple of lads out there we know about who may move in the same circle as the people who may have stolen the pictures. There's two in particular I'm thinking of who have fathers and uncles in prison. The promises of early release can work wonders.'

'Right,' said Powerscourt cheerfully. 'Now, one of those houses not to be watched is called Burke Hall. I think it's on the far side of Louisburg but I'm pretty useless at geography. Suppose now that one of your lads drops the word that Burke Hall is not guarded at all by the Orangemen, it's wide open, so to speak, for anybody. Only it's not unguarded at all.'

'Me and a bundle of policemen are waiting there for them!' Harkness was slapping Powerscourt on the back in his excitement. 'It's an ambush! I like this plan, Lord Powerscourt, I like it very much!'

'Will it work, Inspector? That's the thing.'

Harkness paused for a moment. 'What happens if they don't want to steal any more paintings? If the theft at Ormonde House was all they were interested in?'

'I've thought about that,' said Powerscourt. 'First of all there's the arrival of the Orangemen some day soon. That's going to be like a red rag to a bull to the thieves. Think how brave and clever they would look if they pinched some more stuff from right under the Ulstermen's noses. They'd be heroes overnight. And it would send a message to Dennis Ormonde. Don't imagine we're finished because you've imported these people from the north. I think all those blackmail letters had a deadline, I don't know if it's the same deadline for all four houses, but I do know that the Butler one is pretty close. More stolen pictures would put more pressure on the man from Ormonde House.'

'Let's do it, Lord Powerscourt. I'll think about it some more on the train, but assume we'll do it. God, it's a grand wee plan so it is. I'll have to go back to Westport, wind up the clocks in person if you follow my meaning.'

'Could you or your people do something for me in Dublin, Inspector? I would send Johnny Fitzgerald but I'd like to keep him close at present.'

'What can we do for you now?'

'It's about moneylenders, plenty of those down in Dublin as you know. I want to know if this person has until fairly recently had large debts outstanding with one or two or maybe even three of these sharks. I've put the name and the general description in this letter.' Powerscourt handed over one of Butler's Court's finest envelopes. Harkness put it in his pocket.

'More reading in the train,' he said. 'Regard it as done, Lord Powserscourt. I'll send you word when I have the answer. Discreet word, of course.'

Walter Heneghan, the contractor responsible for the construction of the new chapel at the summit of Croagh Patrick, was holding a crisis meeting with his staff at the end of the day. In one sense good progress had been made. The exterior of the building was virtually finished. It had a stout roof, fit to withstand the winter storms. It had windows with glass in them. But it had no doors, no pews, no altar, no furniture inside of any kind. Clasping The Skedule in his right hand, Walter addressed his troops like a general before a battle.

'Men,' he began, 'you have done well. We are nearly back on Skedule.'

There was a murmur of appreciation from the little band. Being back on Skedule was like winning a prize at school.

'However,' Heneghan went on, 'we have very little time left. I have been consulting with that old sailor with the disgusting pipe who sits all day under the portrait of the Blessed Oliver Plunket in the saloon bar in Campbell's public house, the man who says he can foretell the weather. Tomorrow and the next day, the ancient eejit told me, will be fine. Then it is going to get bad, rain, storms, all of that. So I am proposing a series of emergency measures.'

There was a slight groan from his workmen. Emergency measures probably meant only one thing, getting up even earlier in the morning.

'Charlie O'Malley, where the devil are you?' Heneghan peered at the faces in front of him.

'Here, sir,' said Charlie, who had been thinking of the days of rest that lay ahead of him.

'I'm afraid that the rotation policy with the donkeys will have to stop. We must have Jameson and Powers in action every day now. And I want to see if you can lay your hands

165

on a couple more of the beasts for a week or so. The Church will provide.'

At least, Charlie thought, even though the donkey rotation policy, one day working, one day resting, carried out according to the precepts of the great agriculturalist Turnip Townsend, might have to stop, now he would be able to add a beast called Bushmills to his stable. But he didn't think there were any more whiskey distilleries in Ireland. What on earth was he going to christen the last one?

'For tomorrow and the next day I have hired another six men, three of them carpenters,' Walter went on. 'The pews and the altar are all ready in bits in the Westport workshops to be brought to the bottom of the mountain this evening. I want to see you all up here at the summit by nine o'clock tomorrow morning at the latest. Including the donkeys carrying the pews and stuff.'

You could almost hear the calculations being done by the workmen. They would have to leave home at six or even earlier. Another murmur of rebellion rose from the ranks.

'The day after tomorrow,' Heneghan said, raising his hand to quell the muttering, 'your man Father Macdonald from Westport is coming on a mission of inspection. Some of you may have seen this priest. He's a bundle of nerves, no more courage in him than a brindled cat. Behind him is that great bullock of an Archbishop from Tuam who's coming to consecrate the building on Reek Sunday. He's not a man to cross, Dr Healey. He looks like he could be the model for Goliath in a holy picture, so he does. Or maybe Samson before he had his hair cut.'

Walter was a great devotee of the religious paintings on display in the bars of Mayo.

'So we don't want to upset the man Macdonald from Westport or the big man from Tuam who could throw us all down the mountain with his bare hands. And there's one last thing, lads.' Walter Heneghan was keeping the good news to the end. 'If the pews and everything are in place by the day after tomorrow Father Macdonald will be providing a small thank-you. Free drinks all evening in Campbell's public house at the bottom of the mountain.'

Charlie O'Malley escorted Jameson back down the mountain, thinking desperately about what to call the fourth member of his fleet. Salvation, in the shape of Campbell's public house, was in sight before the answer came to him. He remembered a relation of his wife's, a cousin, he thought, who had done well in America and had come home to show off to his relations. He had brought a couple of bottles of spirits from Tennessee with him to show what native American industry could produce. Charlie felt rather proud suddenly. The links between Mayo and the mighty continent of America had always been close. He would add a transatlantic flavour to his team of donkeys. He would christen the last one Jack Daniels.

Lord Francis Powerscourt and Johnny Fitzgerald were crouching on the hard stone floor of a little tower to the left of Burke Hall on the far side of Louisburg, peering out through the turrets. This was where Inspector Harkness of the Special Branch in Dublin Castle hoped to spring his ambush on the thieves who had been stealing paintings from the houses of the Anglo-Irish gentry. It was shortly before two o'clock in the morning. Burke Hall itself was a fine Georgian mansion with all the usual great windows and fine plasterwork. About eighty years before an ambitious Burke, conscious of the fashion for Gothic revival sweeping through Irish country houses, decided to add a section to his inheritance of two wings with two round towers each, both linked to a square fortification topped with battlements at the end. Work was started but never finished. This Burke consumed so much of his inheritance on the gambling tables of Dublin that the builders downed tools, great piles of stones were still stored at the back of the house to this day, and only one single tower remained.

The Burkes called it the Pepper Pot. The locals called it The Stump. It was commemorated in a local ballad as the Divil's Thumb.

From time to time Powerscourt or Fitzgerald would shift in their position, rubbing at a leg or an arm. To their left was Burke Hall. To their right a curved drive, flanked by beech trees, stretched out towards what passed for the main road a mile or so away. In front of Burke Hall lay a great expanse of grass with tight clumps of trees at the end of the lawn. Beyond the trees, invisible from the house, lay a long beach, marked with great stones and piles of dank weed, and the sea.

Earlier that evening there had been a frightful row about authority and precedence between the policemen. Powerscourt, keeping well in the background, saw at once that it was one of those who's in charge arguments that must have begun when Eve was trying to persuade Adam to eat of the apple in the Garden of Eden. The local Mayo policemen came with their very own sergeant, one Sean O'Callaghan, a man even taller and broader than the Archbishop of Tuam, though not endowed with many mental blessings from the Almighty. O'Callaghan had been a sergeant for fifteen years now. Even his own wife thought further promotion was beyond him. His own mother, after all, had once described her Sean as a little slow sometimes. In spite of, or perhaps because of his limitations, Sergeant Sean had a very acute sense of his own position and his own role. Mayo men, he told Harkness, should come under the command of a Mayo man. When the Special Branch Inspector pointed out that he outranked a mere sergeant from Castlebar, it was like a red rag to a bull. Here was a stranger, a younger man, with the very rank he had aspired to for all these years, giving him orders. The Dublin men, he assured his visitor, could all go and jump into the biggest vat in Guinness's brewery as far as he was concerned. Eventually Harkness gave way, fearful that all the policemen would be marched off if he did not. So it was the Sergeant who made the dispositions. He placed two of his men at the front of the house. His own command post was in the hall inside, next to the dining room where two Burke ancestors, one of them the great gambler, lined the walls. Harkness was with him. One hundred yards up the drive, Harkness's assistant O'Gara and a colleague waited for their visitors. If the thieves thought the place wasn't guarded, O'Callaghan reckoned, they would head straight up the drive for the front door. He believed the visitors might display as little finesse as himself. Two further men guarded the back of the house, with a further two in reserve inside. The Burke family and their friends had been sent early to bed, but they were behaving like naughty children, forever leaning out of their windows to whisper to each other and peering up their drive. Silence only arrived on the upper floors when O'Callaghan threatened to remove himself and his men at once and leave them to their fate. Up in the attics the butler and the footmen kept as still and as quiet as mice. They were lying on the floorboards, staring out of their attic windows into the night. The moon and the stars were hidden beneath thick clouds. There was scarcely any wind. At least, the watchers felt, it wasn't raining.

There had been a couple of false alarms already. Shortly after midnight some animal had charged across the path at great speed, followed rapidly by O'Gara's assistant who thought the beast was a burglar and made so much noise blundering through the bushes that O'Callaghan himself had to come out to restore order. Just before one a man at the back, who had been taking a sip of whiskey to keep awake, just a sip as he had told Harkness afterwards, swallowed too much and had a great coughing fit, sounding, the Inspector told him, like a man on the terminal ward of the Westport Hospital rather than a policeman on duty on a dangerous and difficult mission. Johnny Fitzgerald had smiled at the coughing fit. He too had kept awake on night watch with little helpings of John Jameson. Powerscourt felt glum and responsible. This, after all, had been his plan, his idea, outlined to the Inspector by the banks of the Shannon a short while before. Now he wondered if the thieves weren't coming. Maybe they had smelt a rat. Maybe they were a day too soon. Maybe the robbers knew they had been given false information. Maybe this whole expedition was going to end in failure. Maybe the Sergeant's plan wasn't the best on offer.

Shortly before three o'clock Johnny Fitzgerald nudged Powerscourt in the arm and pointed to his ear. Johnny had heard something. All Powerscourt had noticed was a very faint scraping noise far away as if somebody was dragging a screwdriver up a wall covered in ivy. Silence fell again. Johnny's ears may have been better than Powerscourt's but Powerscourt's eyes were sharper. Five minutes or so after the scraping sound he prodded Fitzgerald and pointed down the drive. Unfortunately for the thieves the clouds had broken and a faint moonlight now shone out over Burke Hall. Coming very slowly, walking in pairs on either side of the grass, a party of four young men were coming down the drive. Powerscourt felt certain suddenly that things were about to go wrong. From his command post inside the house O'Callaghan had no idea they had visitors. He could make no deployments. The coughing man and his colleague at the back could not see the thieves either. O'Gara and his colleague were outnumbered two to one. But instead of sinking back into the trees and letting the thieves go past and so surrounding them, they panicked. O'Gara sprang into the middle of the drive and shouted 'Halt!' for all the world, as Johnny said afterwards, as though he was conducting the traffic on Sackville Street in Dublin. His colleague fumbled in his pockets for his pistol. 'Halt! In the name of the law!' O'Gara tried again. The four figures turned and fled at full speed back the way they had come. O'Gara's colleague fired two shots at the retreating figures and was rewarded by a shriek that turned into a scream.

As Powerscourt and Fitzgerald reached the bottom of their little tower, they heard one of the great windows open on the first floor. 'Bastards! Thieving bastards!' yelled the senior male

Burke figure, leaning out of his bedroom in his finest silk pyjamas and firing three shots from an ancient rifle at the disappearing quartet as they fled up the drive. Powerscourt and Fitzgerald overtook a shaken O'Gara and his trembling colleague a hundred yards from the house. Around the bend the drive stretched straight ahead for another hundred yards or so. There was nobody there. Another three shots sounded out from the first floor of Burke Hall. 'Cease firing! You bloody fool! You could kill one of our own!' Sergeant O'Callaghan had arrived at last to take command. Now the sounds of weeping women replaced the noise of gunfire. At the end of the hundred-yard stretch another bend led into an even longer straight section of drive. O'Gara and his colleague staggered off, O'Gara holding on to a stitch in his leg, his companion wheezing and making slow progress. Johnny Fitzgerald motioned Powerscourt to stop.

'Don't think the buggers are up there at all, Francis,' he said, panting slightly. 'You remember that noise a few moments ago?'

Powerscourt nodded.

'I think it might have been a boat,' said Johnny. 'The noise was the boat being pulled up on to the beach. Our friends may have come by sea.'

'In which case,' Powerscourt said, 'there must be a path off to our left somewhere leading to the beach.' They moved slowly back down the drive, searching for the track. The moon had gone in again. A figure bumped into them, coming the other way.

'Who the devil are you?' said the figure.

'Don't shoot, for God's sake,' said Powerscourt. 'Far too much shooting going on round here, if you ask me. It's Johnny and I here, Sergeant.'

'And what are you doing, may I ask, going the wrong way, when them thieves are up ahead?'

'It's terrible cowards we are, don't you see, Sergeant,' said Johnny, 'but we think they came in a boat. We're looking for a path off this drive towards the beach.'

'Boat?' shouted the Sergeant, 'Boat, did you say? What nonsense! You're holding me up!'

And with that he lumbered off in pursuit of the thieves.

'Bloody fool,' said Powerscourt bitterly. 'If he'd planned the thing properly the whole investigation could be over by now. As it was with all the shrieking and wailing the thing was organized like a pack of nuns trying to rob a bank, for God's sake.'

Fitzgerald tapped him on the shoulder. 'Look, Francis, here's our path, right here.' They ran down the overgrown track as fast as they could. Brambles scratched at their faces. Low branches, virtually invisible in the dark, bumped into their heads. After a couple of hundred yards the path met the beach. Powerscourt pointed dramatically out to sea. In the distance a rowing boat was making good progress away from the shore. Powerscourt thought he could see two figures rowing in the centre and one at either end. The clouds cleared once more. In the ten seconds or so before the moon disappeared Powerscourt noticed two things. The figure at the stern was holding his right shoulder. The figure at the prow seemed to be drinking heavily from a large bottle. The two rowers laid down their oars briefly and waved to the two figures on the beach. A derisive cheer could be heard clearly on the strand. The thieves had got clean away.

'I am so sorry, Lord Powerscourt.' Harkness had joined them on the beach, the rowing boat scarcely visible now on the dark waters of the bay. 'They came as we thought they would. We were there waiting for them. Then that bloody fool Sergeant made a mess of things.'

'Never mind, Inspector,' said Powerscourt, 'we'll just have to try again.' He was about to suggest that Harkness might like to remove the informant who had given the false details for a fortnight or so, but the Inspector had vanished back into the night.

Up in the attics Eamonn the junior footman punched his colleague on the shoulder and pointed out towards the ocean.

'Do you see, Seamus, they're well away, so they are, in their rowing boat. Isn't that grand!'

'It is so,' said Seamus. 'Christ, it's stiff you get lying here on this bloody floor. We'd better celebrate. Won't they be like a flock of sheep at a narrow gate down there below.' He groped his way towards a dilapidated bedside cupboard. 'Is it Jameson's you'd like now, or a touch of John Powers?'

Lady Lucy was waiting for them when they returned to Ormonde House. She knew, from long experience, that sleep would not come until she saw Francis was back. Dennis Ormonde, she told them, had accompanied her in the earlier stages of her vigil until his claret got the better of him and his tiny wife materialized out of the upper floors to order him to bed.

'It was a fiasco, Lucy,' said Powerscourt, drinking deeply from a cup of tea. 'The thieves turned up all right. The local sergeant and his men made a complete mess of everything and the thieves got away in a rowing boat.' He filled her in on the details as Johnny wrestled with a recalcitrant corkscrew.

'Not without its lighter moments, mind you, Lady Lucy,' Johnny said cheerfully, finally liberating the liquid in one of Ormonde's finest bottles of burgundy. 'I'll always remember the man Burke, in his blue pyjamas, firing down the drive with a rifle that looked as if it last saw service at the Battle of the Boyne. And the thieves safe out there on the water, waving to Francis and me on the beach as if they were taking part in some bloody regatta. I thought that had a certain style.'

'I have one question for you, Francis, before I go to bed,' said Lady Lucy. 'I've been thinking about all these robberies, you see, while I waited for you and Johnny to come back. You say there were four of them, four thieves, looking quite young?' Powerscourt nodded. 'Do you think they are the same four people who stole the paintings from Mr Moore and Mr Butler?'

'What do you mean, Lucy?' Powerscourt sat up in his chair and looked closely at his wife.

'Well,' she said, 'I just wondered if there mightn't be different lots of thieves, you see. These ones tonight must have a lot of local knowledge to be aware of the path up from the beach. The other thieves had special knowledge of the houses they robbed. Could there have been two or three different lots of thieves, Francis, all working to the same master criminal?'

Powerscourt smiled. 'How very clever of you to have worked that out, Lucy. I've been thinking about that for some time but I didn't want to cause confusion in the people in these houses here. They're worried enough about one lot of thieves, God knows, heaven knows what they'd be like with two or three sets of them.'

Lady Lucy felt proud to have joined her Francis's thoughts to her own. She went to sleep happily, one arm draped carelessly across her husband's shoulder. Powerscourt couldn't sleep. He was searching for something in his memory, maybe two things. One of them, oddly enough, had been contained in Uncle Peter's narrative of Parnell's funeral. What the devil was it? Some detail in there would help unlock his investigation. As he drifted off to sleep, his mind racing between Dublin City Hall and the shooting star at Glasnevin cemetery, he said to himself that he might have to go back to Butler's Court and borrow Uncle Peter's book. How appropriate in Ireland, was his final thought, that events of 1891 might contain the key to what happened fourteen years later.

In a small cottage up in the mountains between Westport and Newport a doctor was just finishing his work. There was a peat fire burning in the hearth and a kettle of boiling water ready for further medicinal use if required. The young man whose shoulder had been wounded at Burke Hall was lying on the sofa, great white bandages now wrapped round his wound. Another of his colleagues from the ill-fated mission watched from a chair by the fire.

'You're going to be fine. I'll come and see you here in the early evening in a couple of days,' said the doctor, packing his equipment back in his bag. 'I presume you don't want to come to the surgery.'

'Not just yet, doctor, thank you, but I will come when people won't notice the bandages.'

The doctor left. He had asked neither the name nor the age nor the address of his patient. You couldn't tell what you didn't know. Much better to keep it that way.

The wounded young man was called Kevin. His colleague was Brendan and they had sat next to each other right through their education from their very first day at primary school.

'Brendan,' Kevin began, taking another sip of his glass of stout, 'you do realize what was going on out there tonight, don't you? I didn't like to mention it in front of the other two just yet.'

'I'm not sure what you mean,' said Brendan.

'Can't you see? Those bastards were waiting for us. They knew we were coming. We're lucky we're not locked up.'

'You can't be sure. There might have been a change of plan.'

'Gladstone's arse a change of plan,' said Kevin vehemently. 'Somebody sent us a message that that place wasn't guarded. That was almost an invitation to turn up. Well, I'm going to find that somebody. And when I do he'll wish he'd never been born.'

10

The Orangemen surprised everybody. They were well behaved. They had, as yet, started no fights. They were polite to any locals they met. They had brought not a band, but a parson, or a minister as the clergymen of the Presbyterian Church were known. They consumed vast quantities of ham and eggs. The original mountain of potato bread baked in their honour by Dennis Ormonde's cook had disappeared within hours of their arrival. Toasted, fried, eaten on its own with thick slabs of butter, the stuff disappeared like manna in the desert. Dennis Ormonde was delighted with them. Even Powerscourt, who had entertained great suspicions about their impact on the local community, had to admit that so far the experiment had been a success. Johnny Fitzgerald, who kept taking the pulse of local opinion in Campbell's public house at the foot of Croagh Patrick and at one or two other drinking establishments nearby, was not so sure.

'There's a sort of simmering resentment out there, Francis,' he said, sitting on the lawn at the back of Ormonde House. 'They don't like it one little bit, the locals, but they're not sure what to do. The priests have told them to be patient and to focus their attention on the pilgrimage up the Holy Mountain. That's not many days off now, so we should have peace until then. I'm not sure about afterwards.'

Powerscourt had smiled when he heard that the priests had been advising caution. He was not alone. He had a mighty ally, over six feet tall and over five foot wide, in the Archbishop's Palace in Tuam. As ever, God was on everybody's side in Ireland. The Catholics had their God with His very own auxiliaries like the Virgin Mary and all the saints. The Orangemen had theirs, a very different deity, a harsh God from the Old Testament. Lady Lucy had caught the end of one of the minister's sermons when he spoke liberally of hellfire and referred to the Pope in Rome as Auld Red Socks. She was remarkably well informed about Presbyterians, having come across the breed in her youth in Scotland.

'It's like the other religions turned upside down, Francis,' she had assured her husband who was anxious to be better informed about these strange people. 'In the Catholic Church or the Anglican Church authority comes down from the top through the Pope or the archbishops and the ordinary bishops to the clergy. With the Presbyterians power flows out from the congregation. They choose their minister. They don't have bishops or anything like that, just a man called the Moderator who's elected every year. You could say it's not authoritarian, it's more democratic.'

Before they had time for further discussion on comparative religions in Ireland, they heard a great shout from Dennis Ormonde, running towards them at full speed from the house.

'Good news by Christ!' he said, panting from his run. 'Good news at last!' He sank into a chair. 'This letter is from Moore over at Moore Castle. Let me read the important passage to you. "I had meant to write before but I have been confined to bed with a severe attack of influenza. Two days ago, one of my paintings came back."' Johnny Fitzgerald stifled a cheer, remembering the return of the Butler picture. '"It was left at the bottom of my drive, as was the case with Butler's, and again heavily wrapped up with stout twine. It is the full-length painting of my grandfather. I have examined it most closely as you can imagine and I do not believe it has been tampered with in any way. Naturally we are all delighted. I have restored it to its rightful place in the dining room. I hope you will be able to come and see it the day after tomorrow when I should have fully recovered. Maybe, by then, the other paintings will have been returned too."' Butler folded up the letter and put it in his pocket. 'Is that not splendid news?' he said.

'Tremendous,' said Johnny Fitzgerald. 'Hurrah for the thieves who brought it back!'

'I'm sure Mrs Moore must be relieved,' said Lady Lucy. 'Such a worry when your interior decorations get messed around like this.'

'And you, Powerscourt?' asked Ormonde. 'What is your reaction?'

'I am afraid I cannot share in the general enthusiasm,' said Doubting Thomas Powerscourt. 'Look at the way it was returned, a carbon copy of the Butler painting's trip back to Butler's Court, and we all know what happened to that.'

'But Moore says there is nothing wrong with it.' Dennis Ormonde sounded cross. 'Surely you accept that?'

'I'll believe it when I see it,' said Powerscourt. 'For the moment I would advise caution. They're not stupid, these thieves. What they did to the Butler hunt was really damned clever.' Privately he wondered, as he told Lady Lucy later when they were alone, if Moore had paid up, if he had met the ransom demand, or part of it. The return of one picture might be calibrated with the amount of ransom handed over. Pay a quarter and we'll give you a quarter of the paintings back.

Cathal Rafferty was not a popular boy at his school in Butler's Cross. He was a tubby child of thirteen years with very thick spectacles. At sport he was no good at all, so terrified when he received the ball that he froze on the spot and threw it away, usually in the direction of his opponents. In the playground he tried to make himself as inconspicuous as possible in case he was surrounded by his classmates with the chants of Pig or Fat Boy that preceded another beating or another trip to the boys' lavatories where his head would be unceremoniously dumped in the bowl. In class Brother Riordan had simply given up on Cathal. He had tried kindness for a month, praising his incorrect arithmetic and his dismal spelling, but to no avail. He had tried force, a regular series of assaults with the strap to see if fear might succeed where kindness had failed. Cathal merely reflected that the classroom had become as dangerous a place as the playground. His performance did not improve. So now Brother Riordan ignored him altogether. He addressed no questions to him as he knew the answer would be wrong. Sometimes, in the days before his confession, the Brother wondered if he should not be trying harder with young Rafferty, but the thought of those thick spectacles and the blubbering lips put him off. Cathal had two elder brothers, both of them stars of the Gaelic football team, and they treated him little better than his classmates. Other boys, he knew, had friends they played with, friends who visited each other's houses, friends they could talk to about their life at school and their dreams for the future. Cathal had only himself. He became his own friend. He turned into a solitary boy, given to roaming alone along the banks of the river or in the outer reaches of the demesne of Butler's Court. He grew very curious about other people, as he talked to so few of them, often making up stories about their lives. Those two young people, for instance, the ones he'd just seen going into the Head Gardener's Cottage, there was something strange going on there, he was sure of it. Cathal had known the previous Head Gardener, one of the few people in the county who had ever been kind to him, but now he had gone. Cathal decided to creep round to the back of the cottage where the windows were bigger and have a look inside.

Johnpeter Kilross and Alice Bracken were getting dressed. This was their third or fourth visit to the place and they felt quite at home now. Soon, Johnpeter reckoned, they would be able to come here once a day.

'Why are you in such a hurry?' asked Alice, inspecting herself in a rather dirty mirror.

'I've been asked to see Richard Butler,' Johnpeter replied, 'at five o'clock and I don't want to be late.'

'Sure, you've got plenty of time left,' said the girl. 'You don't suppose he knows about us, do you?'

'I don't see how he could know anything about it at all. I expect it's something to do with these paintings. Maybe he wants to ask my advice.'

'The day Richard Butler asks you for your advice, Johnpeter Kilross, I shall ride naked down the drive and out into the main square in Butler's Cross, so I shall.'

'I expect it's to do with those paintings,' said Johnpeter.

'Those wretched paintings,' said Alice with great feeling. 'I wish oil paint had never been invented. I did enjoy that one that came back, mind you, with Mr Mulcahy and the rest of them on horseback. I thought that was really funny.'

'Richard didn't think it was funny. To this day the man Powerscourt and his friend haven't told him where they put it.'

'Maybe it's in here, up in the attic,' Alice laughed. 'Maybe the Powerscourt man comes down to look at it first thing in the morning. What do you think of the wife, by the way, Lady Lucy or whatever she's called? She seems well set on her husband, I'll say that for her.'

'She's very attractive,' said Johnpeter, fiddling with a shirt button.

'Oh, is she now?' said Alice, turning to reach for her stockings. 'Is she more attractive than me then, Johnpeter Kilross?'

'Of course not,' said the young man loyally. He had frequently noticed with women that any praise of another was taken almost as a personal insult.

Cathal Rafferty was crouching behind the hedge that marked the boundary of the Head Gardener's Cottage garden. He could hear voices coming from the bedroom but he couldn't make out the words. He thought it strange that people were in a bedroom in the late afternoon. If he stood up he could take a quick look in the window. The curtains were not properly closed. He was astonished at what he saw. There was a man and a woman getting dressed. The man had no trousers on and had very hairy legs. The woman had almost nothing on at all and was pulling up her stockings. What on earth was going on? Cathal ducked down behind the hedge and began to move away from the cottage as quickly as he could. There was some sort of grown-up secret going on in there. He remembered an overheard conversation between his eldest brother Michael and his friend in which they talked about a whore taking off her clothes faster than the winners at the Galway Races. It was something grown-ups did in private, though he didn't know what it was. And if it was all above board, why had these two people crept out to the cottage? Why hadn't they just taken their clothes off in Butler's Court? Plenty of rooms there for taking your clothes off, at whatever speed you fancied. It must be something bad. Suddenly he remembered something he had been told only very recently. 'If you see or hear of any wickedness going on round here, you just come and tell me, young Cathal Rafferty. The Devil never sleeps, you know, not even in Ireland.' As he crept out one of the side entrances of the demesne Cathal made up his mind. He would go and tell everything he had seen to Father O'Donovan Brady. He thought the priest might even pay good money for such promising information.

Five minutes later Johnpeter Kilross opened the front door of the cottage and poked his head cautiously outside. 'All clear,' he whispered. 'We can go back now.'

'Look, Lucy, look! Can't you see? Halfway up on the first bit of track that leads to the summit.' Powerscourt and Lady Lucy were in a carriage going to Westport station to catch a

181

train to Moore Castle to inspect the returned painting. They had been on a detour to the fishermen at Old Head to collect a couple of lobsters for Moore and were passing the bottom of Croagh Patrick, where the pilgrims' path began.

'I can't see anything, Francis,' said Lady Lucy rather sadly, peering up at the Holy Mountain.

'Moving very slowly, Lucy, just to the right of a line going up from the chimney of that little cottage over there.'

'My goodness.' Lucy had spotted the little convoy now. 'It's two men and a couple of donkeys. Those donkeys seem to be going very slowly, Francis. Do you think they're all right?'

'I expect they're carrying things up to the top, Lucy, materials maybe, stuff they need for fitting out the inside of the church. Are you looking forward to climbing to the top?'

'I am,' she replied, looking suspiciously at the summit which seemed a very long way off. 'I do hope I get to meet your Archbishop. I've met plenty of bishops but never the top man.'

Powerscourt was not to know it, but the building at the top had been completed ahead of Skedule a couple of days before. Charlie O'Malley and Austin Rudd were actually transporting yet another consignment of bottles of Guinness to the summit, to be sold off at outrageous prices to thirsty pilgrims a safe distance from the oratory when Mass was over. The idea had come to Charlie in Campbell's public house as he finished his first pint after coming down from the mountain in the days of overtime a week before.

'God,' he had said to Austin Rudd, 'how much do you think a man would pay for a bottle of stout when he's reached the top on Reek Sunday? There'll be thousands of thirsty buggers up there, their throats parched like lost travellers in the desert. Think of it, man. If we can get the damned donkeys to ferry enough bottles up there we'll make our fortune!'

Johnny Fitzgerald was not with them on this day. He had, he said at breakfast, an appointment in Westport with a man who claimed to be a defrocked Christian Brother. Of the reasons for the defrocking Johnny was not aware but he thought the man might have a story to tell. Dennis Ormonde was busy on estate business, saying that in any case it was a damned long way to go to look at some picture of one of Moore's bloody ancestors.

'Do you think the painting will be the real thing, Francis?' asked Lady Lucy as their cab carried them up the long drive to the crenellated castle.

'I don't believe it will be the real thing at all,' said Powerscourt gloomily.

One look at a crestfallen Moore at the top of the steps told them that Powerscourt's fears were correct. Moore looked like a man who has just lost his fortune, or suffered a bereavement. His face was pale and his hands were trembling slightly.

'Thank God you've come, Powerscourt, Lady Powerscourt, I'm in despair, I really am.' He led them up the stairs with the stags' heads and across the great hall with its gallery into the dining room. There indeed was the painting, a full-length of Alexander William O'Flaherty Moore hanging above the fireplace. Or rather, Powerscourt thought, inspecting it closely, it might have been turned into the ghost of a painting. The colours were fading, all of them, what must have been the deep blue of the cloak around Moore's shoulders turned pale, the hair no longer receding from his forehead but virtually disappeared back into the off white of the canvas, the colours everywhere ebbing away like the smile of the Cheshire cat. As he looked, Powerscourt thought you could almost see the painting vanishing away in front of your eyes. By the end of the day, or by the end of tomorrow, he thought, it would have disappeared completely, only the canvas and the frame remaining in their place of honour above the fireplace. Alexander William O'Flaherty Moore, here today, gone tomorrow.

'How terrible, Mr Moore,' said Lady Lucy, putting her hand on his arm in a gesture of sympathy, 'and this is your grandfather, I think you said?'

'It was,' said Moore bitterly, 'it bloody well was.'

Powerscourt was looking very closely at the painting. 'When did it start to disappear, if you see what I mean?'

'It was fine for the first two days,' said Moore, breaking off suddenly to sneeze violently. 'Damn, I thought I'd got rid of the wretched influenza. It was on the third day I thought it looked odd but I put it down to the medicinal whiskey. Then yesterday there was no doubt about it, it had started its disappearing act.'

What a way to send messages, Powerscourt thought. It was a form of Celtic voodoo, a desecration of the ancestors to discomfit and almost unman your enemies. If you had no ancestors, even symbolic ones, then who were you? You had lost your past to a cruel and unforgiving present. Your entire family history, a commodity very dear to these Irish patricians in their great houses, was under attack, the history stretching back far into the past to confirm your ancient right to these houses and these lands. That, after all, was why they put these paintings on the walls in the first place, a defiant statement of their right to be here, to be the masters in their Castles and Parks and Courts and Halls. Not for the first time Powerscourt wondered about the mind that had dreamt up this vicious onslaught. He thought briefly of Father O'Donovan Brady nursing his hatred of the Anglo-Irish along with his drink in the evenings in the priest's house. He doubted if somebody who did not understand the mentality of these Butlers and Ormondes and Moores and Connollys could have worked out such a clever plan. It had to be somebody who knew how they thought, somebody who had lived in one of these houses perhaps. A servant with a grudge maybe? He remembered suddenly that some of the greatest fighters for Ireland's freedom – and that would have meant a Catholic freedom, surely – had been Protestants. Lord Edward Fitzgerald, mortally wounded on the run, Parnell himself, the man who nearly brought Home Rule to Ireland. Did the Anglo-Irish generation of 1905 harbour a traitor in their midst?

'Tell me, Powerscourt,' Moore was speaking very quickly, as if he thought the remains of his ancestor on the wall might hear him, 'what does it mean?'

'Come away, man,' said Powerscourt. 'We can talk better away from the poor chap on the wall.'

Moore led them into the sitting area at the back which had once been the entrance hall. He ordered coffee and a stiff whiskey for himself.

'Let me say first of all,' Powerscourt draped himself in an elegant chair and stared out at the lawns and the fountain that led down to Moore's little river, 'that in one sense it is the same as the Butler picture. That isn't the original, I'm virtually certain of it. So, with luck we may recover the real thing in the end and your grandfather can go back on his walls. That picture in there is a copy, maybe done by the same man who painted the different version of *The Master of the Hunt* for Butler's house. And the artist has used some very inferior paint, or he's treated it with some fancy chemical so the paint fades away completely in a week. Some of the Old Masters, you know, in the days before commercially manufactured paint, used to mix their own. Sometimes the very same thing happened to them as has happened to yours – the work just faded away in a very short time.' Powerscourt hoped that Moore might take some comfort in being bracketed with the likes of Albrecht Dürer and Filippo Lippi, but if he did he was hiding it well. He continued scowling at his floor. 'As to what it means, it's the same thing as Butler's. You're not wanted. Your ancestors and what they stand for are repudiated. Your view of history and your family's view of history and your class's view of history are discredited, not valid any more. But it means something else as well, I think.' Powerscourt paused to take a sip of his coffee. A great peacock was strutting outside on the lawn.

'Can I just take you up on one thing you said earlier, Powerscourt? You said you thought we might recover the real painting in the end, that we might get my grandfather back again. Do you really believe that?'

'I do, Moore, I believe it very strongly. I have a feeling, no, more than a feeling, that the paintings are safe. People who manipulate pictures and their significance as cleverly as these thieves must have an understanding of what they mean. They're not likely to destroy them.'

'You were about to say something more when I interrupted,' said Moore, looking slightly happier though Powerscourt suspected it might be due to the whiskey which was disappearing at a rapid rate.

'Yes,' said Powerscourt, 'I must ask you a question. In the original blackmail letter there was a deadline, a day by which you were meant to have done whatever it is they wanted you to do. Is that correct?'

Moore nodded.

'And has that day arrived, or are we very close to it?'

There was a pause. Powerscourt looked over at Lady Lucy who never took her eyes off Moore's face.

'It's very close,' Moore murmured, 'but it's not quite yet.'

'And have you given in to their demands, the blackmailers?'

'No, I have not.' Moore was firm and defiant now.

'Very good,' said Powerscourt, 'then that is the other message from the disappearing grandfather next door. It's a warning. They're trying to frighten you. If you don't agree to our demands, terrible things are going to happen to you. Vanishing relations in the family portraits for a start.'

'You don't think some more of my paintings are going to come back with things wrong with them, do you, Powerscourt?'

'No, I don't,' said Powerscourt firmly. 'I don't think they'll try that particular stunt again.'

Just what the thieves were going to try next became apparent all too soon. Ormonde House was in chaos when Powerscourt and Lady Lucy returned there in the late afternoon. Groups of Orangemen were searching the woods to the side of the house. Other Orangemen could be heard clumping about in the attics, opening doors and rooms that had not seen a visitor in years. Clouds of dust floated down from the top storey on to the floors below. The butler, Hanrahan, gave them the news. 'It's Mrs Ormonde and her sister Winifred that just came to visit her today, sir, they've disappeared. We can't find them anywhere. The Chief Constable's in with Mr Ormonde now, sir, if you'd like to join them.'

'I don't think we'll do that just now,' said Powerscourt, his brain reeling from the news. The pictures were only a start. Then it's the people. Your own wife, even. He took Lady Lucy's hand absentmindedly into his own.

'Do we know when they disappeared? Do we know where they were when they were taken? If they were taken, that is.'

Hanrahan coughed. 'I'm afraid it's not altogether clear about when they were last seen, sir. Some people thought they went out on to the lawn. Others think they saw them after that in the house.'

'They didn't say if they were going out for a walk with a picnic perhaps, something like that? They didn't go off in one of the carriages, did they?'

'We've checked all that, sir. There was no picnic ordered and the carriages are all there still now.'

They heard the clatter of boots coming from the library. The Chief Constable was introduced, a former military man, Powerscourt decided. 'Colonel Fitzwilliam, Lord Powerscourt.' A grim-faced Ormonde made the introductions.

'Delighted to meet you, Powerscourt,' said the Colonel. 'Heard you were roaming in these pastures. Aren't you the chap who did all that intelligence work in South Africa?'

'I am,' said Powerscourt ruefully. 'I feel I was more successful out there against the Boers than I am here with these thieves.'

'Nonsense, man.' The Colonel at least was in cheerful mood. 'You'll get the hang of it soon enough.'

Powerscourt did not like to admit that he had been working on the case for many weeks now and did not feel any more advanced than on the day he started.

'Ormonde will fill you in on the plans. I've got to get some sort of system organized for finding the women. Won't do it without a system. I've always believed in systems, getting things properly organized. Nothing happens otherwise, civilians even worse than military.'

With that Colonel Fitzwilliam clattered off out of the front door and was driven away at great speed toward his systems. Ormonde drew them into the drawing room. Powerscourt remembered the flood of uncontrollable anger that had swept through this man when he realized his paintings had gone from his walls. He wondered if the reaction would be the same this time, or worse. But he seemed calm at first. Powerscourt thought he could see the terrible wrath lurking just beneath the surface, waiting to explode.

'Let me ask you one thing straight away, Powerscourt,' he began. 'Do you think they're alive, my wife and her sister, I mean?'

'I do,' said Powerscourt firmly. 'Let me tell you why I believe it. This whole affair is about blackmail. The thieves took one lot of chips, if you'll pardon the expression, when they stole the pictures. They thought that would be enough to persuade you to do what they want. It wasn't. So they've helped themselves to some more chips. But they have to keep the two hostages alive, it seems to me. They're no use to them dead. You might get years in prison for stealing paintings and hijacking people. You hang for murder.'

'Thank you,' said Ormonde gravely. Lady Lucy didn't feel she would like to be referred to as a chip as if she was part of a poker game but she let it go. 'Now then, I'll tell you the plan. The Chief Constable is planning a great sweep through a fifteen-mile arc around this house. Every house, great and small, is to be visited, the inhabitants questioned, notes taken about every single dwelling. Just as well Mayo is one of the least populated parts of the country. He's bringing in extra policemen from all of Connaught and further afield if he needs them. Each force will have its own particular area to work on. The working day for policemen is to be extended until eight o'clock in the evening. The Orangemen are to abandon their defensive duties and search as much of the mountain and wasteland as they can in the time. Fitzwilliam wasn't at all keen on their knocking on doors. I've got to go and talk to these Orangemen now, if you'll forgive me. I shall return soon.'

'Just one thing before you go,' said Powerscourt quickly. 'The deadline, the deadline in the blackmail letter. Has it come yet?'

'No,' said Ormonde.

'How soon?' said Powerscourt.

'Middle of next week, actually.' Ormonde looked as though he would much rather not have had to part with this piece of information. 'We've got five or six days to find the women. And,' he glowered balefully at this point, 'the bastards who took them.'

Powerscourt wandered about the house talking to some of the servants who had been on duty that morning. He learnt that there had been an elderly gardener employed raking the gravel on the front drive and he had seen nothing. A couple of foresters had been working in the woods on either side of the road that led to the back exit and they had seen nothing. It was as if Mary Ormonde, wife of Dennis, and her sister Winifred, had vanished into thin air. Powerscourt resumed his deliberations in the garden to the rear of the house. A great terrace with a balustrade ran the full length of the back of Ormonde House. In front was a small statue spouting water and a long expanse of grass. To the right and at the far end of the lawn there was a lake which ran right down to the edge of the demesne. Powerscourt looked at the layout for some time and rushed in to find Lady Lucy who was deep in conversation with the housekeeper. 'Forgive me Mrs O'Malley, I must borrow Lucy for a little while. I'll bring her back presently, don't worry.' And with that he hurried her out into the garden. Powerscourt picked up a chair and placed it on the lawn at right angles to the terrace, so both house and lake could be seen. He motioned to Lady Lucy to sit in it.

'Lucy,' said her husband, 'I want you to pretend to be Mary Ormonde. I didn't think Mrs O'Malley would be quite right for your sister Winifred so you're just going to have to pretend you have an imaginary friend sitting next to you.'

'Like Olivia used to do when she was little?' asked Lady Lucy. Powerscourt remembered his daughter having long and involved conversations with her phantom friend, often involving food and not going to bed for some reason.

'Indeed,' said Powerscourt. 'Now I am going to disappear for a moment or two but I shall come back. You two have a nice little chat, you know how much you ladies enjoy conversation.'

Powerscourt could have been seen from the terrace dragging something along the side of the lake. Suddenly Lady Lucy felt something hard and round poking into the middle of her back. 'Don't make a noise,' said Powerscourt in his nastiest voice, 'or I'll kill the pair of you. Just leave your things there and come to the water with me. If you value your lives you'll climb into that rowing boat as fast as your feet will carry you.'

Powerscourt led the way to the water's edge and climbed into the boat. 'Stern for you,' said Powerscourt, settling himself in the middle of the little craft and rowing as hard as he could. 'Don't we look innocent, Lucy,' he said in his normal voice. 'Nobody would think anything untoward was going on at all. Two ladies being taken for a row by some young man, probably a servant.'

'I think it's quite nice being abducted by you in a rowing boat, Francis,' said Lady Lucy, trailing a hand in the water. 'Do you think we should do it more often?'

'Now then,' said the villainous Powerscourt, taking his little stick out of his pocket and pointing it at his wife once more, 'when we get to the far side, do exactly as I say or you're for it.'

He beached the boat and pointed to a little door that led out into the world beyond the Big House. One hundred yards away was a jetty with two of Dennis Ormonde's yachts moored close by.

'Just pretend, Mrs Ormonde,' he snarled 'that one of those boats is ours.' Powerscourt stared out at the blue water and the islands. 'You could be clean away,' he said in his normal voice, 'in five minutes from the first encounter in the garden.'

'Do you think that's how they were taken, Francis?' asked Lady Lucy. 'It's quite risky, isn't it?'

'Once you've got them out of the garden,' said Powerscourt, 'it's plain sailing, if you'll forgive the expression. With all those Orangemen wandering about nobody's going to look twice at any strange young man or men roaming about. It's all quite normal.'

'So what happened then?' asked Lady Lucy. 'Do they sail away for a year and a day to the land where the bong tree grows?'

Powerscourt laughed. 'I very much doubt it. I don't think they met any pigs selling rings either. I suspect they met something rather nastier than the pig. We'd better go back, I suppose. I'd better tell my theory to Ormonde though I can't see for the life of me how it's going to help finding them.'

Father O'Donovan Brady was on his second sherry of the evening when Cathal Rafferty knocked on his front door. The Father always limited the sherry before his tea on the days when Pronsias Mulcahy came to call with his fresh bottle of John Powers.

'Good evening, young man, what can I do for you?' Father O'Donovan Brady did not sound overjoyed at the prospect of his visitor.

'Good evening, Father,' said Cathal, wringing his cap in his hands, and falling silent. Somehow it had been easier to rehearse this conversation when there was only one of you. It seemed much more difficult when there were two.

'Well,' said the priest, 'I cannot offer you any guidance if you don't speak, you know.'

'You remember, Father, you told me that if I saw or heard of any wickedness going on round here, I was to come and tell you.'

'The Devil never sleeps, not even in Ireland, that's what I said,' said Father O'Donovan Brady, curious now to know what sins this strange young man had witnessed. Sin excited the Father. He found discussion of it stimulating, possibly because the hearing of the sins was as near as he would ever get to committing them. 'What have you seen, young Cathal?'

This was going to be the difficult bit. 'Do you know the Head Gardener's Cottage out there at the back of the demesne?'

'I do,' said the priest. 'I knew the last Head Gardener well. He was a parishioner of mine. But I think the place is empty now.'

'It wasn't empty this afternoon, Father. There were two people in there.'

'And what were they doing? What a strange place to go in the afternoon. Did you see them go in?'

'That I did not, Father, I saw them through the window.' Cathal blushed red now, staring at the carpet.

Father Brady sensed that there might be gold, pure gold, if you could use those words for what he suspected was such a terrible sin, in the boy's account.

'You saw them through the window, did you now? And what were they doing, Cathal?'

The boy was whispering now. 'They were putting their clothes on, Father.'

'Putting their clothes on? God bless my soul. Tell me exactly what you saw. Don't leave anything out now.'

'Well,' said Cathal, feeling relieved that he'd passed the worst, 'the woman didn't have anything on at all. She was pulling her stockings up. The man had a shirt and his underpants on but no trousers. He had very hairy legs.' Cathal seemed to attach great importance to the amount of hair on Johnpeter's legs.

'This was in the bedroom, I presume,' said Father Brady. The hunter had spotted a fox now and was in full pursuit. Cathal nodded.

'I don't suppose,' the priest went on, 'that you managed to catch sight of what had been going on before they put their clothes on?'

'No,' said the boy.

'Pity, that.' Father Brady finished his sherry. 'What sort of people were they? Butler's Court people? Young? Middle-aged?'

'Oh, they were young, Father. I should say they were in their early twenties. And I'm sure they came from the Big House.'

'And I don't suppose you know their names? Protestants, I presume, seeing where they were.'

'They looked like Protestants all right,' said Cathal, 'but I don't know their names, I'm afraid.'

Father Brady dug into his pocket and handed over five shillings. 'That is your reward, young man. I fear great sin is taking place in our midst. I want you to do two things, young Cathal. I want you to find out their names and if they are married or not. And I want you to see if you can watch them before they put their clothes back on. Before we name the Devil's work, we have to know precisely what it is. You did well to come to me today.' He showed the young man to the front door. 'I'm very pleased with you. Remember, Cathal, if doubts should come, that you are doing the Lord's work.'

Johnny Fitzgerald returned late that evening to a depressed Ormonde House. The host had retired to bed early with a bottle of Armagnac. Powerscourt and Lady Lucy were having a disconsolate conversation about where you might hide two women of the Protestant Ascendancy.

'Word of the kidnap reached Westport about five o'clock in the afternoon, Francis,' said Johnny. 'Must have travelled round the town in about half an hour flat, I should think. Probably reached Galway by now. Limerick tomorrow morning, I shouldn't wonder.'

'What of your defrocked Christian Brother, Johnny?' asked Lady Lucy.

'He was rather disappointing, really,' said Johnny with a laugh. 'I'd imagined all sorts of terrible crimes he might have committed but all he'd done was to fall in love with a young widow whose son was in his class. He was going to resign but the authorities got in first. They said he must have broken his vow of celibacy with this woman before he handed in his resignation. He said it would be difficult to maintain your vows in the company of this girl. She was very beautiful. He did have one interesting theory, though, about how to start a revolution in Ireland.'

'And what was that?' asked Powerscourt.

'All you needed, the former Brother Mooney maintained, was the Christian Brothers and all the young men from the Gaelic Athletic Association on your side. You take over the towns of Ireland one by one. Then you march on Dublin. It's revolution by hurling sticks, if you follow me. The only snag, as your man pointed out, was that the whole bloody country would end up being run by the Christian Brothers. He didn't fancy that too much.'

'What do you think about this pilgrimage?' asked Powerscourt. 'It's two days away now and I'm not sure we should do it with all this fuss about the missing women. It wouldn't look right, would it?'

'But I thought you promised the Archbishop, Francis,' said Lady Lucy, 'that you and some friends were going to accept his invitation.'

'That was before this latest tragedy.'

'I think we should do it,' said Johnny Fitzgerald.

'So do I,' said Lady Lucy.

194

'Very well,' said Powerscourt. 'We'll have to look out our stoutest boots and walking sticks. I want to go anyway. Perhaps I'll find inspiration half-way up the Holy Mountain.'

11

They didn't find the Ormonde women the next day. Hundreds of policemen knocked on doors, checked rooms, wrote down details of who might be absent from the house in case they should prove to be the kidnappers. All of this information was laboriously copied into great ledgers whose pages began to resemble the early stages of a census, a Domesday Book of Westport and the surrounding countryside in 1905. More policemen were expected the following day and on the Monday, although their work would inevitably be confused by the pilgrimage to Croagh Patrick. The Chief Constable himself made periodic inspections of the information, making sure his systems were working properly and had not been diluted by human weakness.

Powerscourt roamed round the gardens of Ormonde House. The last Orangemen not out on the hillsides were completing the search of the woods, singing strange Orange hymns and ballads as they worked. He would sit in the meagre library from time to time, cursing himself for his failure. Lord Francis Powerscourt did not like failure. He had rarely experienced it in his professional life. For him, failure in this case would be a scar on his reputation, something he would never be able to erase. Lady Lucy tried to console him, to appease his restlessness. She knew from experience that if Francis worried away at a problem with the front of his mind, as it were, little would happen. The mysteries he set himself to solve did not often yield to a full frontal assault. In Lady Lucy's opinion it would not be the siege engines that broke the defenders, but a flash of insight that said there must be a path up the cliff at the rear end of the castle.

'I'm useless, Lucy,' he said as they took tea in the library. 'The only reason these people haven't pensioned me off is that they're too polite. I'll become a tolerated guest, rather like Uncle Peter back at Butler's Court. Maybe I should start work on the rest of his history of Ireland. He stopped in 1891, you see. That would keep me out of mischief. I couldn't raise anybody's hopes that I might actually improve their lot by solving the mysteries that are ruining their lives then.'

'What nonsense, Francis,' said Lady Lucy, who had seen him in these moods before. 'You know you'll solve the mystery, you know you will. You mustn't be so hard on yourself, my love.'

'Hard on myself?' said Powerscourt bitterly. 'How can I not be hard on myself when I can't even solve the mystery of a few disappearing pictures, for Christ's sake. It's pathetic.'

Lady Lucy suspected that Powerscourt's sense of himself would take a severe blow if he ever failed in a case. But then he never had. Not yet, anyway. Perhaps, she said to herself, anxious to find something that would cheer up her husband, perhaps the pilgrimage would do him good.

It was Charlie O'Malley who found the body in the oratory on top of Croagh Patrick at a quarter to four in the morning. Charlie, accompanied by two of his fleet of donkeys, Bushmills and Jack Daniels, had been making a last push towards profit from the stout. His donkeys had reached the summit laden with the stuff. The dead man was young, not more than eighteen or twenty in Charlie's view, slight of build and with black hair. He had been shot twice, once in the chest and once in the back of the head. Dark matter from these wounds had congealed on his clothing. He had been placed, in a sitting position, with his back to the altar. Dead eyes gazed down at the empty pews and the non-existent congregation. 'Jesus Mary and Joseph!' Charlie had said and knelt down beside the corpse. He said two Hail Marys and one Our Father. At first Charlie thought it was a punishment sent by God to warn him of his sins and wickedness in intending to sell alcohol at greatly inflated prices to the penitents after they had attended Mass on the summit. Perhaps he should bring his prices down to those at ground level. That thought didn't last for long as Charlie reasoned that God would not have bothered to have somebody killed just to reprove him for a few bottles of stout. He said a Creed and a couple more Our Fathers and staggered out into the open air.

The omens were not good for the pilgrims that day. Low cloud enveloped the mountain from about halfway up. A fine but persistent rain was falling. Five to four in the morning on Reek Sunday, Charlie said to himself, surely to God somebody is going to arrive soon. Charlie knew that the body would have to be moved out of the church. It couldn't be left there, not on this day, of all days, but he felt reluctant to take the responsibility himself. And what would they do with the body when it was outside the church, for God's sake? You couldn't take it down the mountain to meet all these pilgrims coming the other way. Some of these buggers, religious maniacs in Charlie's view, liked to come to the summit very early to pray. There were even, Charlie knew, some fanatics come from Australia for this pilgrimage today. Charlie wasn't quite sure where Australia was as a matter of fact, come to think of it he didn't think the geography Christian Brother, whose name Charlie could never remember, knew where it was either, he always shifty about the place, but Charlie did know Australia was inhabited by convicts who liked playing cricket and counting sheep. You couldn't very well pass the time of day with one of these devout Australians or some other zealot, 'Have a good pilgrimage, I've just got to take this corpse to the morgue if you don't mind.'

Charlie thought it was an insoluble problem. He went to check his two donkeys had not run away. Then he heard a wheezing sound, as if from a man very short of breath from the climb. Walter Heneghan materialized out of the cloud. For the first and last time in his life Charlie was glad to see him. Walter Heneghan of Louisburg, chief contractor for the little chapel, had lived for most of the construction work in a tent at the top. His men were unaware of the reasons for his residence on the spot. His doctor had told him that if he went up and down Croagh Patrick twice a day for six months he would probably be dead before it was finished. And his wife, a woman with a fearful tongue, had told Walter with the candour that had so endeared her to him over the years that as far she was concerned, he, Walter, would be much more use to her living in a tent on top of a bloody mountain than he would be cluttering up her house in Louisburg. Walter did travel up and down the mountain occasionally for meetings with Father Macdonald about The Skedule but he had not attained the expertise or the fitness of Charlie O'Malley and the rest who could go up and down at speeds they never spoke of to Walter in case the working day grew even longer.

'Is that you, Walter?' cried Charlie O'Malley.

'Who else would it be at this terrible hour?' said Heneghan, sinking down for a rest by the side of the chapel.

'Walter, brace yourself now. It's God's truth I'm going to tell you, so I am.' Charlie peered at Walter to make sure he was ready for the news.

'What is it, Charlie?' Heneghan was rubbing his leg vigorously as if he had cramp.

'As God is my witness, Walter, there's a dead body in that chapel, so there is, God rest his soul.'

'A dead body? In my chapel? How the divil did it get here? Did it walk?'

'Can't have walked when it was dead, Walter, might have walked up when it was alive, I suppose. Hard to tell.'

'Come on.' Walter rose to his feet with difficulty. 'Show me.'

The two men tiptoed into the little church. The body was still there, like a ghost at a feast.

'God in heaven!' said Walter and he rattled off a quick volley of Hail Marys. 'He's very dead, isn't he?' he went on as he knelt beside the corpse.

'What are we going to do, Walter? We can't leave the dead bugger in here. Do you have the boy with you?'

'He's hanging round the summit somewhere, eating an apple.' Heneghan made it sound as if his son had brought the Garden of Eden up to the top of the Holy Mountain. Maybe Eve was hidden in the clouds. Walter's son Matthew had frequently been used as a runner to take messages up and down the mountain during the construction work and sometimes even spent the night in the tent.

'Look here,' said Heneghan, 'we've got to get the body away from here. It's no good trying to hide him a couple of hundred yards away, there's nothing higher than a grasshopper's knee for miles. I didn't spend six months of my life building this damned chapel, some of it in the month of February in Christ's name, to have the opening day ruined. It's not for us, Charlie, to say whether or not the bloody pilgrims get told about it, that's for Father Macdonald and the Archbishop man. I'll send Matthew off at full speed this minute to the priest's house in Westport. I think the big man is staying there too.'

'You said we've got to get the body away from here, Walter. How do you propose to do that?' Charlie had a sick feeling in his stomach. He didn't know what was coming, but he knew he wasn't going to like it. They heard a whistling noise coming up the final stretch.

'Tim Philbin, is that you?' Walter Heneghan shouted into the murk.

'It is,' said Tim.

'Thank God you've come,' said Heneghan. 'You're just in time to help Charlie here carry a corpse down the mountain the other way, the Louisburg route. You and Charlie and two bloody donkeys are to take our dead friend down to ground level and into the nearest police station. That's your mission for the day.'

'Fine, Walter,' said Tim, fully visible now. 'You did say corpse, didn't you? Corpse as in dead man?'

'I did,' said Walter. 'Doesn't look too heavy a chap to me. Slight sort of corpse. You'll be down the bottom in no time.'

News reached the clergy shortly before seven o'clock. Father Macdonald, the Administrator of Westport, and the Very Reverend Dr Healey the Archbishop of Tuam were finishing a hearty breakfast when the housekeeper showed in a rather dishevelled Matthew Heneghan. One look at him plunged Father Macdonald into despair. You knew, he thought, you just knew, looking at this sad face, that here was bad news. Terrible memories of his disastrous role in the construction of the new convent outside Ballinrobe in his previous post came flooding back to him, the building unfinished by the day of the opening, the ceremony postponed, the windows with no glass, the kitchen with no cooking facilities, the unfinished cells for the sisters. He remembered the rebukes of his superiors and the articles in the local newspaper which more or less accused him of being a fool. Well, it was just about to happen again. He felt his heart beating faster already, even before he had heard the news, and he felt certain that one of his nervous headaches was going to start very soon.

'Well?' said the Archbishop in his let's be friendly with the young, they are the congregations of the future, voice.

Matthew Heneghan coughed slightly. 'I am Matthew Heneghan, Your Grace, son of Walter Heneghan the contractor. Forgive me, Your Grace,' his father had told him five times before he left the summit that you called an archbishop Your Grace, 'there's a dead body in the chapel, sir, the chapel on the summit.'

A piece of toast, well smeared with Father Macdonald's housekeeper's finest home-made marmalade, was arrested halfway towards the Archbishop's mouth. 'A dead body, lad? Are you sure?'

'My father and the others were absolutely certain, Your Grace. The man had been shot twice, once in the chest and once in the back of the head.'

The Archbishop's toast, rather like Father Macdonald's spirits, sank back towards his plate.

'May the Lord have mercy on his soul,' he said.

'Your Grace, Your Grace,' Father Macdonald had turned red with worry, 'we'll have to cancel the pilgrimage, won't we? We can't go on after this terrible news.'

'Cancel the pilgrimage? What nonsense!' boomed the Archbishop in such a loud voice that the housekeeper dropped her second best teapot on to the kitchen floor where it broke into hundreds of small pieces. 'People die every day, after all, let's not forget that. Somebody probably dies in the Westport area every year on Reek Sunday. It's just they don't choose it to do it in the chapel on the top. God's will works in mysterious ways and I am sure He would want the event to continue.' The Archbishop crossed himself with great ceremony. 'We couldn't stop all those special trains bringing people here anyway even if we wanted to. Tell me, young man, what's happened to the body? Is it still there? In the chapel, I mean.'

'Oh no, Your Grace, it's being brought down the mountain the Louisburg route, that's the opposite route to the one the pilgrims take. Then they're going to hand it over to the police. I have to go to the police station here in Westport, sir, after I've finished with your reverences. To tell them about it, Your Grace.'

'I presume,' said the Archbishop, resuming work on his toast, 'that nobody as yet knows the name of the dead man?'

'No, Your Grace, I don't think anybody up there had seen him before.'

'Well, thank you, young man, thank you for coming down to tell us this terrible news. We mustn't keep you from your duties with the police. And please give my best regards to your father when you next see him.' That message, Matthew knew, would keep his father happy for weeks. What happiness you could bring into people's lives if you were an archbishop. Matthew wondered briefly about joining the priesthood as he set out through the early morning light for the officers of the law.

Father Macdonald's anxiety had not abated. That little red vein he so wished he could have removed was throbbing busily in his forehead. 'We'll have to keep it a secret, Your Grace, the death, I mean. Nobody must know.'

The Archbishop frowned. He glanced briefly at a painting of the disciples on the wall, one of them a man called Thomas. 'I don't think that would do, no, not at all. I have no idea how many people were at the summit when the body was found – it sounds as if the poor man was murdered now I think about it – and I have no idea how many people young Matthew will tell here in Westport. Word will get out. Much better to let the pilgrims know. That way they can't accuse the Church of covering up unpleasant truths.'

'B-but how?' stammered Father Macdonald. 'We can't get anything printed in time. If you tell somebody on the way up the rumour will have multiplied it into half a dozen corpses or more by the way down.'

'I expect there may even be a ballad about it before the day is out,' said the Archbishop. 'The answer is simple.' He saw he would, as so often, have to take command. 'I'll do it. I'll tell them. Find me three priests or Christian Brothers to act as stewards and we'll hold the pilgrims up for ten or fifteen minutes or so at St Patrick's statue. Then I'll tell that batch what happened. Ten minutes later I'll tell the next batch and so on until I have to set off for the summit. You can take over then.'

Father Macdonald nodded feebly. The prospect of having to address a crowd of a thousand people or so filled him with dread. The little red vein was working overtime already and he wasn't even on the mountain. Oddly enough, for a man ordained into the priesthood, Father Macdonald hated public speaking.

The route to the summit of Croagh Patrick is not one that would be taken by a flying crow. It begins at Murrisk a couple of miles from the mountain itself and the path goes up to the top of the hill and then turns right to snake its way across the scree towards the peak. At the bottom the going is fairly benign, but later on the surface is composed of loose stones where the pilgrim slips back almost as far as he advances.

By eight o'clock there was a thin trickle of penitents beginning the climb, dressed as if going to church, the youths and the men in sober suits of dark grey with white shirts and caps on their heads, the women in long skirts with matching jackets in sombre colours, and hats, often purchased specially for the occasion. Powerscourt and Johnny and Lady Lucy were all soberly dressed as they arrived to start their ascent just after half past eight.

'Don't go and get converted now, for Christ's sake,' had been Dennis Ormonde's parting words. 'I'd never live it down.'

'Are you going to say any prayers on the way up?' Lady Lucy addressed her two men in turn.

'Think I might manage the Lord's Prayer a couple of times,' Powerscourt said with a smile, 'but not in the numbers these good people have to say. They have to get through industrial quantities of Hail Marys and things, I believe.'

'If I think I'm going to fall off the edge of this damned mountain further up in that cloud,' said Johnny Fitzgerald, 'I shall start praying like a bloody Jesuit.'

There was a family of four in front of them, young parents with children who must have been about eight or ten years old. The youngsters were larking about on the edge of the

204

path, running further up to ambush their mother and father later on, the parents trying to persuade the children to conserve their energy for the more arduous territory ahead. A group of four nuns overtook them, their hands on the rosary beads, their lips moving silently. Powerscourt suspected they were going to pray all the way to the summit, and possibly all the way down, a whole day of pilgrimage and prayer and penitence. They passed an old couple, the woman bent, the man carrying a stick in his right hand and trying to help his wife with the other. Powerscourt thought they must be over seventy years old. They weren't going to go all the way, the old woman assured Lady Lucy, just as far as their old legs would carry them and then they would have a rest. Within half an hour they had reached the statue of St Patrick, a great beacon of a thing with the bearded saint gazing out to sea. Here the procession seemed to halt. Powerscourt could see a couple of priests barring the route with a pair of long sticks held out over the path. After a few minutes, with the crowd behind them growing ever deeper, there was a great shout from one of the men in black.

'Pray silence for His Grace the Very Reverend Dr John Healey, Archbishop of Tuam!' The voice went right back down the mountain. Somebody seemed to have found some kind of impromptu platform for the Archbishop to stand on, raising him well above the crowd at the front and easily visible to those at the back.

'Pilgrims of St Patrick!' he began, his arms extended to encompass all his flock. 'Brothers and Sisters in Christ, I welcome you to Ireland's Holy Mountain today!' There was a murmur of approval from the penitents. It wasn't every day or every pilgrimage that you received a greeting in person from such a prince of the Church. The Archbishop raised his crook above him to quieten the noise. 'I bring sad news for us all on this day. I want to tell you about it in person. Over the last six months, as many of you know, a new oratory or chapel has been constructed on the summit of this Holy Mountain.

Later today we shall celebrate Mass in this place and you will have the chance to observe the skill and devotion which have gone into the construction of the building.' The Archbishop paused for a second. The crowd were completely silent. He could ask each person to kill his neighbour, Powerscourt thought, and such was the hold of his personality, they would probably do it. 'This morning,' Dr Healey went on, 'this morning of all mornings, a dead body was found resting in the chapel. It was that of a young man. He had been shot. We do not yet know his name. God moves in mysterious ways, my friends, even on the mountains devoted to his glory. I was asked if I would consider cancelling the pilgrimage in view of this terrible event. My answer was No. I could not deny you the opportunity of penitence and devotion which mark Reek Sunday. I could not deny you the chance of the spiritual nourishment and the experience of God's grace which so many find on this barren hillside, wrapped in cloud today, symbol of God's mystery. I ask you to pray for the soul of the dead man whose body has been taken away to the appropriate authorities. I ask you to pray that he may find peace with our Father in heaven. Finally, let me repeat what I said at the beginning. Whether you live in Westport and the surrounding villages, or whether you lodge with us from distant parts for the duration of this pilgrimage, you are most welcome. May the Blessing of Father, Son and Holy Ghost be upon you.' With that the Archbishop made the sign of the cross very slowly and climbed down from his improvised pulpit.

Most of the crowd surged on up the hill. The very old stayed behind. There were three stations for the pilgrims to make on this climb and St Patrick's statue was not one of them. But it became a place of prayer for those who felt they could go no further. The murmuring noises Powerscourt was to associate ever after with this day began to float upwards into the air.

'Did you know about this young man, Francis?' Lady Lucy whispered.

'I did not,' replied Powerscourt, 'and I hope most sincerely that he is not the young man I am thinking of.'

Before Lady Lucy or Johnny had the chance to reply there was a great booming noise.

'Lord Powerscourt! Lord Powerscourt!' went the boom, coming down a few yards to greet them. 'How very good to see you, even in such unhappy circumstances!' The Archbishop shook him by the hand. Powerscourt made the introductions. 'Lady Powerscourt, a pleasure to have you with us here today. Johnny Fitzgerald, you're not by any chance related to Lord Edward Fitzgerald of the '98 Rebellion?'

'I'm afraid I am,' said Johnny. Powerscourt and Lady Lucy looked astonished. Johnny related to one of the most famous rebels in Irish history! Why had he never mentioned this before? 'It's on my mother's side,' he went on, grinning sheepishly.

'What an honour for us here today,' said the Archbishop. 'But tell me, Lord Powerscourt, do you by any chance have any knowledge or any theories about this poor young man found dead on the summit?'

'I have only just heard of it, Your Grace. I do have a theory, I'm afraid, but I would not wish to tell anybody about it until I have more information, his age, for instance, and the people he consorted with.' Powerscourt looked into that strong and powerful face again. If the Archbishop asked, he knew he would have to tell him. The Archbishop did not ask.

'I must return to my duties,' he said. 'I hope you will feel able to tell me later, if the facts bear out your theories. Now,' he beamed at all of them in turn, 'I cannot tell how much it pleases me to see you here today. Thank you for coming. I must continue my mission here. I have to make my little speech every ten or fifteen minutes to tell the pilgrims what has happened. Maybe I shall see you at the summit.' The Archbishop marched back up his hill. Powerscourt turned to look at the old people clustered round St Patrick. The noise was louder now. Snatches of prayer came across the hundred yards that separated Powerscourt and his party from the penitents.

'Thy kingdom come, Thy will be done . . . The third day He rose again from the dead . . . The Lord is with thee, Blessed are thou among women . . . Was crucified dead and buried, He descended into hell . . . Thy kingdom come, Thy will be done . . . And blessed is the fruit of thy womb Jesus . . . As we forgive them that trespass against us . . . He ascended into heaven and sitteth at the right hand of God the Father Almighty . . .'

'Quite hypnotic, those prayers,' said Powerscourt as they renewed their ascent, the cloud beckoning a few hundred feet above them. 'They go round and round in your head, like a top. But tell me, Johnny, I never knew you were related to Lord Edward Fitzgerald and I've known you for a very long time. Why did you keep so quiet about it, you old rogue?'

'You never asked, Francis. I didn't want to make a fuss. It can be very dangerous being related to a dead martyr in Ireland. People endlessly expect you to stand rounds of drinks in pubs and clubs in memory of your ancestor, that sort of thing. But I couldn't tell a lie to an archbishop, for God's sake. Not here. Not on his very own mountain. He might have turned me into a bloody statue like your man Patrick over there.'

They climbed on towards the mist. A party of six Christian Brothers, clad entirely in black, shot past them as if in a race to the summit. Now they were entering the cloud and a fine rain began to fall. Fast-moving pilgrims were clearly visible a few feet in front of them, then they vanished into the broom. The colour seemed to drain out of the day, apart from the dark red which stained the rough stones that now constituted the path, the blood of those who made the ascent in their bare feet, shoes or boots tied around their necks. Johnny Fitzgerald was panting slightly. Lady Lucy moved steadily on, holding on to her husband's arm when the going got rough. Powerscourt heard that muttering noise again, louder this time, a hundred feet or so above them. You couldn't make out any words yet, just a rumble ahead.

The first station the pilgrims had to make on their way to the summit was called Leach Benain and it was situated at the base of the cone that formed the final stage of the ascent of Croagh Patrick. There was a cairn of stones about the height of a man and instructions for the faithful to walk round the station seven times saying seven Our Fathers, seven Hail Marys and one Creed as they went. Powerscourt and Johnny and Lady Lucy stood to one side as a mark of respect and watched as an enormous serpent of people circled the stones, ring upon ring of them, many of them holding on to their neighbours. '. . . I believe in the Holy Ghost, the holy Catholic Church . . .' Small children clutched their parents' hands as they went round and round, not in some game in the playground but on God's business. '. . . pray for us sinners now and in the hour of death Amen . . .' The six Christian Brothers were moving very slowly now, perhaps as a mark of respect for one of the sacred places of Reek Sunday. '. . . lead us not into temptation but deliver us from evil . . .' One young man stifled a scream as his bare foot stamped down on a particularly sharp piece of rock and the blood spurted from his sole. '. . . born of the Virgin Mary, suffered under Pontius Pilate . . .' More and more people kept joining the circling pilgrims, a thin trickle peeling off, their prayers complete, to continue their journey toward the summit. 'Our Father which art in heaven, Hallowed be thy name. . .'

'How long does it take their feet to get better, Francis?' whispered Lady Lucy. 'They must be in agony by the time they get to the bottom again, these poor people.'

'I don't know. I expect it's some form of extreme penance,' Powerscourt whispered back. 'Maybe you get forgiven some of your sins in exchange for the bare feet.'

'Hail Mary full of Grace . . .' The cloud was beginning to lift now. Looking back down the mountain Powerscourt saw a human chain curling its way upwards, tiny specks further down, assuming normal size further up. '. . . the communion of saints, the forgiveness of sins . . .' Behind Leacht Benain, on the far side of the mountain, a barren landscape, dotted with lakes and ponds, stretched away to a grey horizon. '. . .give us this day our daily bread . . .' Gazing backwards again Powerscourt saw the huge figure of the Archbishop, making great strides up his Holy Mountain, his three priests struggling to keep up. '. . . and in Jesus Christ, His only son, our Lord who was conceived of the Holy Ghost . . .'

The sounds followed Powerscourt and Johnny and Lady Lucy as they set off towards the summit. Johnny Fitzgerald had turned quite red and was panting heavily. Powerscourt wondered if the drink had finally caught up with him, over two thousand feet above sea level. Lady Lucy was looking serious. Her husband thought she might have been praying for their children. The Archbishop and his party passed them in a whish of ecclesiastical garments, Dr Healey waving an enormous wave as he shot past. At eleven o'clock they reached the summit. This was the second station and the faithful had to repeat the performance of the first station, and then some more. Powerscourt and Lady Lucy and Johnny watched as they prayed for the Pope's intentions near the chapel, then made fifteen circuits of the chapel saying fifteen Our Fathers and fifteen Hail Marys, and then, just to finish off, they had to walk seven times round a relic of St Patrick with another seven Hail Marys and Our Fathers and a Creed. The crowd of pilgrims making the station was enormous. Maybe, Powerscourt thought, all this going round and round in circles is a metaphor for sin, the prayers the appeal for forgiveness. Some were lying on the ground, their eyes closed. Many of the barefoot brigade had brought water with them to bathe their aching limbs. Johnny Fitzgerald had spotted some suspicious-looking activity taking place a couple of hundred yards away. 'Don't tell the men of God, Francis,' he whispered on his return, 'but there's a couple of fellows down there selling bottles of Guinness. Bloody expensive they are, but welcome. I'll give them that. It's a miracle, so it is.' A Westport band had managed to reach the summit with their instruments and were serenading the crowd with patriotic airs like 'The West's Awake' and 'A Nation Once Again'.

Dr Healey dedicated the new church to St Patrick. Charlie O'Malley and Tim Philbin, returned from their corpse-carrying duties, had closed their makeshift bar to be there for the great moment although, as Charlie observed, if anybody had told him he and Tim would have moved a corpse out of the church on the day of its consecration he'd have knocked them down. The Archbishop paid tribute to Father Macdonald for his role in supervising the work and Walter Heneghan for the construction. He named almost all of the workmen, including Austin Rudd and Tim Philbin, but not Charlie who thought he was being punished for selling illicit liquor on the summit. But Dr Healey hadn't finished yet. 'Finally,' he boomed, 'we have to thank some other members of God's kingdom. Some of our four legged-friends, christened, not as I would have wished, with names from scripture, but with the names of great distilleries here and overseas, had a role to play. Under the supervision of Charlie O'Malley, a team of four donkeys, Jameson, Powers, Bushmills and Jack Daniels, played their part in the great work carrying material to the summit. We thank them too.' There was a huge cheer from the crowd. 'Finally,' the Archbishop's voice, Powerscourt thought, must be carrying halfway down the mountain, 'I want to thank you, the pilgrims. You alone have always venerated the footsteps of St Patrick and you alone have practised the fasting and prayer of which our patron saint was so bright an example.'

The journey down was more treacherous than the journey up. The loose stones on the scree threatened to throw people off balance. The sticks which had been useful on the route to the top were even more valuable now, jammed down into the ground to prevent a slide down the mountain. Johnny Fitzgerald could be heard muttering, 'Bloody mountain,'

211

'Bloody stones,' 'I'm damned if I'm going to slide all the way to the bottom of this bloody thing.'

Then the sun came out and everything looked different. All those grey and black suits the men were wearing looked less sombre. The white vestments of the nuns sparkled in the light. Suddenly Powerscourt felt a moment of elation. To his left was the blue sea and the islands of Clew Bay scattered like pearls from a necklace across the waters. Above that, clear blue sky with faint wisps of white cloud spangled across the road to heaven. Ahead of him on the path thousands of fresh pilgrims marching towards the summit. In front of him another thousand, going down, circling round the third and last station on Croagh Patrick and saying their prayers to God and the Virgin. They had said so many prayers on this day, the pilgrims. They had never complained. He felt God was here among the rough stones they trod, he was immanent now among these people. In Powerscourt's eyes the pilgrims were translated into a new kind of innocence, cleansed of their sins among the rocks and scree of Ireland's Holy Mountain, their feet washed, not in the blood of the Lamb, but in the blood of their own wounded feet. Lucy was beside him. His oldest friend was by his side. Suddenly Powerscourt's eyes were filled with tears. He knew now what the Archbishop meant when he had talked in Tuam those weeks before about God's grace being present on the mountain on this day. For a brief moment, he, Powerscourt had been filled with it. Tears began to roll slowly down his face. Lady Lucy held his hand very tight, murmuring that she knew exactly how he felt. Then the moment of ecstasy passed and Powerscourt's brain returned to his investigation.

He was trying to remember something the Archbishop had said earlier on down by St Patrick's statue, something that might prove to be a clue in his inquiry. Dr Healey had talked about the dead body at the summit – that wasn't it. He had talked about the need to continue with the pilgrimage – that wasn't it either. It must have been something near the end when Powerscourt's attention had been diverted by a group of fifteen nuns all climbing together.

'When the Archbishop addressed the faithful, Lucy, by the statue early on, what did he say at the end?'

Lady Lucy looked at her husband closely. 'He blessed the faithful, Francis, and I think he asked them to pray for the dead man. Why do you ask?'

'I think it could be something important, my love, did he say anything else? Very near the end it was.'

Lady Lucy frowned. 'He talked about the people who lived in Westport and the people who were visitors all being welcome. Hold on, he didn't put it quite like that.' She struggled to find the word. 'This is it, I think, Francis. "Whether you live in Westport and the surrounding area or whether you lodge with us for the duration of the pilgrimage, you are all welcome."'

'That's it, Lucy! Well done!'

'I don't understand, why should that be important?'

'Lodge, Lucy, that's what I was trying to remember. Not lodge in the sense of stay with or reside but lodge as in hunting lodge or shooting lodge or fishing lodge. Can't you see? It would be a perfect place to hide the two Ormonde ladies, Lucy, miles from anywhere, you could see a rescue party coming from miles away, nobody would think of looking there anyway. They're perfect hideaways.'

'Would the people who took the pictures know about such places, Francis?'

'They knew enough about all the big houses to come and steal the pictures. No reason why they couldn't know about fishing lodges. Let's see what Dennis Ormonde thinks.'

They passed the third station of Croagh Patrick, the pilgrims marching round it in circles once again. The afternoon was warm and the young men took off their jackets on the way down. Johnny Fitzgerald recovered his good humour at the easier passage at the bottom. Powerscourt still found it hard to believe that his friend was descended from one of the

213

leaders of the '98 Rebellion. Lady Lucy hoped that all those poor people who went up and down in bare feet could receive some attention as soon as possible. Just after one o'clock they were back in Ormonde House.

12

Dennis Ormonde was delighted to see his pilgrims return. 'Come in, come in,' he said, ushering them into his dining room. He was accompanied by a young police inspector from Westport. There was an enormous spread of cold food laid out in front of them. 'Thought you would be famished after all that climbing,' he went on, 'didn't know what time you'd be back. There's cold chicken and salmon and a pheasant pie and cold potatoes and all kinds of stuff. And there's beer and lemonade and wine for the thirsty.' Johnny Fitzgerald advanced rapidly towards the drinks department and downed a glass of all three in quick succession, beginning with the lemonade and advancing through the beer to the Ormonde Chablis.

'God, there were a lot of people out there today,' Ormonde continued. 'I took a little walk round about ten o'clock. There's even a pilgrim with a bloody great motor car parked not a hundred yards from my front gates. I saw one of the locals patting the bonnet affectionately and telling his friends: "It is easier for a camel to pass through the eye of a needle than for a rich man to enter the kingdom of God."'

Through mouthfuls of cold chicken and potato salad Powerscourt outlined his theory about hunting and fishing lodges.

'By God, that's clever, Powerscourt. Must be worth the ascent if it puts your brain into that sort of working order.

They'd be perfect places to hide people, miles from anywhere, well equipped, bit of fishing if you get bored. Hold on . . .' He paused for a moment. 'My grandfather had a list of all the lodges round here, don't suppose any new ones have been built in the last fifty years. It's in the library somewhere, I'll go and fetch it.'

Powerscourt asked the Inspector, whose name was Ronan O'Brien, if there was any further news on the name of the body found at the summit, and was told that there was so much confusion caused by the pilgrimage and the vast numbers of people that normal police work was virtually suspended for the time being.

'Here we are,' said Ormonde cheerfully, returning with a map which had a number of lodges marked on it, stretching as far north as Ballina and south into Connemara.

'Is there a lodge belonging to the Butlers anywhere in that list?' Powerscourt asked.

'Not on here,' said Ormonde, 'but I believe there is one on the borders of Galway and Mayo, miles from anywhere. Bloody huge, the place is. Why do you ask, Powerscourt?'

'With your permission, Ormonde, Johnny and I would like to take a look at that one.'

'Is there something,' asked Ormonde, staring closely at Powerscourt, 'that you're not telling us? Some information you have about the Butlers?'

'Coming from you, my friend,' said Powerscourt, 'I don't think any charges of holding back information carry much weight, seeing you have not yet shown me the blackmail letter.'

'Of course you and Johnny can inspect the place. The Inspector here and his men will look after the rest.'

Powerscourt took a long draught of his lemonade. 'This is, of course, premature,' he said, pushing his plate back, 'but I think we should consider exactly what anybody, policeman or ourselves, should do if they find the two Ormonde ladies and their captors. This is especially important for you, Ormonde. It's your wife and her sister we are talking about here.'

'I'm not quite sure what you mean.' Dennis Ormonde looked puzzled.

'It'll be like a siege, for a start, and very few sieges end up with no casualties in my experience. Suppose you find signs of life in one of those places, smoke coming out of a chimney, a horse tied up round the back, somebody going in and out of the house. Do you go up and ring the front door bell? I think not. You might be shot or hauled inside to join the hostages. Another one in the bag.'

Dennis Ormonde looked thoughtful.

'Suppose then' – Lady Lucy wondered if her husband was about to start ticking off his points in the palm of his hand – 'you decide on a frontal assault. One person rings the door bell and tries to shoot his way in, another one breaks a window and comes at the thieves the other way. There's nothing to say they won't shoot the two ladies the minute they hear the sound of gunfire. You could try launching some kind of attack in the night time but they're perilous ventures, those night attacks, you can't see who you're shooting at and you can't see the person shooting at you either.'

'Dear me,' said Ormonde.

'Then there's the problem of messages,' Powerscourt went on remorselessly, 'not just the messages we might want to send back, but the messages going into the house. There are three days left as from today until the deadline expires, as you well know, Ormonde. Somebody's going to want to send messages to the people holding the women. If we're doing our job properly we can spot the messenger before he arrives and intercept any message. But then how do we deliver it, assuming the real messenger is our prisoner? Or do we send a false message, saying Ormonde has paid up, the mission is accomplished, let the ladies go? And then what? If I were them and that happened, I'd leave the house with the ladies inside, lock every door in the place and take away the key. That would give my escape a head start.'

Dennis Ormonde looked confused. Lady Lucy remembered her own time as a hostage, incarcerated in a suite of rooms on the top floor of a Brighton hotel some years before at the time of the Queen's Diamond Jubilee. Francis had used a cunning combination of smoke and fire to effect her rescue on that occasion but she did not think he could use that device again.

The policeman had been looking at Ormonde's map. 'If I could make a suggestion, gentlemen,' he began hesitantly, not accustomed to this sort of company, 'there are two other lodges on the way to the Butler one. It would be a great help if you could look them over on your way.'

'Of course,' said Powerscourt.

'And one more thing, if I may,' the Inspector went on. 'I'd like to send a couple of cavalrymen with you. We've got a detachment of them just now from the garrison in Castlebar. You may need people to send your own messages and so on.'

'Thank you, Inspector, that would be most helpful.'

'Were you involved in sieges in your time in the military, Powerscourt?' Dennis Ormonde seemed to attach great importance to Powerscourt's time in uniform.

'We both were,' Powerscourt replied, 'and damned messy things they are too.'

'Well,' said Ormonde, refilling Johnny's glass, 'you'll just have to use your discretion. I trust you to bring them back if you find them.'

Later that evening Powerscourt and Lady Lucy took a walk in the garden. Swallows were flying in formation round the terrace. A couple of sailing boats could be seen out in the bay.

'You will be careful, Francis, promise me,' said Lady Lucy. 'I'll be thinking of you all the time you're away.' Lady Lucy had never told her husband about the knot of anxiety that twisted its way round her stomach when he was off on a dangerous mission, a knot that sometimes seemed to her to grow into the size of a tennis ball.

'Of course I will,' said Powerscourt, putting his arm around her waist. 'You mustn't worry,' he went on, although he suspected she did worry about him all the time.

'Tell me, my love, why did you ask if there was a Butler lodge? Do you have suspicions about the people in the Butler house?'

'It's a hunch, Lucy, that's all. Sometimes I think the key to the whole affair is in Butler's Court, if only I could put my finger on it. But it's nothing more definite than that. I wish to God it was.'

Early the next morning the four horsemen, not of the Apocalypse but of the rescue mission, set out from Ormonde House. Lady Lucy was there to wave them off. Powerscourt and Fitzgerald both had rifles and binoculars and an enormous supply of the Ormonde House cook's finest chicken sandwiches along with some cheese and fruit. The two cavalrymen, Jones and Bradshaw from the County of Norfolk, looked as if they were equipped to survive out of doors for days at a time. Just ten minutes after they left Inspector Harkness rode up to the front door of Ormonde House. He left a large envelope addressed to Lord Francis Powerscourt. The rescue party made good time in the bright sunshine along the road to Louisburg, Croagh Patrick behind them looking especially friendly this morning, the sea and the islands on their right. In Louisburg, a miserable-looking place, Powerscourt thought, they turned left and took the road towards Leenane across the mountains. This was desolate country, barren hills all around them, not a single soul to be seen, the only sign of life the occasional sheep that wandered across the road and stared at the four riders as if they had no right to be there. Powerscourt reached into his breast pocket and pulled out grandfather Ormonde's map.

'For God's sake, Francis, will you give the thing here,' said Johnny Fitzgerald, holding out his hand. 'We want to find the bloody place this year, don't we? If you're in charge of the map, we'll end up going round in circles like these sheep here.'

Powerscourt handed it over. 'According to this,' said Johnny doubtfully, 'there's a wood with a little river going through it about a mile or so up the road. Inishturk House, the first of these places, is in the middle of that. Quite how we find a wood in this empty space I don't know, but that's what the man says.'

On their left now they could see that the ground had been cut open to reveal black sections where turf had recently been cut. Turf, Powerscourt remembered, the free fuel of the poor, used to heat their homes and cook their food, always taking a long time to dry out before it would burn properly. He remembered an aunt of his who had refused to have it in the house on the grounds that it was tainted with Catholicism, only good for the poor Papists of the west, not the respectable Protestants of Dublin who had the sense to burn proper English coal in their fires. After five minutes or so they came upon the wood, a sad affair now, the trees diseased or stunted, battalions of crows nesting in the upper branches. The little river was behind the house, gurgling its way towards the Atlantic. An overgrown path, heavy with brambles, led off to their right.

'The house must be down there, Francis,' said Johnny, folding up his map. 'What do we do now?'

'I think we stop and listen for a moment or two. If we don't hear any noises, you and I will go and have a look.'

The two cavalrymen stayed on guard at the entrance. Powerscourt and Fitzgerald tiptoed very slowly down the little track. Their feet seemed to be making a vast amount of noise. The brambles scratched their clothes. After a hundred yards Johnny tapped Powerscourt on the arm. Just visible ahead was the roof of a fairly large house. One or two of the slates seemed to have come off and one of the gutters was hanging down the side of the upper wall. Fifty yards further and the whole thing came into view. Powerscourt could just make out the words Inishturk House on a faded sign to the left of the front door. He made gestures with his hands to indicate that he was going to go round the left of the building and Johnny should take the right. He passed what had once been a tennis court or croquet lawn, a lopsided net full of holes still in place in the centre, but with only one post still standing. All the windows on the ground floor were enclosed by shutters that had once been white and were now a grubby grey. On the floor above there were curtains with holes in them. Towards the back of the house he came across a window that stood clear with no shutters. Spiders had been having a competition on the inside to see who could produce the most webs to stretch across the panes. He rubbed at the glass to get a better view. All he could see was a large dresser, looking in pretty good shape, he thought, and a stove where the cooking surfaces were thick with dust. At the back he met Johnny Fitzgerald, trying to rub the dirt off his hands.

'What the devil do you think you two are doing, creeping round this house like a couple of burglars!' An old man with a dog and a shotgun in his hands was addressing them from the front of an outhouse about thirty feet away. Powerscourt and Johnny both reached instantly for their right-hand pockets and then stopped. Was the old man the guard, the sentry for the people holding the hostages? Were they in the stables rather than the house? Was there another building further back where the captives lay?

'We might ask the same of you,' said Powerscourt pleasantly. 'Just what are you doing wandering round the place with a gun in your hands?'

'I'm no burglar,' said the old man, 'not like you two, though quite what you'd find to steal here I don't know. I'm the caretaker here, they pay me a little to keep an eye on the place.'

'Well, we work for Dennis Ormonde back at Ormonde House,' said Powerscourt. 'We're trying to find his wife. She's been kidnapped. All the empty houses round here are being inspected.'

'I heard about the missing wife, and that's a fact,' said the old man. 'Come to think of it now, you don't look very much like burglars.'

'Have you seen any strangers about the place,' asked Johnny, 'some people with a couple of women in tow?'

The old man spat neatly between his feet. 'Couple of women, did you say? Single woman would be a bloody miracle round here. Something went wrong with the breeding business in these parts. Males everywhere. Hardly any women. I think it's the peat in the water myself. One woman would be a bonus. Two would be a gift from God. No, I haven't seen anything suspicious at all now.'

Powerscourt wondered if he was telling the truth. The party could still be hidden round the back somewhere. 'We'll be on our way then, Mr . . .?' said Powerscourt.

'O'Connell's my name. Daniel O'Connell,' the old man replied. 'Named after the Liberator, you see.'

'Splendid, Mr O'Connell,' said Powerscourt, handing over five shillings as a mark of good faith and loyalty to the memory of the Liberator.

'Tell me this, Mr O'Connell,' said Johnny, 'are there any pubs round here at all?'

'Pubs? Pubs?' The old man laughed and spat on the ground once more. 'There's no more chance of finding a pub in this district than there is of finding a woman. Less, I should say. You'll have to go back to Louisburg or further on to Leenane to find a bloody pub and that's a fact.' The old man inspected Johnny carefully. 'I could sell you a bottle of home-made, if you follow me, for a half a crown, so I could.'

Johnny handed over the money. The old man disappeared into his shed and brought back an innocent-looking dark brown bottle that might once have contained beer. 'There you go,' he said. 'I've always found that if you drink enough of the bloody stuff you forget about the women altogether.'

The next house was a couple of miles further down the road. The sun had gone in and dark clouds were coming in from the sea, threatening rain later in the day. They were climbing deeper into the hills, the great empty wastes rolling across on either side of them. Johnny announced that Masons Lodge was just off the road and proposed that they should ride past it and then double back for an inspection. Rain was just beginning to fall as Powerscourt and Fitzgerald set off back down the road with Jones the cavalryman bringing up the rear. Bradshaw was in charge of the horses.

Masons Lodge was in much better repair than the previous one. Every tile was in place on the roof and the pale grey shutters on the ground floor looked as if they had been painted last year. This time Powerscourt and Fitzgerald checked the outbuildings first, stabling for four or five horses, a carriage house, and a large barn half filled with turf. Then they watched the house for ten minutes. Nobody came out to greet them. No old man with a dog and a gun tottered forth from any of the outbuildings. Powerscourt motioned his little band forward. He was trying to think what he would do if he was holding the two women. One person on permanent sentry duty watching the road. Once you see four people go past you go into emergency routine. Close all the shutters. Pull the curtains upstairs. Tell the women they will be shot if they speak a word. Put out the fires if there are any. Was that what had happened here? He checked the rubbish bins. They were empty. You'd need to be really careful to carry your rubbish to some outhouse, he thought. Still he wasn't sure.

Johnny Fitzgerald had found a window whose latch had not been fastened. He began to draw a venomous-looking instrument from a pocket in his jacket. Powerscourt shook his head. If they were wrong, a hand coming through a window could be a death sentence. Always in his mind's eye he included Lucy among the captives. He motioned to Johnny to be still for five minutes. They watched the house as if their lives depended on it. A couple of rooks came and settled on the roof. Then Powerscourt signalled to Johnny to watch his back. He walked very slowly up to one of the windows on the ground floor. The shutter was sealed tight. Then he tried another one. Sealed tight again. The third one had a shutter whose bolt was broken so it did not fit as tightly as it should to the window. Through a small sliver of light Powerscourt peered into the room. It was empty. He thought he could make out dust sheets spread over the furniture to keep it in good condition while the owners were away. He continued his tour and found that once again the kitchen window was in the clear. There was no sign of any living soul inside. Were they all upstairs? He glanced up and wondered if he could find a ladder in one of the stables. Then he made up his mind.

'Don't think there's anybody here, Johnny. Let's go.'

'Christ, Francis, your voice made me jump then, coming after we'd been quiet for so long.'

As a final thought Powerscourt strode up to the front door and rang the bell. They could hear it echoing round the empty house. As they set off again down the road, Johnny Fitzgerald munched on one of his chicken sandwiches and gave a further bulletin from his map. 'The road's going to go between the Sheffry Hills on our left, boys, and some mountains that seem to be called Mweelrea on our right. Bloody odd name, Mweelrea, might be a form of low life in one of Dickens's novels, forever skulking in the dark by the docks and the East End. I expect it means something in Irish, though God knows what.'

'Please, sir,' said Bradshaw, the trooper from Norfolk, 'it means bald hill with the smooth top, sir. In Irish, sir.'

'How the devil do you know that?' asked Johnny. 'Did they teach you Irish in your primary school in the Fens?'

'No, sir. I like climbing mountains, sir. I've got a book about them in the west of Ireland, sir. That's how I know what it means.'

'You should have been with us on Sunday,' said Johnny, whose memories of the climb were mixed. 'You could have

224

gone to the top of bloody Croagh Patrick in your bare feet if you'd wanted to. Bloody mountain.'

'I was on patrol, sir, or I would have done it.' Powerscourt thought they were absurdly young, these cavalrymen, Bradshaw very slim and wiry, Jones a more solid citizen with wavy brown hair.

'Anyway,' Johnny referred back to his map, 'after a couple of miles more of this barren stuff we come to a lake sitting between the hills. On the far side of that there's a little river and a very long drive leading down to Butler Lodge. Or so the map says, and grandfather Ormonde hasn't let us down yet.'

The rain stopped and the sun came out again. Looking behind him from a spur in the road Powerscourt could see Croagh Patrick in the distance. It must dominate the view of over half of County Mayo, he thought, popping into sight sometimes when you least expected it.

Now the road was twisting along the side of the lake. Small ripples crossed the surface of the water. On their left the hills were bathed in sunlight, the green and brown of the land as desolate as any they had passed that day. On the far side of the lake the hills were in shadow, dark, almost black. There was a sudden burst of noise. A lone horseman, riding very fast and going the other way, crashed through the middle of their party. When he saw them the young man tried to increase speed and put a hand over his face. Within a minute he was gone, racing away in the direction of Louisburg.

'Do you think that might have been a messenger, Francis?' said Johnny. 'Some news being sent back to enemy head-quarters? I don't think he was very pleased to see us, mind you. He didn't have the air about him of a man who was going to stop and pass the time of day.'

'Damn!' said Powerscourt. 'Don't you see, Johnny, that we're a kind of message? Four men, two of them cavalry troopers, out on this road at this time. You don't have to be Daniel O'Connell to work out that we are probably looking for the women. That young man will send a message back to where he came from when he can after he's delivered his first one. There's a party of four on the road, lads, and they're coming this way.'

'Let's get a move on,' said Johnny, 'we can't have far to go now.'

At one point the mountains on either side seemed to meet in the distance. It seemed impossible for the little road to pass through. There simply wouldn't be room. Then the perspective changed and a narrow slit opened up for the four horsemen.

Johnny consulted his map again. They were surrounded by tall trees now. 'In a hundred yards or so,' he said very quietly, 'there should be a drive or a road to the right. That leads to Butler Lodge.'

They had passed the end of the lake now. As they trotted up to the turning to the right Powerscourt motioned them forwards. After a couple of hundred yards they found a track on the left. After another hundred yards they came to a little clearing in the wood, great piles of logs all around them.

'I think we should make this our base for now,' said Powerscourt. 'We can't see the road but a man stationed halfway down could. Bradshaw, young man, how good is your eyesight?'

'It's good, sir,' said the young man. 'They test us for it before we enter the regiment. My captain lent me a telescope, sir, just for this expedition. He said it might be more useful to me than it would be to him on patrol round the streets of Westport.'

'Excellent,' said Powerscourt. 'Do you think you could climb further up this hill or mountain or whatever it is and see if you could catch a sight of this house for us?'

'Of course,' the young man replied and began digging about in his luggage for the telescope. He slung it round his neck and disappeared into the trees.

'Jones,' said Powerscourt, 'two things. Can you get back on your horse and ride down into Leenane? Book us four rooms in the Leenane Hotel. I think Dennis Ormonde may have sent word ahead of us. When you get back here I want you to go down the path until you can see the main road. In an ideal world you might be able to make your way through the trees to find a position where you can see the entrance too. Just watch what goes in and comes out, if anything.'

'What do I do if see anybody coming out, sir? Do I arrest them?'

'No, no, not yet,' said Powerscourt hastily, 'just keep watch for now. Johnny and I are going to see if we can get a sight of the place. We've got binoculars but the person with the best view is going to be young Bradshaw up the hill.'

Powerscourt and Fitzgerald made their way back down to the road and turned left away from the entrance. After a hundred yards or so the trees thinned out and they saw another lake in front of them. 'Look, Francis,' said Johnny, pulling his friend off the road. 'That lodge must be very near the edge of this damned lake. If we follow the reeds in the water to the end of the lake and round to the other side we should be able to get a sight of the place. We might have to go right round through one hundred and eighty degrees but it would be worth it, surely.'

'Let's go,' said Powerscourt.

It was just after five o'clock in the afternoon. There were about four hours of daylight left. The cross-country journey round the lake was not difficult. Occasionally the ground turned soft and boggy and the mud level crept slowly up their trousers. Powerscourt kept glancing back over his shoulder to check whether he could see Butler Lodge. If he could see it, somebody in Butler Lodge could see him. But most of the time all he could spot was the lake and the mountains behind it. Now they were further away he was struck by the steep rise of the mountain behind the house. It seemed to shoot up out of the lake at an angle of about sixty degrees. Then they came to another wood and Johnny Fitzgerald pulled out his glasses. He inched his way to a gap between the trees.

'Not yet, Francis,' he whispered, 'can't be far to go now.'

After another hundred yards he looked again. He motioned to Powerscourt to pull out his binoculars. The two men lay on the ground fiddling with their apertures. Through them, across the lake they could see the side of what must be Butler Lodge. It was a handsome Georgian building, well-proportioned, looking, Powerscourt thought, about the size of a decent hotel. There were great windows looking out over a well-kept lawn down to the lake. Behind it the mountains shot up towards the sky. And, coming in a regular flow from two of the chimneys, smoke was rising to mingle with the pure air of Connemara.

Cathal Rafferty spent three afternoons in a row watching the Head Gardener's Cottage. He didn't think Protestants would change their routines for the pilgrimage to Croagh Patrick. Nobody came. Nobody went. He wondered if the two young people were going earlier, or maybe later. He thought of playing truant from school one afternoon so he could begin his vigil around lunchtime, but decided that another beating from Brother Riordan and another summons for his parents to attend the school was too high a price to pay. One part of Father O'Donovan Brady's instructions he had successfully carried out. Through a cousin in the town who worked part time in the kitchens up at Butler's Court he had learned that the young man was called Johnpeter Kilross and that he was single, and the young woman was Alice Bracken, married, with her husband away in India or some other foreign part. Cathal felt the Father would be pleased with him. He did not know what appealed to the priest about this kind of information. He supposed he was curious, like himself. For young Cathal had been thinking a lot about what he had seen through the bedroom window. He couldn't make any sense of it. Why were they taking all their clothes off unless they were going to have a bath – he knew that the gentry went in for baths – and he hadn't seen any sign of one of those things.

So here he sat, in the last lesson of the Monday after Reek Sunday, listening to Brother Riordan droning on about the rivers of Ireland. Quite what use it would be to anybody,

228

acquiring knowledge of these waterways, Cathal had no idea. The bloody man was sticking a great map all over the blackboard now with these damned rivers marked on it. The Shannon, the wretched fellow was saying, pointing halfway down his map. Were they even now setting off for the Head Gardener's Cottage, ready for the fray? The Liffey, running into Dublin, serving Ireland's greatest city, Brother Riordan blathered on. Perhaps they were in the cottage already? Perhaps they were beginning to take their clothes off and he, Cathal, was not there to see it. The Lagan, which flows into the sea at Belfast Lough – did the man never stop talking, even for a minute? – and nourishes many of the great industries of that northern city. And now? Here Cathal's imagination failed him. Only reality would do, and reality was half an hour or more away when the last bell of the day would be rung and the boys would be free to leave.

Then Father Riordan did a terrible thing, quite against all the rules in Cathal's view. He took down his map, told his class to take out their exercise books, draw a map of Ireland in outline and fill in the routes of the three rivers they had been discussing. Not so, Cathal thought. You, Brother Riordan may have been discussing these rivers. We, the boys, have not. It was a low trick asking people to fill in a map of Ireland when they mightn't have been paying full attention. The Brother should have said at the start that the class would have to do an exercise. Then they would have tried to pay attention. Desperate glances were exchanged all around the room. Anybody whose map was deemed unsatisfactory, Brother Riordan declaimed from his desk, would have to stay behind after school.

Cathal opened his exercise book. Page after page contained harsh comments from Brother Riordan. 'Poor,' 'Very poor,' 'Why were you not paying attention in class? See me after school.' Cathal often felt that his progress through the place was marked out by the critical remarks in his exercise book and the lashings of the strap. It wasn't fair. He opened a new page and began to draw what he thought was an outline map of Ireland. It wasn't too bad, except that the south-western section, which should have been filled with the long inlets of Kerry and Dingle, had turned out completely round. And the north was square, completely square like the top of a biscuit box. The Shannon, on Cathal's page, began life at the top of the square and flowed into the sea south of Belfast. The Liffey entered the Atlantic Ocean north of Galway and the Lagan was a pathetic dribble which seemed to begin at Wicklow and terminate at Waterford. Cathal looked at his map. There was, he felt, something not quite right about it. And here was Brother Riordan, strap in hand, coming to inspect his work as most of the class filed out. The Christian Brother looked carefully at the map. His finger ran experimentally down his strap. His face turned red. 'Get out!' he shouted at Cathal. 'Get out of my sight! You're so stupid it's a waste of time trying to teach you! Get out now!' Cathal needed no second invitation. Before the Brother had finished his tirade he was out of the door and heading at full speed for the demesne.

When he reached the Head Gardener's Cottage he tiptoed round the front to look for any signs of life. All seemed quiet. Then he went on the detour that brought him behind the hedge close to the bedroom window. He thought he could hear sounds coming from inside. There was a gap in the curtain once again. Very slowly, so as not to draw attention to himself by a sudden movement, he rose to his full height and peeped in the window. Nobody had any clothes on. The pair of them were as naked as the day they were born. The man seemed to be lying on top of the girl and jolly uncomfortable it looked too. Cathal dropped down slowly behind his hedge. He thought the young man might have been looking out of the window. He ran back to Butler's Cross as fast as he could. After all, he reflected as he went, he had a good start. Anybody trying to follow him would have to put their clothes on first. Surely, he said to himself, this has to be worth another five shillings from Father O'Donovan Brady. Maybe even ten.

13

Powerscourt and Fitzgerald watched Butler Lodge for almost an hour. The smoke continued to pour regularly from the chimneys. The only human they saw was a young man who came out of the front door and returned five minutes later with a bundle of logs. There was no sign of any women. Powerscourt crept back into the wood and beckoned to his friend.

'What do you think, Johnny?'

Fitzgerald pulled his Daniel O'Connell memorial bottle out of a side pocket and took a tentative swig of the clear liquid. 'I think they're in there, Francis. I really do. I know we haven't seen any of the ladies, but I wouldn't let them out of the house if I could help it. Christ, this stuff has got a kick in the tail. At first sip you think it's lightly spiced water or something like that. Then it tries to knock your head off. It reminds me of some Polish vodka a fellow gave me once. It was so powerful the authorities banned its manufacture altogether in case it killed off half the population of Poland.'

'I agree with you, Johnny, I think they're here. I wish I knew what to do tomorrow, mind you. I hope that bloody hotel has got a telegraph.' Powerscourt rubbed his leg, stiff from lying by the edge of the water. 'Could you stay here for a while, and keep watch? I'm going back to see if young Bradshaw has spotted anything up that damned mountain. I'll see you in the hotel about nine o'clock.'

Powerscourt found himself wondering what the cuisine would be like in Butler Lodge. If the kidnappers were all young men of the age he had seen so far, the bill of fare might not be too elaborate. He speculated about how Lucy would survive on a regimen of ham and eggs for five days or so. He had to climb some way up the hill before he found Bradshaw. The young man had veered off a couple of hundred yards to the right to find a better view.

'Have a look for yourself, sir,' he grinned, handing over the instrument. Powerscourt now had the back view of the lodge. He saw part of the drive leading up to it and the woods stretching out on either side. On the far side of the lawn he thought he could see a small river, flowing into the lake. Two of the rooms on the first floor were visible, one of them with a window open to let in the evening sunshine, but his eyesight was not good enough to spot a person inside. He asked the young man if he had seen any female inhabitants of the house on the upper floor, but Bradshaw shook his head.

'Keep watching for half an hour or so and then make your way to the hotel,' Powerscourt said, patting the young man on the shoulder, and he set off to find his other watcher. Jones was so well hidden that Powerscourt walked past him twice before he realized Jones was there. 'Nobody's gone in, nobody's come out, nothing at all, sir,' he said. Powerscourt asked him to watch for another half an hour and then make his way to the Leenane Hotel. He wondered if they should take turns to watch the house through the night but he didn't see what purpose would be served. As far as he knew the kidnappers were not yet aware that there was a rescue mission at the gates.

Later that evening, after enormous helpings of Irish stew, Powerscourt outlined his plans for the following morning. Operations were to begin at first light. He and Johnny were going to watch the road leading from Leenane to Butler Lodge, at a safe distance from the house. Bradshaw and Jones were to maintain a similar vigil on the other side. Anybody who looked as if they were going to the place of captivity was to be seized, and any messages taken from them. Prisoners, Powerscourt explained, were to be taken to a secure room in the basement of the hotel which was fitted with a great many locks. It was, the hotel keeper explained, where they had concealed contraband in days gone by.

'I don't know,' Powerscourt said to Johnny after the two young men had gone to bed, 'how long it will be before those thieves know we are here. Not long, I shouldn't think. Even if we intercept all the messages coming from Westport or wherever enemy headquarters is, it's going to leak out of here somehow. I shouldn't be at all surprised if the hotel isn't supplying them with food. I've sent a message to the authorities saying I think we've found them. I've asked for reinforcements, twenty men, police or soldiers I don't care, but I don't suppose they'll get here until the afternoon at the earliest.'

Johnny took another swig of his stout. His bottle of Daniel O'Connell memorial liquid seemed to have been reserved for emergencies. 'Do you have a plan to get them out, Francis? It's going to be bloody difficult.'

'I'm just trying to make it up as we go along,' Powerscourt said, trying to sound more cheerful than he felt. 'I keep thinking about those two women and what they must be going through. I keep thinking about Lucy too, and how I should feel if she was locked up down there in Butler Lodge.'

As he went to sleep that night Powerscourt reminded himself that there were now two days left until the expiry of the deadline, two days to spring Mary Ormonde and her sister Winifred from the grasp of their captors. And while he knew that they only had value as long as they were alive, he was unsure how the terms of trade would change once the deadline had expired.

Low cloud lay over the mountains the following morning. The party of four rode past Killary Harbour, Ireland's only fjord, snaking its way back into the hills and forward to the sea. We may as well hang a banner round our necks saying rescue mission come to Butler Lodge, Powerscourt thought, as a few of the locals peered out of their windows to watch them go by. Whose side would these people be on? he wondered. He suspected the loyalty of the inhabitants would not be with them. An hour and a half after they had set out Jones and Bradshaw brought the first catch of the day, a defiant young man of about twenty years.

'This is the fellow we saw on the road yesterday, sir,' said Bradshaw, 'or at least it's the same horse. It had a little cross of white in the middle of its head. We've left the horse tied to a tree up the road.'

Powerscourt looked at the young man. Was this the enemy he had been wrestling with all these weeks, a lad scarcely more than twenty who had barely started shaving?

'What's your name?' he asked.

The young man said nothing.

'I said, what's your name?' Powerscourt repeated his question.

Once more the young man said nothing.

'We're not asking for anything other than your name.' Powerscourt asked his question for the third time. 'Remember that if you co-operate with us you will receive much better treatment than if you don't.'

'I'm not co-operating with you,' the lad suddenly found his voice, 'you're a bloody traitor, that's what you are. Doing the work of the occupying power like some posh Uncle Tom. You should be ashamed to call yourself Irish, so you should.'

With that he spat into the road right at Powerscourt's feet. 'Search his pockets,' said Powerscourt. 'I'm sure he was bringing a message to the people in the lodge.'

Jones found a battered envelope in his inside pocket. There was no name on it. Powerscourt ripped it open and laughed. There was indeed a message but it was written in Irish. None of the four could understand a word. It was, Powerscourt realized, even worse than India where they had often intercepted messages written in native languages. There the servants would translate for them. No doubt they could find some Gaelic speaker in Leenane but he would share, almost certainly, the political sentiments of the young man and might suffer from a temporary bout of amnesia. Powerscourt stuffed the letter into his back pocket. 'Take him to the basement down in Leenane, and see if you can find anything about him when you get him there.'

'Traitor!' shouted the young man as he was led away. 'You're a disgrace to your country!'

'If you don't shut up,' said Johnny Fitzgerald savagely, 'you won't get any food for the next two days, so keep your bloody mouth closed from now on!'

Powerscourt and Fitzgerald returned to their position behind a clump of trees overlooking the road from Butler Lodge to Leenane. 'If they send us some policemen,' Powerscourt said, 'rather than English soldiers from the garrison at Castlebar, one of them might speak Irish.'

'I doubt it,' said Fitzgerald gloomily. 'The kind of people who learn Irish round here aren't the kind of people who join the police force.'

They stopped talking. They heard a whistling sound coming up the road. As they stepped out from their cover to intercept the whistler they had a brief glimpse of another youth of about twenty years old wearing a bright green shirt. He turned and fled back down the road. Then they heard the voice.

'Lord Powerscourt! Johnny Fitzgerald! Stay right where you are! You are surrounded!'

They didn't wait to hear any more. They raced across the road and dived into the undergrowth. Both began wriggling down the hill towards the lake. Two shots followed them into the scrub. 'It's no good!' The voice sounded very self-assured. 'You are still surrounded. You'll only get yourselves killed.' Another shot ricocheted off a tree a couple of yards away.

Johnny Fitzgerald wrestled a gun out of his coat pocket and fired in the general direction of the voice. 'God save Ireland from people like you!' he shouted defiantly and was rewarded with a bullet that passed six feet over his head. Powerscourt was cursing himself. If his reinforcements arrived that afternoon he had been intending to surround the house and give the kidnappers an ultimatum. Now, while he and his men thought they were secretly observing the approach roads to and from Butler Lodge, the people inside had been observing them and claimed to have them encircled. Powerscourt doubted if the forces from the lodge had sufficient manpower to have himself and Johnny completely surrounded but he had no idea where the ring would be weakest. He and Johnny had been moving in the direction of the lodge. Now, he felt sure that would be the wrong course of action. However he deployed his forces, the voice would want to be able to bring his men home within the secure walls of Butler Lodge. Powerscourt pointed in the opposite direction, towards Leenane, and began half walking half crawling through the gorse and bracken.

'Give yourselves up now! Come out with your hands up!'

Johnny Fitzgerald fired off a little salvo of two shots and the voice kept its peace. Where were the horses? How far back had they tied them? A hundred yards? Two hundred yards? Certainly they were on the other side of the road. In a straight running contest Powerscourt felt sure they would be out-paced by these young men, if indeed they were all young, but on horseback they might get clean away. Did the voice know they had horses? Had they been apprehended? Were they even now safely accommodated in the Butler stables, ready to serve one side as loyally as they had the other? Powerscourt dismissed his speculations and hurried on through the under-growth. Suddenly he saw the first piece of good news they had received that morning. He could just see the horses fifty yards away by the trees. And lying on the ground beside them was Trooper Bradshaw, rifle at the ready, prepared to fire away at all and sundry. This could be turned to his advantage. Powerscourt and Johnny Fitzgerald shot out of the undergrowth and raced across the road. Then they positioned themselves behind the prostrate figure of Bradshaw. 'Fire!' shouted Powerscourt. Three shots rang out, aiming in an arc down the road. 'Fire!' Powerscourt shouted once more. 'Fire!' he gave the order a third time and then all three mounted their horses and fled back, heads down, in the direction of Leenane, Bradshaw turning round from time to time to send yet more covering fire in the direction of their enemies. They might not have been caught but they had been forced to flee the field. It was not, Powerscourt said to himself as they finally reached Leenane, the most auspicious start to their operations. There were thirty-two hours to go before the expiry of the deadline.

The cavalry came shortly after two o'clock in the afternoon. The man in charge was a Major Piers Arbuthnot-Leigh, a veteran of the Boer Wars. 'I've got twenty-three of my chaps with me, Powerscourt,' he informed his host, 'all well blooded in pursuit of the Boer, not so much experience against the native version over here.' He had one of those braying voices that can cut through the noises on the hunting field. His troops all looked young and fit.

Powerscourt led the Major and a detachment of his men off on a reconnaissance mission towards Butler Lodge. Arbuthnot-Leigh peered down at the house through a powerful pair of binoculars from a position hidden among the trees.

'I say, Powerscourt, that looks pretty damn fine to me.'

'The Lodge, do you mean?' asked Powerscourt.

'No, no, man, not the wretched lodge, haven't had time to look at that yet, the fishing, salmon, I should say in that river, and in that lake in front of the house. Some of the finest prospects I've seen since I was last at my place in Scotland. Bloody fine!'

'I think,' Powerscourt said acidly, 'that our business on this occasion is with the humans in the lodge rather than the fish in the river.'

237

'Quite so, quite so, another sort of bag altogether, what?' Arbuthnot-Leigh turned his binoculars in a slightly different direction and continued staring down the mountain. 'Didn't stint themselves when they built the bloody lodge, these Butlers, did they? Place is huge. Expect they went in for wild parties down there, compliant females of good proportions imported from Dublin, what? Let me see.' He swung his glasses round the exterior. 'With sixteen of my chaps I could have every door and window covered, bag any Paddy trying to make a hasty getaway to the pub or the bog or wherever they come from, seven more as a mobile reserve. Trouble is, don't have to tell you this, Powerscourt, what about the fillies inside? Bloody difficult with the two fillies, if you ask me.'

Powerscourt realized that the Major might not be as dense as he sounded.

'What's the plan?' Arbuthnot-Leigh went on. 'Would you like my chaps to put on a show of force? Ten of them ride down the hill, rifles in hand, like something out of the Wild West and shoot a few rounds in the air? Give the Paddies something to think about, what?'

'They might panic,' Powerscourt said rather sadly, 'and think this is a full frontal attack. Then they might shoot the women.'

'Pity, that,' said the Major. 'We could launch an attack in stages, like a proper siege. Begin firing at the little green people from the top of the hill, work our way down, surround the building, knock on the front door and offer them surrender terms, if there are any of them left, what do you say?'

'Same objection as before,' said Powerscourt.

'Fillies?' said Arbuthnot-Leigh.

'Fillies,' nodded Powerscourt.

'Bit like real life, don't you think, Powerscourt, damned women causing a lot of trouble, whichever way you look at it.'

The Major looked round at the six men under his command, all staring down the hill at Butler Lodge. 'Tell you what,

Powerscourt, what do you think of this as a suggestion? These six chaps of mine here, all damned good at tracking the enemy, creeping about in the bushes, not making a sound, that sort of thing. Bit like the fox in the hen coop, only know he's been there after he's gone, if you see what I mean. We need to know how many Paddies are on guard duty in that damned place. If I leave these fellows and our sergeant here in charge, they can try to come up with an estimate of the number of the other team. Are we playing cricket or rugby or tennis, what? Be damned useful to know that. What do you say?'

'Good idea,' said Powerscourt, 'it would be very helpful to know how many of the rogues there are.'

'Good show,' said the Major, and moved off to confer with his sergeant. A few moments later he was back. 'Operation's going to start in a few moments,' he announced. 'I'm going to stay with them for a while, Powerscourt, so I'll see you back at the hotel. Must remember to organize nosebag and sleeping bag for my chaps. I'm completely hopeless at all this crawling about in the undergrowth business. My ghillies tell me I make more noise than a herd of cattle but I'll see my chaps started. Bloody poachers in an earlier life, three or four of them, the buggers would crawl through the jaws of hell if they thought there was game on the far side.'

Powerscourt thought he was dreaming when he walked into the reception area of the Leenane Hotel. He thought he saw Lady Lucy sitting in a corner by the window drinking tea. He thought the phantom figure waved at him. Then the phantom spoke.

'Francis, my love, how very good to see you. You're looking rather dishevelled, I must say. I've changed our room upstairs, you know. We've got a huge place now and I've moved some of the furniture and I've filled as much of it with flowers as I could. Would you like some of this tea? It's rather good.'

Powerscourt held the ghostly apparition in his arms and realized from the strength of the embrace that this was no apparition but the wife of his bosom and the mother of his children.

'Lucy,' he said, looking into her face, 'what on earth are you doing here? How did you arrive? How long are you staying?' Part of his brain said he should add 'Are you out of your mind?' to his list of questions but he resisted.

'One thing at a time, Francis,' she said brightly. 'I was talking to that nice Dennis Ormonde yesterday and he was wondering how his wife and her sister were going to get back from a place as remote as this. That Chief Constable person popped in to tell us you'd found them, you see. And Mr Ormonde said he wanted them back as quickly as possible and that he would send his coachman and one of his finest carriages once he heard they were free. He's absolutely convinced, you see, Francis, that you'll secure their release. It's quite touching, really. So I said why didn't he send it today, with me in it, as the ladies would welcome another female to talk to on the way back. So here I am!'

'So you are,' said her husband, unsure of his feelings. For while he was delighted to see Lucy, he didn't like her to be as close to the point of danger as she was now. Still less did he like to have her on the spot when he thought of what he was contemplating for the morrow. 'Is there any news of the paintings, Lucy? Any word of any more people being taken? Orangemen still behaving themselves, are they?'

'There was one rumour, Francis, about that man Connolly, the one who sent you away.'

'What did it say?'

'Well, Mr Ormonde told me the rumour was that all his paintings had been returned intact. No Christian Brothers replacing the ancestors, none of that. But then he tracked the rumour down and he found it came from a man who travels the country selling horses. Mr Ormonde didn't think he was reliable, if you see what I mean.'

Powerscourt frowned. 'Don't see why it should be doubtful just because it comes from a man who sells horses, Lucy. Half the bloody country spend their time buying and selling horses, for heaven's sake. Don't see why he should be any less reliable than any of the rest of the inhabitants.'

'Ah,' said Lady Lucy, 'but Mr Ormonde had actually bought a horse from this fellow once. He said the animal was so lame it could scarcely trot the length of his drive. And by the time he discovered that, the man had taken his money and disappeared off in the direction of Ballinrobe.'

'If it's true,' said Powerscourt, resisting with difficulty the urge to walk up and down the little reception area, 'then Connolly must have paid up, in whatever currency the thieves were dealing in. His deadline must have arrived too. How very interesting. Any other news, Lucy?'

'Only this, Francis: Young James has disappeared from Butler's Court. Everybody is very worried about him. They think Young James might have been taken hostage too.'

'Don't think he's close enough to the family to warrant a kidnapping. Distant cousin, isn't he? How very curious.'

'If you think you might have found the women, Francis, does that mean that you are closer to solving the mystery?'

Powerscourt laughed bitterly. 'I don't think I'm ever going to get to the bottom of this one, my love.'

Their conversation was interrupted by a great shout from the doorway. 'Lady Lucy! By God, here you are in Leenane! This calls for a celebration!' Johnny Fitzgerald embraced Lady Lucy and disappeared briefly to order some refreshments. When he came back he looked cheerful. 'They've got some Pomerol in this place, who would have thought such a thing. I've ordered a couple of bottles in case the first one's a fluke if you follow me. Now then, Lady Lucy, was it the scenery that brought you here to this place, or have you other intentions?'

She explained that she had come in the carriage that was to bring the Ormonde women home, that her role was to provide company and conversation on their long journey back.

'Three women cooped up in one of those posh carriages,' said Johnny, 'probably be able to talk non-stop all the way to Dublin. Seriously though, Francis, I have some news. When you were off showing our aristocratic friend the lodge I went off on a great loop round that lake in front of the house. I went behind the hill, if you follow me, and then I crept down through the wood opposite Butler Lodge. Amazing view you have up there.' Johnny sounded like a recent convert to the beauties of nature. 'The lake in front of you, the lodge sitting on its lawn like a doll's house, that bloody great hill shooting up behind it. Anyway, what do you think I saw? Two ladies walking about the lawn escorted by one young man of about twenty, I should think.'

'Good God!' said Powerscourt. 'So we were right. They are there.'

'How did they look, Johnny?' asked Lady Lucy. 'Did they seem to have been maltreated in any way? Did they look pale?'

'They looked fine to me,' said Johnny. 'They were laughing with their young guard at one point as a matter of fact.'

'Were they now,' said Powerscourt, remembering somebody in South Africa telling him how captives often grew close to their captors. Maybe this happened in Butler Lodge too. Maybe the ladies were just looking after their own interests by charming the young men.

There was another arrival at their table. The Major was introduced to Lady Lucy and gazed at the Pomerol in astonishment. 'Good God! Did you bring that stuff with you, Johnny?' he asked.

'No,' said Johnny cheerfully, 'there's a heap of it here in the cellars. It's in pretty good shape. You'd better try some.'

'Now then, Lady Powerscourt, Powerscourt, Johnny,' the Major was making his report, 'I bring news from the front. I stayed at my post rather longer than I intended, I must confess. Thought I might catch a sight of some of the damn fish the lodge was built for but no luck. Wrong time of year.

My chaps went through their full routine of crawling about on their bellies, shinning up trees without making a noise, the usual tricks. They report a total bag of five or maybe six, all aged about twenty or so, all carrying out various tasks inside the house. My most expert wallah, fellow by the name of Healey, claimed he heard one of the villains complaining he'd been made to do the cooking three days in a row. Didn't hear the reply.'

Powerscourt told the Major about the sighting of the two women on the lawn.

'Fillies in the paddock, eh? That's damned good work. Now then, Powerscourt, your show here, of course, do you have a plan for tomorrow?'

Powerscourt did indeed have a plan taking shape in his mind for tomorrow but he was not going to mention it at this point or in this company. 'Yes and no,' he said, 'Sorry for such an Irish reply. Do you have any suggestions, Major?'

'Well,' said the Major, rubbing his hand together, 'I can't see a way round the women and that's a fact. My natural instinct, as taught by those clever chappies in the Staff College, would be to infiltrate the place. Trooper at every window, rifles drawn, pack of seven or eight lined up at the front door. Stand and deliver. Under normal circumstances that should loosen their bowels all right, the damned Paddies, all come out with their hands up demanding a glass of Guinness, that sort of thing. But it wouldn't work with the fillies inside unable to flee the coop.'

'Do you think they'll try to make a run for it, Francis, now they know we're here?'

'Would you, Johnny?' Powerscourt replied.

'I think I would,' said Johnny, emptying another glass of rich red wine. 'The longer they stay, the more heavily the odds are stacked against them.'

'I'm not sure,' said the Major, screwing an elaborate monocle into his right eye for a closer inspection of the wine bottle's label, 'that it makes any difference if you have fifty fellows camped outside their front door or five hundred. As long as they have the fillies they hold the ace of trumps.'

'I wonder if they're waiting for something,' said Powerscourt, 'the day of the deadline perhaps. I forgot to tell you, I haven't been able to find a single person here who speaks Irish and could translate that message we intercepted. There's a bloody menu in Irish, for God's sake, at least I presume it's Irish. Hardly likely to be written in Bulgarian out here. There's a helpful page written in what I presume is Irish with drawings of boats and horses which I imagine is some sort of guide to the local attractions, waterborne excursions up Killary Harbour, best places to hide a couple of Protestant women, that sort of thing, but not a soul will admit to being able to translate a few sentences.'

'I think we should put a guard on the place tonight, Powerscourt,' said the Major, eager for action. 'They might well try to make a run for it. Fox's last stand, what?'

'Please do that, try to keep the villains awake, might dull their wits tomorrow,' said Powerscourt, and the Major marched off.

'Do you think they know they've had it, Francis,' said Johnny Fitzgerald, 'that the game is up?'

'I don't think that's how they see it,' Powerscourt replied, 'not yet at any rate. If Ormonde gives in to the blackmail tomorrow, then they've won. They leave the ladies behind and try to escape. In one sense, you see, our arrival has made the ladies' position much safer, though I don't know if they have worked that out yet. If they had killed them before we came and made good their escape, how could we have linked these young men to the deaths? Very difficult, if not impossible. But now they know they're surrounded. If they kill the ladies they'll be caught. Then they'll hang. Even a Mayo jury would have to convict them. It'd be committing suicide. You're not going to advance the sacred cause of Irish freedom by murdering a couple of harmless Protestant women. So why kill them? I can't see any advantage at all, only the gallows waiting for you after a short spell in Castlebar Jail.'

'Would you like to put that to the test by trying to storm the place tomorrow?' Lady Lucy sounded very serious.

'I would not,' replied her husband.

'I'm just going to sort something out in our room, Francis,' said Lady Lucy, 'and maybe I should dress for dinner. I'm sure they always do here in Leenane. I'll see you both in a little while.'

Powerscourt took his friend out into the little garden that looked over the water. A stone nymph was blowing water on to the roses. A couple of fishing boats were coming in to land at the little jetty a hundred yards to their left. Powerscourt leaned over the wall and told Johnny of his plan. Johnny looked at him closely and took a great gulp of his Pomerol. 'If I'd known you were going to say something like that, Francis, I'd have brought the whole bloody bottle with me.' Johnny looked out towards the mountains, brilliant with sunlight. 'Well,' he said, 'of course I'll do it. Wouldn't do it for anybody else, mind you. Have you told Lady Lucy?'

'I'm not going to tell her this evening. It can wait until the morning.'

'One other thing, Francis,' said Johnny, looking at the tiny harbour, 'don't you think our friend the Major should mount a guard here too? The buggers could escape in a boat and nobody would know where they'd gone.'

After dinner that evening Powerscourt outlined part of his plan. 'First thing in the morning, Major,' he began, 'could you send a couple of chaps up to the front door with a white flag. They're to deliver this letter and wait for the reply.'

Lady Lucy was looking anxious. 'And what does the letter say, Francis?'

Powerscourt pulled a sheet of the hotel's finest notepaper from his pocket. 'It says,' he began to read, '"Lord Francis Powerscourt and Johnny Fitzgerald propose to call on your leaders at eleven o'clock this morning. They will not be armed. They suggest that a truce should be in operation from the receipt of this letter until the end of the meeting. Please give your reply to the man who brought this letter. Yours, etc, Powerscourt."'

'Spot of chinwag never did any harm in these circumstances,' said the Major. 'Mind you, the way these Paddies talk you could be in there till dinner time at the earliest.'

'Expect we'll be lectured about our desertion of the Irish cause for the King's shilling,' said Johnny gloomily. 'There's no fanatic as fanatical as a young fanatic, especially if they've been educated by the bloody Christian Brothers.'

'And what are you going to say to them, Francis?' Lady Lucy sensed there was something her husband was not telling her.

'I'm going to try to point out to them,' said Powerscourt, 'that their position is hopeless. They're outnumbered and outgunned for a start. In any fight they're going to lose. I don't think I'll put it quite like this, but they have a choice between a bullet at Butler Lodge and the rope on the gallows. If they give themselves up peacefully, we will ensure that the authorities treat their cases with sympathy.'

'I don't think Dennis Ormonde would see it in quite those terms, Francis,' said Johnny. 'If he had his way, they'd be stripped and tied to those punishment triangles at the Octagon in Westport and flogged until their blood was running down the street.'

'Well, he's not here,' said Powerscourt realistically. 'We are.'

'I've been thinking about the problem with the fillies,' said the Major, looking suspiciously at a large glass of Irish whiskey. 'Do you think we could mount a raid in the night? Get a couple of chaps inside, shouldn't be difficult, find the ladies, whisk them out. Blast the rest of them to hell first thing in the morning.'

'It's worth considering,' Powerscourt replied diplomatically. 'Once we know the results of the meeting we will have to review all the options left. That would certainly be one of them.'

There was a full moon shining over Killary Harbour and the little garden of the hotel. Powerscourt and Lady Lucy were leaning on the wall, looking at the water, dark grey, almost black. A couple of fishing boats were pulled up on the shingle near the quay. The mountains to their right were dark and menacing. Somewhere up there, Powerscourt said to himself, the two ladies were spending another night in dangerous captivity. Did they know there was a rescue mission just five short miles away, eager to devise a plan that would restore their liberty?

'How do you think they'll be bearing up, Mrs Ormonde and her sister, Lucy?'

'I expect they'll be managing, anybody who can cope with Dennis Ormonde should be well equipped to handle anything.'

Powerscourt laughed.

'I'm more worried about you, to be honest, Francis,' Lady Lucy went on.

'Do you think you'll be all right, going to confer with these people?'

'I'm sure I've talked to worse in my time,' said her husband, wondering if now was the moment to give her the whole picture. He decided against it. As he fell asleep that night, realizing that the deadline, so long awaited, was about to arrive, he wondered if this was the last night he would ever spend with Lucy sleeping by his side.

14

Lord Francis Powerscourt delayed his breakfast as long as he could. He spent a great deal of time shaving. He pottered about in the bedroom for so long that Lady Lucy was quite stern with him, saying he should come along to breakfast now and stop daydreaming like one of the children. The Major interrupted them during the kippers. 'Had to borrow a hotel sheet for the flag of truce, Powerscourt. Told the hotel fellow we'd make it up to him. Expect we'll be charged some giant bill in recompense. My chaps are just about to totter off now. Back soon, I hope. Do you think these peasant people will recognize a flag of truce? Just thought I'd ask. Tough luck on my men if they don't. Never mind. Tally ho!' With that, Arbuthnot-Leigh strode off to the stables to supervise the troopers' departure. Powerscourt and Lady Lucy had moved on to the toast and marmalade now. Suddenly Powerscourt could bear the deception no longer.

'Lucy, my love, there's something I've got to tell you. I meant to tell you yesterday but my courage failed me.'

As he told her Powerscourt thought he could see the tears forming in her eyes, then she fought them back. Her family, the Hamiltons, he remembered, had been soldiers for generations. Her first husband had been a soldier, lost with Gordon at Khartoum. Now, he knew, she was thinking about losing another one. 'I'll be perfectly safe,' said Powerscourt. 'It may never happen. I'll come back. I promise you.'

He took her hands in his. She was sobbing now. 'Just let me go to our room alone for a few minutes, Francis. I'll be back. Just a few minutes.'

She took the key from the table and went off. Powerscourt wondered, not for the first time, if he was doing the right thing. Johnny Fitzgerald appeared, took one look at his friend and fled. The waiters began clearing the breakfast things away. Powerscourt looked at his watch. The two troopers should be at the house by now. He wondered if the two ladies would be able to watch them come, messengers from another world, a world they had left behind.

Lady Lucy came back, looking more cheerful. Powerscourt marvelled at her courage. It was nearly half past nine.

'Powerscourt, Lady Powerscourt!' The Major was back, slightly out of breath. 'Good news. Our lads are back. The meeting is on for eleven o'clock.'

'What happened exactly?' said Powerscourt.

'Might have been an exchange of invitations to afternoon tea in Tunbridge Wells by the sound of it,' said the Major cheerfully. 'My chaps ride up, waving white flags vigorously as if they had just relieved Mafeking. Red-headed Paddy answers the doorbell. Disappears off to find Head Man Paddy or maybe Head Boy Paddy – why are they all so bloody young, for Christ's sake – and comes back inside a minute. "That's fine," he says. "Truce. Ceasefire." Then he closes the door. That's it.'

'Good,' said Powerscourt, part of whose brain had been hoping the meeting would be rejected. He had told the army man the details of his plan the night before. 'If, for whatever reason,' he had said finally, 'I don't come out and the kidnappers do, follow them, follow them all the way home or wherever they are going to. Unobtrusively, of course, but all the way.'

'Of course,' the Major had replied. 'Let's pray it doesn't come to that.'

'Look, Lucy,' Powerscourt turned to his wife, 'there's nearly an hour before I have to go. Why don't we take the hotel boat out on the water? It's a lovely morning.'

Five minutes later Powerscourt was stroking the little boat up the dark waters of Killary Harbour. Lady Lucy was wearing an enormous hat to shade her from the sun. She thought you could hide all sorts of things under a wide brim. 'Is Butler Lodge up there, Francis?' she said, pointing towards the mountains on the right.

'It is, my love,' said Powerscourt, 'it's on the far side of that mountain with an unpronounceable name, Mweelrea I think it is. It's got its own lake in the front and a river that's supposed to be full of fish.'

'Is it pretty?' said Lady Lucy. Powerscourt knew she was trying to form a picture in her mind of the site where she might lose another husband, another one lost not to the fogs of war but in the mists of civil strife.

'I can't say that I have been inspecting it with the eyes of a tourist,' said Powerscourt, 'but it would be very beautiful if it was being used properly.'

Lady Lucy fell silent. A couple of fishermen shouted good morning at them from a hundred yards away. A herd of cows was making a leisurely progress towards Leenane, mooing loudly as they went. Powerscourt turned the boat round and began the return journey towards the hotel.

'Francis,' she said at last, 'you will be careful, won't you. You see, I've just worked it out, we've been married for thirteen years now, it's scarcely credible, is it, and I love you as much now as I did on the day I married you. More even. I couldn't bear it to end. Not here. Not now. Not like this. I want to be with you till the end, Francis, as I hope you'll be there for me. Please remember that I love you so much. Take care. Take very great care. I shall be thinking of you and praying for you every moment of every day until you come back.' She held his hand and kissed it. 'Now, I won't say any more. Semper Fidelis, Francis.'

Semper Fidelis, forever faithful, was a sort of motto, or talisman, between the two of them. It had first been mentioned to Powerscourt by a young man who killed himself in an earlier investigation when he first met Lady Lucy. It had followed them through their lives ever since, a punctuation point on their journey through love and time.

'Semper Fidelis, Lucy,' said Powerscourt gravely. Out there on the still waters of Killary Harbour, under the wide Connemara sky, he wished he did not have to continue his investigation, to embark on his hazardous mission to Butler Lodge. He wanted to be somewhere else, to stay with Lucy and row out to the mouth of the great fjord. Then he thought of the Ormonde family, of husbands whose wives had been abducted, of the Butlers and the Moores whose very identity was under threat from forces they neither knew nor understood. He kissed Lady Lucy after he handed her out of the boat and set out to prepare for his ordeal.

Half an hour later he and Johnny Fitzgerald were standing by the front door of Butler Lodge. They knew that the hills around the house concealed the Major's troops, rifles at the ready in case things went wrong.

'Your round or mine, Francis?' said Johnny, looking at the bell.

'Mine, I think,' said Powerscourt and pushed it firmly. A clear peal could be heard inside. Powerscourt wondered if the two ladies had heard it. They heard footsteps. The door opened to reveal the redhead who had answered it earlier that day. Perhaps he was acting as butler for the duration.

'Come in, please,' said the young man politely. 'Would you wait here for a moment now?'

Powerscourt looked around the hall. The floor was marble, you could find marble everywhere in Connemara, he remembered. A couple of hurling sticks were resting in an umbrella stand. There was a table to the left of the door. A pair of fish in glass cases looked across at them from the opposite wall. Powerscourt suddenly remembered the fascination of stuffed creatures for the Anglo-Irish. The birds of the air and the beasts of the field were all fair game for the taxidermists, owls and badgers, voles and squirrels, pike and salmon and trout, otters and owls, bream and perch, all ended up stuck on the walls of the Anglo-Irish in their glass coffins. Powerscourt had been to houses in his youth where they were so numerous that he would not have been surprised to see a stuffed human staring out at him from hall or passageway. Privately he suspected that the gentry identified with these dead creatures. Were they not preserved too, pickled in their past and their history until they had little relevance to the modern world?

'Come this way, please,' the redhead interrupted his reverie and showed them into a little sitting room on the left of the hall. There were bookcases here from floor to ceiling and a great window that looked out over the lake. The redhead motioned them to a sofa and indicated they were to sit down.

'Posh dentist's waiting room, Francis?' said Johnny.

'Doctor's, I think,' said Powerscourt. 'No magazines at all here.'

Two slim young men of average height came in through the other door and sat down on the chairs opposite the sofa. They were both wearing dark trousers and green shirts, some kind of private uniform, Powerscourt suspected. One had black hair. The other one was so fair he was almost blond.

'Which of you is Powerscourt?' asked the black-haired one.

'I am he,' said Powerscourt.

'Then you must be Johnny Fitzgerald.'

'The same,' Johnny nodded gravely, wondering if he should mention his ancestor. Not yet, he thought, not yet, maybe later.

'Traitors, the pair of ye,' muttered the blond.

'You can call me Seamus,' said the black-haired young man, making it abundantly clear that whatever he was called, it was not Seamus, and that he had no intention of revealing his true identity. 'And he's Mick,' he added, pointing to his companion. 'Now then,' he continued, 'it was youse who asked for this meeting. What do you have to say for yourselves?'

'Principally this,' said Powerscourt, 'I think it's time you considered your own position. You have pulled off a most daring piece of kidnapping. But for our good fortune in finding you here, everything would have gone your way.'

'We were betrayed,' said Mick viciously, 'another bloody traitor in the ranks. Well, he'll get what's coming to him, youse mark my words.'

Powerscourt did not bother to tell the blond that they had not been betrayed. Dissension in the ranks might work to his, Powerscourt's, advantage.

'But now,' he continued, 'think of it. You are surrounded here. Over twenty cavalrymen are on patrol in the woods. More are expected this afternoon. I do not know how many of you there are in this house but I do not believe you number more than six or seven at the most. And with the greatest possible respect, these men outside are more experienced in battle than you are. They fought in the Boer War after all.'

Even as he said it he knew mention of the Boer War was a mistake.

'Imperialist racket!' said the blond in anger. 'Whole war just so the City of London could get its hands on the South African diamonds! Women and children herded into concentration camps to die! Bloody disgrace!'

'Then think of the position of the two women you have seized. I presume they are still alive, they certainly were yesterday afternoon. If anything were to happen to them now, the authorities would know who to charge.'

Powerscourt sensed as he spoke that he was not making much impression. Rational argument might not be the best way to reach these young men. He felt that they rejoiced in what they saw as their emotional and moral superiority. They probably thought he was old. He suddenly remembered the appeal of a glorious death fighting in Ireland's cause against overwhelming odds. He wondered if they would prefer death to a prison sentence, a blood sacrifice in the cause of Ireland's freedom. That, he felt, might be their most likely and the most dangerous option. He ploughed on.

253

'If anything were to happen to the women, if they were to be killed for instance, it would go very badly for you. I am certain you would hang. If you give them up, and give yourselves up, the authorities would, I am sure, look at your cases sympathetically.'

He felt even more like a schoolteacher who has lost all rapport with his pupils. He felt that he was probably making things worse.

'Is that what you came here to say?' Mick was almost on his feet. 'Hand ourselves over to the authorities, as you call them? We'd rather die.'

'I don't think you do want that really,' said Johnny Fitzgerald affably. 'You're young, for heaven's sake. You've got your whole life in front of you. Think of all the wine and women and song waiting for you in the years ahead. Give yourselves a chance, lads.'

'The wine and the women and the song may appeal to people like you from the Big Houses,' said Seamus. 'We have a higher cause, the rights of the Irish people to their freedom, the rights of the Irish people to own the land of Ireland, the rights of the Irish people to govern themselves in their own way.'

'Fair enough,' said Johnny, 'but you won't be able to advance that cause very much if you're in a wooden box. By the time you become a hero and a martyr in Ireland you don't know about it, it's too late, you've gone to join your ancestors in the cemetery up on the hill.'

'What about the two of you?' said Seamus. 'Intelligent men, well educated, plenty of talent. And you're Irish. Why do you run around doing the bidding of those people in the Big Houses? Why are you trying to support the crumbling Protestant Ascendancy? For I tell you, I am certain that I will see it disappear in my lifetime. The struggle may be long, it may be bloody, or the whole pack of them may fall in like a pack of cards, but their day is passing. I'm sure of it. Why support all that if you're Irish? Wolfe Tone rose above his

Protestant heritage to advance the cause of liberty in Ireland. Charles Stewart Parnell was a bloody Protestant landlord in County Wicklow, for Christ's sake, and he nearly brought us Home Rule. Why can't you join the right side?'

'Perhaps we're too old,' said Powerscourt, nodding at Johnny by his side on the sofa, 'and perhaps you're too young. I was brought up into one world, it may be passing now, I grant you, but it was the world my parents lived in. It was the only one I knew. You are growing up in a different world. Each fresh generation embraces a cause, certain with all the certainty of the young that their mission is just and all earlier missions misguided and wrong. As they grow older, that generation is surprised in its turn by the fact that their children espouse different causes, take up another mission. Their creed, their beliefs that they held so strongly in their youth are now ancient history. They've been washed away, like sandcastles on a beach. So it goes on, down the generations, like the rising and the setting of the sun or the passing of the seasons. I don't apologize for my beliefs. I don't condemn you for yours. All I would remind you is that you're going to be better placed to advance them if you're alive rather than if you're dead.'

Powerscourt suddenly realized that he had another problem. Pride, the pride of the young, the pride that would not let them lose face. He remembered himself as a young man, willing to argue on long after he had lost because he did not want to back down. He suspected it would be almost impossible for Seamus to agree to his requests. He would only show himself to be a leader without courage, a general who surrendered without a fight. He tried to find a way to ease his path but he couldn't do it. There were no inducements he could think of offering.

He tried all the same. 'Perhaps you'd like to take a break from our conversation and confer with your colleagues elsewhere in the house? Give yourselves a bit of time to think? As long as you go on holding those two women, I think your position is very difficult. If you start a fight here and they are injured or killed you're in a desperate state, Seamus, you really are.'

It was Mick who replied. 'Weasel words!' he cried. 'Time to think? You people have had centuries to think and you haven't come up with anything better for Ireland than croquet on the lawn and hunting six days a week in the winter. You're a bloody disgrace, the pair of you!'

Seamus was boxed in. He could not, Powerscourt knew, give way now in face of the defiance of his friend. Powerscourt felt sick inside.

'I have made my mind up,' said Seamus finally with an air of slight reluctance as if he might have behaved differently on his own. 'Thank you for coming. Your offer is rejected. One of my men will escort you to the front door. The truce will end half an hour from now.'

This is not the best of times, Powerscourt said to himself, it is the worst of times. It is not the season of Light, it is the season of Darkness. Suddenly he remembered reading Charles Dickens's *A Tale of Two Cities* at the age of fourteen, lying on the grass in the summer at Powerscourt House, oblivious to the noises of his sisters, and weeping uncontrollably at the end.

'Perhaps I could make another proposal,' he said firmly.

'And what is that?' replied Seamus.

'Take no bloody notice,' cried Mick, 'it'll just be another piece of Protestant trickery!'

'My proposal, quite simply, is this. You let the two ladies go. They must have suffered enough by now. Johnny and I replace them as your hostages. You lose nothing. You still hold a couple of hostages of some value to the authorities here and in England.'

'Just let me make sure I understand you, Lord Powerscourt, I find it hard to comprehend. We let the women go. You volunteer to replace them. Is that right?'

'It is.'

'Well, I'll be damned,' said Seamus. 'You're sure about that?'

'Quite sure,' said Powerscourt.

'This time I do need to talk to the others,' said Seamus, 'I think I may have to put it to the vote. Wait here. Don't try anything stupid.'

So, Powerscourt said to himself, their fate was to be decided by half a dozen twenty-year-olds, their heads probably filled with the nationalist rhetoric of the Christian Brothers and the wild songs of rebel Ireland. He took comfort in one thought. He did not think that these young men would have felt happy holding female hostages. They might have rejected orthodox religion or they might have not, but the Marian cult was probably stronger in Ireland than in any other country in Europe. They had been looking at statues of the Virgin Mary by the roadside, paintings of her on the walls of convent and schoolroom, huge representations with halo and sanctity on the altars of their churches, further icons no doubt displayed in their own homes since before they could walk. She was everywhere. Reverence for her was instilled into every generation. The young men would probably be relieved to be rid of the two women. Then he realized to his horror what else the Marian cult meant. Seamus and Mick would have fewer scruples killing men. Especially Protestant men.

Johnny strolled over to the window and stared out at the lake. Powerscourt took a close interest in a stuffed badger standing to attention in another glass case. They did not speak. Suddenly Powerscourt remembered the system of hand signals they had learnt in India, a private language without words. With their backs to the door so they could not be observed, they ran through a bewildering variety of gestures involving hands and feet, fingers in a variety of combinations, slight movements of the feet. Fifteen minutes passed, then twenty. Their revision class was complete. Johnny tried to work out how many of the Major's troopers he could see, hiding in the woods. Powerscourt wondered if indeed it was a far far better thing they were doing now than they had ever done, if it might be a far far better rest they were going to than they had ever known. Half an hour had gone now. Powerscourt found himself wondering how the Major would behave if their offer were accepted. He hoped he would be calm in making his plans and ruthless in carrying them out. Forty minutes. Powerscourt found himself thinking of Lady Lucy in her wide-brimmed hat out on Killary Harbour so very very long ago now. He wondered what she was doing. The door opened to reveal Seamus and the redhead who had opened the door.

'Very well,' said Seamus, 'we accept your offer. We will exchange the two of you for the wife of Ormonde and her sister. Please listen carefully while I outline the other arrangements. When we have finished our conversation, you, Powerscourt, and my colleague here will go outside under another flag of truce and explain the position to your friends skulking in the bushes out there.

'In half an hour the two ladies will be escorted out of the house to the top of the drive. What happens to them from then on is up to your companions. Half an hour after that four of my colleagues will leave and set out towards their homes. They are not to be arrested. I am sure they will be followed but it is an essential part of this bargain that they are allowed home to see their families. That great carriage that came here the other day is to be brought here. You and I and Mick and Mr Fitzgerald here are going on a journey in it. The coachman can drive us. Any attempt to intercept us, to attack the vehicle, to impede its progress in any way and you will both be shot. Do I make myself clear?'

'Perfectly clear,' said Powerscourt, 'and I am grateful for your decision about the two women.' Not quite so keen on the decision about the two of us, he said to himself, but he kept his counsel.

'Could I ask you about one aspect of your proposal, which may be hard to sell to the people outside?'

'You may.'

'Your four colleagues who are to be allowed to go home in the first instance. Do you think the people outside will feel able to permit that?'

'I have two things to say to that, Lord Powerscourt,' said the one called Seamus. 'The first is that they were not involved in the actual kidnap in any way. Mick and I did all that. Those four joined us here to help look after the women. If you care to ask the women before they go how they have been treated, I am sure they will agree they have been well looked after. Only yesterday Ormonde's wife was telling one of the lads that he must come and see them when all this is over. The two women have never seen either Mick or myself, not properly. We wore balaclavas when we seized them and we have kept out of sight here. So what would the charge be? Not kidnapping because they weren't involved. Holding people against their will? They weren't the ones making the decisions. Harsh treatment of poor women in captivity? Hardly likely when the women might testify in their defence. Indeed the two ladies have already said they would appear in court on behalf of the four young men if things turned out that way. And the second thing is quite simple. If the people out there don't agree, then the whole deal is off. The women stay as our hostages. You two could go.'

'That's very clear,' said Powerscourt with just a trace of bitterness in his voice. The redhead appeared again wrapping the tattered remains of what had once been a white shirt round a hurling stick The flag of truce was prepared. As Powerscourt and the young man stepped outside the front door, they could hear a faint rustling in the undergrowth ahead. A couple of crows flew past to explore the lake and the desolate hills beyond. The sun was shining. Major Arbuthnot-Leigh was wearing civilian clothes today, a tweed suit that might have seen stalking duty in the past and a hat that looked as though it could once have belonged to Davy Crockett. Powerscourt outlined the plans.

'Not a particularly good hand, what?' was the Major's first reaction.

'It could be worse,' said Powerscourt. 'All things considered, I think we should accept the offer.'

'Are you sure? You don't think the Paddies have got too many aces?'

'I don't think we have any choice,' said Powerscourt. 'At least one of those young men would rather die than make a deal of any kind. Blood sacrifice, that sort of thing.'

'Bloody fool,' said the Major. 'Well then, I'll get the carriage brought up. We've got a couple of spare horses here for the ladies to go to Leenane first of all. Damned pity their carriage has been hijacked – just like they were, I suppose, what? Never mind. The ladies coming out to the top of the drive in half an hour, you say? Do you think we should have a sort of honour guard to welcome the fillies home? Troopers lined up, rifles in the air, serenade of shots to greet them?'

'No,' said Powerscourt and turned back to the house. He didn't see Mrs Ormonde and her sister go. He didn't see the carriage arrive or the four young men depart, two to a horse and moving out on the Louisburg road. Nor did he see a group of six horsemen following them after a five-minute interval.

'Now then,' said Seamus, carrying a rough pack over his shoulder, 'we're ready to go. Let me tell you the rules. Mick and I have a pistol each, so we do. Any hostile move from either of you and you'll be shot. You're not to converse on the way. Any attempt at a rescue mission from the authorities and you will be shot. When we have reached our destination safely and unimpeded, you will be allowed to go. Is that clear?'

Powerscourt had a sudden vision of tens of carriages like this one sweeping up to Butler Lodge in the days of its glory, visitors come for the fishing or for parties or for balls, the music wafting out over the waters of the lake and disturbing the fish in the river. As he was ushered into the red velvet interior he saw himself being shown into a different sort of vehicle, the rough cart that had carried Sydney Carton to the guillotine, the doomed aristocrats packed close together, hair shaved off, a last journey across the streets of Paris to the mocking gibes of Madame Defarge and the awful finality of the guillotine. The worst of times.

He and Johnny were on one side of the conveyance, the two young men opposite. The Ormonde coachman, warned no doubt to be on his best behaviour, perched in his place on the top and muttered to his horses as they cantered slowly down the drive. The windows were tightly closed. Powerscourt had a slight sense of being in a luxurious coffin on its way to the grave. The two young men were conversing in Irish. Powerscourt tried to work out which direction they were going in as they reached the top of the drive and turned into the main road. If they went uphill they would be heading for Louisburg and Westport. If they went downhill they were going towards Leenane and Lady Lucy.

Five minutes after the coach departed, a group of horsemen, the hooves of their animals muffled, trotted slowly down the gravel track. As the road joined the main thoroughfare to Westport it passed a small waterfall, much favoured by local watercolourists and picnickers. After a few more miles along the side of Killary Harbour it crossed a bridge into Leenane. There the road forked, the right hand turning into a winding road that skirted the coast to Clifden, the left hand climbing up into the hills towards Maam Cross. Had Powerscourt or Fitzgerald been able to look out, they would have seen a female figure, standing back from the road to watch the coach and see where it went. The figure still had a hat with a very wide brim on top of her curls, and it made no move at all. She waited some more and received grave salutes from Major Arbuthnot-Leigh and his troopers as they passed. At least I know where Francis is going, Lady Lucy thought to herself, he's going into the mountains. She had learnt the news of the exchange of the hostages when the man came for the carriage. She hurried back to the hotel and stared for a long time at a map on the dining-room wall. She could not see anywhere inland where the young men would want to go. They could catch a boat at Oughterard on Lough Corrib and escape detection for a couple of days on one of the islands. But she didn't think these young men would be happy with that. Then she realized. She knew where Francis must be going. If you went on past Maum, over Teernakill Bridge and across the mountains to Maam Cross, on past Lough Bofin to Oughterard, down through Roscahill and Moycullen, you would come to Galway. Galway had many amenities, Lady Lucy thought, though she would not have classed herself as an expert. But she felt sure there were boats, plenty of boats. There might not be boats that sailed straight across the Atlantic from there, but there would be boats that could take you, discreetly, no doubt, to places where you could sail to America, Cork probably, the young men stowed away in some obscure cabin, or pressed into service as waiters in the restaurant. Galway – Lady Lucy suddenly remembered the song:

> If you ever go across the sea to Ireland
> Then maybe at the closing of your day,
> You will sit and watch the moon rise over Claddagh
> And see the sun go down on Galway Bay.

She didn't like the bit about the closing of your day very much. She prayed that Francis would find a way to escape long before he could see the sun go down on Galway Bay.

Powerscourt knew that the road would be bumpy whichever direction they went. He was sure that they had gone down the hill towards Leenane but which fork in the road they had taken he could not tell. There were occasional shrieks from the wild birds and loud bleatings from the sheep whose tenure of the road was so rudely interrupted by the carriage. He and Johnny could only wait.

He began piecing together in his mind random thoughts that might have a bearing on his investigation. They were like fragments of unsolved code in his brain, or strings of numbers that could mean so much to a mathematician, looping and circling round each other, spiralling away on a journey of digits that could lead to chaos or infinity. What had the young man called Seamus said that morning? He talked about the right of the Irish people to own the land of Ireland. Somebody else had talked about land, Connolly, that was it, the very first man with the vanished paintings he had seen, who had virtually thrown him out of the house. Hunger, Connolly had said, there's a hunger for land so strong out there that on market days you could practically smell it. He thought of the tall, impossibly slim figure of Young James at Butler's Court, saying very firmly that he never played cards for money. He thought of Uncle Peter's account of Parnell's funeral and the honour guard of young men from the Gaelic Athletic Association with their hurling sticks who accompanied the dead hero all the way from the railway station around the city to his final resting place at Glasnevin Cemetery. Why, only that morning he had gone out to meet the Major under a home-made flag of truce that consisted of a battered shirt wrapped round a hurling stick. He thought of Johnny Fitzgerald's drinking companion, the defrocked Christian Brother, and his account of how to seize power in Ireland. He thought of the young man opposite, Mick, saying he'd rather die than capitulate. Suddenly he remembered a different young man singing 'The Minstrel Boy' in the concert party at Butler's Court, Thomas Moore's lament for his friends slain in the '98 Rebellion. In the ranks of death you'll find him. Maybe, Powerscourt thought, defeat had to be celebrated because victory never came. Maybe Ireland's glory compensated for failure, the failure of every rising, the failure of every land campaign to dislodge the English from Dublin Castle. When the men with the pints of porter in their hands belted forth the words of 'The West's Awake' or 'A Nation Once Again', they could, briefly, believe in Ireland's glory. For, in truth, the west was not awake, the nation was as far away as ever. The songs took over from the truth, a whole nation incapable of distinguishing dream from reality. A nation once again, his history tutor at Cambridge had once asked acidly, when was the again? How far back did you have to go, to the High Kings of Tara or Finn McCool or the Firbolgs or the Tuatha De Danann, creatures all well dressed and clad in Irish myth? It was all nonsense, his tutor said, in a dusty room in Cambridge where reason thought it had long ago defeated the myths of glory.

He raised his eyes briefly for his first eye contact with their jailers. They were no longer conversing in Irish. The one called Mick was reading a slim volume extracted from his pocket. Somehow Powerscourt doubted if it was *Patriotic Ballads of England*. Seamus was staring at the floor. They were beginning to look a little drowsy – it was now quite hot in the coach with no fresh air coming in and the Major's men had kept them awake for most of the night – but they were not asleep. This was not the spring of hope, it was much closer to the winter of despair. The worst of times.

Lady Lucy had a strange conversation with the liberated ladies. The Major had escorted the freed fillies, let out into the paddock, as he mentally referred to them, into the main sitting room of the hotel and brought a bottle of champagne. Then he fled, saying he could not bear the thought of not being with Powerscourt and Johnny Fitzgerald in their time of need. They had, they assured Lucy, been well treated, apart from the food which was bad except for the days when a very slight young man made them his grandmother's Irish stew. The first time, said Mary Ormonde, it was excellent, the second time it was acceptable, the third time it was revolting, the young man seemed to have forgotten some of the ingredients, like the meat and the potatoes. They absolutely refused to go back to Westport until Lady Lucy's ordeal was over. If Ormonde wants to come and see his own, his wife declared, he could get on his horse and ride here.

As she and her sister departed to their rooms to rest after their ordeal, Lady Lucy wandered out into the little garden on the edge of the water. The battered nymph was still spouting erratic bursts of water on to the flowers. A red rose beside it was losing its leaves, perfect red petals drifting down to lie on the ground, the colour of blood. Lady Lucy thought of Francis rowing her out there that very morning, the time passing impossibly quickly. She remembered the look of complete pleasure on his face as the two of them lay back in their gondola in Venice several years before and were transported up the Grand Canal to the art gallery, the Accademia. She remembered the ecstasy on his face as he stood, transfixed, in front of Giovanni Bellini's altarpiece of the Madonna and Child with Saints in a side chapel of the Franciscan church there, the Frari. He had quoted Henry James to her, she remembered, nothing in Venice is more perfect than this. She tried to blot out the memories of Francis and the children but they kept coming in like the tide. Francis bowling for hour after hour to Thomas in their makeshift nets at Rokesley Hall, teaching his little boy some of the strokes of cricket. Francis out riding with Olivia, trekking all afternoon through the paths of Rockingham Forest before they returned, exhausted, for an enormous tea. Francis chasing the twins round and round the dining-room table and up the stairs in Markham Square. She began to pray. Our Father which art in heaven, Hallowed be thy name. The words of the pilgrims came back to her as they walked round and round the first station on the Holy Mountain. Hail Mary, full of grace, the Lord is with thee, blessed art thou amongst women. Lady Lucy could see no reason why it couldn't be a Protestant prayer as well. She found it comforting, even the last words, pray for us sinners now and in the hour of our death, Amen. There between the hills and the mountains with Killary Harbour in front of her, Lady Lucy said seven Our Fathers and seven Hail Marys as the faithful had done at the stations on Croagh Patrick. She called it the Leenane Station. She offered it up to her husband, wherever he was.

Johnny Fitzgerald had fallen asleep. Occasional low snores broke the silence in the red velvet carriage. The one called Seamus was drifting away, sitting up suddenly every now and then to remind himself that he was on duty. The one called Mick had the book open on his lap but it was some time since he had turned a page. Powerscourt too drifted in and out of sleep. The heat was making him feel uncomfortable and he longed for a glass of water. He wondered when they planned to change the horses, these present ones couldn't last much longer. Then the road surface seemed to improve. The great lurches that had marked their progress so far were, for now, a thing of the past. Powerscourt could only guess where they were. His sense of geography, never very accurate at the best of times, had abandoned him altogether. All he could tell from the regular bleatings of the sheep was that they were somewhere up in the mountains. He wondered what a shepherd would have made of this strange vehicle, doors closed, no sign of life inside, rattling along near Maam Cross.

After ten minutes on the good road, Powerscourt decided it was time to move. The two young men were dozing or asleep. He nudged Johnny Fitzgerald very gently in the ribs. They both arched back very slowly on their seats to gain maximum purchase. Then, in unison, they drew their knees up to their chins and they launched themselves as hard as they could, boots first, into the crotches of their enemies. Powerscourt followed this up with an enormous punch with his right hand into Seamus's cheek. Out of the corner of his eye he could see Johnny doing the same thing. Seamus fell to his right. Powerscourt reached out his left hand and opened the door. He grabbed the young man by the top of his shirt and the seat of his trousers and propelled him towards the door. Two vigorous kicks were enough to send him into the outside world. Powerscourt closed the door and turned to administer a final kick to the departing figure of Mick on the other side. Johnny closed the door. They had left the season of Darkness behind them.

'By God, that was good, Johnny,' said Powerscourt. 'Give it ten seconds or so and go tell the coachman to keep going for another four hundred yards as fast as he can. Then we can review the situation.'

No pistol shots followed them up the road. Powerscourt rubbed at the knuckles of his right hand. They would be sore for some time from the punch that felled the one called Seamus. Johnny clambered out and took up his position beside the coachman. Now they heard shots behind them, three fired at brief intervals first, and then two volleys of about eight or nine rounds at a time. A scream echoed round the mountains and its noise and the gunshots sent the sheep scurrying for whatever cover they could find. Johnny stopped the coach. Powerscourt had picked up the book Mick had been reading. It had fallen on the floor at his departure. *The Wind Among the Reeds*, Fisher Unwin, London, 1899, the title page said. W.B. Yeats. And him, Powerscourt thought, a Protestant poet from Sligo, a man of the Anglo-Irish, read by such an ardent and uncompromising Catholic nationalist as the young man called Mick.

They could hear horses coming at speed. 'Powerscourt,' shouted the Major, 'are the two of you all right?'

'Never better,' Powerscourt replied cheerfully, 'bit thirsty, that's all. Catering department non-existent among these nationalists. Thirst must be meant to be good for you. What was that firing a moment ago?'

'Young fool,' said the Major, 'the one you must have thrown out on the left-hand side of the road, thought he'd take us on. Must have seen he was outnumbered about twelve to one. Maybe the natives never learn to count out here. Anyway he loosed off a few, couldn't shoot straight incidentally, so we had to reply. He's gone,' the Major looked round at the desolate landscape for a moment, 'to the great peat bog in the sky.'

'I think he always preferred death and glory, that one,' said Powerscourt. 'Nothing finer than giving your life in Ireland's cause. What about the other fellow? He told us his name was Seamus but he's really called something else. I think he was the brains of the enterprise.'

The Major laughed. 'Brains, was he? Well, he's not looking too clever at the moment. Doubled up, he is, whichever of you two kicked him in his private parts did for him good and proper. Pity we've only got one in the bag, but better than nothing.'

Powerscourt thanked the Major for his swift appearance on the scene. 'We were right behind you all the time,' said the military man. 'Had a bet on what time you'd break out, actually, Powerscourt.' He looked at his watch. 'Damn it, I think I may have won. I said you'd see off the little green people five minutes ago. Good show, what?'

Johnny made a special request. 'Does anybody have anything to drink in this godforsaken place?'

The Major looked at his troops. 'I am blind,' he said, 'I cannot see a thing.'

Half a bottle of John Jameson was handed over to Johnny Fitzgerald who took an enormous swig. 'Thank you,' he said, 'thank you so much. By God, that tastes good.'

'I say,' said the Major, 'I'm forgetting my duties. We've got a couple of spare nags with us. Thought you might like to totter back on your own. Leave all this mess to us,' he waved his hand at the corpse on one side of the road and the doubled-up figure on the other, 'we'll clear it up.'

As Powerscourt and Fitzgerald began the ride back to Leenane a vicious hiss pursued them down the road. 'Traitors, bloody traitors to Ireland, both of you.' The face of the one called Seamus was doubled up with pain as he spoke but there was no doubting his sincerity. One of the troopers kicked him hard on the side of the head.

'Shut up, you piece of Fenian shit,' said the trooper. 'From now on you can learn some bloody manners. Don't speak, unless you're spoken to first.'

Lady Lucy Powerscourt was still at her prayer station in the garden late that afternoon. She watched the street that led up to the Maum road. Twice in the last half-hour she had heard horses' hooves and human voices but it was only a farmhand and a man come in to buy some tea from the store. Still she waited. She said more prayers. She looked at some fishermen unloading their catch and a man from the hotel kitchens obviously haggling about prices. A priest went by on his bicycle and smiled at Lady Lucy. Three small boys trotted past her kicking at a stone in the road. Then she heard laughter that she thought might be Johnny Fitzgerald's. Johnny had a very distinctive laugh. She wondered if she should run down the road to meet them, if it was them. Something told her not to. If her prayers had been answered, then it was only proper to wait in that place for her deliverance. She heard Francis's voice. The two of them were hidden temporarily by a bend in the road. Then she saw them, rather dirty, rather dishevelled as if they had been in a fight, but not wounded or hurt. She pulled out a handkerchief and waved it furiously.

'Francis!' she shouted. 'Francis!'

One of the horses broke into a gallop. 'Lucy, my love! Lucy!'

Then Francis was beside her, holding her tight in his arms. 'My own love,' she said, 'you've come back! Thank God! Oh, thank God!'

Half an hour later Lord Francis Powerscourt was lying in

his bath. Lady Lucy was plying him with champagne as she listened to his adventures.

'There's to be a great dinner tonight, Francis,' she told him. 'To celebrate the release of the ladies and your escape. The Major organized it before he left. He said he might sing a song, the Major.'

'God save Ireland,' said Powerscourt, 'if the Major sings a song.' He wondered if a wake had been organized too in case he and Johnny had not returned but he didn't like to ask.

'And Dennis Ormonde is coming from Ormonde House,' Lucy went on. 'He'll be so pleased to see his wife again.'

Lady Lucy left to attend to some matters in the bedroom. There was still some time before dinner. Powerscourt rose slowly from the waves and draped himself in a series of towels. He thought of *A Tale of Two Cities* again. It is a far better thing I do now, he said to himself with a wicked grin, than I have ever done before. He advanced into the bedroom and kissed Lady Lucy firmly on the lips.

'Francis,' she said, and then in a different tone altogether, 'Francis!' She moved to close the curtains. The worst of times were over.

PART FOUR

TREAD SOFTLY

The Minstrel Boy to the war is gone,
In the ranks of death you'll find him;
His father's sword he has girded on,
And his wild harp slung behind him.

Thomas Moore

15

Father O'Donovan Brady had made Cathal Rafferty tell his story of the strange goings-on in the Head Gardener's Cottage three times. He made copious notes. He wrote the names of the two participants in a small black book in large capital letters. He knew he would return to reread this material over and over again in the days ahead. He gave Cathal ten shillings with instructions to keep watching. Cathal, after all, was carrying out the work of the Lord. Then Father Brady poured himself a generous glass of John Powers and sat down to plan his campaign.

Central to this strategy was the Protestant parson, the Reverend Giles Cooper Walker, the man who had read the prayers at the concert party at Butler's Court. Ordinary Protestants, the Father had been taught at theological college, were little better than heretics. Protestant clergymen were worse, much worse. The priest wondered if he should consult with his bishop about the move he was planning, actually calling on the rector and, much more difficult, being polite to him, something he knew he would find much more taxing. Nevertheless, he told himself, unusual times need unusual measures. Our Lord would never have succeeded in His mission here on earth if He had carried on according to the ancient principles of the Pharisees. It was time to seize the hour and tackle the vicar in his own quarters. So it was that at eleven o'clock a few days after Cathal's visit Father

O'Donovan Brady was knocking on the front door of the Protestant rectory, a handsome early Georgian house with roses blooming in the small front garden.

The two men were as different in appearance as they were in religion. The Catholic was short and round. The Protestant was tall and very thin, as if he didn't have enough to eat. Father O'Donovan Brady was ministered to by his striking twenty-three-year-old housekeeper. The Reverend Cooper Walker was ministered to by Sarah, his wife of fifteen years, who might not have had the bloom of youth of the housekeeper but was still a handsome woman, regularly admired by other clergy at diocesan conferences. The Catholic had no children. The Protestant had three, two boys and a girl, who were only a trouble to him when he contemplated the expense of educating them and bringing them out into society. Father Brady had never left Ireland, indeed he had only once visited the north where his visit accidentally coincided with the parades of Orangemen on 12 July, where hatred of Catholics was a central feature of the proceedings, and left him determined never to return to such a place again. The Reverend Cooper Walker had been attached to a parish in Oxford for a time – he had been a noted theologian in his youth, and his professors had tried with all their might to persuade him into an academic career, but Cooper Walker turned them down, saying his version of God called him to the service of real people in what he naively called the real world rather than that of the saints and sinners of the second and third centuries AD. Among the rich of North Oxford and the poor of Jericho the Reverend Cooper Walker had seen the pain caused by unhappy marriages, the damage that could be done by a love that went wrong or alighted in the wrong place. Father O'Donovan Brady's God resembled Moses on top of the mountain, tablets in hand, entrusted by a fierce and unforgiving God with the salvation of his people, however harsh the punishment. The Reverend Cooper Walker's God resembled Christ feeding the five thousand

and saying blessed are the meek for they shall inherit the earth.

The two men had never met before. Father Brady struck the Reverend Cooper Walker as rather coarse, with a crude but effective faith. The Reverend Cooper Walker struck Father O'Donovan Brady as a Protestant intellectual – both words of extreme condemnation in his book and, taken together, virtually the same as heretical – who would be prepared to argue for tolerance rather than rigour, for forgiveness rather than punishment, for turning the other cheek rather than inflicting the wrath of a jealous God. The Catholic Church in Ireland, Father Brady felt, would never have reached the position of authority and power it held today if it had had truck with doubt or uncertainty.

In spite of their differences the meeting went well, the two men of God circling each other like boxers at the start of a fight, each reluctant to enter into what might be dangerous territory. Sarah Cooper Walker fed them with tea and some of her special scones that always did well at church fêtes and harvest festivals. Surprisingly quickly, they agreed on a plan of campaign to be put into action the following Sunday. Their methods might be different, but the message would be the same. As Father Brady walked back to his house, past the queue at Mulcahy and Sons, Grocery and Bar, and the drinkers already assembling outside MacSwiggin's, he felt he had scored a notable victory. He had brought the Protestants, even if only for one occasion, into the orbit of the true faith. The Reverend Cooper Walker had too subtle a mind to think in terms of victory or defeat. He thought of the words of the Bible and felt he had little choice.

Mass in the Church of Our Lady of Sorrows in Butler's Cross began at eleven o'clock. Father O'Donovan Brady had processed up the nave and genuflected. The Father kissed the altar and the congregation rose.

'*In nomine patris et filii et spiritus sancti.* In the name of the Father and the Son and the Holy Spirit.' Father Brady felt oddly nervous as he began his service.

'Amen' said his congregation.

'*Gratia Domini nostri Iesu Christi et caritas Dei, et communicatio Sancti Spiritus sit cum omnibus vobis.* The grace of our Lord Jesus Christ and the love of God and the fellowship of the Holy Spirit be with you all.'

'*Et cum spiritu tuo,* and also with you,' came the response.

There was always a large congregation at Mass at eleven o'clock on Sunday mornings. At the front Pronsias Mulcahy sat in his pew with his wife at his side. She was a formidable woman in her late forties, Mrs Mulcahy, dressed as ever on Sundays in a dark blue suit that had once been fashionable for a slightly younger clientele. Sylvia Butler and Young James had spotted her once months before wearing this same suit on her way to the service. Sylvia had nudged James in the ribs and pointed to the grocer's wife. 'Would you say that was mutton dressed as lamb, James?' Young James carried out a lightning inspection. 'No, I would not,' he had replied quickly, 'I should say that was mutton dressed as mutton.'

Behind the Mulcahys was a platoon of Delaneys, the solicitors, and the Delaney wives, all growing over time to look remarkably like their husbands. For the only time in the week MacSwiggin's Hotel and Bar was closed while the owner and his wife heard the word of the Lord. O'Riordan the bookmaker and his wife were there in their Sunday best, bets forbidden on the Sabbath. The agricultural machinery man Horkan was there in a new suit that was slightly too large for him, and his wife in a spectacular hat. Behind the Catholic aristocracy was a great throng of servants from Butler's Court, farmers, blacksmiths, farriers, stable hands, horse dealers and small tenant farmers, most of them working land that belonged to Richard Butler in the Big House. All the children had been sent to the Church Hall for instruction in Catechism and Commandments.

> 'There is a green hill far away,
> Without a city wall,
> Where the dear Lord was crucified
> Who died to save us all.'

The Protestant congregation in the Church of St Michael and All Angels were singing a hymn written by one of their very own. The green hill far away was the work of a Mrs Frances Alexander whose husband went on to become Archbishop of Armagh and Primate of all Ireland. The few, the very few in the church that day gave it their best.

> 'There was no other good enough
> To pay the price of sin,
> He only could unlock the gate
> Of heaven and let us in.'

The church had been built in times when the Protestant population of Butler's Cross was much greater. If Father Brady had been faced with so few worshippers in Our Lady of Sorrows he would have thought that a catastrophe must have struck, a second famine come to decimate his flock. Richard Butler was there, of course, Sylvia by his side. Several other members of his family and friends come to visit managed to fill up a couple of pews. Jolingeter Kilross was there, feeling rather hung over, and Alice Bracken in a summer dress. There were some more Protestants from outlying districts who travelled miles to come and show the flag at Sunday Matins. Behind them stretched row after row of empty pews, dust gathering on the wood, the prayer books unopened, the hymn books abandoned.

> 'O dearly dearly has he loved,
> And we must love him too,
> And trust in his redeeming blood
> And try his works to do.'

277

At the back of the Catholic church the young men were trying to attract the attention of the girls who looked so unattainable in their Sunday best. Father Brady moved on.

'*Kyrie eleison,*' he intoned, Lord have mercy.
'*Kyrie eleison,*' replied the congregation.
'*Christe eleison,*' continued the Father, Christ have mercy.
'*Christe eleison,*' came the response.
'*Kyrie eleison,*' boomed Father Brady.
'*Kyrie eleison,*' said his parishioners.

The Reverend Cooper Walker had resolved to read the first lesson himself. He had changed the reading, which was meant to come from the Book of Isaiah, to one from the Book of Samuel.

'Second Book of Samuel, Chapter Eleven,' he began. The lectern was magnificent with a great gold eagle on the top. '"And it came to pass in an eveningtide, that David arose from his bed and walked upon the roof of the king's house: and from the roof he saw a woman washing herself; and the woman was very beautiful to look upon.

'"And David sent and inquired after this woman. And one said, Is not this Bathsheba, the wife of Uriah the Hittite?

'"And David sent messengers, and took her; and she came in unto him and he lay with her".' The Reverend Cooper Walker looked directly at Johnpeter Kilross for a fraction of a second. The young man's face had turned bright red. The vicar carried on. '"And she returned to her house. And the woman conceived and sent and told David, I am with child."'

Maybe it was the colour of Kilross's face or Alice Bracken hiding her head in her hands, but a current of excitement was running through the tiny congregation now. What was going on? Did the vicar know something they didn't? The Reverend Cooper Walker carried on, outlining the device used by David to have Uriah the Hittite killed in battle so Bathsheba might become his wife. The vicar paused before the final words of the chapter: '"But the thing that David had done displeased the Lord."'

At twenty minutes past eleven Father O'Donovan Brady climbed the steps to his pulpit. He stared at the young people whispering to each other at the back of the church. He paused until there was complete silence in the Church of Our Lady of Sorrows.

'The Devil is abroad in Butler's Cross,' he thundered to his congregation. 'On our peaceful streets, in our community of Christian souls, Satan is doing his work. Let me remind you of the seventh of God's commandments, handed down to Moses on the mountain for the guidance and instruction of his people.' Father Brady paused again. 'Thou shalt not commit adultery.' He repeated it in case some of his flock had not heard, this time with a heavy emphasis on 'not'. 'Thou shalt not commit adultery. Do not get me wrong, my friends.' The priest had noticed some members of his congregation looking decidedly sheepish and wondered if Cathal Rafferty might not have been better employed on his snooping missions closer to home. Still, there could always be other fishing expeditions later on. Sin was sin wherever it was to be found. 'These are not members of our congregation here, devout Catholic souls, who are breaking the laws of God. It is two Protestants who are staining the pure air of Butler's Cross. Even Protestants claim to believe in the Ten Commandments. They too subscribe to Thou shalt not commit adultery. But what do we find? We find two of their number doing the Devil's work in broad daylight.'

At twenty-two minutes past eleven the Reverend Cooper Walker climbed into his pulpit. This was going to be one of the most difficult sermons he had preached in his entire ministry.

279

'In the first lesson this morning,' he began, 'we heard the story of David and his lust for Bathsheba. We also heard at the end how God was displeased by what David had done. For he had broken not one, but two, of God's commandments. Thou shalt not kill, by his plotting to have Uriah the Hittite, Bathsheba's husband, killed in battle. And he had broken the Seventh Commandment, Thou shalt not commit adultery.' The vicar paused and looked round his little band of worshippers. Most of them looked bemused. But not all of them.

'I have not come here this morning to name names,' the vicar went on. 'I do not think that would be helpful. But I ask each and every one of you here this morning to look into your hearts and ask yourselves if you have broken the Seventh Commandment. It should not be a difficult question to answer.'

'Johnpeter Kilross! Alice Bracken! These are the sinners who reside in Butler's Court and who have broken God's holy law and commandments!' Father O'Donovan Brady was in full flow, thumping the side of his pulpit. 'These are the people, one a single man, the other a married woman with an absent husband, who have committed adultery in a cottage on the Butler estate! So great is their contempt for their Saviour, they didn't even close the curtains properly! These are the wretches who have brought disgrace unto themselves and despair into their families! I bring you this message this morning. If you work in Butler's Court, think before you serve them their food. Think before you are asked to wash their garments, befouled and besmirched no doubt with the sins they have committed. If you are asked to clean their quarters think rather if they would not be better left in the squalor they deserve. If you are a shopkeeper in the town think before serving them any sustenance that might give them strength to continue their sordid debauchery. Their behaviour might be fitting in the souks of Cairo or the brothels of Bangkok: it is not fitting here, in St Patrick's island.' Father O'Donovan Brady stopped briefly. 'This is the message of God's teaching. Abide by God's commandments. Keep God's word. Let not sin intrude into innocent lives. Let us work together to banish Satan from our midst for ever. *In nomine patris et filii et spiritus sancti*, Amen.'

'We are few, here in this land, we who belong to the Church of Ireland,' the vicar went on. 'I would not say a happy few, not today, nor would I refer to us this morning as a band of brothers. But the fact that we are few, our numbers small, means that our responsibilities are great. We must be seen to lead virtuous lives. Our Catholic colleagues may think we are in the wrong Church but they must not think we are not decent Christian souls, intent on leading as good a life as we can in this world in the hope of finding salvation in the next. When people in our faith commit adultery, they not only demean themselves, they demean all of us. I would ask you to pray for the sinners, pray that they may sin no more and be brought back into the light of God's gracious mercy and forgiveness. If you have sinned, I would ask you to repent. Above all I would ask you to be mindful of Christ's words to the woman taken in adultery, "go thou and sin no more."'

It was not long before the full scale of the disaster hit Butler's Court. The servants, with their normal invisible sources of information, learnt very quickly what had happened in the Protestant church. The steward, acting as spokesman for the footmen and the parlour maids and the kitchen staff, informed Richard Butler of the sermon of Father O'Donovan Brady. The steward felt it was only fair. Richard Butler turned pale but merely thanked the man for his news. The soup that lunchtime came in a silver tureen and was ladled into the Spode bowls by Richard and passed down to the guests. Butler

281

himself carved the meat with a great German carving knife and handed it round. Disaster struck with the vegetables. These were being served from a large silver salver by a pretty parlour maid of about twenty years who looked very correct in her smart black and white uniform. When she reached Johnpeter Kilross she simply walked straight past him as if he wasn't there. The same fate, accompanied by a slight toss of the head, awaited Alice Bracken. Everybody else was served in the normal way. The girl took the empty salver back to the kitchens. There was complete silence in the dining room. The blank spaces on the walls where the paintings had been stared down at them. Alice Bracken burst into tears and fled the room. Johnpeter Kilross followed her a moment later. Richard Butler stared helplessly at his wife. The rest of the meal was taken in complete silence. The boycott, or a form of boycott, had come to add to the woes of Butler's Court.

Richard Butler and his wife held a crisis meeting in his study after lunch. 'Did you know this was going on?' he asked her.

'Certainly not. Do you know precisely what was going on?'

Richard Butler made a disagreeable face. 'From what I was told just before lunch, Father O'Donovan Brady named Kilross and the Bracken female as having carried on in broad daylight in the Head Gardener's Cottage. He told his flock, if they worked here, that is, to think before they served their food or washed their clothes, that sort of thing.'

'My God, Richard, this is terrible! So soon after the paintings and everything. What are we going to do?'

'I don't think we have any choice,' said Butler. 'They'll have to go away. They'll have to go almost at once before things get out of hand.'

'We can't do that. They may have misbehaved, those two, but they're our kith and kin. We can't let them down. What will people say? That Father O'Donovan Brady, that horrible little man, preaches a sermon at half past eleven and the Protestants cave in first thing in the afternoon? You can't take a high and mighty line with the blackmailers, Richard, and then betray your own after they miss out on the carrots and the cauliflower!'

'Ah, but there's a difference,' said her husband. 'We're in the right over the paintings. We're in the wrong, very much in the wrong, about the adultery. Would you have the locals say our house is a refuge for adulterers, that the people who break God's commandments can find sanctuary at my house? It won't do. My mind is made up, Sylvia. They've got to go. You might tell them to pack their bags right away. I wish Powerscourt was here. He'd have something sensible to suggest. I'm going to speak to the vicar. Maybe he'll have some thoughts about where they could go. I don't think anywhere in the south of Ireland is going to be safe for them. The word will shoot round the Catholic grapevine at lightning speed.'

Five days after his escape from his captors on the Maum road Lord Francis Powerscourt was sitting in the reception area of Messrs Browne and Sons, Land Agents and Valuers, of Eyre Square in the heart of Galway.

The dinner at the Leenane Hotel had been a riotous affair, graced with lobsters and champagne. The Major had indeed attempted to sing a song, 'The Ash Grove', deemed too English by local taste and drowned out by Dennis Ormonde and Johnny Fitzgerald belting out 'The West's Awake' and 'The Wearing of the Green'. The dining room, the landlord observed to his wife, was little better this evening than the public bar on a Saturday night. Ormonde had brought some correspondence for Powerscourt, the letter from Inspector Harkness that had arrived at Ormonde House just ten minutes after he left in search of the missing women. It was cryptic. 'It is as you thought. Here are the dates and the figures for the person you mentioned. H.' And there was a note from the Archbishop's Chaplain reminding Powerscourt that the Archbishop of Tuam was anxious to see him before he left Ireland. An appointment had been fixed for later that day. Johnny Fitzgerald had been dispatched on a fishing expedition to locate and investigate Pronsias Mulcahy's brother, Declan Mulcahy, believed to be a solicitor somewhere in the west of Ireland.

Richard Browne, senior partner in the firm that bore his name, was a small, silver-haired man in his middle sixties. He was wearing a very elegant dark suit that Powerscourt did not think had come from a Galway tailor with a cream shirt adorned by ornate silver cufflinks. He carried about him an air of great respectability. The room was large, with a fine marble mantelpiece, a desk by the window, a sofa and some easy chairs loosely grouped round a Regency table. Powerscourt was relieved to see that there were no stuffed animals in sight.

'Lord Powerscourt, a very good morning to you. How can I be of assistance?'

'Dennis Ormonde of Ormonde House suggested I call on you, Mr Browne,' Powerscourt began. 'Let me give you a little background, if I may. I am an investigator, sir, summoned to Ireland to look into a delicate matter of stolen paintings. So far there have been two deaths and a serious kidnapping during the course of my inquiries. I need to know about land, who is buying, who is selling, the general state of the market. Land is always central to what goes on in Ireland, I think. Dennis Ormonde said you would be the best person to consult in the whole of the west of Ireland.'

The old man laughed and began filling his pipe. 'He flatters me, Lord Powerscourt. I shall be happy to oblige though I find it hard to detect the link between land and pictures. But tell me, didn't your people once own a huge estate in County Wicklow? And Powerscourt House itself? All sold now, of course, but in its day, surely, it was one of the finest of its kind in Ireland.'

'We did own it, Mr Browne. It was I who sold it, for reasons I won't burden you with. There are no lands or houses owned by Powerscourts in Ireland now, I'm afraid.'

'Pity, that,' said Richard Browne. 'The family went back a very long way. Now then.' He forced a final lump of tobacco into his pipe and began fiddling with his matches. 'Land, Lord Powerscourt, land in Ireland. Dear me. Where should I start? Two years ago, I tell you, I was going to retire. My wife and I had spent over a year planning a great journey round Europe by train. It was going to take three months. I have always wanted to see some of the great art galleries. My wife is very keen on gardens and great chateaux. We had the route planned, we even had the names of the hotels where we were going to make reservations. Then I heard about this Wyndham Act, the one that encourages the landlords to sell out and gives them a bonus of twelve per cent on the price for doing so. You know about this Act, Lord Powerscourt?'

Powerscourt remembered William Moore talking about it. He nodded.

'Mabel, I said,' the land agent went on, thin wisps of smoke beginning to curl out of his pipe, 'in forty years in this trade I have never seen an opportunity like this. Business for a while will be brisker than we have ever known. I could not sit happy in Gstaad or Portofino and think of all those missing profits. So we postponed the trip. I had to buy Mabel a new house to make up for it, mind you, a Georgian place out near the coast, cost me a packet but it was well worth it.'

'Did business boom, Mr Browne? Were your expectations justified?'

The land agent laughed. 'It has been better than my wildest dreams, Lord Powerscourt. These Anglo-Irish landlords, you know, they've never been very good with money, most of them. They're extravagant. If a neighbour builds a Gothic extension to his property, then you have to do the same. Most of those estates are lumbered with loans and mortgages of unimaginable size. Sometimes half or even two-thirds of the income goes on servicing the debts. If agricultural prices are good then the rents can be high. But they've not been too good for a long time with all these foreign imports of wheat and so on. So when George Wyndham proposed this Act, the landlords thought it was manna from heaven. Sell some of your land, sell all of your land, collect the bonus, and it's a golden opportunity to pay off a lot of those debts and still be left with plenty of money. I've had people coming in here at a rate you wouldn't believe, as if I was the bookmaker round the corner.'

'So you have lots of sellers,' said Powerscourt. 'Who is buying? And might I make so bold as to raise the religious question? Dennis Ormonde said you dealt with all the Protestant sales. But it doesn't sound as if there are many Protestant buyers on the market.'

Richard Browne puffed vigorously. 'Good question, my lord, good question. Very rarely will a Protestant enter the market to buy. Some of the most efficient farmers have increased their holdings, it is true. But most of the time the land is offered to the existing tenants. That's only fair, after all. It's after that the business really takes off. Many of these people – we'd have called them peasants in days gone by – didn't have very much land. If they sold it they might have enough money to emigrate or to pay off some of their debts. Or they could stay on and work on the land for the new landlord. Some of the larger Catholic farmers have amassed enormous amounts of land by buying out their co-religionists. Sometimes, I understand, they're even harsher landlords than the ones who sold up. The key point is this shift in the ownership of land towards the native population and, in particular, the acquisition of these huge holdings. It's history running backwards, my lord. Out go the Protestants who acquired or stole the land from the Catholic population hundreds of years ago, in come these great Catholic speculators buying up the Protestant land with the help and encouragement of the British Government in London. It could only happen in Ireland.' Browne's pipe had gone out. He began again the difficult search for matches, never to be found in the pocket where you thought you had put them.

'Is that clear to you, my lord, the general picture, I mean?'

'Admirably clear, Mr Browne, you have explained the situation very well. Might I trespass on your knowledge yet further and trail a couple of names before you, names of Catholic gentlemen who might be buying up the land in the manner you adumbrated so well?'

'I'm afraid, my lord,' Richard Browne had finally managed to relight his pipe and was now blowing great lungfuls of smoke in Powerscourt's direction, 'that at certain points the priorities and preoccupations of investigators, however distinguished, diverge from those of humble land agents like myself. We have a duty of confidentiality to our clients. It is not as rigorous as the duty that binds the priests in their confessionals, but we break it at our peril.'

'Goodness me, Mr Browne,' said Powerscourt, 'forgive me, I was not thinking of anybody with whom you might be doing business here in Galway or Clare or however far your remit runs. I was thinking rather of somebody in the Midlands, somebody whose land agents would probably come from Athlone rather than Galway.'

'It's very unusual, my lord. I'm not sure I could coun- tenance giving out any information where I was not in the full possession of the facts.'

Powerscourt threw his hat into the ring. 'Mr Mulcahey, Mr Pronsias Mulcahey of Butler's Cross – does that name ring any bells, even distant bells, with you, Mr Browne?'

Something in the land agent's face told Powerscourt that he had scored a direct hit.

'I couldn't say, my lord, I really couldn't say. Pronsias Mulcahey, grocer and moneylender of Market Square, Butler's Cross. I couldn't say, but you might be on to something there.'

Jameson was unwell. His owner, Charlie O'Malley, was very worried about him. He was not old, for a donkey. He still worked for his living but his performance was sporadic.

Occasionally he sat down in the middle of the road and refused to move. He was not eating much. After their heroic efforts building the chapel on the summit of Croagh Patrick, Charlie and his animals were currently employed building a new hotel and bar near the beach at Old Head, a few miles from Louisburg. The land was flat and the effort involved for donkeys bringing materials out to the site was minute compared with the long haul up the Holy Mountain. Charlie had consulted widely among his cronies in the bar of Campbell's public house. One had recommended large doses of whiskey, another great helpings of vegetable soup, another swore his granny had cured a dying donkey by feeding it a diet of potatoes soaked overnight in stout. The goodness of the Guinness, according to Charlie's informant's aged relative, soaked into the spuds and effected the cure. Charlie had tried them all. He had mentioned to his wife the possibility of the vet and been soundly berated for his pains; how were the children to have clothes on their backs and shoes on their feet if all their hard-earned money was to be squandered on a delinquent donkey?

Charlie had virtually decided to have Jameson put down. The two of them and Bushmills had finished early for the day and Charlie was thinking of celebrating his release with a glass of refreshment in the public bar at Campbell's when it happened. Jameson stopped at the bottom of the track that led to the summit. He stared upwards. Then he began trotting purposefully up the path.

'Jameson!' shouted Charlie. 'Jameson! Where are you going, you stupid animal?'

The donkey did not deign to turn round. He continued, at a regular pace, in the direction of the statue of St Patrick. Charlie tethered Bushmills to the post outside Campbell's and set off in pursuit.

'Jameson!' he shouted, spying the beast some two hundred yards further up and cruising steadily past St Patrick. 'Where the hell do you think you're going?'

Jameson gave every indication of having a very good idea of where he was going. He was going up and nobody was going to stop him. By the time Charlie caught up with him, the donkey was almost at the first station and looking as if he might break the All Ireland Donkey record for the summit of The Reek. Charlie himself was panting heavily. The fitness established on those trips up and down to the chapel had long gone, eroded by the flat lands of Old Head and the stout of Campbell's public bar. Anybody looking at the two of them now would have said that Jameson was the healthy one and Charlie the invalid. Onwards and upwards went the animal, five hundred yards from the summit, then three hundred, then eighty. Charlie was feeling rather unwell and had taken to reciting a series of Hail Marys. Jameson gave one triumphant bray when he reached the chapel he had helped to build and he peered out into Clew Bay, master of all he surveyed.

'For Christ's sake, Jameson,' said Charlie, sitting down by the edge of the chapel, 'won't you take a rest? Sit down, in God's name. You're bloody well killing me.'

Jameson took no notice. He trotted past Charlie without even a glance and set off back down the scree. Charlie floundered after him, slithering on the rough stones, and once sitting down very uncomfortably. Charlie knew he had to stop Jameson disappearing off down the road at the bottom and escaping into some kind of donkey liberty. He redoubled his efforts but Jameson was too quick for him. By the time Charlie eventually reached the bottom, holding on to his side and panting heavily, Jameson was next to Bushmills. They appeared to be having a conversation in donkey language on the inadequacies of humans. Charlie tied the donkey up and staggered into the public bar. He had to be helped to a seat. He was too exhausted to speak. A variety of remedies were proposed.

'Plain water, that's what he needs,' said a farmer from nearby Murrisk.

'Plain water?' said a carpenter from Westport. 'You must be mad. When did plain water do anything for anybody, for God's sake? Stout, that's what he wants.'

'No, no, not stout. It'll puff him out like a football,' said a small farmer. 'whiskey, that's the thing.'

'Brandy,' said the landlord, who had left his seat of custom for a close inspection of Charlie. 'Here, take this very slowly. Don't rush it or you'll be ill.' He handed over a large glass half filled with cognac and Charlie sipped it gently, like a man taking his medicine after a long illness. Gradually he felt himself returning to something approaching normal. Certainly the state of semi-inebriation brought on by the brandy was a condition well known to Charlie. And when he outlined the recent events concerning Jameson, he had the attention of every single person in the public bar.

'He's mad, the animal,' said one. 'Who ever heard of a mountaineering donkey?'

'Take him to the Alps, Charlie,' said another, who had not excelled at geography with the Christian Brothers. 'See if he can climb the Horn of Matter!'

'Matterhorn, you eejit,' said his friend. 'Why don't we organize a donkey race up Croagh Patrick every summer? Jameson would be hot favourite. I'd put five shillings on him now, so I would.'

'It just goes to show,' said a solicitor's clerk, 'that all donkeys are mad. You can never tell with them, they're so stupid.'

'The spirit of St Patrick has entered the animal,' said a teacher who had once contemplated a career in the priesthood. 'Jameson has taken on the mantle of the patron saint.'

Charlie paid little attention to any of these theories. Jameson had certainly returned to health. He even attained a brief moment of local fame when the editor of the *Mayo News*, a veteran of the journalistic profession, florid of countenance and portly of figure, heard about the mountaineering donkey and sent one of his brightest young men to interview

Jameson. The reporter quickly realized that donkeys, like the dead, cannot sue for libel and that he was therefore free to print whatever took his fancy. Jameson, he informed his readers, was an avid supporter of Home Rule as he much preferred staying in the field next to Charlie O'Malley's house to going to work. And he deduced from the considerable amount of time the donkey spent outside Campbell's public house that Jameson would favour a relaxation of the licensing laws and a lowering in the duty on the spirit that bore his name. Parties of schoolchildren would make appointments to come and see Jameson after this, bringing gifts of vegetables and stroking him happily. Twice a month Charlie took him up to the summit of Croagh Patrick to keep his health up. Charlie rejected all the theories about his donkey's behaviour. Charlie knew the truth. Jameson was a pilgrim.

The Archbishop of Tuam, the Very Reverend John Healey, was perusing a large pile of documents on his desk as Powerscourt was shown into his study.

'Lord Powerscourt, how good to see you again. Please take a seat. Is your mission to Ireland nearly completed?'

Powerscourt quite liked the thought of his mission. It linked him to the saints and scholars of Ireland's past, perhaps even to Patrick himself out here in the country where a great mountain was named in his honour.

'I believe I am on the last lap, Your Grace. I hope so anyway.'

'So you think you have found the answer?'

'In this case, Your Grace, I think it will come down to answers in the plural rather than answer in the singular. So often in my investigations there has been one perpetrator, one single individual who committed the crime or murdered the innocent or forged the paintings. Here I think there may be a number of individuals. It has made it very difficult to work out the links that held them together.'

'I'm sure you will get to the bottom of it all. Tell me, Lord Powerscourt, I have received a great many letters complaining about the shooting of a young man on the Maum road very recently. My correspondents say that the young man was totally innocent and was victimized by the soldiers for no reason. And his companion, another young man, had been badly beaten up. Do you know anything about this?'

Powerscourt smiled. 'Is it possible, Your Grace, that some of these letters are in the same hand? Or that the words in one are remarkably similar to those in another?'

The Archbishop frowned. He riffled through the stack of letters. 'God bless my soul! Both of those statements are true,' he said in surprise. 'How very strange. Do you think somebody is orchestrating this campaign?'

'That might indeed be the case, Your Grace,' said Powerscourt, 'but let me give you the facts. You see, I was present, or almost present, at the time. Those two young men were responsible for the kidnapping of two Protestant women from Ormonde House. They kept them locked up in a fishing lodge near Leenane for some days. The ladies were only freed when Johnny Fitzgerald and I substituted ourselves for them, and became hostages in our turn. We were all going to Galway in the finest Ormonde coach, with Johnny and I told not to move or we would be shot.'

Dr Healey's ample eyebrows shot high up the archepiscopal forehead. 'Goodness me,' he said, 'what colourful lives you people lead. I'm sure Lord Edward Fitzgerald would have been proud of his descendant's gallantry, mind you. Please go on.'

'Well, Your Grace, we managed to set ourselves free by a violent assault on the young men when they were nearly asleep and kicking them out of the coach. Then they were intercepted by a party of troopers who were following our progress at a discreet distance. The young man who was shot could have allowed himself to be arrested. He must have known he and his colleague were outnumbered. But he did

292

not. We only knew him as Mick, Your Grace. That was not his real name and he was a very excitable young man. He fired at the cavalrymen. They fired back. He was killed. I am sure he preferred death and glory to capture and a prison sentence in Castlebar Jail. No doubt there will be a ballad about him soon.'

'I think there already is,' said the Archbishop. 'One of the grooms here heard it last night in the Mitre across the road. I see, Lord Powerscourt. I feel I should pay little attention to these protesters. But tell me, I only saw you on the way up the mountain, not on the way down. Did you enjoy the Croagh Patrick pilgrimage? Did it have meaning for you?'

'It most certainly did,' replied Powerscourt. 'It was, for me, a spiritual experience. I am most grateful to Your Grace for inviting us. Could I extend, on behalf of Lucy and myself, an invitation to you, Your Grace, to come and see us when you are next in London? You could meet the children. We live in Markham Square in Chelsea. Sir Thomas More lived not far away, we have the Royal Hospital close by, one of the most beautiful buildings in London, designed by Sir Christopher Wren, we have the river Thames, but we have no mountains and no pilgrimages.'

'Thank you, thank you.' The Archbishop beamed with pleasure. 'Are you familiar with the works of John Donne, Lord Powerscourt? He began life in a very distinguished Catholic family and ended up as Protestant Dean of St Paul's. I have had this quotation from him on my desk these twenty years now.' The Archbishop opened up a little notebook which Powerscourt saw was filled with neat copperplate handwriting. 'It comes from the passage about for whom the bell tolls: "And when the Church buries a man, that action concerns me: all mankind is of one author, and is one volume: when one man dies, one chapter is not torn out of the book, but translated into a better language; and every chapter must be so translated; God employs several translators; some pieces are translated by age, some by sickness, some by war, some by justice; but God's hand is in every translation, and his hand shall bind up all our scattered leaves again for that library where every book shall lie open to one another." Donne talks of many translations, my friend. I like to think there are many mountains, too, not only ones made out of stone and rock and rough scree like our Croagh Patrick. There are mountains of hatred and bigotry in men's hearts here in our little island which the Church must try to remove. There are mountains or lofty places of the spirit, if we are to believe Donne and the mystics and the poets, where love can take its adherents to the highest peaks of happiness or ecstasy. There are many translations, Lord Powerscourt. There are many mountains too and many different paths to the summit, whether in Mayo or Chelsea.'

Two days later Powerscourt was back in Butler's Court, reading another letter from the art dealer Michael Hudson. 'You will be as astonished as I was to hear of the response to our advertisements in the Irish newspapers. So far we have had eighty-seven replies! When Mr Farrell has inspected them I will let you have further details. Unfortunately not one of them is on your lists. It may be that the thieves did not steal them in order to sell them on. It may be that they are biding their time. In my experience thieves are usually anxious to dispose of their booty at the earliest possible opportunity. Yours etc.'

Powerscourt laughed out loud. For all their protestations about their devotion to their ancestors, the Anglo-Irish were queuing up to sell their forebears for American dollars in great numbers. There might, he thought, be more to come when word about the high prices travelled round the thirty-two counties. The answer to his problem did not lie with selling the stolen paintings.

He had met with the land agent in Athlone earlier that day and been given a report very similar to the one he had received in Galway. Some of these Protestant patricians, he had been told, were so happy with the Wyndham bonus that they were even building new houses for themselves, though little thought appeared to have been given to how they were to be maintained. What they ought to have done, the agent from Athlone had informed him, was to invest the proceeds from the sales in sensible stock and maintain their standard of living from the income, but that had little appeal. One single man from Tralee was believed to be working his way through the proceeds of the Wyndham Act at the gambling tables of Monte Carlo. The name Mulcahy produced the same instant frisson of recognition as it had done in Eyre Square but no details of his dealings could be extracted. Powerscourt had also met with Inspector Harkness to co-ordinate the final arrangements of his investigation. 'If this works,' he told the Inspector, 'we'll be heroes, temporary kings for twenty-four hours. If it fails we'll be humiliated.'

Powerscourt filled Lady Lucy in with the details in the Butler's Court gardens late on the Sunday afternoon. 'At nine o'clock tomorrow morning, my love, Inspector Harkness and a team of eight men, all from areas remote from here in case of leaks, are going to search Mulcahy's premises. If that fails, they'll try his house. If that fails they'll try the priest's place. I'd love to see Father O'Donovan Brady's face when they start ripping his house apart.'

'Is all this legal, Francis? Can you actually raid those places?'

'Oh, yes, Lucy,' replied her husband, 'the Inspector has got search warrants falling out of every pocket in his suit. And, at the same time, exactly the same time so there can be no tip-offs, another party of police, escorted by Johnny Fitzgerald, is going to raid the offices of the solicitor brother Declan Mulcahy in Swinford. His speciality is land and he is believed, Johnny said in his note, to have parcels of land coming out of his ears. Johnny also tells me that there is some mass grave over there from famine times with over five hundred and fifty souls in the ground but our boy Declan isn't going to starve. Not by any means. There's property and land and prize cattle in his empire apparently, and it's growing by the hour.'

'Are you sure you're right?' Lady Lucy looked worried suddenly.

Powerscourt smiled and took her hand. 'We'll find out tomorrow. Let's go and see what's on the menu this evening, Lucy. But, please, don't breathe a word of any of this to anybody. If a whisper of a rumour goes down the hill, we're sunk.'

16

Lord Francis Powerscourt slept badly that night. In his dreams he watched as grave Anglo-Irish gentlemen walked out of the frames on their walls, sat down at their dining tables and demanded food. He saw another empty beach where the sandcastles were being washed away by the tide. He found himself in an enormous throng of persons walking very slowly through the streets of Dublin. He thought they might be mourners at Parnell's funeral, but he had lost Lady Lucy and the press of people was so great he could not break out to find her. He was locked again in the red velvet of the Ormonde carriage, Johnny Fitzgerald by his side. They seemed to be hurtling down a hill with no coachman on top to halt their progress. He knew without being able to see them that there were rocks and boulders at the bottom. Just when he felt they were certain to crash into them and perish, he woke up and grabbed hold of Lady Lucy who muttered to him sleepily that they were on the first floor of Butler's Court and the birds were already singing outside. It promised to be a beautiful day.

Shortly after half past eight Powerscourt set out to walk down to the main square. He told Richard Butler that he would like to see him about half past ten, if that was convenient, nothing important, he assured his host, just a couple of pieces of routine administration for his accounts. Lady Lucy followed him about fifteen minutes later. She did not go all the way to the bottom but seated herself on a bench halfway down the hill. She had brought a book of poetry to keep her company if the wait proved long. At precisely nine o'clock Inspector Harkness and a sergeant from Longford called Murphy marched their men into the main square of Butler's Cross. At three minutes past they were lined up outside the front entrance to the emporium of Mulcahy and Sons, Grocery and Bar. The rest of the square was empty except for a stray dog who limped along the road by Horkan's the agricultural supply people. MacSwiggin's Hotel did not begin to serve breakfast to its clients until ten o'clock except in cases of emergency. There was one customer in the shop already, an old lady preparing to pay for a couple of slices of bacon and half a dozen eggs. Sergeant Murphy escorted her gently to the front door and closed it firmly behind her.

'Pronsias Mulcahy!' said Inspector Harkness in his best Ulster accent. 'I have a licence to search these premises. You are to wait outside in the square. One of my men will accompany you. If you attempt to flee you will be transported immediately to Athlone Jail.'

'You can't do this to me, you northern bastard,' Mulcahy spat, 'this is my shop! You've no rights here!'

'Oh, but we do, Mr Mulcahy,' Harkness replied, waving the search warrant in his face. 'Now I suggest you go outside and wait quietly. I should let you know,' he added cheerfully, 'that we have a warrant to search your house as well. Any misbehaviour and we'll be in there too, tearing up the floorboards and poking about in your attics. Now get out!'

A burly constable escorted Mulcahy out of his premises. A chair was provided for him to sit down by his own front door. Harkness's men began working their way methodically through the main shop, peering behind the backs of cupboards, tapping regularly on the walls. Powerscourt headed straight for the back office where Mulcahy did his accounts among the hams hanging from the ceiling and the barrels of stout awaiting final delivery to the bar. He picked up the three books where Mulcahy kept note of his business. He discarded the two concerning the grocery and the bar and took the third, the blue one concerning the loans, out into the open air where he could get a better view.

'That's private!' yelled Mulcahy. 'That's mine! You can't steal that, you fecking traitor!'

'You just shut up, you!' said the burly constable, giving the grocer a hefty clip round the ear. 'Any more disturbances and you're off to jail.'

It was not yet ten past nine. Powerscourt was to tell Lady Lucy afterwards that he had no idea how it was summoned, but a crowd was already gathering outside Mulcahy's. It could not have been the old lady's doing for she lived next door and spoke to nobody on her brief return journey. Two Delaney solicitors were there, muttering to the constable about habeas corpus and due process and whatever else they could think of at that hour in the morning. Father O'Donovan Brady had arrived, the buttons on his soutane not all fastened, escorted by a group of young men with hurling sticks. Two bleary-eyed drovers had tottered out of MacSwiggin's Hotel and were sitting in the sunshine, watching the proceedings with great interest. Father O'Donovan Brady began a prayer for the afflicted one in his hour of need until told to shut up by the constable, this wasn't his church and it wasn't bloody Sunday morning either, so it wasn't. The stray dog too had heard the summons, calling two more of its kind to patrol the periphery of the crowd. Every few minutes another figure would amble into the square to look at Pronsias Mulcahy, who had so much influence in the little community, sitting on a chair, virtually under house arrest, while the constabulary searched his premises. Then a group of women appeared and began shouting insults at the constable until Inspector Harkness poked his head round the door and told them they would all be charged with a breach of the King's peace if they did not keep quiet.

Inside the searching party had almost finished with the main body of the shop. Powerscourt had told the Inspector that he thought it very unlikely that anything would be hidden there. But he also said that he doubted if any great attempt at concealment would be made. Mulcahy, he felt, would have thought there was about as much chance of his premises being turned over as there was of his being chosen as Tsar of all the Russias. Powerscourt retired behind the gates of Butler's Court and checked the dates and the entries on Mulcahy's loan ledger with the details in Harkness's letter. A slow smile spread across his face. In one respect, at any rate, he was not wrong.

A couple of hundred yards away, further up the hill, Lady Lucy had left the book of poetry in her lap. The sun was quite warm already. She was daydreaming now, wondering if Francis was going to take her away for a holiday when this investigation was over. He usually did. She checked through various places in her mind, Rome, probably too hot, Nice, probably too crowded, Naples, too dirty. She was wondering if she could persuade him to take her to New England when she fell asleep.

Harkness's men were in the outhouses now. There was a slight air of frustration among the constables. Various piles of stores, carefully laid in by the grocer in case they should prove to be in short supply in the near future, were kicked over. Outside in the square Mrs Mulcahy had made an appearance, wearing, not the blue suit she wore to church, but a well-worn apron over a cream blouse and a dark skirt. She advanced towards her husband, still sitting defiantly on his chair, a lawyer Delaney on either side of him in case his enemies should assail him from the left or the right. Far from offering comfort, Mrs Fionnula Mulcahy brought wrath. She came not with peace but with the sword. 'Just look on the disgrace you've brought on us all! Stuck there like a common criminal in the stocks! I always told you you'd go too far. Me own father Seamus Dempsey warned me you'd bring shame down on us all and you have! Just don't expect me to come visiting you in the jail in Athlone with little packets of barm brack and fruit cake, Pronsias Mulcahy! Don't even expect to find me waiting for you when you come out, if you ever do!'

She shook her fist at him and returned to her home. A small cheer of support from the hurling stick youths followed her back.

At the back of Mulcahy's they were now halfway through the outbuildings. A faint tremor of anxiety passed across Powerscourt's face as he contemplated the fact that their prey might not be there. Inspector Harkness was sweating slightly. A party of children had arrived in the square and were playing hopscotch by the Butler's Court gates. Three Christian Brothers joined Father O'Donovan Brady in silent prayer for their troubled comrade. MacSwiggin's Hotel and Bar opened its doors early to cater for the demand. A potboy carried a glass of stout to Pronsias Mulcahy who seemed to be in need of refreshment. The policeman scowled but could not think of any laws or regulations that were being infringed. This was Ireland, after all.

It was Inspector Harkness who solved the problem. In the last outhouse but one he thought that the internal dimensions were less than the external ones. The area inside was smaller than it should have been. He stalked round the outside knocking on the walls with a crowbar he had apprehended in an earlier building. He looked suspiciously at what might have been a new internal wall, recently assembled in wood and draped with black tarpaulins. He pointed out his suspicions to Powerscourt.

'Knock the bloody thing down,' Powerscourt said, 'and let's see what's on the other side.'

One of the constables had worked as a blacksmith before he joined up. He borrowed the crowbar and struck a number of fearsome blows. Quite soon he had opened up an entry, large enough for one man to pass inside. Inspector Harkness gave a shout of triumph and handed a large parcel out of the opening to Powerscourt. Five more, of different sizes, followed, then more still. Another constable returned with a torch, for the outhouse was rather dark and had no electricity of its own. Powerscourt took out his penknife and worked his way very carefully through the wrapping. After a couple of minutes he found himself looking at an eighteenth-century gentleman, almost certainly a Butler from the set of his cheekbones. He checked all the others to make sure they had not been defaced in the manner of *The Master of the Hunt.* Then another set of paintings appeared. These were the ones from Moore Castle whose theft had caused such upset to their owner. Inspector Harkness whistled.

'I'll get one of my men to saddle up the Mulcahy cart, my lord. We can take these back home.'

The Inspector arranged the transfer so that every painting was carried out right in front of Pronsias Mulcahy, still sitting by the front entrance to his shop. When the parade had finished and the paintings were safely stowed away, a constable on guard on either side of them, Inspector Harkness raised his voice till it carried to the far corners of the square. 'Pronsias Padraig Mulcahy, I arrest you on the charge of being wilfully in receipt of stolen goods. I have to warn you that anything you say may be taken down and used in evidence against you. Take him away!' More policemen ushered Mulcahy into a police vehicle and drove him off. One of the Delaneys started to run after it, saying there was an absence of due process, but the constables took no notice. Father O'Donovan Brady turned on his heel and took the Christian Brothers back to his house. The good Lord Himself, Father O'Donovan Brady told them, would not object if they took drink at a time like this.

A small triumphal procession made its way up to Butler's Court. In the van was Mulcahy's cart with the paintings and the two constables on guard. Behind that marched Inspector Harkness and his remaining forces. Behind them, a rather grubby Powerscourt, a dirty hand holding on to one of Lady Lucy's with great pride and affection. They must have been spotted from one of the windows at the front for Richard

302

Butler came out and eyed the cart suspiciously. He remembered the earlier painting that had returned with the faces changed.

'They're all right, Richard,' said Powerscourt, 'these are the real things. They've come back. After all this time they've come back. I think you should rehang them straight away. And you'd better tell Moore to come over as fast as he can. We've found his too.'

An hour and a half later Richard Butler carried two bottles of champagne into his dining room. His ancestors and his Old Masters were back on the walls. Next door *The Master of the Hunt* in the correct version was also back in its place. The entire family was present. Inspector Harkness had borrowed a red smoking jacket for the occasion and was puffing happily on a large cigar. Powerscourt was sitting at one end of the table.

'Ladies and gentlemen,' said Butler, raising his glass, 'I ask you to drink the health of Lord Francis Powerscourt who has secured the miraculous return of these paintings. Lord Powerscourt!' The toasts rang out into the great hallway. 'And now, Powerscourt, perhaps you can tell us all what has been going on!'

Powerscourt remained seated. 'Let me begin,' he said, 'by saying how steadfastly everyone has behaved throughout this business. Except for Connolly. I have no brief for Connolly. I expect his pictures were guests of Mulcahy's as yours were, but were released when he paid up. But without the courage of all of you, even when the Ormonde women were seized, this strange battle would have been lost long ago.' He paused and looked at the Butlers and the Moores, who had only just arrived to be reunited with their ancestors.

'Let me begin, if I may,' said Powerscourt, 'with the theft of the paintings. One obvious reason would have been to sell them. The market for Anglo-Irish ancestors might be limited, but they do have a certain value. Yet all the inquiries Johnny and I set in motion in Dublin and in London and in New York

303

revealed that not a single one had been put on the market. So, unless we were dealing with an obsessive collector who wanted a basement full of dead gentry, there had to be another reason. And here, I think, we come to a question of psychology. It seemed to me that the only people who would understand what these ancestral portraits meant to families like the Butlers and the Moores would be Protestant. Only they would hear the tribal beat that echoes back down the centuries. Catholics tend to have different kinds of paintings on their walls. So my first theory was that a Protestant dreamt up this particular plot. But for what purpose? And in whose interest? Protestant or Catholic? Then we had the return of two pictures, the Moore one that faded away, and *The Master of the Hunt* that was returned here with a completely different cast of characters on horseback. Whoever thought of that was clever, extremely clever. I don't think Mulcahy or anybody like him would have thought of either of those ploys in a hundred years. So there had to be somebody behind the Mulcahy figure, Mulcahy's brains, as it were. But why should anybody volunteer for such a position?'

Powerscourt paused and took a sip of champagne. His little audience was transfixed. Lady Lucy smiled at him from halfway down the table, Thomas Butler, 1726–1788, behind her head. 'Now we come to the blackmail letters, or the absence of them. I must say that the denial of their existence for a long time caused me considerable problems. For I was sure there were blackmail letters. There had to be. The thieves didn't want to sell the paintings. They obviously wanted to wound their victims, but surely there was more to it than that. I remember Richard Butler telling me once that he had sworn to his father to preserve all his inheritance and to pass it on to the next generation. The others may have made similar vows, I don't know, it may be the custom in these families. Only Dennis Ormonde, in his fury, confirmed that there had been such a missive. His anger, incidentally, confirmed to me that the thieves had indeed chosen a powerful weapon in the paintings, guaranteed to destabilize their victims. Even then you all refused to tell me precisely what was in the blackmail letters. I presumed, wrongly, that it had to do with money, and that was a subject any Irish gentleman would be reluctant to discuss with his peers.'

Uncle Peter shuffled slowly into the back of the dining room. He was wearing a tattered blue coat and clutching a bottle of white wine. He nodded amiably to Powerscourt and sat down.

'Now I would like to address one of the thorniest aspects of the matter,' Powerscourt went on, 'put simply, how many lots of thieves were there? One? Two? Three? Four? Eventually I came to the conclusion that there were two. The thefts from here and from Moore and Connolly were all the work of one lot. The proof is in the fact that Moore's paintings were found in the Mulcahy outhouse. But who were the others? Mulcahy has a brother, one Declan Mulcahy, a solicitor in Swinford with branch offices in Castlebar and Ballinrobe. He specializes in land, you'll be surprised to hear, and is a rising power in County Mayo. I think our Mulcahy mentioned his plan to his brother and they decided to try it on at Ormonde House, both with the theft and with the kidnap. It was Uncle Peter, oddly enough, who put me on to how the manpower was recruited. In his account of Parnell's funeral he mentioned the honour guard of young men with hurling sticks from the Gaelic Athletic Association who guarded the coffin all the way through the streets of Dublin to the cemetery. Even then it was thought that they were linked to extreme elements of Irish Republicanism. There were a couple of hurling sticks in the front hall of Butler Lodge. The Archbishop of Tuam told me he was very worried about some of the younger priests and Christian Brothers because their politics are so extreme and they preach their message of violent opposition to English or Anglo-Irish rule to the young. Johnny Fitzgerald had a conversation in Westport with a defrocked Christian Brother who said you could use the young men of the Gaelic Athletic

Association, the GAA, to take over Ireland. I believe the Swinford Mulcahy got in touch with these people, maybe through a priest or a Brother who coaches one of the football or hurling teams, and asked for volunteers to strike a blow in Ireland's cause. Steal a few pictures, make off with a couple of women, that sort of thing. Those kidnappers who took and held the Ormonde ladies were fanatical nationalists to a man. They said we were traitors. I believe the kidnap, incidentally, was in part to do with the blackmail and in part a sort of revenge for the arrival of the Orangemen. The blackmail letters may have said that the women were next after the paintings, I don't know.'

Outside the windows they could hear the shouts and cries of the children playing, the children who had been so well entertained until recently by Young James.

'Now I come to the death of the young man whose body was found in the chapel at the summit of Croagh Patrick on the morning of the pilgrimage. He had been shot in the chest and in the back of the head. I will always feel responsible for that. The Inspector and I concocted a plan to lure the thieves of the Westport paintings to a house that they thought wasn't guarded by Ormonde's Orangemen, but was, in fact, guarded by a different lot of police. A young man with a father in jail was persuaded to tell the group that contained the thieves that Burke Hall was not guarded. I don't know what inducement was offered, early release for his parent perhaps, but the message got through. One of the ringleaders of the thieves was shot in their attack but they got away. When they discovered who had betrayed them, they dragged the young man up Croagh Patrick, tortured him and shot him. Inspector Harkness was told the torture had been quite frightful before he died.'

'You mustn't punish yourself, my lord,' said the Inspector. 'If the plan had worked, we would have captured one half of the thieves and the investigation would have been half over.'

'But we didn't catch them,' said Powerscourt sadly. 'The young man's dead.' He looked down at the table for a moment or two before he continued.

'It was late in the day when I realized that the motive was not money at all. It was land. It could only be land. The four houses where the paintings were stolen have some of the richest, the most valuable land in Ireland. Irish landlords are selling up in droves after the Wyndham Act, but not these four. Connolly talked to me about a hunger for land round here, a hunger so strong that on market days you could almost smell it. Mulcahy wanted land. I believe he has made offers for some of the Butler and Moore estates in the past and always been rebuffed. The other Mulcahy wanted land. They were desperate for it. Sell them so many hundred acres, or so many thousand, and you get your paintings or your wives back. I'm sure they'd have been happy to pay a reasonable asking price. Connolly paid up. He sold them the land they asked for. The land agent in Athlone admitted to me that he had had recent dealings with Connolly. It's caused terrible trouble, land in Ireland, lack of it for so many in the famine years, the Land War, the boycotts. Land, the hunger for land, was at the bottom of the whole affair.

'I have left what I am sure is the most painful part of my account of the affair to the end, painful, that is, to the people in this room. What I am about to say is going to upset many of you. It certainly upsets me. As with so many of my theories in this investigation, I doubt if I could actually prove it in a court of law. You will remember that I raised earlier the question of Mulcahy's brains, the mind behind much of the enterprise. Young James, as we all know, has now disappeared. Young James said, in a very pointed fashion when we were all playing cards some weeks ago, that he never played cards for money, never. It was said with such feeling that I suspected there was some secret behind it.

'I asked Inspector Harkness here to find out if Young James had incurred any gambling debts in his time at Trinity. He would not be the first. He will not be the last. The Inspector discovered that Young James had run up fifteen hundred pounds of debt, playing at cards for money, in his last year at university. However,' he could read disbelief in the faces all around him, 'all those debts were cleared, paid off, in May, before the paintings began to disappear. In Mulcahy's loan book, which I have in my possession, there is a record of a loan of fifteen hundred pounds to a James of Butler's Court, also in May. One loan paid off the others. But there is more. I think Young James sold the idea of the robberies of the paintings to Pronsias Mulcahy in return for an alleviation of his debt. James was the brains. Mulcahy supplied the rest. Two days after the Butler paintings were taken, seven hundred and fifty pounds was deducted from Young James's loan. The day after the Connolly pictures were returned, a further quarter was deducted. It was a bargain, pure and simple.' The reason I asked, after the abduction of Mrs Moore and her sister, if there was a Butler Lodge in the west, was that I already suspected Young James, and he would have known about Butler's Lodge. He lived with the Butlers after all.

'Why did he disappear?' asked Sylvia Butler, who had been particularly fond of the young man.

'He disappeared shortly after the body of the young man was found on Croagh Patrick. I don't know if you are aware of it, but bullets in the back of the head can be the mark of the execution of a traitor in the world of the Fenians or the Irish Republican Brotherhood. I think Young James panicked. He hadn't intended to have anything to do with these violent characters. He thought it would be better if he cleared off, disappeared in case he was next for the shooting.'

More champagne was circulated. Throughout Powerscourt's account Richard Butler had been looking at his ancestors on the walls rather than his investigator at the end of his table.

'I'm nearly through,' said Powerscourt, 'I've gone on far too long already. I'm sorry it took me so long to find the answers. I was looking at things the wrong way, you see. In most investigations there is one thief, or one murderer, or one blackmailer. Here there was a much larger cast, Young James, the Mulcahy brothers, the young men of the GAA and so on. I'm sure that ghastly priest Father O'Donovan Brady had something to do with it all but I'm damned if I can pin anything on him. Maybe he was the link with the young men with the hurling sticks, I don't know. Anyway,' he opened his hands in a gesture that might have been of completion or might have been resignation, 'it's finished, it's all over now.'

'What about the attempt on your life, Francis?' said Lucy. 'When the bicycle was tampered with.'

'I didn't think you knew about that, Lucy,' said Powerscourt, wondering if he had a rival in detection in the person of his wife. 'I think it was a warning shot from some local hothead. I don't think they meant to kill me, they just wanted to frighten me.'

That afternoon Powerscourt and Lady Lucy sat under an enormous awning on the Butler lawn and Powerscourt fell asleep. He was roused by a vigorous clap on the back from Dennis Ormonde.

'Well done, man, I cannot thank you enough! Wife back! Paintings back! Happiness back! Bloody Orangemen can be kitted out with thousands of rounds of potato bread and sent home to bloody Ulster!'

Late that afternoon Ormonde, Butler and Moore all disappeared into Butler's study for half an hour and then emerged, grinning hugely. As the company were taking drinks before dinner, Richard Butler rose to his feet and appealed for silence.

'Lord Powerscourt, Lady Powerscourt, I, or rather we,' he nodded at Ormonde and Moore, 'wish to make a suggestion. In the normal course of things we would even now be preparing to hand over a most generous cheque in recognition of your services. But this evening we have a different proposal to put before you.'

Powerscourt had no idea what was coming. Were they going to offer him a painting? Please God, not some bloody horse.

'The name of Powerscourt has been absent for too long from the land registers of this country,' Butler went on, 'a name that stretched back to the Normans, a family rich in history and devoted to the service of the state. We want to set that right. We want the name of Powerscourt back where it belongs in the bosom of the Anglo-Irish gentry. Will you accept, for your family and all your descendants, in recognition of your service in this matter, the gift of Butler Lodge and all the land and waters that go with it?'

Powerscourt was astonished. Those wide open skies. The desolate beauty of the lakes and the mountains. Fishing with Thomas. The Atlantic Ocean pounding at the coast. Yachting with the children. The light, so bright in summer that things were impossibly clear.

'You're pulling my leg,' he said at first. 'You must be pulling my leg.'

All three assured him they were deadly serious. 'Then I accept,' said Powerscourt, rising to his feet. 'I accept with great pleasure on behalf of Lucy and myself and all Powerscourts yet to come. What a very great honour! What a very great privilege! What joy!' He was almost in tears as he sat down, Lady Lucy moving to his side.

After this investigation Powerscourt and his wife did not go abroad for a holiday as they usually did at the end of a case. They went west to Butler Lodge, shortly to be renamed Powerscourt Lodge by the Archbishop of Tuam with Butlers, Moores and Ormondes as guests of honour. The new proprietor spent his days quietly, pottering about his estate to establish how much land and mountain he actually owned. The new proprietor's wife began moving the furniture about on the second day, just making the place more comfortable, as she put it, and commencing a detailed inventory of china, bed linen and other necessities of life. They were both supremely happy.

EPILOGUE

Ten days later Powerscourt and Lady Lucy were back in Markham Square. Powerscourt was peering at an envelope with a strange postmark that had come in the second post. There was something familiar about the handwriting. Then he remembered where he had seen this distinctive, rather ornate hand before. He had noticed it when he picked a page of script up off the floor at the children's concert in Butler's Court. He called for Lady Lucy and opened the letter. He smiled.

'Lucy, he said, 'you weren't there for Uncle Peter's account of Parnell's funeral, were you? At one point Young James interrupted at the mention of a young woman called Maud Gonne who was a friend of the poet W.B. Yeats.'

'I was reading Yeats that last day at Butler's Court, Francis, when you raided Mulcahy's.'

'Maybe that's an omen. Anyway, Young James said Gonne was Yeats's bitch goddess, she wouldn't marry him, she wouldn't leave him alone.'

'What's that got to do with this letter, Francis?' asked Lady Lucy.

Her husband held it up. 'It comes from Boston, Massachusetts. This is Young James's handwriting. There's no precise address, and no date. The front side says Bitch and the back says Goddess. Then the front side says:

'Fasten your hair with a golden pin,
And bind up every wandering tress;

311

I bade my heart build these poor rhymes:
It worked at them, day out, day in,
Building a sorrowful loveliness
Out of the battles of old times.

'You need but lift a pearl-pale hand,
And bind up your long hair and sigh;
And all men's hearts must burn and beat;
And candle-like foam on the dim sand,
And stars climbing the dew-dropping sky,
Live but to light your passing feet.'

'It's so beautiful, Francis,' said Lady Lucy. 'Do you think the poet is still writing to his bitch goddess?'

'I'm sure that's what Young James thinks. He was always very fond of Yeats. But don't you see, Lucy, he's letting us know that he's alive, that he's in America for the present. Maybe Young James will come back some day.'

'And what does the other side of the letter say?'

Powerscourt read very quietly, pausing every now and then to look into Lady Lucy's eyes.

'Had I the heavens' embroidered cloths,
Enwrought with golden and silver light,
The blue and the dim and the dark cloths
Of night and light and the half light,
I would spread the cloths under your feet:
But I, being poor, have only my dreams;
I have spread my dreams under your feet;
Tread softly because you tread on my dreams.'